Stone Angels

Paula R. C. Readman

www.darkstroke.com

First Dark Edition, darkstroke. 2020

To my dear friend and mentor, Ivy Lord
(aka author Maggie Ford) forevermore
my guardian angel, without
wings of course.

About the Author

Paula R C Readman grew up at Moulsham Mill in Chelmsford where her father worked as a master miller. She now lives in a village in Essex with her husband and two cats. After leaving school at 16 with no qualifications, she spent her working life mainly in low paying jobs. In 1998, with no understanding of English grammar, she decided to beat her dyslexia, by setting herself a challenge to become a published author.

She taught herself 'How to Write' from books which her husband purchased from eBay. After 250 purchases, he finally told her 'just to get on with the writing'.

In 2010, she had her first taste of success with fiction when English Heritage published her short story in their anthology, Whitby Abbey-Pure Inspiration. In 2011, Paula took the opportunity redundancy offered her to take up writing full-time and started concentrating on writing short stories for publication in anthologies and for competitions while mastering the skills needed to write novels. Paula has had over fifty-nine short stories published, one collection of short stories, Days Pass Like a Shadow, published by Bridge House publishing, and a crime novella. The Funeral Birds, published by Demain Publishing.

Also in 2011, she had her first overall win in the World Book Day short story competition run by Austin and Macauley Publishers, and then 2012 the Writing Magazine and Harrogate Crime Writing Festival short story competition, when the crime writer Mark Billingham selected her dark crime story Roofscapes as the overall winning entry.

In 2014, Paula decided to take the main character James Ravencroft's point of view from ***Roofscapes*** short story and turned it into the Stone Angels novel.

Acknowledgements

A big 'thank you' to Darkstroke for all their encouragement, words of wisdom and for the opportunity to see my novel ***Stone Angels*** published. Huge thanks to Laurence for helping me to knock my book into shape.

A big thank you to Debz Brown, Kim Martin, Nicola Slade, Sally Zigmond, Gill James and the members of the Ivy League writing group, Derek Corbett, Linda Gruchy, Linda Payne, Mark Readman, Maxine Churchman and Carol Simmons whose words of encouragement kept me writing. Thank you to my husband, Russell, for all his support and belief in me even when I failed to believe in myself. My darling son, Stewart and daughter-in-law Kathryn and not forgetting Dave, Joan and Ana, thank you for being there.

And, for everyone else who has briefly touched upon my life. Good or bad, you've created the writer I've become.

Stone Angels

Chapter One

The First of Nine
1971

The first painting in my urban *Roofscapes* series now stands on a mahogany easel in my drawing room. Heavy faded velvet curtains surround a stone-arched window through which pale sunlight floods, giving the room a shrine-like appearance. My agent Basil has been studying the painting for some time. He leans forward slightly with his broad back to me. I recline on a threadbare velvet sofa, swirling whisky around in a crystal glass.

I'm an artist. And, like all artists, I was born to create. Creativity flows through my blood and is in everything I see and do. The world is a series of lines that I must draw, and then reproduce in paint on raw hessian.

When I begin a painting, I place a new canvas on the paint-spattered easel and breathe in the smell of the paints, turps, and linseed oil. On closing my eyes I allow my mind to clear and fall into a sickness.

It's like misery, all consuming. The darkness envelops me, I feed on its strength and it empowers me. I lift a paint-filled brush and mark the canvas. She appears. Her beauty wraps itself around me. Her smiling face haunts me almost as much as my father's steely stares. Then, just as quickly, she leaves. Passion spent, my desire gone, my heart stills. Weak, I am unable to hold my brush. It falls onto my palette.

I awaken.

The virgin whiteness of the canvas is gone. In its place is a work of art in shades of grey, dull green, blue, and inky black

– my trademark.

I'm jolted out of my thoughts by a comment from Basil.

"I do believe this painting is one of your finest so far, James," he says as he straightens and offers his empty glass.

"Help yourself to another, old boy." I wonder what's different this time. He normally helps himself to my whisky.

"Thanks. And less of the old boy," Basil protests as he crosses to the drinks cabinet. In midstride he pauses to study a small collection of my mother's watercolours. "Dear God, I do so love this room. I cannot make up my mind whether it's the clash of styles, or its sense of history. To think, I didn't know who you were when we first met. And here we are, surrounded by all this fame and fortune." He holds out the bottle of Johnnie Walker Blue.

I shake my head, holding up the half-filled glass. He nods and fills his glass to the brim before dropping into father's old chair next to the fireplace. I take a sip, allowing the layers of richness to separate, and close my eyes. I roll the smoky liquid around my mouth, pushing it through the small gap in my front teeth before swallowing the sandalwood taste. As I do so, my thoughts settle on how we met eight years ago.

***

In the summer of 1963 I bumped into Basil at the opening of a new art gallery in London. I was squatting with a bunch of beatnik artists in all that remained of a once handsome Edwardian four-storey terraced house. It had survived Hitler's bombs enough for its spacious rooms to become studios. With no real income between the artists, they spent most of their days spattering paint over large canvases in the style of Jackson Pollock as they dreamt of fame and fortune while smoking themselves into oblivion. I steered clear of the drugs, busy rebranding myself, into a poor artist called Tommy Blackbird. I knew how dangerous fame was after witnessing the damage it had done to my mother. Though living with them had its rewards.

Joe, who ran the squat, believed we were the reincarnation

of Pre-Raphaelite Brotherhood by all agreeing to help each other. While they were happy to share everything from beds to food, paints and clothes, and even their girlfriends with me, I was being far more self-centred. Only one girl sparked my interest, the unobtainable girlfriend of Joe. I certainly appreciated Candela's shapely form, a willowy blonde with dark green eyes.

Candela and her friends, Trudy and Dor, worked as picture hangers in the major galleries around the city. Most evenings they would supply us with a meal while keeping us in the loop with the latest art news, information on art competitions, or galleries that were on the hunt for new and up and coming artists from across the city, and sometimes from New York.

One evening over supper, Candela told us about a new gallery that was to have a celebrity launch party. As we sat feasting, we made plans to gate-crash.

A few days later we arrived at the gallery to find the party in full swing. Posters covering the front windows proclaimed that the exhibition was for the art critic, Lawrence Alloway's 'Pop Art' artist, David Hockney. I stood in awe of the large white space with its pale grey carpet and loft-style gallery. The fluorescent lighting seemed to bring the modern abstract paintings alive. Transfixed, I wanted nothing more than to grab a paintbrush and start work.

My conspirators seemed more focused on the gathering masses. Candela tugged on my arm. "Oh my God. Tommy just look who else is here!"

Over my shoulder I saw Joe moving towards a group of new arrivals. Among them was a young up and coming singer, Mick Jagger, with his latest flame clinging to his arm, as well as celebrities from film and TV, all milling about, chatting with artists and agents. They stood before the large canvases, holding up their wine glasses, smiling into the cameras, pleased to have their pictures snapped in the trendiest, newest hotspot.

As the others wandered off to mingle with the famous, my attention returned to the paintings. Soon I was looking for a quiet corner so I could sketch down a few ideas. As I made a few notes on colours and positions of figures, I became aware of a couple talking.

"I can't believe it. He's here!" an excited woman said.

"You're having me on. Where?" a pretty boy replied. "I've been here since it opened. He wasn't here then. I went over the whole place and didn't see him."

"He's upstairs in the main gallery. You know, where it says private."

"Oh well, that's no good for the likes of us, dearie."

I slipped the notebook into my jacket pocket as their excited laughter faded. Unable to locate Joe or Candela, I headed for the stairs to see if I could catch a glimpse of Hockney.

Of course, I wasn't the only one. The place swarmed with his admirers. Well, who wouldn't want to be around him? The guy had the Midas touch. That's the trouble with fame. You become the property of the masses. Everyone wants a piece of the action.

While barging through the milling crowd on the stairs, I somehow locked arms with a tall guy dressed in a striped boating blazer with cream trousers. He deposited his red wine down the front of my white shirt.

"Jesus bloody Christ. I'm so sorry mate!" he yelled over the din.

"Hey, it's all right. I thought I was blending in too well with the walls anyway." I laughed.

For a moment I thought he was on something as he stared blankly at me. Then his grey eyes widened, and he began to laugh.

"I'm Basil Hallward." He offered me his hand.

As I took it, I became aware of his tightening grip, and he pulled me away from the steady conveyor belt of people that were pushing to get past and guided me to the corner where I had taken refuge earlier. I'm not sure at what point he mentioned he was an agent, or whether I told him I was an artist looking for representation. The next thing I remember clearly about that night was leaving the party early, after Basil and I exchanged contact details and he had made an appointment with me to view some of my work in his London office a week later.

As for Hockney, I never did meet him.

I left the launch party and made my way back to the squat. I decided it was the right time to leave Tommy Blackbird in London, and head home to Halghetree Rectory.

At the squat I took the stairs two at a time, wanting to be gone before anyone else arrived back. I paused on the landing below mine when I became aware of someone crying. Joe's studio door stood slightly ajar. I placed an eye to the gap. Suddenly transported back to my childhood, within the paint-splattered studio, I saw my mother amidst spilt paints and torn canvases. I shook my head in an effort to clear the awful image from my mind. I struck the door, causing it to swing open. Mother turned with a bloodied knife in her hand.

I froze.

"Christ, Tommy! I thought it was Joe!" Candela shrieked, and mother vanished.

I tried to make sense of the torn paintings strewn across the room. It wasn't blood covering them, but paint.

"What the hell are you doing?" I shouted.

"What the fuck do you think?" she said, tossing the knife into the disarray. "I can't take any more of his lies, so I'm leaving him a farewell surprise."

She picked up a couple of bags and pushed past me.

"Where are you going?" I called after her.

She paused, her hand resting lightly on the banister and looked up, her eyes red-rimmed. "As far away as possible," she said with a shrug of her thin shoulders before continuing down the stairs.

"How are you getting there?" I ran after her.

"Train, bus, I don't care. I just want to be gone before he gets back."

"Wait! Give me a moment and I can take you. I have a car. I can drop you off anywhere you want or… Come with me. It's up to you."

As her green eyes locked with mine, I recognised the

bitterness that burnt within them. I inhaled deeply. The smell of paint, spilt turps and linseed oil caused something inside me to snap. I knew whatever happened next; Candela had to come with me.

***

The squeaking springs in my father's chair brought me back to the present. I open my eyes, my breath catching in my throat. It still shocks me to find someone sitting in it beside the fire. I try to squash the displeasure on seeing Basil relax as he surveys the room, glass in hand. I let my breath out slowly and wait for him to comment on my painting. It's the only reason I have allowed him into my inner sanctum.

After doing a series of land and seascapes in my own unique style, Basil suggested I should try something urban. It amazes me that he should have suggested such a subject matter. The idea was not new to me. What I'm showing him was actually painted eight years ago. It's why I'm more than a little intrigued to know his thoughts on my interpretation.

Within the painting, a semi-naked, grisaille-style woman posed in shades of grey, dull green, blue, and inky black in a bleak cityscape. Her arms were tied behind her as she leaned forward like a figurehead on a sailing ship, among the saintly statues and gargoyles on the side of a Gothic building. The rain plastered her hair to her head while four small metal clips held her eyelids open, causing blood to trickle down her cheeks.

Oh how I recall the power of the muse as she played with my emotions. Within every sweep of the brush I built the paint up, layer upon layer to convey the symbolism and eroticism in the way the halter strap of the model's body harness emphasised her breasts. I wanted the art connoisseurs to search for answers within each stroke as they do when discussing other great works of art.

Basil clears his throat, and I'm jarred out of my thoughts. I took another gulp of my drink and try to clear my mind of Candela.

"Hmm," he utters before taking another sip of his drink. "There's something quite dark about your painting, James. Something unspoken."

I smile, satisfy that he's hooked. There's a sparkle of delight in his grey eyes, though. It could be just his bank balance sparkling. You never can tell with Basil.

"James, my dear man, finally you've found your voice. Your last series of paintings was brilliant. And I must say they've made us a small fortune, but... this is outstanding!"

He crosses to the painting again and studies it. I can see the muscles in his back twitching as he scans the painting. I'm sure he's calculating just how much each brushstroke is worth.

He takes more than his fair share in extra commission on each sale he makes on my behalf. It doesn't bother me. If he has his hand in the cookie jar, I hope for his sake he's lined his nest well. One day soon the axe will fall, and he won't know what has hit him.

With fame, I know if you have a big enough fortune, it allows you to get away with things ordinary folk cannot. Basil constantly reminds me he's a friend, someone I can confide in.

Now that's not something I find easy to do. We all have things we like to keep to ourselves. I know his, but he doesn't know about mine yet.

Tommy Blackbird was too kind and didn't know how to paint. James enjoys playing among the shadows while painting in his unique style.

Basil reaches for the bottle again. "They say behind every great piece of art is a story. So, what's yours? What's your inspiration, James?"

I shrug. "I paint what I see."

A puzzled look crosses his face. "Has it a title? Is it painted from real life, or just your imagination?"

"It's an idea I've been toying with for some time. I've called it '*Roofscapes*,' but it is really 'a work in progress'."

"Oh, so it's an on-going. Part of a series like '*Of Land and Sea*?'"

"You could say that. I'm already working on the next one."

"That's great. I can't wait to see it."

I drain my glass, not telling him that I've already finished nine.

Chapter Two

Something Urban
The First Painting
1963

Still buzzing with excitement at Basil's astonishing reaction to the first of my nine '*Roofscapes*' paintings, I recalled how it all started in 1963. Once my patronage was large enough, I wanted the freedom to paint whatever I chose. After my initial meeting with Basil at his London office, a month later I received a phone call from him.

"Hi James Ravencroft? It's Basil Hallward."

"Yes — I'm James." The telephone receiver betrayed my nerves as it shook in my hand.

"Good. I've phoned with some wonderful news. I've sold your painting and secured a further five commissions for your *Of Land and Sea* series."

"That's marvellous, Mr Hallward."

"Do call me Basil. So you better get painting, James. I can see us having a long partnership. I will get my secretary to draw up a contract and send you a copy. We can sort out the payment next time you are in town."

The prestige of having an agent to sell my work excited me, but my series of land and seascape paintings was not the kind I wanted to build my reputation on. I should've been grateful, considering I was an unknown artist, but the money was the least of my problems.

Prestige is a funny word. The Latin 'praestigiae' means *conjuring tricks.* It's what we artists do. We're a kind of magician, though we conjure with canvas, charcoal, lines, colours, and paints to create our illusions.

I used more than a sleight of hand the night I made Candela disappear.

Candela and I sat in my Ford Consul with its engine idling waiting for her to make her decision. Through the misty window, a streetlight flickered, highlighting the dreariness of the dead-end road where we sat away from the squat.

"I can't believe you had a car all the time you've been living with us."

She rubbed her wet hair with a towel. A growing puzzlement slipped across her face as we hastily load my sparse belongings into the car boot before the others returned. She hadn't understood why I had left my paintings, brushes, paints, and most of my clothes behind. I had even waited for her to ask why, but it never came.

Candela began to comb her hair as I climbed out of the car.

"Tommy, where are you going?"

"I won't be long. There's something I need to do." I closed the door before she had time to protest.

Back at the squat I set about making Tommy Blackbird disappear. Joe had always been secretive about his work-in-progress. Only Candela had access to his studio. I carefully lifted the knife, by its blade end, from where Candela had tossed it. I sliced the palm of my hand and dropped it back among the damaged paintings.

After clenching my fist to get the blood flowing, I spattered the room, staining Joe's paintings and made a trail towards the door. Upstairs I carefully unlocked my studio door, trying not to disturb Candela's fingerprints. Once I had what I needed out, I got her to close the door behind us. I ignored the stinging pain and deepened the cut with a penknife. I splattered the doorframe, door and floor just outside Tommy's studio hoping to eliminate him from police's suspect list. Once I had stage-set the studio to have a look of expectancy, as though at any given moment the artist, Tommy Blackbird would return to finish the painting on the easel, I was ready to leave. I wrapped a rag around my hand so no droplets of blood would give me away. I locked the door and kicked the key under it.

Relief washed over Candela's face as I climbed in. She was eager to leave, but I wanted to be certain it was with me. I drove a few streets away and parked in a narrow back road.

"So have you made up your mind?"

She looked into the distance. The road before us was empty, though every now and then a brave cat appeared out of the darkness and sauntered between the pools of streetlights. When Candela spoke, her answer was noncommittal as though she wanted me to make the choice for her.

"Home, or with you?"

"What about your job?" I flexed my hand. It stung like hell. I saw the white rag looked darker in the semi light of the car's interior.

"I don't give a shit." Candela spat the words out. "And as for Joe — well, I've wanted to go home for quite a while now. I wrote to my family the other day saying as much. Mum was right. Men should look after us, not us them."

"So what's your choice?" I focused on the water gushing from a broken drainpipe. I sensed her moving and turned. She sat with her legs under her, facing me. The force of her gaze woke sensations within me. The pounding of rain on the car roof mimicked the beating of my heart. Candela broke the spell as she twisted round to face forward again. "Can I tell you something, Tommy?" Her fingers played with the ends of her hair.

"Sure. If you've made up your mind."

"Yeah, I'll come with you."

I turned the key, starting the engine, and slipped the car into gear. As we left the dreariness behind, Candela said nothing. She settled into the seat with her eyes half closed as though needing a moment to process her thoughts. I drove on.

At last she spoke. "Do you remember seeing a tall, good looking guy at the party, Tommy?"

I laughed. "Which one, if you're not including me?"

She giggled. "Yeah, you're handsome, but I meant the

unmissable one. He towered over the rest of us, well-dressed in a blue and green striped blazer with shoulder length brown hair."

"Nope. Too many beautiful people. Why?" Outside, the streetlights reflected our journey back at us in the wet bonnet.

"Oh, well. It was crowded," she said.

"What about him?"

"Well, according to Joe he's an agent. To me he was a dirty old git. The bastard hit on me. Do you know what Joe said when I told him?"

"What?"

"Sleep with him, and while he's fucking you, tell him what a brilliant artist I am. He simply *must* see my paintings!"

Unsure whether she wanted my opinion on Joe's behaviour or not, we drove on in silence. When she spoke again it was more to herself than to me. "Joe and his frigging free love. Got a bloody nerve to say I do fuck all for him. Bloody cheek! Whose sodding money has he been living off all this time! Unlike Dor and Trudy, I haven't slept around until now."

"Sorry —" I kept my eyes on the road ahead.

"Don't be. It's what I want." She brushed her hand across my leg. "Only you haven't shown much interest in me until now. Why?"

"You were Joe's."

"I'm not now." She giggled.

The rain, heavier now, slowed our progress as we hit the A12. All I could think about was how much I needed to lose the car and find a replacement. It reeked of her cheap perfume and Camel cigarettes. I needed to put some distance between Candela, the squat and myself.

By the time we left the A12, Candela's constant chatter about her hatred of Joe had died away along with the rain. When I switched off the wipers, I realised she had fallen asleep. In the silence, my mind had free rein to bounce a few ideas around for the sort of painting I hoped to create using Candela as my model. Soon I pulled the car off the main road and onto a rough lane that led to the old Halghetree Rectory.

As I swung the car round, Candela stirred, stretching like a cat.

"Where are we?" She stepped from the car and looked up at the house. "Is this where you live, Tommy?" Silhouetted against a full moon, its buttresses and pinnacles shone in the moon's light after the heavy rain.

"Yes." I lifted her bags from the car and set them down at her feet before taking out my boxes and carrying them to the house. I placed them on a seat in the porch while I unlocked the door and switched on the hall light. Candela seemed reluctant to follow me.

"I'll soon have the place warmed up," I called over my shoulder. I placed the boxes on a hall table, went through to the drawing room, and switched on a light. The room was dusty after my time away.

Other homecomings had been full of delicious smells like homemade bread, cakes furniture polish and bees wax when the house sparkled. Then it echoed to the sounds of Mrs Page's laughter as she welcomed me home from school.

"At last, Master James. Put your case down, wash your hands, and come into the kitchen. Tea's ready." Dear Mrs P. She possessed the magic to turn a sad, cold house into a happy home.

In the hall, Candela held her hair back from her face as she studied a framed photograph hanging in an alcove. "Do you live here alone?"

"Yes, all alone." I opened the cupboard door under the stairs and pulling out some old newspapers. In the drawing room, I set about working building a fire. Candela hovered in the doorway.

"Come in." I added coke to the fire. "Once it really gets going, I'll light the Aga in the kitchen. That heats the whole house. There'll be hot water too. You okay?"

Candela studied me for a moment. Then I knew it wasn't me she was studying, but something over my shoulder. She began to gesture wildly. "What I don't understand is why you pretend to us you were penniless if you have all of this. You could've easily got into the party with the mere hint of your mother's prestige. Hell, you could have bought yourself a first-class ticket to the New York opening."

I tried not to let my annoyance show. "My Mother's—"

"Why the hell not?" She came further into the room. "Bloody hell, Tommy. Everyone else in the squat would've done it. What leverage! Shit, you could be anyone you want to be."

I added another log to the fire before facing her. "You know nothing."

"Bloody men!" She shook her head. "Get this; I'm not a dumb blonde. Yes, I worked as a picture hanger, but I have aspirations too. No fancy education, but then I didn't have a mother who could afford to pay for one."

"And, your point is?"

"Guess what, Tommy Blackbird? Or whatever you call yourself. I know who *Jane Elspeth Maedere* was. I guess you would see my art as daubs the same as Joe did." She narrowed her lovely eyes. "I guess you men feel threatened by us women, but we just want recognition as much as you do. Only the establishment doesn't take us seriously. We have to have more than just talent, as your mother found out. It's all down to how we look rather than our talent."

"Do you want a drink?" I held up a bottle of whiskey.

"No— thank you. The photo in the hall is of you with your mother?"

"How observant of you. Take a seat." I gestured to the sofa.

"I've never seen any photos of this one before—" She nodded in the direction of the painting above the fireplace. "It's an amazing self-portrait." Candela sat on the edge of the sofa closest to the door.

"Please relax. You're making me nervous." I poured myself a large whisky, glad it wasn't the crap I'd been drinking for the last six months. As its burning quality slipped down my throat, I became aware that Candela's nervousness had returned. She perched uncomfortably on the sofa's edge, like a bird hanging on to a branch in a strong breeze. It was as if she was about ready to make a quick dash, not that she was ideally dressed to run across muddy field in her Mary Quant pale yellow trouser suit and flat green suede shoes. Even so, she wouldn't get far as the surrounding Suffolk countryside outside the rectory laid in pitch-black, unlike the streets of London, with its streetlighting.

"Why all the pretence, Tommy? Why not just use your given name, Tommy Maedere, the son of the great artist, Jane Maedere?"

"My father was Donald Ravencroft. Maedere is my mother's maiden name. I'm James Ravencroft."

"Raven— Blackbird. I get it, but it makes no sense. Why not call yourself James Maedere, if Tommy isn't even your real name."

I gulped more whisky before answering. "Then you understand nothing. Why should I use my mother in the same way others did?"

"But why lie?"

"Did I lie?"

She pondered the question.

"Exactly." I set my glass down and dropped into my father's chair. "You never asked. I never said. End of story. Anyway, what about you? For all I know, you might be a poor little rich girl— Daddy drives a 'Roller'"

"Nope. Daddy drives a taxi! Mummy is a cleaner. My parents couldn't afford to send me to college. I read about your mother while working full-time to pay my way in life. She's so talented—"

"Was," I snapped. She flinched as though I had struck her. I softened my tone, trying to keep calm. "She isn't anymore."

"I'm sorry. Of course there was some sort of an accident."

I reached for my glass in an effort to block out the image of my mother with the knife and the sound of father's pleading voice. As I fell silent Candela studied the room, while I studied her. The tilt of her head and the shape of her profile against the flickering fire light made me want to pick up a pencil and capture her, to strip back the layers of eye make-up to bring out her real beauty, the raw beauty that only

I saw.

"Please feel free to look about," I said softly, though still managing to startle her. The make-up that already widened her eyes now exaggerated her agitation. "I won't be long. I am just going to light the Aga. The house will soon warm up." I left and went through to the kitchen.

Like the rest of the house, the kitchen was covered in a film of dust. I should've hired someone to clean while I was away, but it would have been impossible to trust anyone not to snoop around when all they needed do was clean the kitchen and bathrooms. I washed the dried blood and the coke dust off my injured hand. I'd just finished redressing it when Candela appeared in the doorway.

"What happened to your hand?"

"Nothing. Just caught it on the coal scuttle."

She stepped forward, keeping the table between us. "Do you want me to take a look at it?"

"No, I'm good." I held out my bandaged hand.

"Well, if we're going to eat in here, I better give it a clean." She opened the cupboard under the sink and began looking for cleaning products without even asking where they were kept.

I watched her closely. She washed down the surfaces, ready to prepare our meal. I took in her loveliness, noting that she seemed to have lost her apprehension. Every muscle in her body relaxed into the task. Candela was city made. Her knowledge of the metropolis, like that of her father and all London cab drivers, would be useless in the vast countryside that I knew like the back of my hand.

Candela fell easily into playing the part of the wife in unfamiliar surroundings as she finished cleaning the kitchen. I put away the few groceries I had brought from London. We sat down at the freshly scrubbed pine table in the kitchen and dined on cheesy baked beans and toast. Candela chatted about her plans to clean the rest of the house, while I was busy contemplating plans of my own.

With my first serious collection of paintings *Of Land and Sea* almost finished, I was on the search for something new.

My time in London had eaten its way into my soul. The architecture had made the biggest impression on me, especially St Paul's Cathedral. As Candela waited for the sink to fill enough to begin the washing up, she leaned forward slightly. The light in the kitchen gave her face the appearance of stone. The words *urban landscapes* filled my mind with new possibilities.

Candela's appearance reminded me of the statues on St Paul's the Golden Gallery. They stared unseeing with vacant eyes across the city while far below people hurried ant-like, with their heads down, focusing on nothing else but making money. Even when Hitler's bombs destroyed the heart of the city, those stone figures watched unmoved by man's inhumanity. As Candela washed our plates, she became my first muse, and my first stone angel.

The next morning I was up early, desperate to begin working on an idea that had come to me in the early hours. In the kitchen, I added coke to the Aga to build up some heat while waiting for the kettle to boil. Candela had put me off the idea of going to my studio after I heard her snooping around in the drawers and cupboards of my sister Lydia's old bedroom.

It's funny how things happen. No matter how well you may make plans there's always an element of the unexpected. It's like looking at a blank canvas. In your mind's eye, you know what it will look like once you've finished. The hardest part is finding the best starting point, and then planning your route to your final destination. You can do as many preliminary drawings as you want to find the best route to take, but once you lift a paint-filled brush and make that initial stroke, the painting takes on a life of its own.

Everything fell into place at breakfast. I gazed across the kitchen table into Candela's beautiful but sad green eyes and knew I had found my starting point.

Chapter Three

Candela gathered up the cleaning products from under the sink and nipped through to the utility room just beyond the kitchen.

"Are you sure you want to clean?" I called after her. "You could come with me."

"No, I'm fine. How long are you going to be?" she asked, stepping back into view. She looked every inch the domestic goddess, with her hair braided and tied back into a ponytail. Even her smile reminded me of a washing powder commercial.

"I'm not sure." I leaned against the doorjamb. "The car was making a hell of a din last night."

"I didn't hear anything."

"You were sound-o. It's a wonder it didn't wake you. It happened mainly when I accelerated. Anyway, I need to get it checked out. Living out here, I don't want the car dying on us."

"Oh, right." She checked Mrs P's tidy-box before looking up. "Do you want me to fix lunch or just wait and see what time you get back?"

"Best wait." I crossed to the pantry. "We're getting low on milk, butter, eggs, and potatoes. I'll pick them up from Jimmy's on my way back."

"Jimmy's?"

Candela came towards me. "Yeah. It's a smallholding not far from here. If I see anything we need, I'll just buy it. It shouldn't take me all day. Please just stick to the rooms I've said if you're up to cleaning, but if you just want to sit and read in the library, or do some drawing, you can. I could sort out a canvas, and some paints, before I go. The light in the lounge is good, if you want to paint."

"No, it's all right. I'm looking forward to putting a shine on the house. Maybe tomorrow I'll do some painting. I noticed a statue in the garden, this morning, a stone angel of sort. If it's nice tomorrow I might sketch it."

"Okay. I better get going. Remember, you don't have to do any cleaning. I'll be back as soon as I can."

It was crazy to think I could trust her, but what else could I do? The car had to go. I couldn't risk her coming with me. I drove like a man possessed to Shottisham to pick up the car I had phoned about yesterday evening. Soon after our arrival I disconnected all phones, not wanting to risk Candela telling anyone where she was or having someone phoning to speak to me and Candela picking up.

By the time I returned it was late in the afternoon. After parking my newly acquired car in the garage, I carried the shopping into the kitchen, via the side door from the courtyard. I stood in the hallway and called to Candela letting her know I was back. On getting no response, I returned to the kitchen. After putting our supplies away, I went through to the drawing room. Candela had been busy. The sun poured through the clean windows and reflected off the highly polished glasses on the drinks cabinet. The freshly vacuumed carpet and rugs gave off a sweet lemon scent, while every surface from the bookshelves to the picture frames looked fresh and clean. She would've impressed Mrs P.

I took the stairs two at a time. On the landing, next to the window, I found Mrs P's tidy-box on a seat with some discarded cleaning rags. The door to mother's studio stood ajar, but I knew I had locked it before leaving the house. As I pushed the door open my chest tightened as a wave of nausea washed over me.

In mother's studio, on the left, was her dressing room and en-suite bathroom. To the right on a raised platform stood her bed, she would often lay here, looking out at the view of the fast-flowing river and broken trees. I held my breath, praying Candela hadn't touched anything. No one had the right to touch mother's things, not even me.

Nineteen years ago father had locked mother's studio door and handed the key to Mrs. P, telling her not to let it out of her sight. Only after I had inherited the house did I enter the room. There before me were the faint traces of my footprints on the dusty floorboards. I had tiptoed to the window to see the view mother had constantly painted, and then retraced my steps by treading in my footprints back again. On other occasions I had stood in the doorway just gazing in, or relived my childhood by peering through the keyhole, hoping to catch a glimpse of her ghost.

My heart hammered as I followed Candela's footprints. On reaching the open door to mother's dressing room, she stood, with her back to me, transfixed before a large dressing mirror, twisting from side to side as she held out a hem of the white georgette evening dress, trimmed in deep burgundy lace.

The bright light of the dressing room emphasised the richness of the lace and the narrowness of her waist where a velvet sash hung. For a brief moment I became a child again. Candela became mother.

Mother stood at the top of the stairs, dressed for a long-awaited evening out. Father stood at the bottom of the stairs. *"Oh my sweet darling. You look stunning. The car is on its way."*

"Will there be many there, Donald?" she asked, her bottom lip trembling. Fear clouded her fine features as she floated down to his side. He placed her mink wrap around her narrow shoulders.

"No, I shouldn't think so. You know what Major Bygraves is like, my dearest. Just the usual crowd."

"I hope that dreadful Yarwood man won't be there this time."

"You mean Major Yarwood? I don't know, my dear. Would you like me to phone and find out?" Father's face took on a resigned look, aware that, no matter what he said, they wouldn't be going anywhere together.

"No dearest," she sighed, easing the wrap from her shoulders. *"I think I will go and lie down again, if you don't*

mind. Please go out and enjoy yourself. It's such a waste having a car driven all this way for nothing."

Mother went back to her room, shutting us out of her life again.

***

"Oh, God. James, you're home— I'm so sorry!" said a frightened voice coming from afar. It filled the room, cutting across the years, banishing the shadows of people waiting to return.

Then everything blurred.

"Please let go of me, Tommy! James don't—!"

Voices mingled with words that made no sense. The terrifying screams of a woman and a man's urgent shouts mixed with long forgotten voices. A fury exploded within me as my fingers circled something soft.

After a second or an hour— I lost track of time— the voices became silent. I released my grip and opened my eyes, aware of where I was. "Candela?"

She lay on her back, bathed in a shimmering white and red aura, with her arms trapped beneath her amid the fallen gowns and dresses. I found the paleness of her skin confusing, but something about the angle at which she lay mesmerised me. Her twisted body reminded me of a figurehead on a ship, as the dress wrapped around her legs hid their natural form.

Candela's braided hair was pulled tight under the weight of her body and gave her head the appearance of a skullcap. Her black eyeliner stained her face, like that of weatherworn marble statue where the elements gave it the appearance of crying. I carried her over to mother's bed and gently laid her down. She showed no signs that she was breathing, I leant over her and placed my fingertips on her neck. Relief flooded through me as I felt a slight pulse, and I reached for the phone. As I lifted the receiver I paused, unsure of what I should say. Then the ghosts of all those people who had crowded into the house on that fateful day reminded me of what father had gone through with all the endless questioning about the state of mother's mind.

The image before me sparked my imagination. Desperate to capture it, I pulled open drawers and scattered mother's drawings and broken pencils. On finding what I needed, I dragged her artist stool over to the bedside and began to sketch. Once the page was full, I flung it aside. My pencil flew across the paper capturing every detail.

As I gathered up the fallen drawings another idea came to me. I moved her head slightly to one side and peeled the dress from her shoulders, ignoring the raw scratch marks on her neck. Candela's breathing seemed a little stronger. I worked on while the ideas flowed. As if possessed, my excitement growing, I prayed nothing would interrupt me as the image of my '*Stone Angel'* revealed itself.

A low inhuman groan emanated from the bed sending chills through me. As my mind comprehended the sound, the pencil hovered in mid-flow. On the bed, a white butterfly-like creature lifted. It hovered briefly before disappearing. I threw the drawing pad aside and dashed along the landing to father's study. I hunted among his bottles and potions, until I found what I was looking for, I grabbed a large wad of gauze.

On the bed Candela sat, like a discarded ragdoll, caressing her throat. The bruising on the back of her neck clearly showing imprints of fingers in her skin. She sensed my presence and turned. I gasped as our eyes met. Her beautiful green eyes were now blood red.

"Don't hurt me—" Candela rasped, turning away. "Please don't— come near me."

"Candela, it's okay— I'm sorry."

"Why did you hurt me?"

"I told you not to. Mother's things are precious to me."

"Sorry—" She slumped onto the pillows, weakened by the effort of speaking. "I want to go home, Tommy."

"Here— this will help you sleep." I leaned over her. Her eyes widened as she lifted her hand in protest. I knocked it aside and pressed the chloroform gauze on her face until her body slackened.

I carried Candela to the lift at the end of the corridor and took her up to the attic studio where I worked. In a small adjoining room, I placed her on a daybed and covered her with a blanket. In mother's studio I tidied up. Once satisfied it was as mother had left it, I collected up my drawings, relocked the door and hurried back to my studio.

As the muses gathered, begging me to start work, I placed the largest canvas I had on the easel. Once the background was sketched in with charcoal I stood back, satisfied with the layout. I hunted through the sketches I had done for the right pose, but frustratingly there wasn't the exact one I wanted, and cast them aside.

The mound on the daybed hadn't moved and I wondered if it was possible to get Candela to stand in the position I needed. I offered up a silent prayer to whatever god was listening and, to my surprise, was rewarded with an answer. There in the ceiling were a series of hooks. In the past the maids brought the damp washing up to the attic through a hidden doorway at the end of the corridor which now housed the lift. On a series of drying racks, suspended from the ceiling, the maids hoisted the washing up using a set of pulleys. Then opening the large French windows on either side of the attic, they created a through-draft.

The image of my angel hovering over a city flashed through my mind as I stared at the hooks. A body harness was what I needed. I dashed downstairs to the outbuildings. Once again, the gods had been kind to me. In father's workshop I scoured among the clutter in two of the stables. In the third one on a hook, covered in dust and cobwebs, hung a couple of old horse harnesses, which were perfect for what I wanted. Back in the studio I used linseed oil to soften the straps and, with only a few adjustments, I created a body harness.

I knelt beside Candela and with a struggle eased the straps over her shoulders. She let out a low moan but didn't stir. Once the body harness was fitted to her front, I rolled her onto her stomach and placed a large metal O-ring in the centre of her back. Then I slipped a rope from the hoist through the ring and lifted her into the air. Her body shuddered as she struggled, but I took no notice. Once her legs were strapped into place, with her arms behind her, I manoeuvred her body into the pose I wanted. Finally, using a horse chinstrap, I pulled her head into the right position and wheeled the daybed away. Candela hung like a wingless angel with her chin held aloft from the ceiling. After admiring my handy work I was ready to paint. But something wasn't right. Her eyes needed to be open.

In mother's dressing room I found what I wanted. I lowered Candela onto the bed again and clamped her head between my knees. I dug the top half of the skirt lifters into her forehead. As the claw penetrated her skin, Candela stirred, woken by the shock. She whimpered and tried to turn her head. A thin trickle of blood bubbled up and ran down her face covering my hands as I held her face still.

"Noooo— Please don't!" she sobbed while rattling the straps that held her arms out. I ignored her protests and continued to hook the other half of the skirt lifters over her eyelids, before placing the chloroformed pad to her face. Once I knew her eyelids would stay open, I lifted her back into position.

Like a magician about to do a conjuring trick, I lifted my palette and selected the first colour. I inhaled deeply allowing the smell of turps, paints, and linseed oil to fill my nostrils. As the shadows gathered around me, I squeezed Prussian blue onto the palette and then selected my favourite brush, allowing its bristles to come in contact with the dark blue paint. As the two met, my muse appeared. I raised the brush to the virgin whiteness and, with sweeping strokes, the power of light, colour, and shadow began to take on a physical form.

Chapter Four

Stone Angels
The Second Painting
1964

By the time I was born my half siblings from my father's first marriage, Lydia and Robert were young adults, which meant I was the only child in the house. Father educated me at home. Sometimes he hired a tutor when his reoccurring illness left him unable to teach. Being home-schooled meant I didn't come into contact with other children or their mothers. This left me at a disadvantage because I didn't know how different my mother was from other mothers nor did I know the full extent of her success as an artist.

At the age of fourteen I made two important discoveries. The consequences of timing and adults aren't always honest. Father decided it would be best for me to finish my education at a boy's boarding school. The lessons that caught my imagination were art history and theory, but my peers found the art teacher far more appealing than her lessons.

Ms Dearborn was younger and far prettier than most of the other teachers at the school. She conducted her lessons perched, cross-legged in short skirts and low-necked sweaters, on the front of her desk, giving the boys much to think about late into the night.

I enjoyed her art classes, but not her special attention. One day, while I was working on a painting, she leaned over my shoulder, pressing her ample bosom hard against me.

"James, your creative flair for mixing colours is just like your mother's." Her husky voice caressed my ear as her perfume choked me.

"How— how do you know my mother?"

It was shocking to me that someone like Ms Dearborn knew my mother when she spent so little time outside of her studio. Aware that the rest of the class was watching, Ms Dearborn straightened and, giggling, said, "My dear boy, everyone knows of your mother. She's famous."

Tucked up in bed that night I cried for the mother the rest of the world knew better than I did. In the morning, as sunlight broke through the thin, faded curtains of the dormitory, I made a promise to myself. Whatever fame was I wanted it as it gave you the ultimate power over others.

I had grown up surrounded by my mother's paintings, unaware of their significance, not fully understanding she was a legend, an inspiration to others, and an enigma. Her paintings, like father's bell jars, were valuable to me because she had created them. Each contained not only her love, but also her sanity. Like angels' kisses, I felt their presence without seeing them. If I was to compete with her, I had to get under her skin and find the source of her creativity. What compelled her to paint such powerful pictures?

All Father would say on the subject was that she was my mother, and what more did I need to know?

"Why did she lock herself away from me?"

"My dear son, all you need to understand is you were very important to her. Unfortunately, her time was not her own. There were deadlines to meet if she was going to be paid."

Then I asked for the truth.

With a look of disdain he said, "You'll have to find that out for yourself, my boy. If you do, you'll be a better man than I am." The conversation ended and he refused to discuss her anymore.

As father's illness progressed, he sought his God for comfort. At night, Mrs P read the Bible to him. Sometimes I would take over while she prepared lunch or saw to some other chore. This would give me the opportunity to question him further about mother, but his mumbled answers left me confused.

Within his befuddled mind she had become part of his butterfly collection, a pale clouded yellow butterfly that hovered on the periphery of his mind. He longed to be with her but, as in life, she never quite wanted him enough to spend all eternity at his side.

In my childhood I had accompanied father on his butterfly hunts. Together we ran across the meadows on a bright summer day, nets in hand. Once he had enough specimens we would return to his study, normally forbidden to me, like mother's studio. The dark, jar-lined room was a place of sadness, yet splendour.

Both my parents had a creative flair and sought some form of everlasting beauty. Father's was not on canvas, but under bell jars. After catching the butterflies he would gas them in his killing box. Then, carefully opening their wings, he would glue the delicate creatures onto dried flowers so they looked to be feeding. Once they were dry, the flowers were placed under the glass to look as though they were growing naturally.

***

One sunny morning in 1964, I was busy amusing myself in shades of darkness by adding bold strokes of colour to a new canvas. Then the phone rang and shattered my concentration, cursing I snatched up the phone and yelled, "Hello!"

"Hi James. Basil here."

At first I didn't recognise who was speaking and was ready to slam down the receiver.

"Look— I know you didn't invite me, but—"

"Sorry. Who's this?" I glanced up at my latest muse.

"Basil! I know it's at short notice, but I was in the area. I've just sold another couple of your amazing land and seascapes and thought—" He inhaled sharply before continuing. "Look, you're probably busy. Well, at least I hope you are, but would you mind if I dropped by?"

"What? Of course I'm busy!" My stomach somersaulted.

My agent knew my address, so the possibility of an unexpected visit was always on the cards. I should have been more prepared, but normally Basil would phone to explain what the client wanted. Once the painting was ready, I would deliver it to his office in London. There his secretary would pass on any further instructions to me.

I breathed out slowly, wishing to be alone with my muse. I relaxed and asked, "Whereabouts are you?"

"About an hour away." He hung up.

Left staring at the humming receiver, I slammed it down, and turned to my muse. "What the fuck am I to do now?"

I ignored her condemnation and cleaned my brush with a rag. A dreadful thought struck me. Basil would expect to see my studio and the latest work-in-progress. I tossed the rag and brush onto the table, snatched up an unfinished landscape, and hurried downstairs to my mother's studio.

After clearing the dust away from around her easel I swapped her unfinished painting for my landscape. I looked about to see what else I needed to do to make her studio look like mine. Mother and I were organised, her set up mirrored my own. Satisfied everything was in place; I squeezed fresh paint onto her old palette and began to paint.

Lost in the moment I added in more of the finer details in shades of greens and blues. Just as I began to blend the colours to the shade I needed, a car crunched over the gravel outside. I dropped my brush into a jar of turps and hurried downstairs.

Basil climbed out of a brand-new Jensen CV8 and looked up at the house.

"Nice car," I said with a nod.

"Nice house, James. You kept that a secret. Is it the family pile?"

"I suppose you could call it that, but my mother bought the old rectory for my father." I looked up at it as though seeing it for the first time through someone else's eyes. Mother had purchased the property before I was born using the money from the sales of her first major exhibition, though I didn't tell Basil that, instead I said, "My father was Reverend

Donald Ravencroft."

"What? Your father was a vicar?" He gave a light laugh while scrutinising me. "I never expected that."

"What do you mean?"

"I suppose I thought an art teacher. You don't give me the impression that you're religious, James."

"Father was all for guidance rather than a zealot. His parishioners loved him."

"Do your parents still live here?"

"No. They're both dead."

"Sorry." He peered through a window, as if he doubted me, expecting to see them sitting either side of the fireplace.

"The place looks old." He turned back to me.

"It's mentioned in the Domesday Book."

"Really?" Basil traced the lettering carved in the stone on the porch, with his fingertips. "What's Halghetree?"

"The name of the original village. It means 'Hallow Tree'. All its inhabitants died during the Black Plague. The only parts of the village that still exist are the remains of the old church, and part of its graveyard. These are within the structure of the rectory and its garden." I pointed to the back garden through the side gate.

"How creepy."

"Yes. I suppose it is, though our old housekeeper, Mrs. P, said my mother found it to be a fascinating place. That's why she bought it."

"Really."

Basil entered my home without waiting for an invite. As I closed the door, he took in the beamed, vaulted ceiling.

"Nice." He ran his fingers over the oak panelling. "Lovely."

"Come through to the drawing room." I held the door for him, but he remained where he was, studying a photograph and some small sketches. A stunned look crossed his face and I knew he saw what Candela had seen a year ago.

"Whisky?" I asked.

He glanced over his shoulder as I stepped away from the door. By the time, I had poured a couple of whiskies he'd entered the room. His jaw dropped, and I knew he had recognised the artist of the portrait over the fireplace.

"Thanks," he muttered, as I pushed the glass into his outstretched hand, his eyes never leaving the picture. I watched his stunned expression as he continued to study mother's portrait.

In the style of Gustave Klimt, Mother had painted herself nude using bands of colours and broad strokes of gold. She lay on her side in the centre of the picture. An ornate bracelet, shaped like a snake, was wrapped around her wrist, while her open palm supported her head. Her dark green eyes were wide and inviting. They peered out from under a mass of black curly hair that cascaded over her shoulders, covering her creamy breasts, but allowed her nipples to be exposed. Her other arm rested along the full length of her body. On her hip she held a red apple that had a bite taken from it.

Placed discreetly and far enough forward to hide her modesty sat another red apple. Sitting upright on the top of the apple was a large cartoon-like worm. At the bottom of the apple was a hole where the worm had entered. A simple wash of colour surrounded the figure and the worm to keep the viewer focused on what she, the artist, wanted them to see. Beyond this were a patchwork of gold and an array of colours.

The symbolism within the painting explained everything, if you knew how to read her work. A small plaque at the bottom of the painting read, '*Eve was as perfect as the apple until her destruction.*'

"Your mother— was *Jane Elspeth Maedere*?"

"Yes." I sipped my drink and leant back. Some might find it strange, but I have a bit of an Oedipus complex. There were too many unanswered questions. I want to understand mother more. In a Freudian way, by understanding her, I could understand the artist in both of us.

"Why didn't you tell me?"

"Tell you what?"

"That your mother was—"

"I'm quite aware of who my mother was, Basil."

"But—don't you understand, James! What a huge selling point you have by adding her name to your work." He gaped at her painting as though willing her to agree.

"No— Basil."

Puzzlement clouded his face. "Sorry! No! You mean you didn't know, or no as in—"

I smiled. He couldn't bring himself to say it. "No, as in I wish to sell my work on its own merit."

"Oh— of course." He lowered himself into my father's chair, disappointment lining his face. He gulped his whisky and leant forward, keeping eye contact with me.

"I understand totally, James. But once it is known, your sales will increase by a small fortune. Everyone wondered what happened to her when she disappeared."

"She died, Basil."

"Oh, I assumed that she disappeared from the limelight, rather than went missing. I didn't realise she had died. In my research on your mother I found no details about her death—or that she had married."

"Your research?"

"I'm a bit of an expert on Jane Elspeth Maedere. What happened to your mother?"

"Are you really? My parents enjoyed a private life. Her funeral was a low-key affair. Anyway, no one needs to know unless someone tells them." Basil lowered his eyes and studied his empty glass. I changed the subject. "So why did you come to see me?"

"I was interested to see where you work. What inspires your pictures?" He set his glass down.

"Really."

"Okay, not quite, but I'm glad I did." He pulled out a slip of paper from his jacket pocket. "As we're on the subject of going missing, I wanted to ask you about a picture printed in yesterday's paper." He held out a newspaper cutting to me. "You might have already seen it though."

"I don't have the dailies." I took the well-thumbed cutting and unfolded it. A grainy photograph of a girl stared out at me. My hands trembled as if it, too, remembered its part in capturing her forever on a canvas, my first of ten. I looked up. Basil was studying me.

Chapter Five

"The quality of the photo is very poor, Basil." I studied the image on the cutting. "Is that you in conversation with a good-looking woman?"

Basil gave a sharp nod. "Take a good look at her, James." His eyes never left my face.

"From an artist's point of view," I began, knowing it wasn't what he wanted to hear. "She holds herself well, high cheekbones and a strong jawline— in a well-cut dress. Makes quite a presence when entering a room, what more can I say?"

I smiled and offered him the cutting back.

He raised his hand in protest. "Does she look familiar to you, James?"

"Nope. Should she?"

"Went missing from the art exhibition we attended last year."

"We attended?"

"Yes, where I met you"

I re-read the headline, *'Hockney Exhibition 1963 Missing Girl.'* "The place was heaving, Basil. How would I recognise one ordinary girl when there were so many famous faces? Anyway, after meeting you I left."

"It's important. You might remember seeing her."

"No. Sorry, I don't." I handed the cutting back. Basil scrutinised it as though looking for something he might have overlooked.

"The police came to see me the other day—" Basil said while pocketing the cutting.

"The police." I leant forward in my seat and gripped my glass with both hands. "They questioned you, and now you're questioning me. Why?"

"I've been hoping someone else saw her that night. As you were there, you might have seen her too."

"Right after we met, I left. Anyway, why did they question you?"

"For the same reason they questioned me a year ago." Basil rose. Without asking, he poured himself another drink.

"Hang on, are you telling me you've been questioned before about the girl's disappearance?"

"I wasn't the only one. They spoke to everyone on the guest list." He turned, bottle in hand and pointed it at me. "Just a minute—" his tone was almost threatening. "If you weren't questioned previously then you weren't invited. How did you get into the launch party?"

I grinned. "Gate-crashed, along with the reporters. That's why I left before anyone realised I wasn't meant to be there."

"I don't know whether to be pleased for you or not. Anyway, I told them the same thing I did a year ago. With the passage of time, along with too much to drink, everything was a little hazy. It's a wonder I can even remember our meeting on that night." He smirked and ran his hand over his face. "I had no idea who they were talking about when they first questioned me. Evidently Candela Waterbrook worked as a picture hanger at that gallery and quite a few other well-established ones around London. It's funny how some odd little things happen at the most awkward of times." He recapped the bottle and set it down. "To help me identify who they were talking about, they showed me a drawing of the girl. It made quite an impression on me. Miss Waterbrook's boyfriend had drawn it."

Basil sat down in my father's chair and took a swig of his drink. "I remember desperately wanting to know more about the artist. He was quite an accomplished one. Shame it was an inappropriate time. Apparently they found a bloodied knife among his damaged paintings."

"Do they think he might've done away with her?"

"No idea. Not that they would've told me. Even so, I wasn't a suspect then."

"Are you now?" I asked while pouring myself a drink. I was glad I had my back to him as his next question threw me.

"The least said. When you were living in London, did you ever hear of an artist called Tom, Thomas, or Tommy Blackbird?"

My hand shook causing the bottle to rattle against the glass. "No— why?"

"Are you sure?" Basil's tone echoed his question.

"Of course." I swung round. "Such an unusual name, not one you're likely to forget."

"It's not just his name that's odd. He's a bit of an enigma."

"In what way?" I glanced out the French windows. The shadows on the lawn told me the afternoon was nearly over. And here I was wasting time.

"After living for six months in the same squat as the Waterbrook girl, all anyone knew about Tommy Blackbird was just that, his name." Basil pulled at his cuffs, as though he had a card trick up his sleeve.

"Did the police think they've left together?" I returned to my seat.

"It's hard to say. I wasn't privy to their evidence. According to a friend, if the police hadn't discovered blood in Blackbird's studio, they might have followed up on that line of enquiry. The blood threw a kind of spanner into their investigation."

"Whose blood was it?"

"According to my friend, no one bled out at the scene. They had nothing to compare it with. There was no sign of a struggle, so the police felt it was staged. They identified the fingerprints as Waterbrook after lifting some off a hairbrush found in the boyfriend's bathroom. Her prints matched those on the knife they believe was used to damage his paintings."

"Are they looking for Blackbird?"

"Your guess is as good as mine. It's a mystery to my friend."

"Your friend knows a lot."

Basil ignored my comment. "Why would a struggling artist leave behind such valuable art materials if he wasn't coming back? There's no evidence of him ever entering Waterbrook's boyfriend's studio. Most of her belongings were gone, so it was believed the girl went off on her own volition."

"If it's the girl's choice, why the fuss?" I relaxed back into my seat, eager to hear more.

"The girl's parents received a letter saying she was heading home. She was pissed off with her boyfriend. Her parents said she wasn't the sort of girl to make them worry unnecessarily."

"So no evidence of foul play?"

"After twelve months of nothing, it seemed that way. Until this picture turned up." Basil flexed his slender fingers before playing nervously with a ring on his little finger. "Now the police are re-questioning everyone on their list. I cannot tell them anything more than I did a year ago. I knew neither Waterbrook nor her boyfriend. Others reported seeing the girl and her boyfriend having a blazing row about me. God only knows why."

"Surely the people who witnessed the row were questioned."

"Of course they were. Some remember seeing the boyfriend afterwards, but no one saw Candela. Her disappearance would've remained a cold case if the mysterious owner of the photograph hadn't sent it to the police."

"The police had the picture published in the paper?"

"No. The newspaper received a copy at the same time. They published it to see if anyone could identify themselves among the people milling around behind the girl and myself."

Basil pulled out the cutting again and pointed to the grainy photograph. "It would've been helpful if Blackbird appeared in the background, but no one really remembers what he looked like. At the time, the police were unsuccessful in tracing everyone who lived at the squat as most of the artists were itinerant. Since the exhibition, the whole area has undergone regeneration. None of his belongings at the squat helped the police in tracking him down."

Basil refolded the cutting. "I just hope that if one new photo can surface, then maybe others will follow proving I wasn't the last person to see her alive that evening."

"So they can feel just as shitty as you do?" I laughed, trying to lighten his mood.

He swirled the whisky around in his glass. Lines of fatigue etched across his forehead. He took a gulp before slipping the cutting into his pocket. "No, this might seem funny to you, but another young woman has also gone missing. This time it is from my local bookshop. The missing girl, Bella Wright, had sorted out the order my secretary Jenny had placed for me. I collected it the day Jenny was off work." He took a deep breath before continuing. "The day Miss Wright went missing. Of course the police got very excited about this and put my name at the top of their suspect list."

"Woo— damn unlucky old man," I chuckled, trying not to look up, knowing that Bella, my latest muse, waited for me.

He glared. "Hang on a minute. Wasn't that the day I saw you coming out of the bookshop, just as I was arriving? Now I remember we were due to meet at five. Was it that week or the following one when we bumped into each other? God, I hate it. Now I even doubt myself." He set his glass down. "Once they've finished questioning you, you're so muddled." A frown crossed his face. "I'm not good at remembering things at the best of times, especially when Jenny's off work."

I refilled his glass. Basil took a large gulp of his drink. With his free hand he ran it through his hair as if to wipe away any lingering tension, before relaxing into the chair. He surveyed mother's portrait again. His grey eyes absorbed every detail as though, like an artist, he was sketching her. "Oh, for God's sake, I've nothing to worry about. It isn't as if I knew the girls personally. I'm not even sure I even spoke to that girl in the bookshop. Most of the time, Jenny takes my orders in for me. On the odd occasion I had to collect it myself I don't know whether I dealt with the shop owner or not. Anyway, we've more important things to think about, James. Your paintings, I'm pleased to say, are selling well.

I've been thinking it's time to up the ante."

"In what way do you mean up the ante?" My stomach churned. When he didn't answer, I wondered if he had heard me. The dark smudges under his eyes told me he hadn't slept well for some time.

Up the ante? I swallowed the rest of my drink as I waited for him to elaborate on what he meant. My inner demon screamed, '*you'll never be better than her!'*

"Hmm," Basil sighed. His eyes focused on mother's portrait. "How about doing something that reflects our society, something urban?"

"Urban." I smiled.

Basil smacked his lips together and lifted his glass to the portrait. "Cheers old girl." He leered at mother as he ran his tongue around his lips. "She was quite the stunner. I would've loved to have met her."

The lewd tone of his voice made the bile in my stomach rise. I had heard him use the same tone when discussing his latest conquest over drinks and nibbles at other artists' exhibition parties. He surveyed the young female artists more than the paintings on show which had earnt him the reputation of being a bit of an alley cat.

At forty-two, Basil was fifteen years my senior, and unmarried. His athletic build and flirty grey eyes meant he was never without a string of girlfriends. They all believed they would become Mrs Hallward. Most were gullible young artists who were convinced he had their best interests at heart, but I knew better.

His past conquests would be of great interest to the police. I was sure they would get the wrong impression of him. Many of those young women would still hold a grudge after discovering just how little Basil thought of them.

"You certainly inherited your mother's looks as well as being a bloody genius." His eyes rested briefly on me before turning to the portrait again.

"Not quite all mother's looks. Her eyes were green. Mine are blue."

"How odd? Well, you have her dark wavy hair. I wish she

was alive. Such a talented beauty."

"I'm sorry that she's not alive too." I peered down into my empty glass and caught sight of my white knuckles.

"Good God, James. I apologise, I meant I would've loved to have discussed her work with her." Basil leant forward in his chair to reach for his glass. On taking a sip, he realised the glass was empty and set it down with a thud. "She was a bit of an enigma in the art world." Basil leant back in his seat. "No one really knew what happened to her. She seemed to have dropped off the radar just before the end of the war."

"I guess in Britain at that time everyone was a little preoccupied with staying alive," I mumbled, though he wasn't really listening.

"*Jane Elspeth Maedere...*" Basil breathed mother's name out like a lover whispering to his sweetheart. He turned his attention back to me. "So, James. Why didn't you tell me she was your mother?"

"As I've already said, Basil, I'm selling my own work, not my mother's." I was wrong. I didn't have his attention, but the son of Jane Maedere did.

He rose and I thought he was about to leave, but he crossed to the drinks cabinet and helped himself again. As he recapped the whisky bottle, I noticed some deep scarring at the top of his little finger, almost as though he had lost part of it. I made a mental note to ask him about it. As he returned the bottle to the cabinet, his attention went to a small group of mother's framed sketches.

"You certainly have your mother's eye for detail. It's quite recognisable." He took a sip of his drink and moved to examine the next set of pictures. "Hmm, I'm surprised I didn't see the likeness before. I'm a bit of an expert on your mother's work." He dropped back into father's chair again. "During wartime I maintained aircraft. By the end of the war I was sick of Britain, rationing and wanted something new so I moved to America. While there I came across a piece of your mother's work. I was in a junk shop, looking for some pieces to decorate my apartment, when I spotted a couple of small paintings. Did you know your mother spent time in

America?"

"I knew she'd lived abroad before I was born. Mrs P had told me that much, but not that it was in America. I've always been curious about how my parents met."

"Mrs P? Of course, your housekeeper." Basil studied his glass.

"Mrs P told me mother was a world-weary artist seeking a quiet life in England after living abroad. My father, a widower with two small children, rented a church cottage. I guess she must have met him in church, though mother wasn't really a churchgoer. Anyway, three years later they married. Just after their first wedding anniversary I arrived."

"It's strange that your mother married someone with no links to the art world, don't you think? She was a recluse by all accounts, so maybe that's what was so appealing about your father. All those vows of silence."

"Father wasn't a monk, but you're right. Maybe she found solace in his quietness. If mother was such a recluse, where did you gather your knowledge from?"

"Ah, it was a lucky accident. It's due to your mother that the doors to the art world opened for me. Purely by chance, the two paintings I found were earlier pieces by her. The framed watercolour sketches depicted the same woman's profile. In both paintings, her hair streamed out behind her head and was interwoven with stars, the moon and setting sun. The pictures were a mirror image of each other. The style of paintings spoke volumes to me, so I bought both. I took the paintings to my friend Cindy to see if she recognised the name. It was as if I'd brought her the Holy Grail. She was ecstatic, explaining the paintings were rare and were worth a great deal of money. Of course, I wanted to know more, and that's when Cindy introduced me to someone who knew your mother well."

"Who?" I demanded.

"An American art agent, Chuck Sparks. He specialised in Native American works. He showed me some amazing photographs of her. According to him she wasn't only beautiful but a prolific prodigy too. Her drive to paint was unprecedented according to him. Her style was a form of surrealism, like Salvador Dali's. I loved her hidden messages within the paintings. You had to fully understand the piece to unravel the conundrum."

I nodded. Prolific Prodigy. What an amazing title. I knew that she had the temperament of a diva rather than of a prodigy. She didn't believe in making life easy for anyone, least of all for me. Father struggled to appease her every time the crew from the London gallery arrived to collect her work for an exhibition. Father knew that if she opened one crate none of the paintings would be going anywhere.

On many occasions I stood at the top of the stairs watching the ghost of my mother, or with my eye pressed to a keyhole, or from behind curtains, or a door. The distance between her and me was unbridgeable. If she caught me watching she would fly into a rage, screaming her green eyes full of anger. I wanted so much to please the strange paradox who was never my mother, always an artist.

Mrs P was my mother, a constant figure in my life. From my earliest memories, it was always her who bathed me, put me to bed and read to me. In the morning, she made my breakfast. During the day she made me laugh and played games with me. The woman that lived in the room, who smelt of turps and linseed oil, who constantly needed to paint, day and night, was not my mother.

The only time she would emerge from her studio was when she had an exhibition. Her agent dealt with everything but, even then, they were unsure whether she would attend, or even allow her paintings to leave the house. If father wasn't there to watch over her, during the night she would destroy her work.

Mother's agent would get her to sign the paintings over to them. Then a team of picture movers cased them up into wooden crates and secured them in our cellar overnight. The following morning they would be collected and taken to London.

According to Mrs P, *'Too many people expected too much too soon from her,'* after the success of her first art exhibition.

She wondered if stress had been the catalyst that brought them together. She, an artist in search of spiritual guidance, and his quiet, ecclesiastical ways, made for a perfect match.

"So are you going to show me what you are working on now?" Basil broke into my thoughts. I stood, and Basil was out of the door before I'd even taken a step. We made slow progress up the stairs. He stopped to take a look at every picture. I went ahead of him and waited at the studio doorway. Basil's eyes never left the wall as he made his way towards me.

"Unbelievable, James. Simply unbelievable," he said, finally making it up the stairs.

I stepped back, allowing him to enter first. He pivoted on the balls of his feet, slowly taking in the room. Once he realised where he was, all interest in seeing my latest work faded.

"This is *her* studio," he gasped, more a statement than a question.

I removed the cloth that covered my painting. The smell of the paints caressed my nostrils, reminding me of the unfinished work waiting for my attention in the attic studio. Basil stood fingering some large canvases leaning against mother's desk, untouched since her death. As he thumbed through them, pleasure lit up his face. Basil pulled out one of the paintings. It depicted a naked figure of a mature woman knelt with her back to the viewer. Strands of golden light played off her hair and the smooth skin of the model. The artist had focused on the shape of the back, the length of the neck and upper arms of the sitter bathing them in a golden sheen.

"I've never seen this one before—none of them." Excitement edged his voice. "They're not listed in any catalogue of your mother's works I've seen."

I shrugged. My painting had more depth to it than mother's. Each brushstroke captured the power of the stormy sky with its fast-moving clouds reflected in the turbulence of the tide-driven estuary as it approached the harbour mouth. Its emanating forcefulness was clearly visible, which pleased me.

"This painting could help you make quite a name for yourself," Basil said, his voice barely containing his excitement.

"You think so? I'm very pleased with it, particularly the strength of the colours in the sky. I was a little unsure of it at first, but now I feel they work really well."

"Brilliant as always," Basil muttered dismissively.

My agent's attention wasn't on my painting but mother's canvases. "What do you think of *my* painting?" My childhood angst surfaced, as I was unable to contain my annoyance. My constant wanting to please a parent whose attention was elsewhere.

"James, the world needs to see these. They're amazing."

"Those paintings are not for sale." I focused on draping a damp cloth over my painting before I snatched the one he was holding and returned it to its place.

"But—" He reached for another. I knocked his hand away and stepped between him and the canvases. Our eyes locked. He lifted his arm as he studied my face. For a fleeting moment he looked as though he considered striking me. Then, seeming to second-guess my thoughts, he let his arm drop. I pointed to the door, but he wasn't about to give up.

"Please—can I see the rest?"

"No."

Basil stood his ground. For a moment I thought I might physically have to remove him.

"I'm sorry. You need to leave now. If mother had wanted the world to see these, you would've known about them."

He backed out of the room, speaking to me as though reasoning with a naughty child. "They're stunning works, James. Please, at least let me catalogue them. It would be such a shame if they were lost forever."

"Only I need to know where they are."

I closed the door behind us and started down the stairs.

"Can't I persuade you?" Basil remained by the studio door, reminding me of my childhood. The locked room I wasn't allowed to enter. "No. I'm sorry."

"But James she's—dead!"

"To you she may be, but for me she's very much alive and living in this house. I won't go against her wishes."

I continued down the stairs.

Chapter Six

We returned to the drawing room and Basil finished off his drink in one gulp and slammed the empty glass down. "When you've finished the painting, bring it to my office," he said, heading out into the hall.

I rose to follow him. Basil called back over his shoulder as he entered the hallway. "I'll see myself out."

As he closed the front door, I turned towards the kitchen. I set the kettle on the stove and watched as Basil's car swung around and disappeared from view. Just before the kettle began to whistle, I thought I heard the distinct click of the heavy front door closing. I glanced out the window to see if Basil had returned for some reason, but a large overgrown shrub blocked my view so I couldn't see as far as the entrance gate. If he had returned, the sound of a car crunching over the gravel would've alerted me.

Eager to get back to my studio I placed Mrs P's teapot on a tray and added a jug of milk along with a tin of biscuits before carrying it up to my attic studio. On passing mother's studio the contents of the tray rattled as I recalled a cold wet morning six years ago.

At the age of twenty-two when I felt couldn't endure the loss of another loved one, after the loss of both parents another the bombshell hit. It came without warning. Mrs P and I were sitting in the kitchen having our first relaxing breakfast after an insane few weeks of organising father's funeral and sorting out his estate when the doorbell rang.

"I wonder who that is, James." Mrs P undid her apron strings, tugged it off and dropped it on counter before hurrying to the front door. On her return she held a letter. The look on her face told me it wasn't good news.

"Oh dear, James. I'm so sorry, but my sister needs me."

"Will you be away for long?" My hand shook as I set my cup down.

"I'm sorry, James, but you're old enough to look after yourself now. I must put my own family's needs first."

I patted her thin hand. "You're right, Mrs P. It's about time I became responsible for my own life. Would you like another cup of tea?" I lifted the pot.

"Yes please. I'm always at the end of the phone if you do need any advice." She passed me her cup. "You can afford to hire help to run this place. Mr Jarman isn't just your gardener, but quite a handyman too. Always happy to help out and earn a bit extra for his young family. I know a couple of reliable women in the village, if you would like their names."

"Let's see how I get on first by myself, Mrs P. If need be, I'll give you a call. Can I help you with anything?"

"Please. Could you order me a taxi? It'll only take me a couple of hours to pack. I don't have much." She began to clear away the breakfast things.

Two hours later we stood in the hall saying our goodbyes while the taxi driver finished loading Mrs P's case and boxes. Mrs P seemed tiny in my arms, as we hugged goodbye, her thin shoulders dug into me while her snowy white hair tickled my cheeks. She pushed lightly on my chest and stepped away.

"James, remember all I've taught you." She pulled a hanky out of her coat pocket and dabbed at her cheeks. "I know you'll be wise with your money. Any problems, just call me. Here, these are yours now." She dropped a bunch of keys into my hand and picked up her handbag. "Look after yourself, won't you?"

I nodded, lost for words.

"Right, I mustn't keep the taxi waiting, James." She kissed my cheek one last time.

I grasped the keys hard and my chest tightened. Hastily I wiped my cheeks and followed Mrs P out to watch her leave. On closing the door after the taxi left I shed tears, which surprised me as I hadn't for my father.

In the hallway the emptiness swallowed me up. Suddenly aware of a stabbing pain in my hand I looked down. Clenched in my fist were the keys Mrs P had given me. Some were familiar to me, especially the front and back door keys. Some had little tags attached to them, stating shed key, outbuildings, and store cupboards. One had a fine gold chain attached to it. A wave of unexpected excitement washed over me, drowning out the sadness of Mrs P's departure. In bounding steps, I took the stairs two at a time as I headed for the locked door of mother's studio. For years I had wanted to paint in there, to breathe in her creativity, to feel the weight of her brushes in my hand, and to play with her muses. Father had refused, insisting that Mrs P keep the door locked, and that she carried the key with her at all times.

With a racing heart, I wiped my clammy palms on my jeans before inserting the key. Its click echoed around me. I pushed the door open and was hit by stale, musty. A wave of nausea rose sent a sickening pain shooting through my stomach. I bent, clutching my sides. The ghost of mother rose before me, her pale face veiled in the darkness that made her haunting green eyes shine. Her lips were a perfectly radiant smile. She lifted her arm and swung the bloodied knife. I screwed my eyes shut and waited.

As the pain and nausea subsided, I opened my eyes. There wasn't a ghost, just an empty studio. I opened the French windows and took a few deep breaths. Mother's easel stood facing a large picture window that overlooked a balcony. On it rested an unfinished masterpiece that depicted a dark sky with skeletal trees against a setting sun. Through the window, I saw on the far side of the river the subject of mother's painting a row of storm-damaged trees. Mother seemed haunted by their sadness, their fallen leaves and broken branches. She had painted them throughout her life. Maybe through them she recorded her own fractured life. Every spring, the warmth of sunlight brought rebirth to the surrounding countryside, but the skeletal trees remained the same just empty shells. The view of the fast-flowing river and the shattered trees made me wonder why the love I had for her wasn't enough to fill her empty heart.

I traced the diagonal slash across her last masterpiece mother's final violent act towards the art world, and wondered, what drove her to paint. Was it the fear of failure, or the fear of rejection by the ones that loved her the most?

I picked up one of mother's brushes hoping to feel some connection to her creativity. Its weight nestled too comfortably in my hand. A sudden burst of electricity rushed up my arm and swamped me with a feeling of uneasiness. I dropped the brush and dashed from the studio. After locking the door, I left her to play among the shadows of my childhood.

I threw a few belongings into an old suitcase, secured the house and left for London. Months later on my return to Halghetree, I moved into father's bedroom. It was cell-like in its bareness, with just a metal framed bed, plain walls and floor. The only changes I made in the room were to add two bookshelves and fill them with paperback novels.

***

Just past mother's studio, at the end of the corridor, I set the tray down, and slammed my hand against a carved raven in the centre of a wooden panelled wall. The panel slid back and revealed a staircase that led up to my roof studio. Basil's unexpected visit had irritated me.

I cursed myself for allowing him to see the inside of her studio, but on reflection the pleasure of knowing how eager he was to get his hands on mother's paintings meant a couple of aces up my sleeve. He was a desperate man, and I was going to use it to my advantage.

As the panel closed slowly behind me, the knowledge that I had unexpectedly cleared myself of any links to the disappearances dispersed my anger. I picked up the tray and climbed the steps into my studio.

My suspended muse disturbed my thoughts as a plea broke the silence. "Please… Please…Let me down— I need water."

I banged the tray down, and hastily poured some tea into a mug and added milk. I scrutinised the unfinished painting, pushing all thoughts of Basil aside while sipping my tea. I picked up the palette and checked to see whether any of the paints had dried and scraped them off, before adding fresh paint. I reached for a brush my eagerness returning.

"For fuck's sake—" The girl's rasping voice echoed through my concentration. "Why are you doing this to me?" she struggled, the cords binding her wrists cutting into her pale flesh.

"Damn it!" I tossed the brush and palette aside, nearly knocking over my mug. "Bloody Basil!"

I kicked the daybed over to where the fastened pulley ropes were on the wall and lowered her enough so she knelt before me. The body harness continued to support her full weight.

"Don't!" She tried to twist her head away from me, but the chinstrap held her fast. "Please—get me down—" Her tongue flicked lizard-like over her dry, cracked lips.

"Don't keep asking!" I gritted my teeth in an effort not to raise my voice. It wasn't her fault we'd been disturbed. "I'm sorry. Until I've finished this painting, you're not going anywhere." I lifted the child's beaker to her lips. "Here, drink this, Bella."

"No!" She pinched her cracked lips.

"Shh— it's only water." I softened my tone. "You'll be pleased to know you've been reported missing." I forced the spout into her mouth. "Slowly now, otherwise you'll start choking." I moved the beaker away to allow her to swallow.

"Let me go. I won't tell."

"Please drink just a little more. It'll help you." I pushed the spout between her lips again. "Now suck gently, Bella." I tipped the beaker in an effort to encourage her. She sucked hard on the spout causing the water to flood her mouth. While waiting for her to stop coughing, I wiped around her mouth and neck. Once Bella had regained her composure, she flexed her shoulders, trying to release her hands while her eyes continued to search my face. Confusion clearly visible in her eyes, but I had no time for explanations. I covered my nose and mouth before pulling a fresh chloroform-filled pad out of a plastic bag. She shook her head.

"No— please, not again," she wheezed as the straps rattled. I held the back of her head while gently pressing the pad onto her face. After a brief struggle her head dropped and rested against the chinstraps. I winched her back into place and set to work again.

It saddened me how quickly Candela's beauty faded. I had hoped both Candela and Bella's beauty would remain long after their death like that of the butterflies. Neither Candela nor Bella had died at my hand. Their lives were snuffed out as a by-product of my creativity. I hadn't physically harmed them. Like my father's bell jars, my paintings are a way of capturing a thing of beauty forever.

The loss of Candela had shocked me. Once the painting was completed, I no longer needed her for inspiration. While lowering her onto the daybed, I noticed how clammy her skin felt to the touch. I checked for a pulse and found a shallow one. Once the chloroform wore off completely, I was sure she would recover. After wheeling the bed through to the storeroom I unfastened the clips from her eyelids. She moaned as her eyes closed. Next, I removed the chinstrap. Deep red lines showed it had dug in. I gently massaged her neck and chin to get the circulation moving before peeling the white silk gown from her shoulders. Carefully I freed her arms from the sleeves of the dress and rolled it down over her stomach and off her legs. After hanging the dress on a mannequin, I unfastened the body harness, starting with the straps on her shoulders. I rolled her onto her side and covered her with a sheet and a blanket. I checked her breathing again. She wheezed slightly, but the rise and fall of her chest told me she was okay. Before leaving the room I placed a small table next to the bed, with a glass of water and a bowl of cut fruit within easy reach for her.

For days I abandoned sleep and barely ate as I added little

dabs of colour here and there to the painting to create the difference between the light and the shade. Finally, unable to keep my eyes open any longer the brush fell from my hand onto the discarded palette. I staggered from the studio, down the stairs, to my bedroom. Without undressing I fell into the bed.

I'm not sure what woke me but I was ready to start work. I headed for the bathroom, stripped and stepped under the hot water. Refreshed, I hastily threw on fresh clothes, eager to prepare my studio for the arrival of my next angel.

In the studio I placed the wet painting into the drying rack then began to clean my brushes and palette, sorted out the paint tubes, discarding any used-up ones and made a mental list of what needed replenishing. Satisfied that the studio was now reorganised, I went through into my storeroom to collect the paints I needed.

On opening the door a blast of cold air hit me, followed by an overwhelming stench. I gagged and covered my mouth and nose. Light cutting through the darkness revealed the white dress hanging on the mannequin, like some watching angel. On the daybed I could just distinguish an unrecognisable lump.

"Oh dear God." I dashed to the bed, knocking over the table. In the half-light a dark stain fanned out across the white sheet that covered the lower half of a body. Retching, I backed from the room. On the balcony I inhaled deeply. In the garden below, the stone angel beckoned to me and I knew what I needed to do.

In the garden I hunted among the fallen gravestones until I found a suitable one. Half hidden among the branches of a huge rhododendron bush stood a large tabletop grave. The roots of the shrubs had lifted one side of the tomb slightly, revealing a cavity within. I placed my shoulder to the lid, but it was far too heavy to lift. With no other choice, I went to the shed to fetch a spade to dig a grave.

I decided the spot under the bush would be an ideal site and began to dig. As I lifted the first shallow spade full, I noticed that the lid of the tomb had a lip. I dropped to my knees and took a closer look. With the spade flat, I inserted its blade under one corner of the tomb's lid. Then, using the spade's handle as a lever, I lifted the lid easily. Though pleased with my discovery, I realised there was a second problem. I needed to keep the lid where it was, because I hadn't the strength to lift it back into place on my own. I returned to the shed to hunt for inspiration.

Back at the gravesite I placed a straw bale next to the tomb. The bale was the right height to support the tomb lid once opened but I feared it wouldn't support its weight. Sweat ran down my back as I inched the lid over enough until it rested on the bale. The clearance gave me enough room to be able to peer in. The torchlight showed the coffin had imploded leaving a chasm at the bottom of the grave. I checked the straw bale, it held the weight. I increased the size of the gap, eager to get the body out of my studio.

I brought Candela to the grave using the wheelbarrow, not wanting to handle her. With unexpected ease, I slipped her through the gap. After collecting a barrow full of compost from Old Bill the gardener's heap, I covered her, and was able to give her a decent burial. With a bit of a struggle I replaced the lid.

It wasn't pleasant finding Candela dead. Her lack of beauty in her demise had disappointed me. I had seen death as a beautiful thing after witnessing the expiry of father's butterflies. No unpleasant smells, leaking liquid, or faeces. Once they settled onto the bottom of the killing box, they looked as beautiful as in life. Mother's passing had been the same.

The day before she died, mother had been radiant in her beauty. In my childish innocence, I had wanted to capture that moment forever like father did with his butterflies. As a child, I loved hunting for them with him. Later I observed, in silence, as he gassed the delicate creature. With fascination, I watched as they beat their fragile wings against the glass, frantic in their desire to live. As their beating slowed, I held my breath until my chest heaved. Once they became still, father lifted them out, and then flattened them. From a box, he took a shiny silver pin and stabbed each one through their belly before pinning them to a board to dry. Now their beauty was captured for all to see.

On my seventh birthday, I heard the best news ever. Even father looked excited as he hugged me. "James, I have some wonderful news. Your mother has finished her painting and will join us in the garden for your birthday party."

"Mrs P. Oh Mrs P, Guess what!" I dashed into the kitchen and threw my arms around her waist. With flour still on her hands she laughed and dusted the end of my nose with a fingertip. "I know, James, I know. Now if you help me, we will soon have your birthday tea ready."

I assisted Mrs P in the kitchen by helping her to make some little jam tarts. While rolling out the pastry I prayed nothing would spoil the day. By the afternoon, the sky was so blue I wanted to cry with relief. In the warmth of the sunshine the heady smell of honeysuckle perfumed the garden. Father decided to set the table and chairs up in the sunken Italian garden under the arbour. While I helped to carry the things we needed out, I constantly watched the sky terrified that a black cloud would appear from nowhere.

"Come on boy, what are you waiting for?" Father said on his return with a tray loaded with plates and cutlery.

"I don't want anything to stop mother from coming to join us."

He knelt before me, his hands resting on my shoulders. "You've nothing to worry about today. She's very happy. It's your birthday and, of course, she'll want to help you celebrate it. Now we mustn't leave everything to Mrs Page, there's more to bring out."

Once the table was set I took my seat, leaving the one next to me free. Mrs P brought out a cake with candles, and the small tarts along with the rest of the party food. While father went to fetch mother, I sat with my hands clasped saying over and over, *"please come, please come."* Between watching the path from the house I swatted the wasps and flies to keep them away from the food.

Mrs P reappeared carrying the small teapot for me and wine for the adults. As she waited with me, I saw her lips move as though she was saying a silent prayer too.

"Is everything all right, Mrs P?"

"Of course, Master James." She patted my hand. "Now, don't you go worrying about your mother. She wouldn't want to let you down after all the help you've given me. Not once have you asked about your birthday presents. Most children I know would have wanted theirs straight away, made a right scene about it."

"I just want to see my mother and for her to share just one day with me, and not to be locked in her room where I can't see her."

"Ay I know, lad. I know you do. We'll give her a little more time. Your father told me this morning when I arrived that your mother had finished her painting, and she's very pleased with it. So I'm sure she'll join us."

Father suddenly appeared on the path, with a dazzling smile. I'd never seen him looking so happy.

"She'll be here in a moment, Mrs Page." He glanced back along the path. "She's just finishing getting ready. I've put a film in my camera, so if you'll be kind enough to take a picture. It would be lovely having one of us three together. Lydia and Robert will be joining us later, but for now, it's just us."

"How do I look, Donald?"

Father swung round at the sound of mother's voice. Her footsteps had been so light that none of us had heard them. Tall and elegant, she floated in a cloud of pale, shimmering yellow, reminding me of a glorious *Clouded Yellow* butterfly in my father's collection. Her long black curls hung around her shoulders, and her face was bright with happiness. I wanted to rush up to her, and throw my arms around her narrow waist, but I couldn't move. All I could do was breathe in the honeysuckle perfume that filled the air.

"My darling, you look so beautiful." Father stepped forward and took her small hand in his. He leant forward to kiss her, but she turned her lips away and offered him her cheek instead. Father's smile dropped and then, aware that I was watching, he recovered himself and kissed her lightly on the cheek. He tucked her hand under his arm and led her over to the seat beside me.

"Hello, James." She fixed me with her smile as she settled in the chair, her voice thin and breathy.

Mother's dark green eyes left me dumbstruck as the sweetness of her cologne enveloped me.

Chapter Seven

Death of a Clouded Yellow Butterfly 1944

"A glass my dear." Father poured out the blood-red wine.

"Yes please, my darling." Mother squeezed my hand gently. "We have much to celebrate today, haven't we, James?" Mother's voice flowed smoothly like the drink. "Are you ready for your present?"

I nodded, unable to speak.

The wine bubbled and sparkled in the sunlight as it flowed into the shimmering crystal glass and dazzled me. I blinked back my tears of happiness as mother's gentle fingers caressed my arm. I couldn't take my eyes off her.

"I had your gift specially flown over from America, didn't I, Donald?" She smiled at father.

"Yes you did, my dear."

"Well go and fetch it, Donald." Mother's sudden harsher tone clouded her face and the softness was gone.

Father looked at me. The hurt in his eyes was clearly visible as he passed her the wine glass, and then hurried indoors. I wanted to say something, but the words wouldn't come. Mother sat glass in hand, looking straight ahead. When father returned with a large rainbow-coloured gift, Mrs P came with him carrying a tray of sandwiches. Father placed the gift gently down in front of mother. No words passed between them.

Mrs P handed around a plate of sandwiches. Mother took one and placed it on the edge of her plate. Father sat down and helped himself to a couple of sandwiches. And with a nod he dismissed our housekeeper. Mrs P paused and picked up the camera, but he shook his head, waving her away. The tension between my parents grew. Father took a bite of his sandwich while mother twirled the fluted glass in her hands, swirling the wine around inside. She looked over its rim at him and a dark shadow crossed her face.

I didn't understand what was going on so I bit into my sandwich, just happy to have them together. To me, it was far better than any silly present.

Father shook his head as his mouth twitched slightly. "Please, Jane, not now, for your son's sake."

"Pleeeaasse…" Mother drew the word out sarcastically. "For your son's sake—" she echoed his words and then turned to me, her face radiant.

"James is happy, aren't you, darling? You have what you've wished for, Mummy and Daddy playing at being Mummy and Daddy. My little darling, things are never quite what they seem. Real life isn't like pretty pictures. Oh, we artists can create a world of our own because, in real life, we don't always get what we want, do we, Donald?" Her lips tightened.

"Please, Jane, it isn't the child's fault," father said with a tight-lipped smile.

"So you keep telling me, Donald. It's the war. Well, it's not the bloody war." She raised her glass to her red lips and took a gulp of wine.

"Jane, don't you dare!"

As mother's lips began to tremble, she raised one bejewelled hand to her mouth and wiped her lips as she placed her glass back on the table.

"Mummy—" I tried to stop myself from crying. "I made these jam tarts." I reached for the plate of oddly shaped golden tarts. "Mrs P showed me how to cut the pastry. Please try one. We picked the blackberries to make the jam, too."

"Did you, darling?" She turned to father. "What a clever boy we have here, Donald. Or is he just my son?" She looked at me, her eyes burning like fire under her heavy lids.

I looked from her to my father, confused by her words.

"Don't, Jane. Leave the child alone for God's sake. It's his birthday. Please just give him our present."

"Our present!" She held out the gift. Disdain passed over her features. "This is from your father in America." She glared at father.

I jumped out of my seat and threw my arms around her neck, not caring about the present. I wanted them to stop whatever it was they were doing to each other, and for her to know how much I loved her.

Father's hand shot across the table as a dark red stain raced across the white cloth towards mother. She pushed me away like a discarded rag doll. I fell backwards against the chair just as the red wine landed in her lap and cascaded onto her yellow satin shoes. She leapt up and lifted her wine-soaked dress as if she was about to curtsy. "You stupid, stupid boy!" Baring her teeth, her eyes wild now, a pair of soulless pits, she leaned over me. "Get up!" Her spittle sprayed my face.

I pulled myself to my feet, too frightened to take my eyes off her face. The glass. Why hadn't I seen the glass of red wine? A sob lodged in my throat and closed my eyes as a warm sensation trickled down my leg mixing with the red wine and covering the beautifully wrapped gift at my feet. Mother snatched up the present and grabbed my wrist. Her face twisted out of all recognition, her hair a tangled mass of black curls while her dress and shoes looked blood stained. With a violent yank she dragged me along the path towards the house. I stumbled, unable to match her long stride. All the time she called me names, some I didn't understand. "You dirty little bastard!" was one of them.

"In the name of God, Jane, let the child go!" Father hurried after us.

The kitchen door burst open and Mrs P appeared, teacloth in hand. Her eyes widened as she took in the situation. I reached for her but she did nothing. Mother tossed the birthday present at Mrs P. It hit her leg causing her to step backwards.

"So this is what you've been teaching my child," mother screeched as if a demonic creature had taken her place, her gentle tone gone. "This filthy wretch." Her long red nails dug into my upper arm as I tried to pull away, "has disrespected me by urinating all over his birthday present." She shook me hard as she began to raise her free hand.

"Don't hit the boy, Jane!" father demanded.

Ignoring his plea, she landed me a stinging slap across my cheek causing my head to snap back.

"Dear God, Jane." Father tried to stop mother, but she pulled me towards her. I tried desperately to stand.

"What I do with my son is my business, not yours!" She gave me another hard shake before pointing a bony finger at Mrs P. "And certainly it has nothing to do with this woman, your mistress!"

Father straightened, his eyes dull and distant. "You take that back, Jane," he said, his tone measured. "Apologise to Mrs Page. You can say and do whatever you want to me if that makes you happy, but leave the boy and Mrs Page out of it. What in God's name has the child ever done to you apart from love you?"

Mother shoved me. I covered my face as I fell backwards, fearing another slap. I crawled towards the kitchen door too scared to stand up in case she lashed out again. Mrs P swept me up into the safety of her strong arms and carried me away. Over her shoulder, I saw my distraught mother lashing out at father as he held her at bay.

By the time Mrs P had bathed and dressed me in clean pyjamas, peace had descended on the house as my parents' raised voices and slamming of doors receded. Lydia and Robert, my half-siblings never came to my party. I knew they wouldn't, as they feared mother's outbursts too. My birthday had passed for another year. The day dissolved into nothingness. I lay in bed restless, with my eyes shut, listening for Mrs P's gentle footsteps on the stairs. I hoped she would come and read me a story before I fell asleep. I guessed she was busy preparing a meal for father. Mother would be back in her studio working on another painting. As I lost the fight to stay awake, something heavy rested on the side of my bed. I opened my eyes to find Mrs P smiling down at me.

"Master James, you are still awake. Are you ready for a story?" she asked, picking up a book. I shook my head. My face still stung from mother's slap. "Why doesn't mother love me or daddy?"

"My dear child." She took hold of my hand. "I wish I could answer your question, but I can't." She leaned forward and kissed my forehead. I threw my arms around her neck, burying my head into her shoulder and sobbed. "I'm sorry I wet myself, Mrs P, and upset mummy. Tell daddy I'm so sorry I spoiled my birthday."

She hugged me and whispered, "Master James, you dear, sweet child. I'm sure your mother does love you. But she doesn't know how to show it. Your father knows it wasn't your fault. You must never forget he loves you."

The sunshine poured through a gap in the curtain and woke me. After yesterday's upset, an air of indifference hung in my attic bedroom. I slipped from my bed and went to investigate why my door stood ajar rather than locked. Normally I had to wait for father to let me out, as mother hated being disturbed when she was working. I paused only for a second. Then I pulled on a white t-shirt and bright red shorts before dashing downstairs. I wanted to see mummy so I could tell her how sorry I was for upsetting her yesterday.

On the landing below, I pressed my eye against the keyhole in her studio door. She stood with her back to it, muttering to herself. She wore a long white lace nightgown and rocked side to side. The cascading lace fell around her feet like a waterfall and imitated her movements. I couldn't make sense of what I was seeing. Something was wrong with a painting that rested on an easel behind her. In an effort to see properly, I pushed my eye closer to the keyhole and hit the door with my knee. I froze. Mother let out a low moan and spun round.

I stifled a cry at the sight of the deep gash that ran the full length of the painting. With my hands over my mouth I was unsure of what to do next. I didn't want to upset her again. I took a deep breath and counted as Mrs P told me to do if I felt a panic attack coming on.

"Was it red paint that soaked the front of her nightgown?" I pressed my eye to the keyhole again.

Mother, with a pained expression, faced the door with her eyes shut. She held one of her painting knives against her arm. Red paint dripped onto the bare floorboards and splashed against her gown. I reached for the door latch, wanting to rush to her, but for some reason, the sight of the knife stopped me. Then I heard voices.

I did not want to be told off for disturbing her, so I dropped to my knees and shuffled backwards, hiding beneath the heavy, velvet cloth that hung over the side of the table just outside her studio door.

Below, Mrs P asked young Kelly, her daily helper, "Where did Madam sleep last night?"

"In her studio again, I suspect..." came the reply. Their voices faded as they moved from the hall in the direction of the kitchen. I slid from my hiding place but remained on my knees while peering through the banisters into the hall below. I hesitated, not wanting to upset mother. I left.

Outside the window the river sparkled in the morning sunlight. Freedom called to me, a chance to explore the river on my own. I dashed down the stairs and hid in the coat cupboard just before the kitchen. The musty smell coming from the collection of old coats, shoes and boots, made me pinch my nose as I waited. All was still as I shot across the space between the cupboard and the backdoor out into the brilliant sunlight.

On leaving the courtyard, I ran bare foot along the path that led to the river, avoiding the other one as Kelly would take it to collect vegetables from the garden. The mowed grass path ran between swathes of long sun-bleached grasses and wildflowers and hummed with buzzing insects. The warmth of the sun on my face and the sound of the birdsongs lifted my spirit as I quickened my pace. The only sadness for me was not bringing a bug box to collect some butterflies. The grass path petered out, and I arrived at a high hedge with a wooden gate at its centre. I stood on tiptoe and reached for its latch only to discover the gate was padlocked. I slammed my fists against the gate and sunk down with my back to it.

I sat smacking the grass and kicking my legs in frustration when a fluttering movement caught my attention. Against the glaring sun four large flashing eyes danced above me. I stumbled after the peacock butterfly, eager to possess such a beauty. It landed on a clump of yellow flowers and made me wish I had brought father's net. I reached forward and closed my fingers over it.

On opening my hands enough to peer in, I held nothing in my grasp. I tore at the flowers, scattering the petals. As I surveyed my destruction the teasing butterfly danced overhead. I snatched at it, but it floated just out of reach. I punched the nettles. Not daring to lose sight of my prey, I ignored the stinging sensation crawling over my bare feet, up my legs and on my hands as I followed the butterfly to a patch of white flowers.

Moving slowly, with my hands cupped I expected the butterfly to take flight again, but it remained where it was. It fluttered madly as though caught by an invisible thread. I leaned over, trying to make sense of what I was seeing. Within the flower's petals was a white spider. It embraced the butterfly twice its size in its outstretched front legs. I ignored the red swellings that appeared all over my hands, feet and legs while watching with fascination as the butterfly struggled to free itself. The spider twisted the prey in its legs, drawing it towards its mouth. With a single bite the butterfly was dead. The spider manoeuvred itself to feed on a well-earned meal, but I snatched the butterfly from its grasp.

A sense of pleasure overtook the stinging pain in my hands and legs as I watched the spider search for its missing meal. I plucked a piece of dried grass and poked it; enjoying the power I had over it.

"What in God's name have you been doing, child! Just

look at the state of you!"

I swung round to face father. Dressed in black with a white collar, he reminded me of a strutting jackdaw.

"Why aren't you in your bedroom? Your mother is still upset after yesterday."

Tears gathered in the corners of my eyes and I dropped all that remained of the butterfly.

"James, I won't have you upsetting her again. I'll give you such a hiding. Now come here." As father reached for me, an unearthly scream rang out, causing the rooks and crows to take flight. We turned in its direction. I glanced up at father. Something flashed across his face causing his eyelids to droop. He seemed to be praying. In the silence that followed, father dragged me across a patch of stinging nettles onto the footpath.

"Come on, boy! Something's wrong."

I could only just keep up with him as we hurried towards the house. A sound of excited voices and pounding feet came towards us. Then Mrs P appeared, red-faced and panting around the corner.

"Oh, Reverend— it's the Mistress. She's—Oh dear God…" She rubbed at her eyes with a floral tea towel while stifling a sob. "I've called the doctor. You best let me take the boy."

Father released my arm and pushed past Mrs P, almost knocking her over. As she steadied herself, she called after him. "She's in her studio!"

At that moment I slipped round Mrs P and sped after him. Crashing through the back door, I bolted up the stairs and tore into her studio. Father lay slumped in the centre of the room. "Why, Jane? Dear God, why?" he pleaded.

Mother lay with her eyes closed and her right arm hanging off the side of the bed. Red paint had run down the heavy tapestry cover, across the floor and pooled just before her easel.

"Is mother asleep?" I asked. "I wanted to tell her that I was sorry for spoiling my birthday party. She was busy painting with a knife and had it all over her nightgown."

Father, with wet cheeks, pulled me towards him. In his softly spoken Sunday school voice he said, “I’m so sorry, child. Your mother has left us to live with the angels in heaven.”

“Left us? When will she be back?”

“They won’t let her come back, son. They need her there to help paint the stars and keep them shining until it’s our time to join her.”

“But I need her awake now,” I sobbed, rubbing my eyes. “I have something important to tell her.”

“I know, my son. But heaven needs her.”

“I need her more!” I screamed, running from the room.

To this day I’ve never understood the reason why I had to learn to share my mother with everyone, but I couldn’t have her to myself. On that fateful day, when the darkness shattered the dreams of a child on his birthday, no amount of praying to my father’s God could answer my prayers.

Chapter Eight

Stone Angels
The Third Painting
1965

"I find London far more fascinating when I'm not here," I muttered, knowing that Basil wasn't really listening. I regretted joining my agent on his trip into the city centre when I could've been heading home. My hope had been to locate my next angel but, so far, no one suitable had sparked my interest.

"Have you been to Grafton Gallery before, James?" Basil asked as we turned into a narrow alley way off Old Bond Street in Piccadilly.

"No, but I've heard of it. It has quite a history." I was excited to be walking in the footsteps of other great artists. As Basil peered intently over the top of his glasses at one of the paintings he had agreed to see, I didn't understand what his excitement was all about. My paintings were far more superior than the crap before me. The artist Joseph Easter was new to the market and unknown to me, yet somehow he had caught Basil's attention.

No matter how hard I tried to muster enthusiasm, the paintings left me cold. The tawdry collection of watercolours depicted a series of pastoral scenes from a bygone rural England with an array of farmers leaning on five-barred gates, pipes in hand, watching their cattle, while in the distance thatched cottages and church steeples peeped above the hedgerows. The scenes showed golden crops and wildflowers, ploughed fields with waves of rooks and crows heading skyward, as well as winter views of snow-covered sheep and cattle standing in wind-swept fields. In among all the trappings from a bygone era, the artist had inserted modern mechanical machinery as if to remind the viewer that time isn't static.

I had arrived at Basil's office earlier than expected. I was heading up as he came down.

"My dear boy, you're keen."

I held out my latest finished landscape to him wrapped in brown paper, like some peace offering. He gave a disinterested nod and continued.

"I've just received some good news. An artist whose work I came across last night is having an exhibition at Grafton Gallery in town. I'd like to add him to my books today if possible. He has potential to become a top seller. I'm desperate to sign him up but wanted to see more of his work before I do." Basil smiled broadly as though expecting me to react to his news. I dropped my gaze to the package I held. "Why don't you give that to Jenny and join me?"

My impatience grew while waiting for Basil. I tried to look for something positive to say about them. They bored me rigid. Grafton Gallery was a spacious area divided into small sections by wooden moveable screens. On these screens, two rows of paintings hung so that buyers could clearly see the wide variety of pictures they had on offer. Basil moved with assured confidence to the next picture. He fixed it with his critical eye, no doubt counting the pound signs in his head.

It surprised me that Basil didn't pick up on my annoyance. A third painting by mother had gone missing. Since her death, Basil was the only other person to enter her studio. Of course, there was Candela, but she didn't take them. While sorting through the dust-covered canvases I discovered Basil's distinct handprints on some of the pictures further back from where he had stood when I had shown him into the studio. In the short time he'd been with me, he couldn't possibly have touched them then.

Basil wasn't the expert he thought he was on Jane Elspeth Maedere. She kept meticulous records on all her works, including the ones she destroyed. I knew exactly what was in her studio. Every painting bore a unique code she had devised. The code told the history of the painting's existence from when she created it to where they were exhibited, who bought them and for how much.

When the time came to confront Basil, I had more than enough evidence, but my desire was to catch him red-handed. He couldn't sell them on the open market. Three unknown works by a major artist would cause quite a stir. No doubt that's what he wanted them for, but it came at a price to his career. There would be questions, their whereabouts for the last twenty-one years. Eventually someone would track me down. I would be horrified at their theft. In my distress I would let slip that the police were already questioning Basil about the disappearance of some young girls.

Basil looked up as though sensing my attention on him. I gave a nod and then refocussed on the paintings. I wanted to find one I liked. For some reason the artist had called them *'Of the Lost Age'*. A more fitting title was *'Victoriana Rubbish'*.

I pondered the artist's use of burnt oranges, reds, yellows and soft greens to which he had added rock salt, sand, eggshells, and other materials to give texture and depth to his pictures. Lifting a price tag, I was surprised to see how much they were asking for it and muttered, "Do people really buy this stuff?"

"Yes, of course," came a softly spoken voice in reply to my question. I spun round to find a petite woman with short bobbed brown hair that framed her delicate features. She wore a tight-fitting, light brown tweed two-piece suit. The skirt just brushed the tops of her knees while flat brown suede shoes encased her small feet. She held out her hand to me. As our hands met, a tingle of excitement raced up my arm. I returned her pleasant smile and looked into a beautiful pair of dark green eyes.

She pulled her hand from mine as Basil's voice boomed from the other side of the dividing screens.

"Hello, Charles. Thank you for allowing me a private viewing of Joseph Easter's exhibition."

"That's quite all right, Basil, my good man," Charles replied in a high-pitched nasal tone.

"Have you met James Ravencroft before?" Basil said.

"Ravencroft? He's here? I'm a great fan. His work's so dark. It's almost a physical presence; you can hear, see and touch. It's powerful. You're a dark horse yourself, keeping him back—"

"James! He was here a minute ago."

I turned to apologise to the girl only to catch a glimpse of her back disappearing through a door. Disappointed at not having a chance to speak to her, I made my way through the maze of screens to find Basil.

"Ah, there you are. James, this is Charles Jefferies, the owner of the gallery. We were at college together."

Charles, a short, stocky man with thinning, oily hair, held out his hand. Reluctantly I took it, feeling its sweaty grip. "I'm so pleased to make your acquaintance, James. I've always admired your work. It's an honour to have you here." He gave my hand a firm shake, before turning his attention back to Basil. They chatted about the paintings that lined the screens. Pleased to be free to wander again. I went in search of the girl. The door she went through was marked private.

"James! Where on earth are you now?" Basil's voice boomed. On returning to Basil's side at the front of the gallery, I was delighted to find the girl seated at the reception desk talking to Charles.

"Emily, please make a note of any calls which come in while I'm away having lunch with Mr Hallward and Mr Ravencroft."

"Yes of course, Mister Jefferies."

"Is everything ready for tonight?" he asked while tapping his fingers on the desk.

"Yes, I'm just waiting on the arrival of the catalogues we've ordered for tonight's showing."

"Aren't they here yet?" Panic edged his voice.

"Please don't worry. They're en-route. We've allowed for up to two hundred with postal orders, which we'll send out after tonight."

"Thank you. You're a star. You'll be working tonight, won't you?"

"Of course, Mister Jefferies." She pushed a strand of hair behind an ear.

"You'll be coming won't you, Basil?" Charles asked as we left the gallery.

I trailed behind them. After checking to see which restaurant they were heading for, I went back to the gallery. Through the window I saw the girl was still sitting at her desk. As I entered, she looked up, puzzlement flitted across her face.

"Hi Emily. The exhibition, I didn't catch what time it opens." I pulled out a small notebook.

"Here, take this." She handed me a leaflet. "All the details are on it."

"Thank you." I examined the leaflet. "So you'll be here until the end of the show?"

"The bitter end I'm afraid. It's all part of my job." Sarcasm edged her tone. "Though it's given me a great insight into the working of a gallery."

"Thanks for this." I folded the poster and slipped it into my pocket.

In the restaurant I looked for Basil and Charles among the diners but couldn't see them. For a moment I wondered whether I was in the right place. Through the large picture window Grafton Gallery was clearly seen nestled among the other businesses on the far side of the street, which meant I had to be in the right one. As I made my way towards the back of the building, the manager cut me off. "Can I help you?"

"I'm looking for—" A burst of raucous laughter filled the restaurant, making everyone, including the manager turn.

"I've found my friends," I said as he followed me to their

table. The manager handed me a menu as I sat.

"Did you get lost, James?" Basil said peering over the top of his menu.

"No. Just saw something in the gallery window."

"Ah-ha, Max, my good man," Charles said to the manager. "We'll have three of your finest, please."

"Will that be with new potatoes and green beans, Sir?"

"Yes, Max. I do hope you two don't mind me ordering for you," Charles addressed us. "They do such bloody good steaks here. You really must try them."

With a nod in Charles' direction, I handed the waiter the menu. As Charles and Basil droned on about their shared past, my thoughts returned to deciding how best I could capture my next angel on canvas.

Once the meal was finished, I wanted to leave, but politeness made me remain. After all, I wasn't paying. My head buzzed with excitement as I planned the evening ahead.

"You were right about the steaks, Charles. The best I've had in a long time." I held my hand out as I stood up and made my excuses.

"You'll be coming back tonight, James?" Charles asked as he took it.

"I'm looking forward to it."

"Good." Charles freed his hand and topped up his glass from the second bottle of wine. Basil dismissed me with a wave of his hand. Their chortling followed me out onto the street as they tried to outdo each other with the reminiscences of their college day pranks.

Once back at Basil's gallery, I collected my car. Not wanting to waste time, I set out to familiarise myself with the narrow backstreets around Grafton Gallery. Earlier in the day I had spotted an entrance to an alleyway. I turned off the main road and onto a lane with red-bricked yards backing onto it. The cobbled road didn't allow much room for parking among the discarded rubbish. Panic set in.

I drove slowly in hope of finding somewhere to conceal

my vehicle among the back-to-back terrace houses with their small yards. As the car rattled over the cobbles it led onto an open area where the occupiers were able to park. Here the large Victorian houses rubbed shoulders with their Edwardian counterpart. A few of these were bomb-damaged or stood empty. The crumbling walls of their gardens had allowed the overgrown shrubs and plants to spill out onto the road. One of these looked suitable, so I parked up and went to check that the house was unoccupied before reversing into the overgrown garden. I set off on foot to see where the alleyway I had spotted earlier took me.

After fifteen minutes I came to a dead end and had to retrace my steps. As I slowed to catch my breath, I noticed overgrown ivy partially covering an archway between two of the terraced houses. On pushing the ivy aside, I found it was obscuring a cobbled footpath. The path took me onto another alleyway. The increasing sound of traffic reassured me I was heading in the right direction. Soon business premises with their frontage onto the high street replaced the cramped Victorian housing. Painted on the gates at the back of the businesses were the names of the shops I recognised as the ones nearest the gallery. The shop owners used the area outside their yards to dump broken furniture and other rubbish, but the alleyway was still wide enough to get a vehicle down.

I hid behind a discarded wardrobe and looked up at the rear of the gallery while trying to decide what to do next. Apart from asking Emily where she lived, or even if she had a car parked nearby, there wasn't anything I could do but wait until after the exhibition and then follow her. I had just decided to search for the entrance to the alleyway to bring my car around when I heard voices.

In the fading afternoon light, from where I hid, I saw Emily, cigarette in hand, chatting to a tall, slender woman.

"I'll be back before nine, Kat." Emily dropped her cigarette and crushed it under her heel. "I'll need to wash my hair to look my best. I mustn't forget to feed Millais." She picked up her bag and set off in my direction.

I stepped into the garden behind me and waited. Once her friend disappeared from view, I followed. Two alleyways later, Emily stopped beside a broken gate. She was just about to push it open when a large black and white cat appeared. She scooped it up and elbowed the gate aside. For a moment she disappeared from view in an overgrown backyard. Then I caught sight of her again running up some stone steps. She unlocked a door on the second floor. The cat ran in after her. I stepped back into the shadows.

Night settled in and the streetlights came on. The only light that shone in the alleyway was an oddly placed streetlamp a few feet away for where I stood. I leant against a wall and checked my watch. Emily had fifteen minutes left if she was going to make it back to the gallery on time.

Moments later a shaft of white light cut through the night as the door to what I guessed was her apartment opened briefly then banged shut. I pushed away from the wall ready to follow her when the dustbin lids next to me suddenly clattered. I caught my breath and relaxed at the sight of Emily's cat with a dead rat hanging from its mouth. On checking my watch again, I saw my muse was going to be late.

The door of Emily's flat burst open and then slammed shut. She flew down the steps and bustled past me, disappearing into the gloom of the alleyway. I followed at a safe distance.

***

I returned to my car and moved it closer to her flat, hiding it in a dilapidated garage at the end of an overgrown garden. With nothing else to do but wait, I decided to use the time to plan my next painting, so I headed to a pub directly opposite the gallery.

A wall of smells hit me as I pushed the pub door open - nicotine, damp clothes, cheap perfume and stale sweat clawed the back of my throat and made my eyes sting. In the far corner a group of men played a noisy game of dominoes as the drinkers battled to hear each other over the laughter and shouting. The regulars jostled me aside at the bar as the barman served them first.

I moved further along and tried again, pushing between two people seated at the bar.

"What would you like, sir?" A young barmaid asked.

While waiting for my drink, I saw I could keep an eye on the gallery over the heads of the regulars. Through the pub window, a queue was already beginning to form outside it.

Basil would be impressed with the growing hordes of art lovers waiting to go in, but it wasn't as busy as the exhibitions that included my work, nor was it full of celebs like Hockney's back in'63. But still it was impressive to see.

"Hey, isn't it about time you were across the road, Joe?" a voice rang out.

A tall, impressive black guy dressed in a purple velvet jacket and black leather trousers headed towards me.

"Let them wait!" shouted a man slumped on a barstool next to me.

"Hey Man," the black guy said. "You've worked your arse off to get your paintings into that place. You should be over there revelling in it."

"Yeah, I know, Morris," the artist snapped back before taking a sip of his drink. "It won't hurt them if I keep them waiting, will it?" The man lifted his glass to the barman for a refill. "Anyway, I've finally got myself an agent sniffing around, so maybe big bucks will be calling me soon. Won't that be dandy? At least then I'll be able to invite my real friends instead of a bunch of wankers who know nothing about real sweat and hardship."

"That's cool, man." Morris patted the artist's back, "We know and understand, but still you should go and shine in your glory. We'll still be here when you get back."

The artist rose unsteadily to his feet. I was surprised to see he hadn't dressed up for his debut exhibition but wore a paint-spattered khaki jacket and trousers. It made me wonder how long he had been sitting there drinking. I wasn't the only one. Morris, with a concerned look, grabbed his arm, but his friend shook him off. He reached for his glass and, in a sweeping gesture, he held it aloft. "For my sweet Candela, wherever you are." He downed his drink in one go.

"Sweet Jesus…" I muttered as his dark eyes locked mine. I turned and headed for the door, leaving my hard-earned drink untouched.

Two years had certainly changed Joe. His unkempt look shocked me. Gone was his neat-cropped hair, goatee, and pencil thin moustache. His full beard was matted, and his shoulder-length hair sported rat tails. Without his toast to Candela, I wouldn't have given him a second look.

I hurried across the road, past the queuing art lovers and ducked down the alleyway that ran between the gallery and a bookshop.

Chapter Nine

Death of the Ghost Swift Moth
1951

I returned to my hiding place at the back of the Grafton gallery, among the dustbins and wind-swept rubbish. A quick glance at my watch reminded me that I could've wasted another hour and a half in the pub, but at least the fresh air kept me alert. The tedium of watching what I guessed was a bathroom light going off and on brought back memories for me of being an outsider once again. In the summer of 1951, I found myself sitting shivering in the hot sun beside a lake. At the age of fourteen I learnt my first and most crucial lesson thanks to Miss Dearborn, my art teacher. I learnt the importance of timing.

***

Five years after losing my mother, father sent me away to finish my education at a boarding school. In two short years a devastating illness changed him from a strong upright man to a weak and crippled creature in a wheelchair.

During my first term at Priory Cross School in the heart of Hertfordshire, I had noticed a marked difference between my physical development and that of my classmates in our dreaded physical education classes. Being stronger, leaner and taller marked me out straightway as being different. My father loved fitness, and his belief that we should look after the body, soul and mind as a single entity had me out cross-country running in all weathers, while he followed behind on a pushbike with a stopwatch. These workouts built up my strength and endurance.

I enjoyed my lessons at school and got on well with the teachers, but I found it harder to relate to the other boys. In the eyes of the adults my mother was a famous artist, but to my classmates I was known as the kid with a dead mother. Even if my appearance and the death of my mother hadn't marked me out as being different, my holiday arrangements certainly did. I was devastated at not being able to return home but understood that Mrs P's hands were full while caring for my ailing father.

During the first few days of the holiday I aimlessly wandered around the grounds and buildings of the old priory. Without the normal dash to lessons I was able to absorb the atmosphere and began to imagine what the place looked like through the eyes of the monks who had lived there in the 1300s.

Of course I wasn't the only one not returning home. The housemaster, Roger Elliott and his wife lived on site so cared for anyone unable to go home. They would gather any remaining staff members, along with the boarders into a smaller communal dining room to share breakfast, lunch, and tea as though we were all part of an extended family.

Between meals I spent most of my free time exploring the extensive woodlands and open countryside that surrounded the school. After two days of hunting for the right location, I found the ideal spot to create my painting of the school. The idea behind the image I wanted to create was to show the medieval priory situated on a rise, overlooking two large lakes. I hoped the painting would give the impression that the priory was rising out of the water like King Arthur's Camelot.

On the morning I began work I skipped the cooked breakfast and took some fruit, keen to get started as the light was just right. Once settled among the trees I was hidden from view to anyone following the footpath. At the edge of the lake, and with a clear view towards the priory, I sat cross-legged with my sketchpad resting on my knees and began to pencil the outline before working with watercolours.

After three hours my shirt clung to my back and arms as the sun climbed in the clear blue sky. On standing to stretch my legs and to remove my shirt I heard the sound of laughter. On the far side of the lake I thought I saw movement in the water at the base of the reeds. Excitement made me reach for my binoculars. I hoped it was an otter. Zooming in, I focused on the ripples. My excitement turned to shock as a naked man clambered onto the bank. He turned his pale body towards the woods and shielded his eyes from the sun. I dropped out of sight, even though I knew he couldn't see me as the reeds on my side blocked his view.

A burst of familiar laughter had me crawling on my belly to the water's edge. Through the binoculars I saw Miss Dearborn emerge naked from the lake like one of her goddesses that she was fond of showing us boys. After a few minutes of watching them I felt sick and lowered my glasses. Hastily gathering up my belongings I stumbled along the footpath that led back to the school.

I slept badly that night. The images of the man pulling her to him as his hand kneading her bare breasts flashed through my mind. The sound of Miss Dearborn's laughter ringing in my head every time I closed my eyes. My hand seemed to have a life of its own as it slid over my belly and between my legs. My cheeks burnt at the thought of pleasuring myself with images of their fornication. An old familiar stinging sensation crept up my legs as I rolled on to my side in my disgust for my actions, I wept for my mother.

The next morning, as I ate my breakfast, I thought about Miss Dearborn's appearance at the lake. It puzzled me as she had told the class how excited she was about spending her holidays in Wales, with her family. After swallowing down the last of my bacon I began to gather up my art things from beside my chair.

"Ah Ravencroft, I'm glad I've caught you," the housemaster said, entering the room. "Please don't be late for lunch today." He pointed to my painting propped against the leg of the table. "Once it's finished it'll be a mighty fine painting of the priory."

"Thank you, sir." I felt the warmth radiate from my neck to my cheeks.

"Nevertheless, the priory will still be standing this afternoon, Ravencroft. After all, it's been here for six hundred years." He laughed at his own joke.

"I know, sir. But the light changes so rapidly."

He smiled. "I do understand your dedication, Ravencroft. But it is unfair to expect others to provide a fresh meal for you after everyone else has eaten." He patted my shoulder, "You do understand, don't you?"

I nodded.

***

The banging of a car door followed by a shout snapped me out of the past. I peered down the alleyway that lead away from the rear of the gallery and saw the silhouette of two figures moving towards me. I held my breath, pressing myself against the wall, and hoped they wouldn't see me as they passed by. After a moment I realised they had stopped before a gateway into one of the yards further down. I heard a man's impatient voice whispering, "For Christ's sake, woman. I ain't got all fucking night. Me missus will be expecting me home soon. What have I said to you before, luv, about leaving your knickers off when we go out?"

"But Tony, it's too cold. Can't we just not for once?" a young girl whimpered.

"I 'ope you're not telling me no," the man interrupted, "after me spending good money on you, luv."

In a pool of dull light I could see the profile of a man pushing a short woman up against the wall. I let my breath out slowly and moved further back into the darkness, unable to shut out the sounds of the man's grunting and her soft moans. It sickened me, and I wondered how the woman could demean herself so when he thought so little of her.

"Tony, will I see you next week?" her child-like voice begged.

The man lit a cigarette and drew hard on it, while zipping his flies. "Of course, luv. But no hanging around me place of work. Otherwise, a word will get back to me missus and I won't be able to see you again. That'll break me heart." His contemptuous laughter echoed around the alleyway.

"You love me then?" She grabbed the morsel of affection he tossed her.

"You know how much, luv." He kissed her briefly and then let out a stream of smoke into her face. He slapped her arse and walked off, calling back over his shoulder. "Remember, no knickers next time."

"Shh, Tony. Me dad," she whispered into the darkness, before allowing the yard door to bang shut.

"Why no respect for oneself." I wanted to ask the girl. I recalled having to struggle to stay true to myself because of Miss Dearborn on that hot summer so long ago.

***

After my chat with the housemaster, I returned to my hidden spot in the woods. I focused on finishing my painting to stop me from thinking about Miss Dearborn and her unknown man. Though the light was not as clear as it had been, the sun occasionally burst through the clouds. It shone off the windows, stonework, and red tiled roof of the priory and bathed it in a golden glow. I set my easel up and began to pick out the priory's finer details. My imagination conjured up knights riding alongside exhausted pilgrims as they arrived at the priory looking for rest. While out in the fields and orchards, the monks laboured.

I bent to add a drop of water to my palette, when a fly buzzed around my ear. I flicked it away and looked back at my subject before dipping the tip of my brush into a speck of white. I blended it into a dark brown creating a lighter tone. Once I had the right shade, I began to paint again. No sooner than I started the irritating insect returned, brushing against my ear and cheek. I shook my head, trying to scare it off, but it returned destroying my concentration.

"Damn!" On stepping back from the easel my foot caught it. A movement out the corner of my eye made me turn sharply. The easel toppled backwards spilling the clean and muddy-coloured water over the surface of the painting; washing out the details I had just meticulously added.

"Oh—so sorry, James," said the honey-sweet voice of Miss Dearborn. She stood mirroring my damaged painting as rivulets of water ran from her thick black hair over the contours of her naked body. She held up a reed stem. Its fine seed head fluttered in a light breeze.

"What does a girl have to do to get your attention, James?" She giggled and then flicked the seed head to demonstrate her cleverness at imitating an annoying insect.

I turned away from Miss Dearborn and studied the damaged painting, wondering whether it was possible to salvage it. A twig snapped and something brushed my cheek again.

"James, my sweet boy. Look at me."

"Go away, please." I dropped to my knees, picked up the two water jars, and began to dab at the painting with a dry cloth.

"Oh don't be afraid, James. I won't hurt you. I've seen the way you boys look at me." She wrapped her fingers around my wrist, pulled me to my feet and snatched the cloth from my hand.

"Don't!" my voice cracked as I twisted my wrist out of her grasp.

"What's wrong, James? I thought you liked me." She bit her bottom lip as she lowered her eyes.

***

Miss Dearborn's intimidation of me had begun three days before the school broke up. I was pleased to find out she was going home for the holidays. Her art class was our last lesson of the day. As the class filed out, she had called me back.

"Close the door, James." She used her husky tone, the same one I had heard her using when speaking to the male teachers.

As I pushed the door closed, Jonesy the classroom bully and his pals lurked in the corridor. They stood snickering while sucking their forefingers and pointing at their crotch. A wave of nausea washed over me.

"Pay no attention to them, James. Come here. I have something to show you."

I remained where I was by the door, torn between staying and disobeying her. I wanted to walk out, but the thought of dealing with Jonesy and his mates kept me from leaving. Outside the room I heard Master Elliott's booming voice telling Jonesy and his pals to stop loitering and to return to their dormitory to prepare for mealtime.

I reached for the handle to leave when Miss Dearborn dropped a large book on her desk. The noise made me jump and I turned.

"James, please relax. You're making me nervous."

My brain stuttered. I cleared my throat ready to tell her about the rumours I had heard, when my satchel slipped from my shoulder and hitting the floor with an echoing thud robbing me of my confidence.

"Come here." She drew the words out as she sat down behind her desk. "I want you to tell me how these paintings make you feel?"

I left my satchel where it fell.

"Come see, James. I'm sure you'll like it." Miss Dearborn pointed to the book.

The double-page spread showed photographs of *Botticelli's Venus* stepping off her scalloped shell. Her hair swept across the two pages as it covered her modesty.

"No, James. Come round here." She patted her side of the desk. "Then you'll see it properly." Miss Dearborn moistened her lips with the tip of her tongue.

I concentrated on the book as I moved round but I found myself staring down Miss Dearborn's cleavage as she leant forward.

"James, what do you think of the painting?" She pushed her hair back from her face and pointed to the naked woman.

"How does it make you feel inside?" She spoke in a breathless tone.

I had seen such paintings in books at home. Even father had a painting of mother in a similar sort of style hanging in the drawing room. A question that had always bothered me about *Botticelli's Venus*, I decided to ask. "Wouldn't she have been too heavy to float to shore on a shell, Miss?"

She laughed, making her big bosoms quiver. "Oh, James, you are such an innocent. She's a goddess. Goddesses can do anything."

Miss Dearborn brushed my cheek with her finger as her other hand squeezed my buttock. A whiff of her cheap perfume caught in my throat and my guts heaved. I turned away from her as a prickling sensation circled my legs and raced across my hands. "Please, Miss. I need to go." I pulled away from her and backed towards the door.

"James, don't be like that. I'm sorry I laughed." She came towards me, hands outstretched, lips bright red.

My foot caught the strap of my satchel, nearly tripping me over. I snatched it up and dashed to the door, fumbling with the handle, unable to grasp it with my sweaty palms.

"Calm down you silly boy."

I stepped away from the door, holding my satchel like a shield across my chest.

"Here, let me. There's a knack to opening this door."

Before she had opened it fully, I burst through the gap and, without looking back, I ran down the corridor, not stopping until I was outside. Once there I leant against a wall, wiping the beads of sweat from my forehead, while drawing in deep gulps of fresh air trying to clear her perfume from my nose and throat.

"Hey Ravencroft, you old dog."

The voice startled me, and I turned.

"Did Dearborn give you one of her after-class special tuitions?" Jonesy sniggered and nudged his second in command. "I thought she only liked to play with the big boys." He continued while rubbing his crotch. "Maybe I should see if she could give me some extracurricular too. I'm sure my future girlfriends will appreciate how hard I studied at school." Their roars of laughter followed me as I bolted, my cheeks flushed.

***

As we stood at the lake side, my anger and disgust rose at the sight of my ruined painting. Miss Dearborn showed no modesty, unlike Botticelli's Venus. I bit my lip, trying to control my nausea at the sight of the hair between her legs and underarm and wished she would cover herself.

"James, you do like girls, don't you?" She reached for my hand.

"Yes, I do." I stepped out of her reach.

"That's good. But I'm not talking about liking them in the way one likes a sister or a mother."

"My mother?"

She shook her head and then ran the tip of her tongue around her full lips. "You do understand the word fuck, James?"

I gasped. I hated the sound of the word. Too often the boys in my dormitory used the word. Once the lights were out, they would sit in a semi-circle around a pile of the mucky magazines with their cocks in hand. After perusing the photographs of naked bodies of men and women performing sex acts, they took it in turns to describe their fantasies in fine details to each other while they wanked. With the covers over my head, I would try to sleep, but they were still too close and heard everything they were saying and doing. It disgusted me. I saw no beauty in their kind of magazines.

Father preached that beauty was in the eye of the beholder and, to me, art was about purity and beauty. Women exposing their hidden places for men to lust after was neither art nor beautiful. Sex outside of marriage was nothing but lust. A man's duty was to love a woman not just for her physical beauty, but also for what was within her heart and soul. "That's where her real beauty lies, James," he said.

"Where's the man I saw you with yesterday?" I hoped to

bring her to her senses so she would leave me alone.

"You naughty boy." She giggled and waved her finger at me. "Were you watching us?" She leaned against the smooth bark of a nearby beech tree, tilted her head, and parted her legs slightly as though offering herself to me. I scanned the lake, but there was no sign of movement anywhere.

"James, I'm all on my own. His stupid wife wouldn't let him come out to play. But then I've found you. We can have fun instead."

The bile in my gut rose. I backed further from her, conscious of her nearness.

"Oh no you don't!" Her hand shot out and caught the tail of my shirt." What's making you so nervous? You know me, James."

My brain screamed, telling me to run.

She held on tight to my shirt, like a cat playing with a mouse. "I'm so hungry for your touch." She sighed, her hot breath caressing my face along with the stench of decay and muddy lake water that clung to her. I knew what she wanted of me after witnessing her adulterous behaviour yesterday. I jerked her towards me while guiding her back towards the water's edge.

"Oh yes, touch me, James! Hold me tight."

In one sharp movement she tore my shirt open and began kissing my neck. As she did so, her hand slid over the waistband of my shorts. As her fingers tightened around my cock, my anger exploded as my body betrayed me. I threw myself forward as Miss Dearborn clung to me. A loud splash rang in my ears followed by a sudden coldness that engulfed us. In the depths of the dark water, Miss Dearborn frantically thrashed about beneath me. Just as my lungs felt as if they were about to explode, the heaviness around my waist released, allowing me to break free of the darkness.

***

"I'm so glad you made it back in time for lunch, Ravencroft," the master said with a smirk as I entered the dining room. "How are you getting on with that painting of yours?"

"Fine, sir," I said as Mrs Elliott placed a plate of cold ham on the table as the rest of the boys tucked into their food.

"Help yourself to salad and new potatoes, James." She paused before me; a concerned look flittered across her face. "Are you okay?' she asked, reaching out and touched my forehead.

I flinched.

"I hope you haven't got a touch of sunstroke. You do feel a bit warm and your hair's damp."

"I washed my hands and face before coming to eat." I heaped piles of the buttery new potatoes on my plate. I had disposed of my ripped shirt and had washed the smell of the lake from me before changing my clothes.

After dinner, I headed back to my dormitory to set to work on repairing the damage to my painting. During the rest of the holiday, I avoided the lake, choosing to use the sketches I had created to complete the painting.

By the time the school reconvened, Miss Dearborn hadn't shown any sign of returning from her Wales holiday. The school engaged a new male art teacher. By the end of the autumn term, news reached our schoolboys' ears that Ophelia, in the shape of Miss Dearborn, had been found floating in the lake.

***

The sound of chattering voices drew me back from the past. I checked my watch - it was one in the morning and the exhibition was over. In mid-stretch, as I tried to free the knot in my back and get the circulation going in my legs, I heard the sound of heels coming in my direction.

The time had come.

Emily passed, unaware of my presence, head bent while searching in her shoulder bag. I counted to ten then followed a safe distance behind. My shoes made no sound, unlike hers.

My shadow raced ahead. Every time we passed under a

solitary streetlamp; my shadow brushed against hers on the ground. Emily seemed unconcerned by the darkness of the alley. My hands trembled as I counted down the seconds. Any further along the path and there were too many windows. I lifted the chloroform pad from its container in my pocket as my shadow rose up from the ground. Just as the last lamp came into view, Emily sensed a shift in the atmosphere and turned. I grabbed her, smothering her mouth. As the darkness descended on her, her strength wilted and I dragged her back to where my car waited in the shadows.

Holding her against me, I briefly struggled with the boot to get it open and then lifted her in. A quick check in case she'd lost a shoe, before hurrying back to where she'd dropped her bag. As I closed the boot a pair of golden eyes watched me from the top of an overflowing dustbin. Emily's cat snarled at me as I jumped into my car and reversed out from the garage.

"Farewell, Millais," I said, thankful he was the only one watching. Once clear of the city, I checked on Emily making sure she was still out cold, before heading home.

Chapter Ten

Stone Angels
The Fourth Painting
1966

I clutched a well-earned glass of whiskey to my chest and studied the third completed stone angel painting. Out of the three I had done so far, this one was the largest.

The painting depicted the evening sun bursting through dark clouds, casting a fading golden light across the rooftops. The main subject, a kneeling angel, was caught in the rays of the sun, while silhouetted behind her stood two other stone angels. The kneeling angel rested her chin on her hands, which covered the mouthpiece of a lowered trumpet, as though defeated by humanity's lack of response to her trumpeted warning. Below on the busy streets the preoccupied masses scurried about unaware of the angels watching over them.

It had taken me twelve months to capture Emily's quiet beauty, but it had been worth it. The freshness of her face radiated her beauty within the rosebud softness of her cheeks and her delicate pink lips. Emily immortalised everything I had admired in the Pre-Raphaelite models. Investing so much in one painting was a big gamble, but I felt the outcome had been worth it.

Her petite build was a disadvantage not for me, but for her. I had hoped she would've lasted as long as my other two muses. To create my best, everything needed to be perfectly still, especially my muse. The slightest movement would distract me, but the sounds of the birds outside, the steady ticking of a clock, and her rhythmic breathing cast a spell over me as I slipped into my creative flow. The weight of the brush in my hand helped to focus me. Only when exhaustion no longer allowed me to stand or paint did I rest. That's when I felt my mother's presence the strongest and most powerful.

As a child the only time my mother and I had spent together was with me on the other side of a door. I would press my eye against her studio keyhole and watch her standing before her easel. The power of her concentration radiated from her as she stood in a fine red cotton dress that hung in folds around her bare feet. The movement of her dress mirrored every sweep of her brush across the white canvas. The bright light of her studio highlighted the muscles in her back as she worked. That's when I was at one with her. I imagined holding her brush in my hand, feeling its weight and warmth where she had held it. I wanted to hold her palette while she worked and imagined her telling me in her sweet honey-soft voice what colours to mix for her. I longed to see her eyes shining with happiness when I got the right combination of colours. But instead, all I could do was crouch at the keyhole and watch until my tired eye forced me to leave, or I heard someone coming up the stairs.

The night I arrived home with Emily, my head buzzed with ideas making me want to get started right away. I fetched a fresh chloroform pad ready in case, but I wanted to delay using it. It wasn't a good idea to give her another dose so soon after the first lot.

As I lifted the boot its dull light caused Emily to stir. She moaned and turned her head in my direction and stretched her arms and legs though her eyes remained closed. I was pleased to find the chloroform still subdued her. She slumped against me as I carried her into the house and up the first flight of stairs to the lift.

Once chained to the cot, I left her sleeping while I prepared my studio and myself to begin work. I took a hot shower; the water soothed my aching muscles and calmed me. After a change of clothes and a quick bite to eat, I set a tea tray with a pot of tea, milk and a packet of chocolate biscuits. On entering the studio, I heard knocking coming from the adjacent room and set the tray down. I poured some of the tea into a plastic beaker, adding plenty of milk and sugar. I switched on the light and found Emily sitting up, blinking rapidly.

"Where am I?" Her voice was groggy.

"Safe. Here. Have a drink. You'll feel better." I set the beaker and plate of biscuits down on the table next to her.

"Better." She lifted a hand, making the chain rattle. "My head hurts. Where am I?" She repeated as her hand dropped back on the bed.

"You're safe." I sat beside her, my eyes meeting her questioning gaze.

"Hmm—could I have a drink? I'm very thirsty."

I lifted the beaker placing its spout to her mouth, pleased that she seemed relaxed. She reached for it. "Thank you," she said after taking a sip of the sweetened tea. "Why am I here?"

"I need you."

"Hmm." She let out a long sigh and blinked, her pupils large and dilated "The tea's nice. Very sweet. I'm sleepy."

"Are you?"

"Yes. Sleepy. Tea sweet."

"Yes, I know. Thought it might help you."

"Help me?" she mumbled, collapsing sideways awkwardly.

"Here let me help you." I covered her with a blanket.

"Thank you," she muttered. "All seems so real."

"Real?"

"I'll wake up soon… in… own bed." Emily closed her eyes, her chest heaving as her lips parted, trying to draw in air.

Two hours later I returned to wake her. She was lying on her side, sleeping peacefully. I sat down on a low stool and began to draw her fine features while I waited for her to wake. The easier option would've been to take a series of photographs, but they wouldn't allow me to make an in-depth study of my subject. To understand the joys of still life I needed to draw and paint from real life. In a series of quick pencil sketches, I drew her parted lips as she sucked in air, her closed eyes with their delicate eyelashes and the shape of her jawline, nose, and cheeks. Sheet after sheet drifted to the floor as my pencil skimmed across the page.

"Where am I?" The strength in her voice filled the room.

I looked up. "It's all right you're safe."

"You! You were in the gallery." The chains on her wrists rattled as she swung her legs off the bed and tried to stand. "Oh—my head." Emily flopped back onto the bed, holding her head in both hands. "Why am I chained? Why am I here—?"

"Emily, please. You're quite safe. I'm not going to hurt you."

She tugged hard on one chain and then tried the other. Tears rolled down her cheeks. "Please let me go."

"The restraints are only to stop you from hurting yourself."

"What do you want?"

I gathered up my drawings and walked through to my studio. When I returned she was still sitting on the edge of the cot, but now hugged herself the best she could as the chains restricted her.

"Why am I here?" she asked.

"I need you. I'm an artist and you are my muse. Now relax."

"Relax? You chained me like an animal! And ask me to relax!"

I grabbed her hair at the back of her head and pressed a pad to her face, muffling her cry of shock. She kicked and lashed out with her nails, but I forced her back on the bed. Once the chloroform took hold, I quickly removed the chains and her clothes leaving her undergarments. I slipped the harness over her head and fixed it around her curvy body before adjusting the shoulder straps. I dressed Emily in a white silk dress and then wheeled her in the cot through to my studio. I turned her onto her stomach and fastened her arms and legs onto a framework. Once I'd hoisted her off the floor, I repositioned her as I needed, before raising her to the ceiling.

With rapid brush strokes I filled the canvas with broad lines before adding in the details of the sun bursting through dark clouds, while creating a silhouette for the two angels standing behind the main subject.

The morning arrived with a bright burst of sunlight. It passed over Emily making her crease her brow. I dismissed it as I worked on; knowing the clips fastened to keep her eyelids open allowed no movement for blinking.

As the day wore on and sunlight drained from the room, I added in some finer details. But as I reached for a pallet knife, something disagreeable pricked my senses. I looked up. So engrossed in my work, I hadn't checked the time to see whether the chloroform had worn off or not. Emily's fingers clawed at the air as her chest heaved. I had no idea how long she had been watching me. That's when I decided I needed to experiment further with timing.

***

In the drawing room, the finished painting stood on an easel where it had been drying out for the last couple of months. I had been studying it until hunger had driven me to the kitchen in search for something to satisfy it. For days after Emily's passing, I divided my time between catching up on sleep, cleaning the house and pottering around the gardens. Through the kitchen window I saw the early signs of spring. Among the last year's decay, bright green spears of daffodils leaves showed a promise of things to come, while the yellows of primroses and celandine shone like golden stars in the untidy flowerbeds.

In the bread bin I found a stale loaf and cut a slice to lie on the top of the Aga to toast. On my way back from the pantry to grab the butter dish and a jar of marmalade I remembered that I had a stretched canvas ready for a landscape Basil needed for an important client.

I buttered the toast and tried to focus on where I could find my next muse. I hastily munched while my mind chewed over the problem of the landscape. Not wishing to waste any more of my valuable time stuck for hours on a wind-swept hillock freezing my nuts off, I decided the best thing to do was fake an abstract landscape just to get the thing done. Taking a tea tray with me, I went through to the hall when the phone rang. I ignored it knowing it could only be Basil. On reaching my studio it rang again, and I picked up. "Hello Basil."

Without even acknowledging my greeting, Basil waffled on about some new commission he had taken on. "My client is a beautiful middle-aged woman with a big personality—and an even bigger bank balance. She's desperate to meet you, James. Do you think you could make it to my office by three on Wednesday, dear boy?"

"Of course, old boy," I answered, with a hint of sarcasm.

"Now less of your cheek, James. I've just this minute finished talking to her. She loves your work and has three paintings already. Her husband was big in banking."

"Was big?" I feigned interest.

"Didn't I say? She's a widow and a merry one, too. Looks after herself well and believes in having the best of everything. Not just for herself, but her twenty-one-year-old daughter, too. She's quite a looker, though a lot quieter than her mother. Surprising really. Normally they're just as much of a man-eater as their mothers."

"Of course you would know."

"I do indeed. In my line of work. I've come across a fair number of them. Money makes them believe they can buy whatever they want. Nothing is unavailable to them. Anyway, Tamsin wants—"

"Tamsin?" I interrupted. "So you're on first name terms with her."

"Yes. Her husband Jeremy Loring and I were old university friends. Tamsin Loring and I only became friends fourteen years after her husband's death. We met by chance in the restaurant at my local golf club. I'll be meeting her and the daughter next Wednesday in my office. I want you to come along too."

"Oh—" My annoyance grew. I hated Basil arranging my life. "What does she want me to paint?" I had no desire to meet the merry widow, even if she was a wealthy one.

"I've no idea. She wants to discuss that with you in person over a meal. Unfortunately, on that day I've scheduled a call from America, so I won't be dining with you." Basil inhaled sharply.

"Is something bothering you? You're sounding a bit uptight. Not like you at all."

"I'm having trouble with Easter. The guy's a bloody genius, but a fucking prima-donna. Making demands left, right, and centre. I wish they were all like you, James. So easy to work with, and a born genius. It must be your bloodline."

"Thanks." I wondered if he moaned about me to the other artists. Then I became aware he'd changed the subject.

"James, do you remember coming with me to see some of Easter's work early on, in the gallery in Old Bond Street?"

"Yes, of course. Grafton Gallery? The receptionist was a pretty little thing with bobbed brown hair." I didn't mention that I thought the paintings were pretty crass.

"Oh, so you noticed her then?"

"Yeah, and…?"

"Well, James it's just that…"

"Just what?"

"There's a problem. It's funny she made such an impression on you, James."

"Why? Is there a problem with me noticing the receptionist on that day?"

"No."

"But there's a *But*? Anyway, I wasn't cramping your style. Just window shopping."

"Cramping my style. Oh just, never mind about that. The owner Charles phoned me the other day to say she's still missing."

"Still missing? As in, the receptionist?" The shocked tone in my voice was just right, I thought, as I poured myself a cup of tea and sat down.

"Yes. Apparently she went missing on the night of the exhibition. The girl's parents had been in contact with Charles. They wanted to know if he knew of her whereabouts before they called the police. He hadn't remembered us being there on that day until he phoned me about a problem he was having with Easter."

"Easter?"

"Yes. He was whingeing about the money he says I owed him. He wanted Charles to have a quiet little word in my ear before he takes the matter into his own hands. Says he'll speak to some people I wouldn't want to know."

"He's threatened you? Ha. Normally we arty types are gentle, loving people." I took a sip of my tea and wished the telephone cable was longer so I could look out of the window too.

"It isn't funny, James. Anyway, while Charles was explaining about Easter, he remembered us being there. The police have questioned him twice already. He thought I should have a word with them. The last thing I want, James, is to have the police question me again.

"What did he say when you told him you're already helping the police in connection with two other missing girls?"

"What! Do you think I'm that stupid? I told him I couldn't help. He got upset saying someone must have seen something that night. He's very concerned about her. Maybe it's just my imagination, but it's getting too uncomfortable. I didn't even speak to her."

"An overactive imagination, Basil." I hoped my voice sounded sympathetic enough. The landscape standing on an easel caught my attention, and I wondered whether the varnish had become dry enough to touch.

"Could be, I suppose. Though I get the feeling that somehow there's an invisible thread linking me to the girls. What do you think?"

"What do I think? Well, she might've had a better offer and dumped old Charlie boy."

"If only. According to Charles, she only worked part-time for him, wanting some experience of gallery work as she was a full-time art student. I'm just hoping the police don't come asking me where I was on the night she went missing."

"No alibi again?"

"You wouldn't be so flippant if it was you. Anyway, how's that latest painting of mine coming along? My client has been asking after it."

"Very well, thank you." The blank canvas leaned against the wall waiting for a primer. Did Basil hope I hadn't heard his use of the word, *mine*, as if he owned both me and the paintings?

As he was so quick to point out, those with plenty of money liked to think they owned the world, and that the rest of us wanted to be like them. If that's what he wants to believe, then he's a bigger fool than I thought.

"Good. So I shall see you soon with it then," he said. "Don't forget, next Wednesday, my office, three o'clock."

He hung up before I had the chance to protest.

Tired of Basil's attitude, I crossed to the raw canvas, snatched it up, and took it down to mother's studio. My plan was to use the view from her studio window of the broken trees as a starting point. I selected the largest brush and set to work priming the surface. While waiting for the primer to dry, I started to sketch out my own interpretation of the landscape, but the second my pencil touched the paper, my mind created the image for my next angel.

I found myself high up on a recess above a busy street. The ever-watching and waiting angel opened her wings, calling me into her arms. Her icy limbs wrapped themselves around me in an eternal embrace while her empty eyes showed no emotion as they stared deep into mine. My pencil reignited, danced across the page as the image in my head transferred itself onto the paper. When it came to the fine details of the angel's features inspiration left my pencil hovering over where her face should be. I threw the pencil down knowing I needed another muse.

The phone rang, shattering the peace. I reached for it, noting that I had lost three hours. "Hello!"

"James there's been a change of plan," Basil said.

Chapter Eleven

Death of a Scarlet Tiger Moth
1966

Basil explained that he had rescheduled his meeting with Tamsin Loring. "I've changed the location too," he said without taking a breath. "Can you meet us at the Potter's Bar Golf Club restaurant, instead of the office?"

"Happy to," I said. The thought of getting a decent meal out of Basil's client helped to soften my annoyance.

I set about starting work on the landscape, with no desire to waste my time painting outdoors, I created it from my imagination instead. The following day after Basil's call I left his commissioned painting to dry on an easel in the corner of the studio. Even with a couple of days' grace, I knew the painting would be too tacky to take with me, but at least it was finished.

I began to relax. A break from the studio would help to clear my mind and with some good food lift my spirits too. After burying Emily, something in me changed. Sleep no longer came easily. I knew she was at peace, truly an angel. I tried to keep busy all day hoping exhaustion would allow me to fall asleep easier, but it didn't help. On closing my eyes Emily's pallid face would rise up from under the compost. Her lips so pale they stood out like scars while empty eye sockets scrutinised me. No matter how much I shovelled the compost to cover her, she would rise to the surface again. Her clawing fingers beckoned me to join her and the other angels in their cold grave. I tried to escape only to be caught around the ankles. I fell backward onto the compost the bloodless faces of the watching angels hung over me.

One morning I woke refreshed from an undisturbed sleep, full of inspirations for further paintings. An inner surge of growing pleasure helped to ignite my desire to hunt for my next muse.

On the morning of the meeting, I planned to leave as soon as possible to beat the traffic heading into London. I took a leisurely drive along the country lanes before hitting the busy main roads.

I switched on the radio as the traffic began to slow. The steady, pounding beat of the Spencer Davis Group's '*Keep on Running*' filled my car and I sang along. The flow of traffic picked up again and the scenery flashed past in a haze of colours. I wanted to prepare myself mentally for my next big piece, though I was unable to start planning the specific details yet. First, there was the excitement of the hunt.

The drive was uncomplicated, and the location had been far easier to find than I had imagined as I pulled into the club's car park. I drove past the more expensive cars, deciding to park my Vauxhall Cresta saloon out of sight from the main building.

After turning off the engine, I rolled my shoulders and climbed out. The car park was empty of people, though I could see golfers playing a round in the distance. I stretched my back and legs before pulling on a jacket and straightening my Slim-Jim tie. On my way to the main buildings, I spotted Basil's Bentley parked next to a neat, little red sports car, which I guessed had to be Mrs Loring's, going by my agent's description of her.

I couldn't see an entrance for the restaurant, so I entered through the clubhouse. In the lobby, I looked around for a sign pointing to the restaurant, but couldn't find one. I was just about to find someone to ask when I felt a hand on my arm.

"Excuse me, Sir. Are you a member?" The nervous little man quickly withdrew his hand from my arm before I had time to answer. He continued. "It's a members club only, Sir.

I must insist on seeing your membership card before I can allow you to go any further."

"Please forgive me, but I'm supposed to be meeting Basil Hallward here today." I smiled broadly.

The man's face reddened. "Oh dearie me. You must forgive me, sir, for not recognising you sooner, Mr Ravencroft." He glanced at his list before crossing off my name. "This way please, sir." He gestured towards a corridor I hadn't noticed. As I followed behind, he glanced over his shoulder. "I'm a great admirer of your work, sir, which I might add I would recognise anywhere."

"Thank you."

On entering the restaurant, the concierge took me over to a corner table where Basil sat, with his back towards us as we approached. Basil was talking animatedly to an older woman, dressed in a classic navy-blue jacket with a white blouse, I guessed to be Mrs Loring. She learnt forward, one slender hand playing with the end of her dyed jet-black hair. Beside her sat two younger women. One had a band of roses woven into her long hair and wore a flowery waistcoat over a white blouse. The other woman had the same air of importance about her as Mrs Loring and was formally dressed in a blazer the same as her mother. I couldn't see if they wore trousers or skirts as the table was covered with a white cloth.

The concierge gave a little cough. "Mr Hallward, your guest has arrived."

Mrs Loring, a strikingly good-looking woman, in her late forties, with pencilled eyebrows, and high rouged cheekbones, looked up. She gave a broad red-lipped smile, which caused Basil to turn in his seat.

"Aha, there you are, James." Basil stood and greeted me with a vigorous handshake. "Glad you found the place all right."

The concierge gave a nod in my direction before addressing Basil. "Sir, I shall get a waiter to remove your empty plates too, if you have finished."

"Yes, thank you, Toby," Basil replied.

I realised sadly that they had already eaten without me.

Basil gave a sweeping gesture towards the older woman. "James, this is Mrs Loring."

"A pleasure to meet you, Mrs Loring." I took the chair opposite her and noticed she wore too much eye make-up robbing her of her natural beauty. She offered me her slender suntanned hand. It felt heavy in mine, weighed down by her collection of antique rings.

"Oh no, Basil, you're making me sound so very old." She turned her full attention on me. "Please James; you simply must call me, Tamsin. And this is my daughter, Jeannie."

"Tamsin, it is." I leaned forward and kissed the back of her hand, knowing she would enjoy a touch of the old-fashioned charm. Either from slight embarrassment or a well-rehearsed modesty, Mrs Loring pulled her hand from mine, touching her thin neck in a girlish gesture.

"My dear boy," she threw a glance in the direction of Basil, while still speaking to me, "you are truly beguiling as well as very talented."

I grinned at her in appreciation, but my attention was on the other girl seated slightly away from Mrs Loring's daughter. My hands began to tingle as I studied her. She sat in profile her strong jawline and thick full lips captivated me in the same way as the waiter had her attention. Woven into her thick, dark brown hair a row of delicate, artificial red rosebuds created a garland around the top of her head. Cascading ringlets fell onto her slim shoulders. I wanted someone or at least Mrs Loring to introduce her to me.

"So what would you like to drink, James?" Basil interrupted my thoughts.

Without taking my eyes off the unknown beauty, I answered. "The usual please."

Basil chatted to Mrs Loring while waiting impatiently to get the attention of one of the busy waiters. This allowed me more time to study the girl. I longed for the waiter to finish serving at the next table and come to ours. I hoped by doing so the girl would turn in my direction, and if the symmetry of her face was right…

A sudden burst of raucous laughter from Mrs Loring at

one of Basil's humorous anecdotes caused the girl to turn slightly. She shifted in her seat and caused her tiny pearl drop earring to sway. It seemed to reflect the lustre of the skin on her neck.

I visualised a fresh canvas resting on an easel waiting for me to paint the profile of her face. The weight of the paintbrush was already in my hand as I held a palette of colours ready to match the glow of her skin.

Jeannie leant in towards the girl who then tilted her head as Mrs Loring explained Basil's joke. The girl gave a light chuckle and took a sip of her drink while watching me over its rim. On lowering her glass, she asked, "Are you like Mister Bond, James? Martini, shaken but not stirred?"

"Not at all." I laughed. "My life is much duller than his." I caught a hint of sadness reflected in her eyes.

Basil clicked his fingers again and finally the waiter came over to take his drinks order and to clear the table. The girl showed no sign of her former interest in the waiter as her eyes remained focused on mine.

"Right ladies, would you like me to refresh your glasses?" Basil asked.

"No, thank you, Mr Hallward," Jeannie said, standing. "It's been nice meeting you, but Annie and I have to go shopping. Mother's taking us to New York soon."

Basil stood. "It's been so delightful meeting you both, too," He squeezed Jeannie's hand. "You simply must come along to one of my exhibitions. I will let your mother know about the forthcoming events."

Annie, my mind whispered, *sweet Annie.*

"I work near your office, Mr Hallward," Annie said, picking up her handbag.

"Do you?" Surprise etched Basil's face.

"Yes, we've met before, but I don't think you will remember. You only came in a couple of times. Normally, it's your secretary who comes to pick up your lunch when you're working late. She's lovely."

Basil's features softened and he began to smile. "Oh, of course! Now I remember. I thought there was something familiar about you. You work in the café on the corner. It's only when Jenny is on holiday that I pop in."

The waiter coughed and Basil turned to him. "Sorry about that. Please, could we have one Johnnie Walker Blue? No ice, thank you."

Jeannie pulled Annie aside and they moved away from our table. With their heads together they began whispering. Annie was the taller of the two, dressed in a long flowery bohemian skirt with a matching waistcoat. Jeannie carried a few more pounds than her friend but she wasn't by any means overweight. She wore a plain green blazer and houndstooth patterned cream knee-length skirt. After a few words in Annie's ear, Jeannie turned to her mother, but I was unable to hear what was said.

Tamsin shook her head. "No, my dear, you cannot drive my car. You'll have to call a taxi to take you to London."

"They can come with me, Tamsin, if that's okay with you?" Basil glanced at his watch. "You must forgive me, but I need to be heading back to the office as I'm waiting on an international call."

"What a shame you have to go so soon, Basil," said Mrs Loring, brushing her top lip with the tip of her tongue as she winked at me.

I took a sip of my drink as the bile in my stomach rose. Over the lip of my glass, Mrs Loring seemed to transmute into Miss Dearborn, her red lips parted in a catlike smile. Without looking in Basil's direction she finally answered his question. "Only if taking the girls is not an inconvenience to you, Basil?"

"None at all, Tamsin. What man wouldn't enjoy having the company of two lovely young ladies while travelling back to the city?" He slid his arm around Jeannie's waist. She giggled and stepped away from him. Basil looked a little hurt by the subtle brush off as he pulled his keys out of his pocket.

Tamsin finally broke eye contact with me and looked up at Basil, "Thank you. It's a weight off my mind. At least I know they'll be safe with you. Now behave yourselves, girls. Jeannie, don't be too late home."

"Of course not, Mum." Jeannie bent and kissed her mother's cheek. Then linked arms with Annie and they both moved away while waiting for Basil to finish talking to Mrs Loring. Annie brushed her hair back from her cheek as she altered the strap on her bag, making it more comfortable on her shoulder. She seemed to sense that I was watching her and nodded in my direction. "It's been lovely to meet you, Mr Ravencroft," she said.

"And you too, Annie. The both of you."

"Come, lovely ladies, your carriage awaits," my agent called. As they left, Basil stopped to speak to a group seated at another table. A man stood and shook his hand. Basil nodded and gestured in my direction before coming back over.

"James, I expect to see the commission in the next few days. It looks as though I might have another one for you soon." Basil nodded to the man who lifted his glass to me. I smiled at him and then answered Basil. "Of course, you'll have it."

"Bye, Basil, bye girls," Mrs Loring called, her eyes still on me.

Basil caught up with the girls who stood talking to the young waiter. My mind was already reaching for a paintbrush as I sketched out an image of my next angel onto a primed canvas. Something cold suddenly caressed the back of my hand and the image dissolved. I looked down. On looking up I was met by Mrs Loring's wolfish grin. Within her kohl-rimmed eyes excitement burnt under false lashes. As she spoke, my chest tightened.

"Finally, James, I have you to myself." She lifted my hand into hers. "I'm sure Basil has told you, I'm a great admirer of your work. The reason I asked him to invite you was so I could discuss an undertaking with you. Before we start would you like another drink?"

"No, thank you." I held up my glass.

She called the waiter over to refresh her drink. I wondered whether she'd had enough already. Once her glass was refilled, she began to explain. "I can see a successful future ahead of you, James." She traced the lifeline on the palm of my hand with her long red talons. "I have a proposition I want to put to you."

I said nothing.

She continued. "I want you to work on a personal home commission."

"I'm sorry to disappoint, Mrs Loring." I tried to take my hand back. "But I don't paint portraits of houses."

She squeezed it tight and giggled. "Oh, you silly boy. Please call me, Tamsin. I don't want you to paint a picture of my house but one of my daughter and me at home." She brushed her bottom lip with her tongue. "You do home visits, don't you?" She leaned forward while caressing my palm.

I took a sip of my drink, trying to keep the loathing and humiliation from my face, but I need not have worried. Mrs Loring was too busy cooing about the paintings of mine that she already possessed. I scrutinised the symmetry of her face and wondered why women of a certain age hide their beauty under layers of powder and paint, while an artist uses the same material to capture such beauty on canvas. Finally I freed my hand from her grip and softened my tone, conscious that a woman like Mrs Loring did not take kindly to the word, *No.*

"Mrs Loring, you must be aware, having my work in your collection…" I gave her hand a light squeeze. "My style of painting doesn't lend itself well to portraiture. I would fail to capture the beauty of you both."

"James." She clutched my hand again. "I'm giving you a magnificent opportunity. I believe in your wonderful talent and know I can help you establish your name internationally. I simply won't take no for an answer. Please come to my home on—" She let go of my hand, reached into her handbag and pulled out her diary. She flicked a couple of pages. "Hmm, let me see—what about next Monday?"

Under the table her foot moving up the inside of my leg and then gently pushing against my crotch, I returned her conspiratorial smile and she rewarded me with a wink and another nudge of her foot. I lifted my nearly empty glass to my lips, and whispered over its rim, “But Mrs Loring I don’t know where you live.”

“Darling, its Tamsin. You’re making me feel so old.” She pulled a silver business card holder out of her bag and handed me one of its crisp, white cards.

“Tamsin, a woman with your outstanding beauty shouldn’t worry about ageing.” I looked briefly at the card, then drained my glass and stood.

“Oh, don’t go yet, James. We’re just getting to know each other.”

“I’m sorry but I need to get back to work.” I held up her card. “What’s the best time to call on you?”

“Anytime. I’m sure you will like what you see.” She leant forward exposing the curve of her over-tanned leathery breasts.

I nodded. “I didn’t take you for an early riser, Tamsin.”

She pursed her thin lips. “Let’s make it ten o’clock, James.” Something flittered across her unreadable expression and I wondered for a moment, whether it was fear of rejection.

I smiled. “Ten on Monday it is then.”

Her face brightened. “I look forward to seeing you again, James.”

I left Mrs Loring to finish her drink as I didn’t want to stay in case I said something I regretted. Why do others think they have the right to arrange my life? I had no desire to paint her for any amount of money.

I was just about to start the car when Tamsin emerged from the main building. I waited, before turning the key. Tamsin seemed to be staggering. At first I thought it was her high heels as she swayed to the middle of the car park. She looked around as though unsure of where she had left her car. On seeing it, she shook her head and plunged her hand into her handbag rocking and then catching her balance as she did so. After a few minutes, she finally pulled out her keys.

I waited.

Once I knew she was safely in her car, I drove out ahead

of her, having made the decision to follow her. I turned in the direction of her home, hoping that was where she was going. I drove on to look for an ideal spot to park. On locating one, I reversed in to wait for her to pass. Within minutes she passed in a flash of red. I counted to ten and was about to put my foot down when a flash of British racing green zoomed past.

Annoyed by the interloper I raced after them. Having a Morgan between Tamsin and my car did not help the situation as it meant its driver was now an unwanted witness. I caught up with the powerful Morgan, as it was unable to pass Tamsin. It revved its engine impatiently. I relaxed back in my seat, realising that maybe the gods had something in store for her after all. I just needed to wait and see what happened next.

I wasn't sure how long we had been driving when the Morgan, with an air of impatience, roared its engine and shot forward trying to overtake Tamsin. The little red sports car gathered speed. It snaked back and forth across the narrow road, forcing the Morgan to drop back. Its driver let rip with a blast of his horn, picking up speed to try again. For a moment I wondered if Tamsin was aware of the car behind her as she hogged the centre of the road.

On our side of the road, a steep bank replaced the trees and hedgerows as they petered out. A tight bend loomed ahead. On my journey to the meeting it was at this point I had tried to overtake a slow-moving vehicle and nearly became squashed between the bank and a lorry. Ancient oak trees grew all along the top of the bank, their thick roots hanging down like tentacles onto the road's edge. The behaviour of the Morgan's driver led me to believe he was unfamiliar with the road as I had been. He raced forward, seeming to want to force her out the way.

The road narrowed.

I dropped back, praying for something to come in the opposite direction as there wasn't anywhere for them to go. They raced on with me following at a safe distance. For a split second, Mrs Loring moved back onto the left side of the road. With another blast of its horn, the Morgan risked all. It shot forward, taking the corner at death-defying speed, cutting across in front of the red sports car, clipping it as it went, before disappearing round the bend. I braked hard.

Everything seemed to move in slow motion. Mrs Loring's car launched itself as it flipped onto its side. It clipped the roots of the trees as it bounced off the bank before careering out of control across the road. It missed several trees before ploughing through a large bush and vanishing from view. A loud bang filled the air, sending a cloud of cawing rooks and crows into the sky.

I left my engine running and climbed out. No traffic came from either direction, I crossed the road. There was nothing to see but a few fragments of broken glass and two deep tread marks on a rough verge. With the side of my shoe, I swept the glass into the leaf litter and obliterated the tyre markings before dashing back to my car.

I drove on until a nagging voice caused me to pull off the road and get out. The tranquillity of the woods returned surprisingly quick. Birdsong echoed around me as I walked on, heading towards the crash site, I hoped. I plunged deeper into the woods, moving rapidly not wanting to encounter anyone else investigating the loud bang. I paused and tried to get my bearings.

If she was dead, my problem was resolved. I decided to leave Tamsin to whatever fate had dealt her, when I caught a whiff of petrol in the air. I followed the scent. A sudden burst of sunlight broke through the trees and reflected off something shiny. I cautiously followed the smell of petrol and found Mrs Loring's car on its side wrapped around a large oak tree. The impact made it look less like a mode of transport and more like a work of art, especially as one of its chrome wheels spun slowly as though continuing on its journey to take her to the underworld. The cooling metal clicked as though sending out a message, maybe a warning as the air reeked of petrol. The lower branches of the trees had ripped the top off the car, and I couldn't see any sign of Mrs Loring.

Not wanting to disturb the crash site too much, in case I

left something behind that might alert the police to the fact someone hadn't reported it, I turned to go. It was then I noticed some droplets of blood spattered across some fallen leaves. Had she, by some miracle, survived the impact?

I looked around, but still saw no sign of her. Then, out the corner of my eye, something fluttered for a brief moment. An image of her swaying in the car park flashed across my mind. On a broken branch a piece of navy-blue fabric, the same colour as Tamsin's trousers. Without thinking, I reached for it, but stopped myself from plucking it off the branch. Beyond the damaged shrub, within a shallow dip, I could just make out a sprawling figure half-secluded by fallen leaves and debris.

Carefully I picked my way around blood and oil-soaked leaves. Mrs Loring lay on her back. Her vacant eyes stared at me while her head, twisted at an odd angle, had bones protruding through a gaping hole where once her throat had been. Satisfied there was nothing more to worry about, I made my way around the debris. As I passed her car, I gave a brief nod of thanks in its direction, knowing I was free to focus on the more important paintings.

Chapter Twelve

Stone Angels. The Fourth
1966

Surprised to find my conscience was untroubled by the death of Mrs Loring, I stood naked by the French windows in mother's room. Looking out across the balcony, I mulled over several different settings for my next angel painting.

I guessed Mrs P, in her wisdom, had been right. She always said drinking and driving was not a good combination, especially not for women. She never aired her opinions on mother's drinking in front of me. Though I once heard her say something to father. She never commented on mother's driving, mainly because Jane Elspeth Maedere always relied on a chauffeur.

The phone rang, just as my thoughts were formulating. I attempted to shut out the annoying din by escaping out onto the balcony knowing it would be Basil. A nip in the early morning air sharpened my senses as a chilling breeze caressed my body. It drained the tension that threatened to stifle my creative thought process. Once the ringing had stopped, the power of the muses beckoned me back inside with the promise of fresh paint and the weight of a brush in my hand.

On closing the door the warmth of the room made my skin tingle. Blood rushed into my chilled muscles. I hunted for a large canvas among mother's rack of unused ones, sending up clouds of dust. I located the one I wanted, just as the phone rang, demanding my attention again, but I ignored it. I knew that all too soon, I would have to answer it.

I placed the canvas on the easel and then picked up a stick of charcoal, and began to sketch the image I had settled on. The incessant ringing penetrated my consciousness, robbing me of my artistic flow. I snatched it and shouted, “Keep it short. I’m busy!”

***

On my return home from London late last night, I removed my precious cargo from the boot and took her straight up to my muse’s bedroom in the rooftop studio. Once I was sure she was comfortable and her breathing steady, I took a shower. With my hair still damp, I crept into mother’s bed, only to find I couldn’t sleep.

Excitement tinged with annoyance buzzed through my head. Outside I watched the distant flickering lights as the strength of wind disturbed the trees on the far bank of the river. As the room filled with the chilling night air, I lay warm and secure under the thick blankets, analysing what had happened after I left Mrs Loring’s shattered remains.

Still annoyed with Basil and his lack of progress in allowing me a solo exhibition, I hadn’t gone home as I had planned, but decided to confront him. Would the mere mention that I knew he was stealing from me be enough to embarrass him into giving me what I wanted?

Before heading to Basil’s art gallery I parked my car in an inconspicuous place rather than his car park. Then using the crisscrossing alleyways that ran between the gallery and the high street, I took a little-used footpath back to the gallery. I couldn’t have timed it any better as Basil’s office light was still on.

I was about to cross the road when Basil’s secretary, Jenny, suddenly emerged from a side gate and hastily climbed into a waiting taxi. Once the taxi was gone I crossed over and went through the gate; Basil normally kept it locked to avoid any disgruntled artists, or to allow his more famous clientele privacy while visiting his gallery.

Behind the gate were two access routes. One led on to the

high street, from where I had come while the other led through an overgrown garden at the back of the property. This was where Basil kept his car out of sight in a garage at the bottom of the garden. There was also ample parking for four other cars. From there Basil had easy access onto the main thoroughfare to take him in any direction.

I climbed the narrow-carpeted staircase as quietly as possible. On the landing I strained to hear what Basil was saying, but the only thing that was clear was his booming laughter through his closed office door. I slipped into Jenny's small office opposite where I knew she had an intercom. The small space was brightly lit by a streetlight just outside the office window. Jenny's tidy desk stood in front of a large metal cupboard where she stored the finished works of art, next to it was a freestanding filing cabinet, and some shelving. I made myself comfortable in Jenny's seat and switched on her intercom after turning my end off.

Basil's voice was loud and clear, his excitement tangible as he chatted, singing praises for his latest prodigy.

"Yes, I know the market is different in America, Chuck," I heard him say. "I'm having such amazing results with Easter's work here. I know it isn't to everyone's liking, but I can see him going far. You know as well as I do, it's all about following the money. Here it's the wealthy old-school types that are snapping up his work." He laughed. "You're always telling me most Americans love the English landscape, Chuck. Well, Easter delivers the goods every time."

The American said something inaudible to me, but Basil snapped back. "No, no, Ravencroft isn't ready, not by a long chalk!"

"What!" A pain shot through my jaw as I clenched my teeth. I was ready to crash through his office door and make all sorts of demands but, instead, I paced the floor between the desk and the door, trying to calm myself.

When Basil spoke again there was more control in his voice.

"Yes, Chuck. I know you wanted to see more of his work, but I'm not sure he's ready for the big time yet. His work sells only moderately well here."

My chest constricted as my desire to slap Basil's smug face grew. Instead I switched off the intercom and left.

Back on the street, I turned onto the rat-run of footpaths and made my way towards the café. I had no idea what time Annie finished work, or whether she was even working. The unlit footpath was nothing more than a strip of bare, compacted mud, edged with grass and weeds. It ran between two continuous brick walls that separated the back-to-back Victorian houses. At unmeasured intervals, yellowish light spilt out from the upper-floor windows of the houses, which allowed me to pick my way around discarded rubbish. To dampen my temper I decided to ditch Basil's '*Of Land and Sea'* crap and turn my energy into creating the rest of my major collection. I checked my watch. It was nine o'clock and well within my deadline.

Just as I arrived the abandoned house where I had left my car, I heard a familiar noise above the hum of the traffic. The swishing of soft fabric mixed with the sound of a light footfall.

I strained to listen. Whoever it was came from the direction of the café. I remained in the shadows. Out of the darkness, the blurred figure of a woman emerged. On seeing me she said, "Mr Bond?"

Without a moment's hesitation and before she could even comprehend what was happening, I pressed the chloroform pad hard against her mouth and nose and held her tightly. She briefly struggled until at last, she slipped into unconsciousness. I swept her up and carried her over to my car. After placing her inside the boot I arranged some cushions around her, making her as comfortable as possible before heading home. I drove at a steady speed, not wishing to draw any attention to myself as I tried to contain my excitement.

***

The last thing I wanted that morning was to keep my beautiful Annie waiting. Brush in hand I was ready to start work.

"I'm busy," I snarled into the phone.

"Sorry to bother you so early, James. I know you have the commissions to finish, but…" Basil's apology softened my rage.

"What? You're apologising Basil?"

"I've heard some terrible news." Basil ignored my sarcasm. "I can't believe it."

"You do sound upset." I crushed my impatience.

"It's unbelievable, James. You were the last to see her alive. Her poor daughter to lose her mother so soon after her father, it's too sad."

"I'm too busy for guessing games, Basil."

"Oh, I'm sorry, James. I just received a call from Jeannie Loring. She was sobbing her heart out, poor kid. Her mother died yesterday, not long after our meeting. A car crash. She only realised this morning that her mother hadn't come home last night."

"Car Crash. Mrs Loring is dead?" Suddenly I heard a hammer putting another nail into Basil's coffin. What would the police make of the fact that on the day Mrs Loring died, he was in the company of yet another woman who's gone missing? That alone sweetened the bitter pill lodged in my throat. "That's shocking news, Basil!"

"It's terrible on two levels, James. I've lost a good friend and a huge commission too. It must've happened after you left her. What time did you two finish talking?"

"Not that long after you actually."

"So quickly! Tamsin told me she had a lot to discuss with you."

"Like what? Mrs Loring wanted me to do a portrait of her and her daughter."

"Oh— so you agreed then."

"No—not really. I decided to tell her on Monday that I would be turning down her offer." I laughed. "Guess I won't be doing that now."

"Turn it down? With the sort of money she was offering— I don't believe you, James! You would've been crazy to reject it—" he stuttered. "It wasn't just about the money, but the prestige. A portrait of such a woman would've set you up for life in America. You can't buy that sort of advertising."

"Look, Basil, to start with she never mentioned any sum. Anyway, my style doesn't lend itself to portraiture, which is what she wanted. I'm not bloody Gainsborough!"

"Okay, I'll give you that!" He sounded once more like a hardnosed businessman than someone who had just lost a friend. "How did she seem when you left her?"

"What do you mean?"

"Happy when you told her you'd think about it?"

"Of course. She was bloody happy. I hadn't told her either way. We agreed to meet at hers on Monday." I paused. "Hang on— did you tell her *I would do it*?"

"Of course I did, James. She was excited about having *you* paint her portrait."

"Great Basil! So what if I had said no that I didn't want to do it?"

"Oh, you would've. No two ways about it, Ravencroft."

The temperature in the room dropped, causing my muscles to twitch and gave me goose bumps. I reached for my dressing gown at the end of the bed and slipped it on one arm as I tucked the handset under my chin. "That a threat, Basil?" I pulled the gown shut.

"Don't push it, James. I can make or break you…" His voice faded.

I waited, wondering if he had finished. I glanced towards the canvas. The chloroform would've started to wear off by now. "Basil old boy. I'm sorry to hear your sad news. But I need to work while the muses are entertaining me." I tried to lighten the tension.

"None of it matters now," he mumbled. "Just ignore me, James. I guess it's the shock of losing a dear friend in such a way. I can't believe— she's dead! I'll ring Jeannie and offer my help. Poor kid what she must be going through. So excited about spending time with her mother in New York—

I guess she'll move to America now to be with her mother's family."

"You never said exactly what happened. Was there another car involved?"

"Oh, it looks as though she was driving too fast, misjudged a corner, and clipped the bank, causing the car to flip over. It ploughed through a hedge on the other side of the road, which obscured the crash site. There weren't any skid marks on the road or tyre tracks on the verge no one would've known an accident had happened."

"How awful. So no witness then?"

"A gamekeeper found the car while out doing his rounds."

"How can they be sure what happened?"

"No idea. Police work, I guess. Jeannie said if it wasn't for the gamekeeper, she might've never known what had happened to her mother. It can't have happened long after you'd left, James, so I guess they might want to speak to you."

"I can't really add anything, Basil. I'd already left. She seemed happy enough, busy ordering herself another drink. How many had she had before I arrived? The police might want to speak to you, too."

"Oh no, I can't cope with them questioning me again! I just hope they don't start joining up the dots as well as doing the sums. It'll only muddy the waters further." He changed the subject. "Do you have any finished landscapes for me?"

"One or two."

"One OR Two! What's that supposed to mean? Can't you give me more? How come Easter can give me enough for an exhibition, but all you can produce is… one or two?"

"I'm sorry. Working in oils means it takes longer for the paintings to dry as you well know."

"My apologies, James. You're right."

Then he hung up, leaving me listening to a humming dialling tone.

After a quick shower I dressed and grabbed a bite to eat before collecting the large canvas from my mother's studio.

Annie, dressed in the fine white silk gown, hung from the ceiling in the harness. Her eyes widened at the sight of me and followed my every movement as I set the canvas on the easel.

"Good morning my dear girl. Now, there are a few things I wish you to know before I start work. You must stay perfectly still. I'll give you a drink as soon as I'm happy with the first layer of my painting. Do you understand?"

Annie's reply was muffled, no more than ragged breaths as the chinstrap held her mouth shut. She struggled in the harness, causing the chains to rattle against the framework.

"Calm down dear girl. No one is going to hurt you." I focused on selecting the right brush and picked up my palette. "Now relax, this won't take long and then I'll release you, so you can rest."

She blinked her eyes and gave a slight nod.

"Good. Then I shall begin."

I began by sketching out my idea. Basil was right about landscapes. They were easier to paint, but they bored me. Weary of travelling around Suffolk, hunting out new views to paint along its wild coastline, I had lost my enthusiasm for painting in all weathers just to please some rich old dear with more money than taste. And as for painting repetitive scenes anyone with half a talent could do it. The same old boats, lighthouses, and tidal mills that Basil wanted were mind-numbingly boring. I wanted more drama in my work, to push the boundaries in the same way mother had. I knew all too well what Basil's argument would be.

"My dear boy," he would say in that smug tone of his. "Your work is selling too well to risk losing your established buyers by trying something new that might not please the punters."

If I had the same status as mother, then I could push the boundaries without Basil. He was right about using her status. It would get me what I wanted, but I would always feel that I had sold out, whereas she had made it on her own terms. After overhearing Basil's American plans for Joe's Victoriana rubbish more than pissed me off. My work was far more superior and deserving of a larger audience.

I squeezed fresh paint onto my palette, tossing the tube onto the table before stabbing at the paint with the brush. The brush moved without me directing it with sharp slashing strokes, as I built up the layers. Slowly I relaxed into the creative flow as my anger calmed.

"So, Annie, my dear, let me explain why you are here. You have the pleasure of being my fourth angel."

***

For the first few weeks I felt I was getting somewhere with my fourth angel painting. Annie was holding up well which pleased me. Then one morning on entering the studio the painting reminded me too much of a somewhat poor imitation of Easter's work. Victorian Gothic in style, the towering turrets and buttresses looked more like some fairy-tale castle than the stark modernism I had wanted.

Frustrated with the amount of time it had taken to create the fourth painting, I allowed Annie to rest, and regather her strength between layers. I lowered her onto the daybed and fed her a small amount of food and something to drink after removing the chinstrap, while I sorted out the painting. I scraped off the paint and then added a few clean lines turning the castle-like buildings into skyscrapers of glass and stone.

***

After a week of blazing heat, the strength of the wind had picked up enough to bend the tops of the trees. On the rooftop just outside my studio, with a glass of lemonade in hand, I enjoyed the cooling breeze. Below my lawn was an oasis of green in the parched landscape. In my parents' time, our old gardener sang its praises as he worked among the remaining gravestones of the old church that once stood within the grounds. He told them they had no need to worry about the lack of rain with its underground springs would keep the garden lush.

The only thing that marred his green lawns was the irregular shapes where the grass paid homage to long-forgotten tombs. I paid my own homage by reusing the graves as markers for my fallen angels, which now numbered four. As though reading my thoughts a dark shadow passed over the gravesite as the rain clouds blocked the sun.

Back in the studio I paused to admire the futuristic theme of my latest painting. I had placed my faceless stone angel with her back to the cityscape. I had opted to paint my model with more body strength than she had in real life, by thickening her neck slightly. Annie's beauty for me was in her strong jawline, full lips, long and narrow nose. I decided not to paint in one thing that had attracted me to her, the sorrow I had seen reflected within her green eyes. By opting to paint her eye sockets empty, I felt the painting reflected the impersonal city behind her.

Chapter Thirteen

1966

When I snatched my fourth angel, I was taking a risk. Under normal circumstance I would have made my preparation well in advance. From setting aside a couple of landscapes in readiness should Basil arrive unexpectedly wanting a painting or two, to making sure there was a good supply of food and paints in, so I didn't have to leave the house.

I spent a little time familiarising myself with the area where my angel lived and worked. It helped to know whether she travelled alone and what route she took. This gave me the best opportunity to discover a place to hide a car in readiness. Immediately after I brought her home, I would dump the car and have another one ready to take its place in my garage.

After Annie's arrival, I set to work. Speed was of the essence if I wanted to keep her as fresh as possible. Being unprepared left me concerned that I might not have enough paint to finish the picture. I was reluctant to raid mother's studio, but if I needed to, then I would. That's if the tubes of paint were still viable.

On three occasions my concentration was broken while I worked on my fourth painting. The first time the phone rang, my initial thought was that it was Basil chasing a commission, but instead, it was his secretary.

"Mr Ravencroft?" a softly spoken woman asked.

I hesitated, trying to recognise the voice. "Hello, yes?" I wanted to hang up.

"It's Jenny Flood. Mr Hallward's secretary."

"Oh, Jenny— sorry."

"I must apologise for disturbing you, Mr Ravencroft. Mr Hallward asked me to let you know that he's away on business now. I'm to remind you about a landscape that's needed for a client."

"He's away?" I laid a damp cloth over my paints.

"Yes. Is the painting ready?"

"Nearly. I've been waiting for the varnish to dry. Are you that desperate for it?" I held my breath.

"Hmm, I'm a little unsure why Mr Hallward is in a hurry, especially as the client hasn't been chasing it. I expect it could've waited until Mr Hallward's return."

"Well, if Basil's only away for a few days, what's the rush?"

"He's away for at least three months."

"Three months. So he's—?" I managed to stop myself from saying *in America.* No doubt, Basil has gone with Easter. "Any idea—where he's gone?"

"I'm not in a position to say, Mr Ravencroft."

"Oh, you've signed the official secrets act, then?"

She chuckled. "Well—I suppose it won't do any harm telling you. America. He's meeting up with an old friend—they've been talking about merging their two companies."

"Really. That's interesting. Good for you, I expect."

Jenny laughed. A deep throaty laugh that helped break the ice between us.

"For me? How for me?" I heard Jenny's fingernails tap against the typewriter keys.

"A chance for you to work in the States." I turned to my muse. Annie's skin looked clammy and pale, but I did not want to cut Jenny off.

"Hmm… I see what you mean. It would be interesting, but Mr Hallward will continue to run the British side of the business, so I'll still be needed here."

"I see." Annie's eyes now focused on me, I needed to get back to work.

"From my understanding, he'll have more access to the American market. Anyway, the client hasn't paid for the painting yet. Guess they're not in a hurry. I've enough other jobs to be getting on with, without chasing around after money too. You know what Mr Hallward's like when it comes to dealing with the important clients. It's all about *the personal touch* as he is so fond of saying."

"Of course— he's all for his personal touch." My thoughts had now shifted to Basil's betrayal. How could he select Easter to get the first bite of the American cherry? "Thanks for letting me know about Basil's trip, Jenny. Just give me a bell when you need the painting, and I'll run it in."

"Oh, thank you, Mr Ravencroft."

I replaced the receiver and snatched up a brush, stabbing at the congealing paint as the canvas before me blurred. A sharp kick in the teeth would have been sweeter than knowing that Easter was on track for fame. "Well, that's made the decision for me, Annie. I need to finish enough of the 'Roofscapes' paintings so I can show Basil where my real talent lies."

She gave a slight nod and I realised that the chloroform had worn off.

"Not long now, Annie." I added a few random dabs of paint to the canvas. "And then you can rest."

Two weeks later, I had finished the underpainting on Annie's picture and was allowing it a little drying time. The day was hot and muggy, as I stepped out onto the roof for a breath of fresh air.

From here, in the winter months, I could see as far as Harwich and beyond, but now the trees were dressed in their greenery my view was shortened but at least I could see as far as the main road. A glint in the distance caught my attention. I picked up my father's old binoculars and focused in on it. A fast-moving vehicle abruptly turned off the main road and onto the long and winding lane that led to my home.

It snaked in and out of view between the rows of trees until, at last, it was close enough for me to recognise the make of car. A black Ford Zephyr. My stomach tightened as my fingers gripped the binoculars. "Why now?"

I stepped back into the studio and returned the binoculars to the shelf. "Well, Annie." I lowered her as fast as I could onto the daybed. "It looks as though we have some unwanted visitors today. I can't think why they need to speak to me. It's been over three weeks since Mrs Loring died."

A tremor passed through Annie's body as her feet met the bed. Once down, she lay with her eyes closed. I hadn't used the bird clips on her as the painting's theme didn't require them. I supported her shoulders with my hands and felt the muscles in her neck tighten. I whipped off the chinstrap and once her head was free, I lowered it onto the pillow. She was scarcely breathing and twisted her head away from my touch.

"It's okay, I'm just moistening your lips with some water." I soaked a wad of cotton wool and dribbled a little water onto her mouth then her tongue shot out, trying to lick her lips. Her mouth, no longer full and pink was grim and colourless. Her skin ashen-coloured was clammy to the touch.

Between the drying stages of the oil paint, I had given her a small amount of water and food as well as allowing her four hours rest. Her resilience had surprised me, but the chloroform had taken its toll.

I released Annie's thin arms and covered her before pushing the cot back into the muse's bedroom. There I held a fresh chloroform pad to her face.

"Maybe, by some miracle, they've managed to trace the driver of the green car," I said as she slipped into unconsciousness. I covered the painting with a damp cloth not knowing how long they would keep me talking.

I dashed out onto the roof and peered over the balustrade, hoping they were not already snooping around outside. I ducked down just as the police car swept onto the drive. There was little chance of them finding the entrance to the studio. Not even Basil knew of its existence, but I did not want to take any chances. I closed the studio door and took the stairs two steps at a time to the next floor. After locking the door that concealed the lift and stairway to the attic, I slid the ornate wooden panel back in place.

In mother's studio I groped around to find a half-finished landscape and threw it onto the easel. I snatched up a discarded palette, squeezed a random selection of usable paints onto it and then picked out a handful of brushes. Working as fast as I could I dabbed fresh paint over the surface, just enough to give the impression I had been busy at work.

Just as I stepped back to see how it looked, the doorbell rang causing my stomach to clench. I took my time descending the main stairs allowing my thoughts to settle, knowing that I had nothing to fear. From the stairs, I could see through the frosted glass of the front door, two impatient silhouettes moved about in the sunlight.

I caught my reflection in a full-length mirror on the final landing. Mother had placed there to check her appearance before meeting anyone. I caught a fleeting glimpse of a paint-splattered artist. I wiped some paint off my beard and decided that it really could do with a trim. I inhaled as I re-tied my ponytail, hoping to force the look of anxiety off my face.

The bell rang again, long and sharp as though someone was leaning on it. I hurried down and flung the door open.

"Sorry to keep you waiting. That's the trouble with living in such a big house. How can I help you?"

"Ravencroft? James Ravencroft?" A burly, long-faced man asked.

Behind him stood another shielding his eyes as he studied the exterior of the house. I wondered if he had seen me on the roof, but I knew that was impossible. They both wore similar dark check tweed suits with narrow trousers and highly polished black shoes, though the younger man carried less weight, and more muscle.

"If you're selling insurance, I'm not interested." I began to close the door.

"No sir, we're police officers." Long Face put out his hand as if to stop me from shutting the door.

"Police officers? Why? I haven't called you?"

Long Face smiled as if this would win my trust. "Do you mind if we come in, and have a brief word?"

I paused in closing the door.

"Mr Ravencroft, I can assure you we are police officers," the younger man said, as they both produced their warrant cards.

"I'm Detective Sergeant Reg Heythorp," Long Face said. "This is my associate, Detective Constable Hayden Wicklow."

I opened the door further. "Now I've seen your ID's you had better come in then. I apologise for my apprehension, but I do live alone— and for a good reason too. I hate to be disturbed, while I'm working."

"Then we're sorry to disturb you, Sir," said Heythorp, as he followed me into the hallway.

"Well, it's done now. Anyway, I was just getting to the point where I needed a break. Come through." I led them into the drawing room, with its heavy dark wood furniture, blood red flock wallpaper and its collection of powerful works of art. Framed sketches of mother's paintings dotted the walls in small groups.

"A mighty fine pad you have here, Mr Ravencroft, if you don't mind me saying." Heythorp grinned.

"Thank you." I made my way to the drinks cabinet, hoping a shot of whiskey might help me relax.

Wicklow examined a group of pictures on the wall before looking up at the portrait over the fireplace. He nodded in its direction. "One of yours, sir?"

"Oh, so you know I'm an artist then?" I poured a drink.

"Part of our training sir is being observant," said Wicklow.

I looked down at my paint-spattered jeans and T-shirt and laughed. "I suppose being covered in paint gave the game away." I offered them the bottle.

Wicklow shook his head. "No, sir, unfortunately, this isn't a social call, otherwise we would be delighted to join you in a drink. So is the painting one of yours?"

"No, my mother's." I gestured for them to sit on the large sofa opposite the fire while I took my father's chair next to the fireplace.

"Thank you, Sir."

Heythorp sat, pulled out a small black well-worn leather notebook and thumbed through a few pages. Over Heythorp's shoulder, Wicklow bending slightly forward as he studied the group of pictures Basil had admired so much.

"Well, Mr Ravencroft... or may I call you James?" Heythorp asked.

"James will be fine."

"You don't seem at all curious to know why we are here." Wicklow's voice came from behind my right shoulder, making me turn in my seat.

"In connection to what happened to Mrs Loring, I'm guessing—" As soon as the words were out of my mouth, I knew my arrogance had the better of me. "My agent told me about her car crash."

"Mrs Tamsin Loring?' Heythorp leaned forward, and his blue eyes shone with curiosity.

I took a sip of my drink and became aware that my hand was trembling. "Yes— I was in a meeting with her— on that day."

"You met her?" Heythorp kept his eyes on his note taking.

"Yes." I hesitated to wait for him to make eye connect, checking to see I wasn't lying. Finally, he looked up, and I continued. "My agent arranged the meeting between Mrs. Loring and me at the golf club restaurant, Potter's Bar. Mrs Loring wanted to commission me to paint a portrait of her and her daughter, Jeannie."

"Your agent's name?" Heythorp asked.

"Basil Hallward. There isn't much more I can tell you, I'm afraid." I took another sip of my drink as Heythorp stopped his scribbling and a questioning look flitted across his face.

"Why's that?" Wicklow asked from behind me. I twisted uncomfortably in my seat again; aware that the young police officer was taking a deep interest in looking at all of mother's paintings as he made his way around the room.

"Well, it must be at least what... three or four weeks ago." I tightened my grip on the glass, my knuckles white now. My mind shouted, *shut up you fool*. I took another sip of my drink. "You know what it's like when you're busy, you lose track of time."

"Three weeks, James," Heythorp said. "What can you tell us about that day?"

I turned back to face Heythorp. He seemed relaxed as his pencil hovered over his notebook in expectation of my answer.

"Well… nothing outstanding. At least not on that day as I didn't know Mrs. Loring had died, but the next day when my agent phoned."

"Quite a journey you made for a five-minute chat," Wicklow said as he stood in front of the fireplace.

"My, you've been doing your homework." I leant forward in my seat and finished off my drink.

"We coppers are busy people too. We're just following up on some leads regarding Mrs Loring," Wicklow said. "Your chat with her was rather short after such a long journey?"

I shrugged. "It seemed longer to me, but if you say five minutes then I'll believe you."

"We're only interested in the time you were there with Mrs Loring on your own." Heythorp licked the end of his pencil.

"Right." I crossed to the drinks cabinet, poured another one, and dropped in a couple of ice cubes, aware they were both watching me. The heat of the room made it hard for me to think straight so I unlocked the French windows and pushed them open.

"Tell us why you were there." Wicklow said.

I inhaled deeply, but the air was dry and muggy, with no breeze. I sipped my fresh drink before turning back to my unwanted guests. "My agent called, inviting me to meet one of his important clients. After weeks of going stir-crazy working here, I jumped at the chance. Even better a chance for a good meal. One can get tired of beans on toast." I forced a smile. "By the time I arrived at the restaurant, they had already eaten."

Heythorp laughed. "They didn't wait for your arrival then?"

"I suppose not. I might have misunderstood my agent, though I did arrive late."

"What do you mean by misunderstood your agent? Did he feel you were beneath them, if Mrs Loring was an important client?"

I laughed. "What on earth do you mean by that, Detective Heythorp?"

"I meant… Mrs Loring was a wealthy woman. I wondered if your agent… thought you were a struggling artist." Heythorp stumbled over his words as he looked about the room. "Clearly, you're not. Obviously, your agent has been to your home, so would've known—"

"That's very middle-class of you, Detective Heythorp, to judge a man by his material belongings. Sure, I'm indebted to my parents for my standing in the world."

"Is that so, Sir," he said, regaining his confidence. "So can you tell us why you left so soon after arriving?"

"Why are you questioning me?"

"It's our job to establish what happened. Questioning those who were there helps us to establish a clear timeline leading up to the event, and what happened afterwards."

I nodded. "Okay. Do I need a solicitor?"

"Do you want one, James?"

I rolled my glass between my palms before making eye contact with Heythorp again. "No, not at all."

He looked down at his notes and flicked a couple of pages before speaking again. "You said you'd arrived in the afternoon and everyone at the table had eaten."

"Yes. There were plates on the table. I had only expected my agent and Mrs Loring to be there. She and the two other younger women had also been drinking. Her daughter Jeannie and her friend whose name I think was Annie, though I wasn't introduced to her."

"Why weren't you introduced to everyone?"

"People's manners these days are very relaxed, I guess."

Heythorp nodded. "Go on."

"Not long after Basil had introduced me to Mrs Loring, her daughter and her friend got up to leave. They said something about shopping."

"So how did you know the girl was called Annie?" Wicklow asked. "After all, you told us they were already there when you arrived, so surely they must have introduced themselves."

"I think Jeannie said something like '*she and Annie were going shopping because they were going to America'*. Then Annie told Basil that they had met before as she worked in the café on the corner near his office."

"So Mr Hallward has had contact with this woman Annie prior to meeting her at the restaurant."

"Yes, she said she'd seen him in the café when his secretary wasn't working late, and he'd been in to pick up his order." I took a sip of my drink and rolled the melting ice cubes in my mouth.

"Let's get this straight," Heythorp said, reading his notes. "You're telling us Basil Hallward knew Annie Linton prior to meeting her that day."

I nodded and crunched on the ice cubes. "If Jeannie Loring's friend, Annie, is the girl you're talking about. Though, I wish to make it clear I didn't know her surname."

"Point noted, James. Annie Linton is her name."

"Basil offered to run the two girls into London after Mrs Loring refused to allow her daughter to drive her car."

"Do you know why Mrs Loring didn't want her daughter to drive the car?" Heythorp asked while making a note.

I shook my head. "Maybe Mrs Loring had no other way of getting home without it."

Heythorp smiled. "You said, Jeannie Loring told your agent they were going to America. Did she mean her and her mother, or her and Annie?"

"I can't be sure, but I think Basil said Mrs Loring was taking the two young women."

"Your agent is Basil Hallward of Hallward Art Agency?" asked Wicklow.

"Yes."

"How long have you known him, Mr Ravencroft?"

"About five years."

"Now, let's get back to that day at the restaurant." Wicklow said." You stated they had already eaten when you arrived. So obviously they had been drinking, too."

"Their plates were being cleared as I arrived. Basil offered to buy everyone a drink, but the girls were leaving. He said something about heading back to his office to wait on an international call. He bought Mrs Loring and me a drink before he left with the girls."

"I see," Wicklow said.

"Does your questioning have something to do with the crash?" I asked.

"What makes you think that?" Heythorp interjected.

"I'm not sure." I sipped at my drink and settled back. They could question me all day as far as I was concerned, if it meant I could find out what they knew or didn't know.

Heythorp stood and took a step closer to the fireplace, "You said your mother painted this?"

"Yes."

"Hmm, I don't think my father would've been happy having such a portrait of my mother hanging in the living room. Your father must be pretty laid back about such things."

"My father *was* Reverend Donald Robert James Ravencroft." I emphasised the past tense.

Wicklow glanced at the painting. "Now I get it— Eve with the apple," he said, almost child-like in his discovery. "I guess it's a sort of religious painting, which is why your father was happy to have it hanging here."

I looked at the picture as though seeing it for the first time. Was that why my father loved it so much? As a child, if I needed my father the best place to find him, once mother's uncontrolled eruption had left a cold silence hanging over the house, was in the drawing room, sitting glass in hand before the painting. I believed he felt if he understood her art and by doing so he could get inside her head.

"That's the thing about art. The artists— like you, James..." Wicklow interrupted my thoughts.

"Pardon?"

"You don't always paint what you see. You expect the viewer to make sense of it. The clues are always in what the artist doesn't show rather than what's there. Now photographs— they're a different story. They only show you what the camera sees. As a camera only has a single lens, they only have one viewpoint."

I nodded, but his statement unnerved me.

"Very profound, Wicklow," Heythorp said. "You're an artist, James. A brilliant one at that, so why isn't there any of your work on show in this room?"

I looked from one to the other.

"So you've noticed that too, Sarge." Wicklow grinned. "There isn't one of Mr Ravencroft's paintings here. But then again if you knew who Mr Ravencroft's mother was you would understand why her pictures dominate the room."

"So who is she, lad?" Heythorp asked, lifting his eyebrows in mock annoyance.

"None other than Jane Elspeth Maedere, Sarge."

"Now you understand what I have to work with, James." Heythorp turned to Wicklow. "Okay, so she was an artist but what makes her so special that you assume that I would've known of her."

"Her work is the most sought after by serious collectors. As always rarity makes them worth a small fortune."

Heythorp nodded in my direction. "What this lad doesn't know about art isn't worth knowing. He's planning on joining a special branch of the force that's going to focus on stolen art. Apparently, there's a growing market for it."

Wicklow crossed to the window. "How's your security, sir?" He examined the locks as much as he had mother's paintings.

I smiled at his questions. The Jacobean builder also had security in mind when constructing the house with its red brick. The stone mullioned-latticed windows were enough to put off most hardened burglars. The narrow windows made it impossible for an average-sized man to climb through and made the room too dark to see if there was anything worth stealing in the first place.

"Do you mind if we check the security in the rest of your house, especially after seeing what an amazing hoard of Maederes you have?"

I stood. "Where would you like to start?"

Chapter Fourteen

1966

Heythorp and Wicklow followed me down three steps and along a panelled corridor into the galley-style kitchen. Enlarged during the Victorian era using stones taken from the remains of the ruined church, it overlooked both the drive and the rear garden.

While the coppers snooped about, I leant my back against the sink. Beyond the main kitchen area was a walk-in larder that led through to the tradesman's entrance at the back of the house. Mrs P often complained that the solid oak back door was difficult to open because of its weight. She said the heaviness of its key alone made her feel like a jailer when she locked the door in the evening.

As I waited for the coppers to finish whatever they were doing, I glanced out the front window and saw the police car parked at an odd angle. The sun reflecting off its windscreen almost blinded me. I turned away. Wicklow pointed to the hinged lockable frames of fine mesh fitted to the kitchen windows.

"What on earth are these?" he asked.

"They're to keep the flies out of here. My father had them made for our housekeeper. There's one fitted to the back door too, so she could leave it open in the summertime."

"Hmm, very clever," he said as he and Wicklow went out the back door and wandered around checking goodness knows what. I just left them to it and picked up an apple to munch on.

Once they were satisfied, I took them through to the oak-panelled dining room with its stone fireplace.

"Are these all the downstairs rooms?" Wicklow asked, making a show of checking the window locks.

"More or less. As you can see, my father was strong on security, so I don't think you need to concern yourselves about my mother's paintings."

"You'll be surprised by just how many houses we've seen where the owners thought they'd done everything they could to make them secure." Heythorp leaned against the doorframe. "Only to return home to find the house has been ransacked because they had carelessly left the bathroom window open. The summer months are the worst for break-ins as people often forget to secure windows before leaving the house."

"Well, I'll keep that in mind next time I go out."

"You just do that, lad." Heythorp rolled his eyes as if he had heard it all before. "Don't you get lonely living out here on your own?"

"In my line of work I need solitude if I'm going to create my best. Having a woman about twenty-four seven would be distracting. Maybe when I'm old, and past caring, I might wish I had a wife and kids. For now, if I want sex, I can go to London and buy it." I gave a wink and added, "If you know what I mean."

I stepped into the hallway, wishing they would just sod off and leave me to my work. I became aware of their frantic whispering and called to them. "I suppose you'll want to check upstairs too?"

Wicklow appeared in the doorway. "Where's your cellar, mate?" Without waiting for an answer, he crossed the hall, and snatching open the coat cupboard door.

"My what?"

"Cellar." He raised an eyebrow as if daring me to lie. "An old place like this must have one. I'm sure the Victorians would've stored plenty of wine down there."

"Look, if you want to search my place, don't you need a search warrant or something?"

Heythorp stepped around me. "Yes, you're right, James. But we're not searching, just looking. It would be amiss of us, knowing about your valuable art collection, if we did not do our job properly and give you a security check while we're here. If you want us to leave you've every right to say so, but if you've nothing to hide then why make a fuss, sir." He smiled broadly, as he waited for my reply.

"So you want to see the cellar?"

"If you don't mind." His tone echoed his sarcasm.

"It's fine by me. You need to be aware you enter at your own risk. The narrow stone steps down there are slippery. There's an underground spring, which makes the cellar very damp. Father never liked anyone going down there as it's so poorly lit."

"Aha, so that's your secret to having a green lawn, underground springs. My grandfather would be chuffed to bits if he had piped water under his lawns. I was going to ask you what your secret…"

"The entrance to the cellarage is in here." I cut Heythorp off before he started asking me for gardening tips. A look of confusion crossed the coppers' faces as I stepped back into the room we had just left.

They studied the layout of the room again, trying to see how they could possibly have missed the entrance to a cellar. As they looked about, I sensed their frustration in their body language. On one side of the room, French windows overlooked the rear garden and the fields beyond. A large Turkish rug covered a polished parquet floor. On it stood a long oak table with eight chairs surrounding it. I crossed to the far side of the brick and stone-dressed fireplace and tapped on an ornate panel. A door sprung open after a two-second delay, and I heard Wicklow gasp, sounding like an excited teenager. "Oh my God, Sarge. A hidden room!"

"Not hidden really." I stepped aside. "It's my father's study."

They followed me into the small room. A large oak desk faced a small window. Covering two walls from floor to ceiling were books. On the third wall, a narrow door made from two roughly-cut planks was set into it. I opened the door and pulled a cord. Below, the gloom lightened.

“Please take extra care. The lighting is appalling down there. The steps are very narrow.”
“Don’t worry about us. We can look after ourselves.” Heythorp said, producing a torch. “You just lead the way.”
A chilled air rose to meet us as we descended into a large space. Stone pillars supported a vaulted ceiling that had once been part of the church. The lighting, a modern addition, consisted of four single bulbs that hung at the centre of the arches. Their pale, yellow light made more shadows in the gloom, rather than helping with the visibility.
“Not much to see I’m afraid.” I stepped further into the cellar, guessing that they wanted to explore for themselves. Once their curiosity was satisfied, they would leave, I hoped.
“What’s that?” Wicklow asked. Before I could stop him from charging off into the blackness, he had disappeared.
“Be careful…” was all I managed to shout.
“Fucking hell!” shouted Wicklow.
“Wicklow!” Heythorp called, shining his torch in the direction of his colleague.
“Over here, Sarge!” came his pitiful cry.
Heythorp inched forward, scanning his torch beam in front of him until we found Wicklow leaning against a pillar.
“I tried to warn you.”
“I bashed my fucking shin bones. There’s some sort of plinth.” He ground the words out through clenched teeth. Heythorp pointed the torch downward, highlighting an ornate stone raised platform. “What the hell is that for?” he asked.
“For God’s sake, they’re coffin rests. I did say that you couldn’t just charge around down here. Upstairs, the redevelopment of the house has happened over many years, but down here, little has changed. We’re standing in the oldest part of the church, the original Saxon crypt.”
Heythorp shone his torch on Wicklow’s leg. “At least it isn’t broken. Let’s have a look at the damage, lad.”
Wicklow pulled up his trouser leg. Apart from a dark red mark on his shin, the skin hadn’t broken.
“You’ll have one hell of a bruise tomorrow,” I said. “I hope you’ve seen enough now. I need to get back to my

work."

Heythorp scanned the rest of the cellar with his torch. Its beam disappeared into the semi-darkness, beyond the reach of the ceiling lights. He inched forward slowly and then paused.

I knew what he had spotted.

He focused in on a chink of light at the far end of the cellar where the ceiling sloped down. His torch beam highlighted a few cobwebs, and then out of the darkness, a shape emerged.

"What's over there?" He was unable to conceal his excitement as his torch beam picked out more shapes half hidden in an alcove. "Packing crates?" Heythorp flicked the torchlight across my face, blinding me for a second. "They don't look Anglo-Saxon to me. Relatively new I would say."

I sat down on a stone coffin, the last remaining one, and knew that their search of thc cellar wasn't going to end anytime soon. "You're right— if nineteen forty-four is classed as *relatively new* to you. The gallery that sold mother's paintings used this space as a kind of workshop to crate her finished works."

I didn't mention mother's instability. Her nasty habit of destroying her work just before it was ready to go off to the gallery. After all, some people think madness is hereditary.

Heythorp raised his eyebrows and asked, "So how did they get the crate out of here once it was packed?"

"Through the brewery-type hatch up there." I pointed to an angular shape trapdoor, edged in a sliver of light. "It was the same way coffins were stored in here overnight, and how the stone coffin was brought in. The packers kept doors open when working down here because the lighting was so poor."

"How come we saw no sign of the entry outside?" Wicklow limped over to us.

"Father planted a shrubbery on the other side of the trap door to hide the entrance, which is now overgrown. My father kept a large collection of vintage wines down here as well." I pointed to racks of bottles covered in layers of dust. "Now if you've finished can we go back upstairs, please?"

In the entrance hall a look passed between the two of them as I tried to guide them towards the front door. My concern was for Annie now after leaving her too long.

"Right, the guided tour is over now," I said, trying to keep the humour in my voice. "I need to get on with my work."

"Well, thank you for being so cooperative, James." Heythorp added emphasis to my name. "But we would be failing in our duty if we didn't check upstairs." Wicklow limped towards the staircase.

"Hang on a minute." I dashed after him. "You've no right to search my home, you said so yourself, Detective Heythorp. I want you to go now!"

"You must have something to hide, sir," Wicklow said.

"No, I haven't. There's no need for you to do a security check up there. If anyone breaks in, I won't blame you. Just get out! Let me get on with my work!"

Wicklow pushed me aside. I fell hard against the wall, unable to stop him as he continued up the stairs. Heythorp offered his hand to me. I pushed it away, choosing to stand by myself.

Heythorp shook his head. "Such a highly-strung lad. I'm sorry, but once he latches on to something, he's like a dog with a bone."

"What's got him so excited?" I rubbed my elbow.

"Well, see here, James, it's those missing girls and paintings."

"Sorry? What girls? What paintings are you talking about?" I turned from him and headed back into the drawing room.

Heythorp followed me. "Surely, you've read about the missing girls in the papers, James."

"I don't have time for papers." I poured myself a drink. "If you haven't noticed, I don't possess a television either. I've no idea what you're talking about Detective Heythorp. So maybe now would be a good time to explain why you really *did* come to see me."

"Sarge!" Wicklow shouted. "Come and have a look at this —"

I flinched and caught my breath.

"Well, well. It seems like my lad has found something not quite to your liking, James." A grin spread across Heythorp's blotchy face.

I followed him upstairs. On the first landing, we found Wicklow leaning against the doorjamb of mother's room.

"In there, Sarge. It looks to be his studio, but I think we've uncovered Mr Ravencroft dirty little secret. He's a pansy." He pointed into mother's dressing room.

Heythorp looked me up and down. "A young man like you, with long hair and living on his own, with no sign of a woman around, and a closet full of beautiful gowns hung neatly on their hangers, with matching shoes and handbags. What's a man like me meant to think, Mr Ravencroft in this liberal day and age?"

Heythorp's look of revulsion told me he wasn't accepting of homosexuality. It put me in a dangerous situation. I had to answer the question he hadn't even asked.

"If Wicklow is so knowledgeable about my mother, then he would know she died. This used to be her bedroom and dressing room, I'm just using her studio. My bedroom is just down the corridor there." I pointed to another door. "I can show you if you want."

"When did your mother die?" Wicklow asked.

"1944. I was seven at the time."

"So why keep all her belongings?" Heythorp's hard face softened.

"My father couldn't come to terms with her loss," I moved to the window. "In a house this size, one never needs to throw anything out."

"Well, Wicklow, I think we've seen enough, don't you?" Heythorp moved towards the door "Thank you for showing us around, James. Any problems, just phone us on this number." He handed over a business card.

I dropped it on the table next to the phone as I followed them out, and down the stairs.

When I was sure they had left, I went up to the attic stairs' window and watched until the car became a small dot flashing through the trees in the bright sunshine.

Heythorp hadn't explained about the missing girls or paintings. I wasn't sure why he had mentioned it. I chuckled, knowing that I had just set Basil up. "How perfect is that?"

The promise of rain had been nothing more than a promise. The heat in the attic hit me as I made my way up the final flight of stairs eager to get back to Annie. I'm not sure what I became aware of first as I entered the studio, the sour odour, or the low hum. The first thing I encountered was the odd fly as I opened the door. The overpowering stench made me gag. I threw open the French windows. A swarm of flies hovered around the door to the side room, while others added to the growing numbers coming through the skylight.

I gasped and stepped onto the roof, trying to fill my lungs. The sound of the feeding flies reverberated through me as though they were in my head. It made me retch. I grabbed a strip of material from my ragbag near the sink and soaked it with water before tying it over my mouth and nose. I rushed into the antechamber and pulled the bed into the main room.

A black rippling mass of flies rose up and followed me. Thousands of beating tiny wings moved as one. Unable to look at Annie, I knew the sight would horrify me. The smell of her was enough to know she was dead. A trail of yellowish-brownish liquid dripping from the bed was alive with flies.

"Bloody hell! Why couldn't you wait just a little longer, Annie?" I flung my arms out in an effort to disturb the flies. As I lifted Annie's body, a couple of flies flew out of her mouth followed by a trickle of vomit. I turned my head away and retched. I stripped the dress from her and tossed it aside. The flies began to lose interest and disperse as I wrapped her body in a clean sheet and carried it to the lift. I set to work using wads of rags soaked in bleach and began to wash the studio floor, piling up everything that needed to go into the lift.

Rags, spoiled blankets and the body wrapped in the sheet I

took down to the next floor. I dashed to the outbuildings and manhandled a straw bale into a wheelbarrow. I pushed it across the garden, keeping to the gravel paths, so as not to mark the lawns. Ducking under low branches of a large rhododendron bush, I pulled the wheelbarrow backwards into the centre of it. I heaved the straw bale out and stood it next to the grave. Then I manoeuvred the grave lid half onto the straw bale to support its weight. With the weight of the lid now supported it gave me room enough to squeeze the body in.

The decomposing soil within the grave smelled a lot sweeter than I did. I pushed the empty wheelbarrow back to the house and piled everything out of the lift into it, desperate to finish the grisly task before the gardener turned up.

I dropped the rags and blankets into a garden incinerator ready to burn later, before crossing to the tomb. I struggled with the body as I tried to avoid contact with the fluid that leaked from it. The flies returned in force, buzzed around me. I retched again nearly dropping the bundle into the pool of liquid that had gathered in the bottom of the wheelbarrow. I heaved the body into the open tomb. I dashed to the back of the greenhouse and shovelled compost in the wheelbarrow. Sweat poured down my face and back, soaking the tops of my jeans and plastering my shirt to me as I hurried back to cover the body. I pushed the top of the tomb back into place, relieved that I had finished. All I wanted now was a shower.

I lifted the straw bale back into the wheelbarrow and tucked the spade in next to it. Halfway across the lawn, I heard someone shout my name.

"Oh, Mr Ravencroft, there you are!"

I halted and inhaled. Not quite believing he was back again. I left the wheelbarrow where it was and walked towards him. I wondered how long my visitor had been leaning on the side gate watching me. He drew lazily on his cigarette.

"Hello Detective Heythorp, back so soon?" I leaned over at the gate, looking for his sidekick but I couldn't see him.

"So sorry to disturb you again," Heythorp said. "Doing a

spot of gardening now, sir." He pointed in the direction of the wheelbarrow.

"No, it's my workout. It helps to de-stress me, so I can think more clearly."

"Sorry, did our visit upset you?" Heythorp sniffed the air momentarily and I hoped years of smoking had deadened his sense of smell. He looked over my shoulder. "What's with the straw bale?"

I looked in the direction he was pointing. "My father's idea, he had me run about with it to build my muscles as a child. You should try it yourself." I unlocked the gate and gestured to him to have a go.

"No thanks, sir." His eyes locked on mine.

I had to look away and closed the gate behind me. "So what can I help you with this time?"

"My colleague and I were wondering if you had any idea where Basil Hallward is at the moment."

"Basil?"

"Your agent I believe, sir."

"I'm just one of his artists. If I were you I would try asking his secretary."

"Okay, we'll try his office. Thank you for being so helpful, sir."

As we turned the corner of the house I saw Wicklow standing by the side of the car.

"How old is this house, Mr Ravencroft?" he asked as we approached.

"Some parts date back as far as the 1500s, others to the early 1800s, but I've already told you this. Now, is that all?"

"You've worked up quite a sweat running around with a wheelbarrow," Heythorp said.

"That's the idea. If you don't mind, I would like to have a shower now."

"Of course, thank you for your time." Heythorp said as Wicklow opened the driver's door. "We may need to question you further at a later date Mr Ravencroft."

"My agent is in America," I heard myself say. "Though

I'm not supposed to know that, Detective Heythorp, so if you do see him, please don't mention that I told you so."

"Is he now? That's very interesting." Heythorp opened the passenger door. "Thanks for that, Mr Ravencroft. Us coppers appreciate when the public are being helpful."

As I watched them drive away, I wondered why Heythorp found Basil being in America so interesting.

Chapter Fifteen

Stone Angels
The Fifth Painting
1967

I heard nothing from Basil for months, and guessed he wasn't back from America yet. With no risk of being disturbed, I focused solely on my angel series. Late one afternoon, the phone rang.

"Hello, James. Sorry for the interruption."

"Good afternoon, Jenny." I was disappointed that it wasn't my agent. Since Basil had been away Jenny and I were now on first name terms.

"Mr Hallward asked me to give you a call this morning, and it went clear out of my head."

"That's so unlike you, Jenny. What's happened?"

"Everything here is a little chaotic. No time to explain. Mr Hallward's client has now paid for his painting. So, if possible, could you run it in as I need it pronto?"

"Sure. I can have it with you tomorrow morning if that's okay?"

"That's great. I'll see you then."

As I lowered the receiver, I heard her flustered voice calling, "Oh James, hang on. Are you still there?"

"Yes, what is it?" I scanned the tubes of paint before me. On a scrap of paper, I made a note to recheck my stores of certain colours.

"It's just he didn't leave me any details about which one he wanted!"

"It's okay. Don't worry. I know the one he's asking for."

"Great. That's something I can tick off my list. See you tomorrow."

"Of course, Jenny. Bye for now."

"Thanks, James."

On waking, I was surprised by how eager I was to find out how well Basil's latest trip to America had gone. Not that I wished to share in Easter's glory, more to gloat in Basil's disappointment. My desire for Basil's return was the driving need to locate the next model as soon as possible.

I climbed the stairs to Jenny's office and heard the rhythmic mechanical sound of her work. Her frosty pink polished nails hammered out a flurry of crisp white paper as she worked at her typewriter. Her door stood ajar and I entered without knocking. A large wooden desk dominated the space while a narrow sash window filled the back wall, with its uninspiring view onto the street below.

Jenny's fingers paused as she looked up from under her blunt black fringe and smiled. She had an exotic beauty about her. Her confidence shone out as she rose and took the brown paper-wrapped painting and placed it in a large metal cabinet behind her. On turning back to me a flush crept across her creamy-brown cheeks. "I'm so sorry, James, Mr Hallward isn't here at the moment." She reached into her desk drawer; her thin silver bangles glinted on the cuff of her green blouse. Jenny handed me a thick white envelope. "He asked me to give you this."

I tore open the envelope.

Jenny saw something register in my face and added, "James your land and seascape paintings are so powerful. When I look at them, it's as though I can feel the full force of nature wash over me. Your palette knife style of painting gives a three-dimensional element to your work."

Surprised by her sudden outpouring, I rested on the edge of her desk. "Thanks— that's kind of you to say so." I began reading the letter.

Jenny shuffled some papers. "I—just wanted you to know. It's wrong for me to say, I know but… your work is far superior to Joseph Easter's. It's unfair that Mr Hallward doesn't exhibit your paintings."

So bloody predictable of Basil! I screwed the letter up. Annoyed at another commission and more time-wasting travelling to various locations along the Suffolk coastline to come up with a variation on a common theme just to satisfy some rich bloke and his pretentious wife, I sighed. Suddenly, aware Jenny was apologising, I smiled.

"I'm sorry. Maybe I'm speaking out of turn, James."

"Jenny, you've nothing to apologise for so don't upset yourself. I wasn't upset with you. Don't say anything to risk losing your job, especially not for my sake." I stood.

She laughed. "Oh, James, Mr Hallward would be lost without me."

"That's true enough." I laughed, glad to break the tension. "Anyway, it hasn't been a wasted journey when I get to see you. I better get home and start on this." I waved the letter at her. "Just another one like all the others I've done so far. Not really pushing my artistic potential."

"Our clients love them." Jenny said her long fingers busy typing a letter to another one of Basil's flunkies, no doubt. "Have a safe journey home, James."

I stepped out onto the high street and turned the collar of my trench coat up against the bitter March winds. With my head down I headed towards the art shop to restock my supply of materials before heading home.

The old shop with its black beams and sooty grey plaster had a narrow façade and seemed caught in its own time warp. It would've looked out of place on the high street among the growing numbers of modern buildings. I pushed open the heavy door with its small leaded window and stepped in.

A bell rang within the storeroom alerting the owner that a customer had entered. A muffled voice called from the other side of a glass-beaded curtain. "I shall be with you in a moment."

The interior should have been quite dark due to the collection of paintings filling the two bay windows on either side of the entrance that blocked out the daylight. But inside was surprisingly bright and spacious. One area of the shop had an assortment of artist's materials from paper, notebooks, sketchpads, canvases, stretcher bars, as well as boards and panels. Almost anything, any artist would need.

The other half of the shop served as a downmarket gallery where for a small sum of money, artists without an agent could hang their works in the hope that someone like Basil Hallward might walk in and spot their artwork. The most expensive items like brushes and paints were out of reach behind a large wooden counter.

With my back to the counter, I took in the display of dusty paintings and wondered how long some of them had been hanging. Then the tinkling sound of the beaded curtain alerted me to the fact the shop owner was now ready to serve me.

"Hello. May I help you?"

I expected the stooped figure of old Bert, the shop owner but, instead, a young woman stood bathed in a shimmering golden light before me.

"Hello— can I help?"

For a moment, the composition of the shapes, light and shadow created by the piles of boxes, I glimpsed through the curtain behind her began to transform. Within that split second, the boxes became tower blocks racing skywards on my canvas as my mind transformed the girl into a stone angel.

"Are you all right?" Her question shattered the image.

"Hmm, sorry…" I reached into my pocket. "Just expected Bert. Is he all right?"

"He's fine." She pushed an auburn lock of hair behind her ear. "At his sister's. I'm helping out here until one of his nieces arrives home as they both live abroad."

"Oh. Are you his daughter?" I pulled out the list of things I needed.

"No, just a friend. Bert's helped me out in the past. I'm Jackie. And you?"

"Oh, I'm…Tommy Blackbird," I said with a grin.

"Pleased to meet you, Tommy. So what can I help you with?"

I passed my list to her.

Jackie leant forward and straightened out the list with the side of her hand. Within my mind, I selected the right colours and added them to my palette. The light caught the soft wisps of her hair as she brushed it over her shoulders. Holly green, I decided was the perfect shade of colour for her eyes. I began mixing to create the right shades to mirror mother's tortured soul. In shades of black, greys and greens.

"Are you one of Hallward's artists?" Jackie's question snapped me out of my thoughts. "There's an awful lot of materials on here." She waved the list at me.

"Hallward's?" I reached for the list. "Does it matter if I'm not?"

"Oh no… sorry, but it's just that Bert said I should keep an eye out, that's all."

"Why?"

"You have to be eagle-eyed working in here. Stuff goes missing all the time. Some of them try to pull a fast one. You know the sort of thing—can I pay you when I've made my fame and fortune?" She bit her bottom lip and pointed to the dusty paintings.

"Luckily for you I'm not one of his lackeys then." I laughed.

"Sorry I guess I shouldn't have said that. Bert's words, not mine."

"Do you see many of them in here then?"

"We mostly get 'wannabes'." She gave a slight nod in the direction of the art gallery.

I crossed to the wall of paintings and peered at them.

"You're one of Bert's regulars are you?"

"Well, sort of. I'm from out of town. Whenever I'm this way, I normally pop in. He has everything I need in one hit. Tell Bert I'm sorry to have missed him."

"So you've come quite a distance then?" She ticked each item off the list with her fingertip as though she were crossing them out in her head.

"Yes, I have."

"Will you want to be taking all of this with you now?" She creased her brow.

"I have a commission I need to get started on." I reached for the list and she quickly covered it with her hand. "You're a professional artist, aren't you?"

"I am indeed." I noticed she wore no rings on her delicate fingers.

"Oh…" Jackie chewed at the side of her thumbnail.

"If there's a problem, I could always go elsewhere." The size of my order would boost Bert's takings.

"It's… just… that it'll take me a while to get it together and…" She gave a smirk. "It's half day closing too. A friend is picking me up soon."

"Right. I see we have a problem."

"Could you pick it up tomorrow?"

"Will Bert be back?"

"Unfortunately, no. I'm holding the fort until further notice."

"I'm sure his shop is in safe hands. May I ask— do you know, Mr Hallward? I mean, has he been in here?"

"You mean Hallward of Fine Arts? What do you think?" She gestured to the room.

"I was hoping to start promoting my work in London and wasn't sure what the going rate is to exhibit here."

"Why not pop in and see Mr Hallward. I'm sure he'll be able to tell you if you're any good or not."

"Is his gallery far from here?"

"Not at all— just up the road. You can't miss it. Very modern. Take a look then you'll know whether it's the sort of place you'll want to hang your work."

"Thanks. So it's safe to say Hallward has never entered here?"

She laughed. "I don't think he would risk his business reputation on these." Jackie gestured to the motley collection of paintings. "*Unsellable masterpieces,* that's what Bert jokingly calls them. Goodness knows how long some of them have been hanging here. I'm not an expert, but I can recognise bad art when I see it."

One painting looked to be some sort of farm scene. The artist had painted a series of abstract squares on a blue and green background and called it, *'Sheep on Blue and Green'*.

"I've met him a couple of times."

"Who?" I glanced back at the painting. "The artist who painted that?"

"No." She laughed. "I meant Hallward. He came to my boyfriend's flat to see some of his work."

"Your boyfriend has work here?"

"No." She shook her head. "And that's not one of his."

"Glad to hear it. So Hallward liked his stuff. What happened?"

"Don't know—we split up. He loved his work more than me, I guess. So what do you paint?"

"Landscapes and seascapes. Abstract mostly."

"Are there any on show in London for me to see?"

"Sorry, only in Suffolk. A local gallery there sells my work."

"What a pity. So are you happy to leave this with me until… say tomorrow afternoon? I'll have it ready by then."

"That's fine. What's the latest I can collect it?"

"Say five. That's when we close. I could give you a ring as soon as I have it ready."

"That's very kind of you, but I'll be out and about. I can be here by five at the latest. Could I bring the car round to the back of the shop as the street is very narrow out there?" I gestured towards the front. "Less an inconvenience to others."

"No problem. See you tomorrow then."

I arched my shoulders against the wind while pulling my collar up as I left the shop and nearly collided with an elderly couple coming towards me. I sidestepped them and hurried towards the main road. The windows of Joe's café shone bright with condensation, freeing me from further concerns that anyone else might have seen me.

At the corner, I took the footpath, that ran to the back of

Basil's gallery and on towards the small, neat bistro where Annie once worked. I wanted to grab a hot drink and maybe something to eat while wasting an hour.

In the warmth of the St. Clair's bistro, I sipped my tea and wondered if Basil had started to join up the dots yet. If I were in his shoes, I would've tried to link someone other than myself to the girls' disappearances. In the last four years Basil has been their only suspect, but with no conclusive evidence, the police had been unable to touch him.

I checked my watch. Plenty of time for me to familiarise myself with the route to the back of the shop and watch how long it takes for her to get ready to leave.

The waitress had finished serving at the other table and was heading in my direction, cleaning cloth in hand. "Are you ready to order?" she asked, cleaning the table next to mine. Her grease-stained overall was pulled so tight across her ample bosom that only a small button stopped it from all spilling out. Plastered on her face was a broad red-lipped smile as she waited for my answer. One hand rested on her thick waist, while the other pushed a curl of bleached blonde hair back under the small, grubby cap she wore.

"What do you have in the way of sandwiches?"

"What do you fancy, love?" she asked.

"Cheese and pickle would be nice."

"Coming right up, love," she said, shouting my order to the kitchen assistant as she carried the tray of dirty crockery to the counter.

While I waited for my food, I deliberated about increasing the pressure on Basil. It would be quite satisfying watching him really sweat. My thoughts wandered. My fifth angel called to me. I pondered on whether to use my car to stakeout Jackie or whether it'll be less conspicuous to watch her on foot.

On checking my watch, I decided not to wait. "I'm sorry but I'm going to have to leave. May I take my sandwiches with me?"

The waitress looked up. "Of course, love," she beamed, revealing a row of decaying teeth. "Just wait a moment. We'll wrap them for you."

I hurried back to the junction between the main road and the back street. I was looking for somewhere close enough to the corner that gave me shelter and spotted a boarded-up shop directly opposite.

The shop entrance was set well back from the kerb and perfect for sheltering from the bitter wind and nosy parkers. I leant against the grimy window and pulled the greaseproof package from my pocket. I removed half the sandwich from its wrapper, lifted it to my mouth. I was mid-way through taking a bite when a woman dressed in a long, mauve coat, and Cossack-style hat emerged from the back street and walked in my direction.

As I stepped back, the door behind me swung open. I ducked in and closed it just in time. Jackie stood where moments before I had. She pushed her cuff back and checked her watch before looking up the street again.

My thoughts raced. The possibility of snatching her now hovered, but something stopped me. I took one bite of the sandwich and tossed the remains into the pile of rubbish at my feet.

Jackie stepped onto the pavement and wave as a green Mini Cooper shot across the road and did a U-turn before pulling up alongside her. The driver jumped out and the blaring sound of Dylan singing *'the answer my friend is blowing in the wind'* filled the abandoned shop along with the sound of girlish laughter.

I moved forward enough to see a leggy girl run around the car and throw her arms around Jackie. After exchanging a few words, Jackie wiped her face.

"Forget about him, Jac. Men aren't bloody worth it," Leggy called as she ran back round to the driver's side. "Come on girl, get in. Let's party like there's no tomorrow."

They sped off.

I stepped onto the pavement, barely missing a small dog. It jumped up growling and snapping.

"Sorry, love." The old woman pulled on the dog's lead. "Come on, Buster. It's time we got home." She hurried off in the opposite direction.

I crossed the road, and took the next one along from Back Street, to see if I could find a way to the rear of the art shop.

Chapter Sixteen

1967

I made my way down a road called Back Street. It ran parallel to the shops on Market Street. Five minutes later I turned onto a narrow, cobbled thoroughfare between two boarded up houses. Daylight was fading as I hurried along, hoping I was heading in the right direction.

Along one side of the lane a high brick wall ran with gateways that led into the backyards of the houses, which stood on Market Street. I found a gap lit by the glow of a single streetlamp when the wall finally came to an abrupt end. The gap seemed wide enough for a car or small van to pass through. Beyond this was a wasteland partially covered with overgrown shrubs. Deep ruts—tyre marks I presumed, lined the rough ground, showing that vehicles had regularly crossed over.

The overgrown bushes hid a muddy footpath that ran the full length of Back Street and gave its residents access from their backyards onto the high street. With the help of a streetlamp, I could see a faded painted sign over a pair of double doors that told me I had found the art shop.

I guessed the uneven paved yard at the back of the shop had once been its garden. High brick walls separated the shop's yard from the houses on either side. Some lights came on in one of the houses, but I took a chance that no one was watching and crossed the muddy footpath into the yard to get a better look at the possibility of getting my car in. A collection of discarded boxes and a couple of trashcans littered one side of the yard, but this still allowed enough room for a vehicle to fit up against the doors. Bert had the good sense to use the two boundary walls to create a covered area for keeping his stock dry while loading and unloading a delivery van. It would, of course, conceal my car from prying eyes too.

***

Early next morning I went out to make some preliminary sketches of the landscapes for a commission Basil had requested, but a sudden downpour curtailed my plans. After stripping off most of my wet clothes, I stood, in my underpants, warming myself in front of Aga oven. While my jeans and jumper steamed gently in the growing heat, I tried to get the circulation back into my fingertips. The phone rang as I reached for the kettle to make a hot drink. On snatching it up, I snapped "Hcllo!"

"Hi, James. Basil here. I'd like to apologise for the letter yesterday, but I didn't know when I would get the chance to speak to you in person." Basil said in a rush. "The client is an important one that we cannot afford to lose."

"Are you in some difficulty, old boy?" I stretched as far as I could, without pulling the phone off the wall, for my father's old trench coat and slipped it on. Common sense would've made me wear it when I originally went out.

"Ever since I got back from America it's been a living hell."

"America?" I queried, trying to flex my fingers while holding the phone.

"Yes."

'But that was months ago. Have you been away again?'

"No, I haven't."

"Oh right. So how was it?"

"What— America?"

"Yes." Basil was not quite on the ball. Something was bothering him.

"Bloody good actually. I'm surprised by how well Easter's work sold, especially after Chuck's negative feedback."

"Chuck who?" I added hot water to my cup.

"Chuck Sparks. I've known him for years. He's now my partner, thanks to Easter's sell-out exhibition in America. It became the deal breaker. Now I can move onwards and upwards."

"Deal breaker?" My mind still on the name Chuck Sparks, it sounded familiar to me.

"For years, I've been trying to get access to the American market. I've managed to sell one or two paintings over there, but having a partner and a main office in the States means it'll be much easier."

"Wasn't he a friend of my mother?" I suddenly remembered and was unable to contain my excitement.

"Your mother?" Basil's voice dropped, briefly betraying awkwardness.

"Yes. You've mentioned him in connection with her I'm sure."

"James, you're very much mistaken." He rustled some papers.

"No— I'm certain. A few years ago you were talking about living in America after the war."

"Really?" Basil's tone deepened. The bile in my gut rose as my hatred increased. He was using mother to further his career again.

"Yes, after the war, I did spend time in America, but I never met your mother."

"I didn't say you met her."

"So what are you saying?" He paused, a shade too long. On recovering himself he added. "I'm quite busy at the moment. And I'll need that commission as soon as possible."

"No, no, you don't get out of this. You said when you discovered a couple of mother's paintings in a junk shop in New York, your friend introduced you to my mother's agent. Now I want to speak to him."

"Look James, I'll ask my business partner if he knew your mother, but at the moment, I'm busy dealing with late paying clients, who still demand I find them their next sound investment. What's a man supposed to live on while he waits for his ship to come in? And to top it all, mine could be bloody sinking before it has even set sail."

"The shit's your problem, Basil. I want his number."

"Sorry James, but I need to speak to him first. It's all about privacy. I don't pass your number out to anyone. I know how you like your privacy."

I wanted to argue the point, but, once again, he had the upper hand. Both he and Easter were winning at my expense. I changed tack. "So what's going on, old boy?" I tried to keep the sarcasm out of my voice.

"Another bloody girl has gone missing!"

"What girl?" I swapped the phone over to my other hand.

"I don't need this right now, especially when my new business partner is such a highly principled man. If shit like this gets back to him…"

"How's he going to find out?" Pleased to learn something else to my advantage.

"Oh, you don't know, do you? I forgot you don't subscribe to the papers. Guess who's breathing down my neck again. According to the papers, I'm helping them with their enquiries."

"What? You've actually been named?" I bit my lip to keep my excitement under control and tasted blood.

"Christ, no! It just mentions *someone* is helping them. Luckily no reporters are sniffing around my home or upsetting Jenny at the office. However, I don't suppose it'll take them long to find out who the mysterious helper is. If the police take me down to the station, maybe things will be different."

"Scary for you." I added coffee to a mug to make myself another drink.

"I'm sure before long they'll be camping right outside my home. So far, no one else has identified me in that damn photograph with the first victim. The newspaper office told the police where and when they received the photo. Apparently, there were other photos of the victim talking to the celebrities on that same evening, too."

"Have they questioned the celebrities?"

"No idea. Guess they would be above suspicion."

"No one is above suspicion, Basil."

"Does that include you, James?"

"If you remember, I left soon after meeting you."

"We only have your word for that, James. I couldn't swear to it that you left when you said. The place was heaving that night. Anyway, the negatives would show the police that I wasn't the last person the victim spoke to that evening. It's just the newspapers doing what they love best, stirring up shit in the hope some will stick, and they will have an exclusive to plaster over the front of their rag."

I managed to get the milk out of the fridge and finished making a drink as Basil went on. "The last thing I need right now is another reason for my slow paying customers not to pay up."

"So being an unknown does have its advantages then."

"What do you mean?"

"It's a good job you're not famous. It's strange that after all your gallery publicity launch photos, you would've become a bit of a local celebrity."

"Fame has nothing to do with it, Ravencroft. Didn't you just hear what I said? Another bloody girl has gone missing. I haven't been able to go into my office for weeks because I've been too busy helping the police. They've nothing on me."

"I thought you had gone back to America."

"They were waiting at the airport for me. I've no idea why they thought I might be helpful to their enquiry with these disappearances. Apparently there's nothing linking the girls but me. It's bloody ludicrous, James. Surely someone has encountered them all in the course of their working day, the same as me, or knows them all on a personal level. For Christ's sake, all of them had jobs that brought them into contact with a host of other people."

"I wish I could help. As I said to the police, I thought they wanted to talk to me about the day Mrs Loring died."

"What? When— when did they speak to you?"

"God, Basil, it was ages ago." I sipped my coffee. Out the window the rain clouds had lifted. The sun broke through the dark clouds and highlighted the stone statue that marked the position in the garden, where the last few ancient gravestones stood.

"When, James?" Basil's voice rang in my ear. "For Christ's sake, when?"

"Hmm, let me see." My thoughts were on the stone angel statue in the garden. She wasn't really an angel. She had no wings. Her weatherworn features gave her a sad expression. Her hand, raised in blessing, had lost all its fingers. Just a thumb remained. Originally the statue of the Virgin Mary came from inside the old church father told me. From my locked attic bedroom on warm summer evenings, as a child, I would watch mother through the binoculars as she wandered around the garden ghost-like and barefoot, dressed in a long flowing nightgown. She would often sit beneath the statue on one of the tabletop graves, and talk to it. "When you were in America last year." I finally answered Basil's question.

"Last bloody year!" He bellowed.

I held the phone from my ear for a moment.

"You had a whole year to tell me and you didn't think to mention it sooner?"

"What difference would it have made? You weren't here. This is the first time you've called me. Should I have left a message with Jenny?"

"No, of course not! It's so embarrassing. Not just for me, but especially for Jenny. At least they've been respectful when they've visited the gallery. Jenny has been brilliant; all her records are up to date."

"I thought they came in connection with Mrs Loring's crash, but what they were interested in was you talking to the girl." I lied. It wasn't as though he could ask them.

"What girl!"

"You know— the girl with Mrs Loring's daughter?"

"Jeannie?"

"No—her friend. She worked near your office— in the café."

"Annie Linton!"

"That's it. Annie. Though, I didn't know her surname until

the police mentioned it." I put the kettle on again.

"That's the missing girl, James. That's who the two stooges from Scotland Yard came to question me about."

"Oh, so not Mrs Loring then?"

"Mrs Loring's death was an accident. They're more interested in the disappearance of another girl."

"You only gave them a lift into London."

"You know that. I know that. And Tamsin knew that. Only she's not here to speak up for me, is she? Jeannie is now in America so upset by what has happened to her mother, and now her friend. I can't talk to her. Well, I can if I want to see what the inside of a prison cell looks like, which I don't."

"I see your point old boy."

"Bloody hell, James, lay off the old boy stuff! Luckily for me, no bodies have turned up yet. They haven't any real proof I'm involved. I'm seriously thinking about finding myself a lawyer as this is getting a little too crazy for my liking."

"Isn't that considered to be a sign that you must be guilty of something?"

"No! It means I'm covering my arse. For Christ's sake, James, I just wish you could understand how serious this is for me. I may have to cut back on my artists' list. If I can't sell their work, there's no point in me buying it."

"Does that mean my work too?" I added water and milk to my mug. Pulling out a chair, I sat at the table with my feet off the cold floor.

"Your work sells and the clients that buy it pay on time. Easter's doing well too, especially after his promotional American trip. I've been thinking about bringing you two together. I know both of your styles are very different, but I'm sure that's to our advantage."

"What do you mean together?" The hair rose on the back of my neck.

"Exhibition, James. Look, I need to think about it a bit more. Put some planning and forethought in. You know, the right venue, the right people to invite, that sort of thing. I don't want to waste good money. Anyway, Easter's busy working on a new series of paintings."

"Is he?" I hoped Basil would give me an insight. Though, knowing Joe, he isn't one for giving anything away, not even to Basil.

I put my mug in the sink and glanced out the window. The sun still shone on the garden angel. "Four isn't enough." I said absently.

"Sorry, what's not enough?"

"Oh, nothing. If Easter's creating something new, isn't it about time I did?"

"Hmm, yes, maybe it is…" Basil sighed. I hoped he was thinking and wasn't bored.

While I waited for his reply, I thumbed the sketches I had made for the commission. I thought I could hear someone talking in the background. Finally Basil spoke again.

"Of course, James. I do understand your need to be creative. It's just that your customer base is very sensitive. We can't be sure how they would react to your change of style, or whether they would want to buy it."

"So it's all down to money. So why can Easter work on something new, then?"

"His market is larger than yours. Look, James, put together some ideas, some sketches and let me see them. We'll take it from there. Remember I need to see the sketches before you start painting."

"Right— I'm—" I stopped myself from saying more as anger tore through me. So soddin' Easter can paint what he wants, but I need permission.

"You have plenty of commissions to fulfil, James. We'll talk further after I've seen your ideas. Okay, Jenny, I'll be with you soon… They want what? Got to go James, Jenny needs me. I just hope it's not the soddin' police again."

A quick shower warmed me up and cooled my temper. By the time I was dressed, all I could think about was showing Basil where my real ability lay, but first I needed to get my studio ready for my next visitor. After checking the pantry to see what I needed to replace, as Mrs P always said, "*you must feed the body to feed the mind,"* I headed off to the local farm shop to stock up on milk, butter, eggs and bread. A simple life is the secret to success. By giving yourself enough mind space, you can stay focused on your goals. There are only three things I needed to make me happy; a breathing space, a room in which I can work and most importantly, a muse.

On entering my studio, I found chaos. Paint-smothered rags, discarded tubes and dirty brushes littered surfaces and the paint-splattered floor. After fetching Mrs P's tidy box, I set to work cleaning the studio to remove all traces of my last muse. As I restored order, a wave of peace and tranquillity descended on me. It gave an understanding of mother's passion and her need to stay focused.

The rooftop studio had everything, even a sink with hot water. Thanks to Mrs P's training, the dress was carefully washed and restored to its original crisp freshness and hung to dry on a line outside the studio window.

I placed the latest finished work with the others in a wall rack before cleaning the tiled walls and floor around my workspace. Next the brushes were washed in turpentine and using a fresh rag I cleaned out the old paint, before rinsing them in soapy water taking time reshaping the bristles before leaving them to air dry. I sorted through the paints, tossing any empty tubes into a bin. Then starting with the blues to the left and finished with the reds on my right. I scraped the old paint from the palette, taking it back to the bare wood as best I could. After cleaning up the paint scrapings, I took a last look around before bringing the dress in and placing it on the mannequin in my storeroom. I was ready to bring home my next muse.

Chapter Seventeen

March 1967

I prayed my timing was right. After pulling off Market Street, I drove slowly down Old Lane and reversed through a gap in the wall. Once I had backed over the waste ground and stopped as close as I could to the delivery doors of the art shop, I got out.

My car fitted under the porch with just enough room for me to ease out of the driver's side and walk round to the boot. I checked the surrounding houses. All that could be seen was a thin sliver of light filtering through some of the curtained windows, but most were in darkness. I slipped on my driving gloves, knocked on the door and stood back.

After a couple of minutes, Jackie opened one of the double doors. Bright light spilled out. She stood in the doorway dressed in jeans and a bright green Sloppy Joe. "Hi Tommy. Glad to see you found us okay." She raised a finger to her lips. "Please be as quiet as you can when loading your car. Come through, and I'll explain." She closed the door behind us. "Bert gets complaints about after-hours deliveries, so hopefully we won't make too much noise getting these in your car." Jackie gestured to the boxes stacked behind the doors.

"I've sorted out your order, though I haven't sealed them as I thought you might like to check them first. Bert prefers customers to check so they cannot complain. He even has a saying, '*check, pay, take them away*'."

The sight of Jackie's pale brown lashes framing her bright green eyes made me want her so much more. She met my gaze with an equally intense stare. I dropped to my knees, scooped up my list from the top of the largest box and scanned it, pretending to check the contents.

Jackie squatted next to me, her left hand resting on the side of the box. From the corner of my eye I scrutinised the shape of it, the frailty of her fingers and the slenderness of her wrist. As she leant forward, strands of her hair fell across her face. With a gentle sweep of her hand, she pushed her hair back as she watched me closely.

"I was worried." There was a slight edge in Jackie's voice. "I forgot that I hadn't given you the directions. Did you have to ask?"

"No. Luckily, I used to be a Scout." I smiled and gestured to the boxes. "Yep, everything seems to be here."

"Gosh, that was lucky. Most new delivery drivers have to phone ahead for directions." A look of uncertainty flickered across her face as she reached for a roll of tape and a knife from a nearby counter. "The drivers hate having to reverse across the wasteland, so they park further back when delivering our orders. It's a wonder you could get as close to the doors as you did."

There was a slight change in her demeanour as she began sealing the boxes. With a quick flick of her wrist, she sliced through the tape before moving on to the next one, making swift work of them all.

"Too worried about damaging their company's vans to risk doing what you've done."

"Yes, I noticed some damage on the edge of your neighbour's wall," I replied, hoping to ease the tension that seemed to fill the space between us.

"That's something else our neighbours enjoy moaning about. But Bert's shop was here before them. Funnily enough, both sides once belonged to this building and some of the garden, too."

"So Bert owns that land at the back?"

"Yes, once he owned all of it." She placed the tape and knife back on the counter before asking. "Are you paying by cash or cheque?"

"Cash." I pulled my wallet out.

She dragged down a large ledger and made a note by some figures. Her pen hovered as she waited for me to count out the money. She picked the cash up and recounted it before laying it in a cash drawer. After she put a line through the figures in the book, she locked the drawer and replaced the ledger on the shelf before turning to me. "Would you like me to help you carry them out?"

"Would you mind?"

I picked up the two larger boxes and left the smaller one for her. I opened the rear passenger door, blocking the way out and slid the two boxes onto the back seat before turning to face her.

"That one can go into here."

I lifted the boot and stepped back, positioning myself behind her. Jackie hesitated before turning her back to me. I eased the pad from my jacket pocket, waiting for the precise moment. My excitement took on a physical impatience. As she lowered the box into the boot, I raised the pad.

"Why didn't you—?" She turned towards me, but I cut her off mid-sentence. Her eyes registered surprise. I pinned her against the car as I grabbed her around the waist. She struggled, panting hard and let out a strangled scream as she raged against me. I applied pressure to the side of her neck, fighting desperately to cover her mouth and nose with the pad. She groaned as tears rolled down her cheeks. Suddenly her body weight shifted. She jabbed one of her elbows sharply into my stomach, while her other hand clawed at mine. Her nails found their mark, digging into my wrists. The pain made me gasp. For a split second, I lessened my hold around her waist and pulled her head backwards, her ear level to my shoulder.

"Calm down. You're only hurting yourself."

Jackie crumbled against me, her head lolling. I bent to sweep her up into my arms, but she lashed out. The force of her kick threw me back. We crashed against the doors, the handle jammed into my spine. As I cried out, her compassion weakened her. She stood unsure of what to do next. I reached into my jacket pocket. Jackie realised her mistake and turned. She tried to push the door out of her way, but all it did was hit the wall. I wrapped my arms around her while clamping a fresh pad over her mouth to muffle her screams.

"Calm down." I kept the pad in place. "None of this would've happened if you had just put the box down." She kicked out wildly again, causing the car door to bang against the wall. I pressed my full weight against her, praying the chloroform would take soon. Her eyes began to close as her rapid breathing steadied. Once she was unconscious, I lifted her into the boot and closed it. I stood panting as I inspected the damage done to my hands.

On entering the shop again, I hunted for her handbag and coat before turning off the lights and locking the doors. Outside, all was quiet as I quickly opened the boot and drop in Jackie's belongings. There was no sign that the neighbours had been disturbed by the commotion. Happy that I hadn't forgotten anything, I slid the shop keys under the door, before easing the car onto Old Lane and steadily made my way onto the main road.

Once outside of London, I hit the accelerator. Normally I would have stopped at the city limits to check that my precious cargo was still sleeping, but I decided not to on this occasion. By the time I hit the A12, my back and bruised ribs ached while the scratches on my wrists stung. I yearned for a hot shower and a warm bed.

Back at Halghetree, my back throbbed painfully with every intake of breath as I hauled myself out of the car and went to switch the porch light on. The sound of my footfall on the gravel echoed in the still night. Thank goodness I didn't have any nosy neighbours to worry about.

I placed the boxes on the hall table and went to collect a fresh pad. I prayed things would go down better than they did at the shop.

Outside, before the boot of my car, my nerves buzzed with excitement. I hoped Jackie hadn't been too uncomfortable during the long journey home. I unlocked the boot and lifted the lid slowly. Jackie lay peacefully sleeping on her side, with an array of cushions protecting her from every bump on the road. I leant forward to touch her forehead. It felt cold, but her breathing was steady. I slipped my right hand under her body. She let out a groan. With a little effort, I lifted her clear from the boot and carried her indoors.

I nudged the front door shut with my heel and began to climb the stairs. Halfway up, I registered a change in the suppleness of Jackie's body. A sudden blur of white, followed by searing pain, crossed my cheeks and made my eyes water. I pulled back and found myself freefalling. A flare of brilliant light exploded in my head as an agonising pain travelled up my already inflamed spine.

Jackie sprang away from me.

I lay on my back, on the hall floor, stunned with my heart racing. From the corridor that led to the kitchen, I heard screaming. The throbbing pain in my head held me to the floor until I was able to roll onto my side. I heaved myself up into a sitting position. Nausea rippled through me and I fought it back. Anger boiled up and overtook the pain. How had I allowed her to get the better of me, again?

I used the banister to haul myself up. I couldn't decide what hurt the most, my face, the back of my head or my damned stupid pride. The floor swirled before me, and I bit down on my lip. With measured steps, I staggered towards the kitchen door, aware that blood trickled down my neck.

Ahead of me a door slammed. I heard Jackie's pitiful cries, "Please help me! Oh God! Somebody please help me!"

I knew she would find the phone in the kitchen after missing the one in the hall. I edged towards the door and listened. Jackie began to dial, though it was in vain.

"Oh, help me! Please," she screamed into the receiver. "Oh God, no!"

With my thoughts focused on my reward, I took a deep breath and calculated that she had her back to the door. I heard her hammering on the top of the phone in a fruitless effort to get the dialling tone. With all the strength, I could muster, I threw open the door and grabbed a fist full of her hair, pulling her backwards and down. I pressed the pad hard against her mouth and nose.

She struggled wildly and lashed out. Her fingers tore at anything she could get hold of— my jacket and hair, all became targets. She pushed against my shoulders as she writhed under me, her legs still kicking. Her hair surrounded her chalk-white face as I fought to keep the chloroform-filled pad in place.

"Please. You're making it harder on yourself."

Her eyes widened as she tried to claw at my face. I turned my head away, but she held onto my hair, adding to the pain in my head as her nails dug into my scalp. Finally her grip weakened as the chloroform took hold and her arms dropped to the floor. Her startled red-edged eyes blinked at me and then closed.

I loosened the pressure on the pad, and moved off her, resting my back against the kitchen cabinet. I took a few deep breaths. The fresh scratches on my hands and face stung. I waited until I was sure she was unconscious. I replaced the receiver on the phone, and then ran some cold water into a glass. After taking a few hurried gulps the chilled water helped to clear my head.

"Oh Jackie. Why, oh why?" I squatted beside her and placed my two fingertips on her neck. Her heart rate was steady, although her breathing was shallow. "Right, let's try again." I gathered her up in my arms and headed to the muse's bedroom to keep her safe until I was ready to start work. There was no other choice, but to strap her to the bed. It saddened me when I had allowed my other angels a certain amount of freedom between painting sessions. Whatever they needed for their personal hygiene I supplied, but with Jackie it would be different. Once Jackie was comfortable and secure in her bed, I returned to the car and parked it in the garage before retiring to my own room.

I examined the damage done to my face in the mirror. Though Jackie's nails were short, she'd still managed to gouge out rows of small nicks across both of my cheeks, in my hairline, on top of my head and around my neck. My arms and hands had suffered the same fate, too.

Under the shower the sensation of the steamy water calmed me as its force washed the blood from my hair. Then the soap seeped into the scratches and nicks making them sting like hell.

After an uncomfortable night with very little sleep due to my throbbing head, I was up and dressed early. In the kitchen, I prepared a tray of buttered toast, and fresh orange juice for my guest before heading up to my studio. I set the tray down just outside the sealed room and switched on a light before looking through the one-way mirror. I could see that Jackie was trying to pull herself up into a sitting position, but the straps restricted her.

I unlocked the door and pushed it open with my foot as I carried in the breakfast tray. I tried to ignore the pungent smell of body odours and urine.

"Good morning, Jackie."

"Fuck off you bastard." She didn't even turn to face me.

"What sort of language is that?" I set the tray down and pushed a trolley closer to the bed. She tried to reposition herself by pushing down on the mattress, its plastic cover crackling beneath her feet, revealing a wet stain on the sheet. "You're a guest in my home." I poured some juice into a plastic beaker. "I've brought your breakfast."

"Guest!" She exploded, her shoulders heaving with raw emotion while pulling at the straps. "That's not what I would've called myself."

Jackie's calmness surprised me, though her language was off-putting. I had expected sobbing, screaming, pleading even begging, but her air of spite left me cold. Her red-rimmed eyes narrowed. "Next, you'll be telling me this is your normal behaviour when you bring a girl home."

I smiled and held out the beaker. "Here. It's orange juice."

She studied my face. "You've got to be kidding, right? You seriously think I'm going to eat or drink anything you offer me?"

"It's here if you want it." I shrugged, placing the beaker back on the trolley.

She eyed it and then turned her back to me.

I knew that beneath Jackie's armour, she was holding her emotions in check. All those questions she wanted answered were bubbling up, enveloping her rage. As my respect for her grew, so too did my creativity. It fed hungrily on the thought of it.

"Look, I know you won't believe me, but I am sorry about having to tie you down."

She jerked her restraints. "Yeah, you're so fucking sorry you race up here to untie me the moment you woke up. More's the pity I didn't have my fucking knife."

"For a pretty one you have a mouth like a sewer. Not quite what I had expected when I first met you." Her rage distorted her face as her lips curled in disgust, robbing me of my angel. It angered me.

"Looks can be deceiving," she shot back. "I can't believe I fell for your '*I'm an artist in desperation for some new materials*.' What a fucking load of rubbish. All you wanted was a fuck!"

"Okay, that's enough!" I stepped towards her.

Jackie bit down on her lip and her whole body seemed to shake as she backed further up the bed. The plastic cover groaned in protest.

"As you said, looks can be deceiving. I needed a model and thought you were just what I was looking for, but now I'm not so sure."

"So sorry to disappoint you, Tommy, but if your mother had taught you some manners like just asking politely, it might have saved your pretty face."

I lifted my hand to my cheek. The pain and her betrayal made me lean forward and snarl in her face. "What's my mother got to do with anything?"

She flinched. "Nothing, nothing—I don't know your mother, I meant you could've just asked me."

"I've tried asking before. Didn't get me what I wanted, so now I just take."

"You mean—there've been others?" What little colour there had been in Jackie's face drained away.

"Of course. I'm a professional. I prefer to use models when I paint my still life."

She glanced at the white silk dress on the mannequin and took in the small windowless room with its bare walls. I wondered whether she was looking for signs of the other angels, but I had made sure that nothing remained of them. The room was impersonal. Apart from the bed, the only other permanent fixture was a deep, stainless steel sink, once used by the housemaids to wash out soiled bedding and clothes before transferring them to an old washing machine once housed in the room.

"Look, I've brought you something to eat too." I pointed to the now cold buttered toast. "If you want something else, just ask."

"Please just let me go." She yanked on the straps. "Nothing terrible has happened to me. I promise I won't tell."

I moved towards the door. "I'm sorry but I can't. To start with, it would be irresponsible of me to open the door and let you go. We're miles from anywhere and anything could happen to you. Anyway, I have a deadline to meet and I need you."

"Need me?"

"Yes. You're my muse."

"Muse? I don't understand. Why me? What makes me so special?"

I rested my hand lightly on the door handle. Jackie sat hunched with her legs curled under her and clothes dishevelled, and hair matted.

My heart raced at the thought of my brush, weighty within my hand, the white of the canvas, blinding me as it begged me to add colour and texture. "Dearest Jackie, you're very special to me. As soon as I looked into your eyes, I knew you were the one. I could see your soul and it spoke to me. Telling me everything I needed to know about you. To capture your beauty forever with my brush, so that everyone can bathe within it."

I closed the door behind me.

Chapter Eighteen

Stone Angels
The Sixth Painting
1968

When I arrived at the gallery, Jenny was just unlocking the front door into the showroom. I followed her in. She asked me if I had heard the news.

"About the assassination of King?" I hoped that's what Jenny meant, rather than what I had seen posted on a nearby newsagent's billboard.

"Yes. Isn't it terrible? I was just having my breakfast when they announced it."

"We must've heard it about the same time. The news flash came over my car radio just as I pulled onto the A12."

"It's so sad. He was a kind and gentle man."

On our way to the stairs at the back of the showroom, we passed rows of paintings that depicted the rolling English countryside, Welsh castles and Scottish lochs. Jenny adjusted the strap of her shoulder bag after taking out a bunch of keys.

"The good die young."

"So true." Jenny hunted through the keys. "One of these days I'll label these. Right, this should be—"

The showroom back door suddenly opened cutting Jenny off mid-sentence.

"Oh—Good morning, James." Basil stepped into view. He wore his trademark pressed grey suit, but his usual clean-cut appearance was a little less sharp. As though he hadn't been home last night, or maybe, he hadn't had time to shave. "Glad you're here nice and early."

"Well you did ask me to come in as soon as possible,

Basil."

Basil addressed Jenny. "I need to have a quiet word with you before you start work. Please show James into my office and take him a drink."

"Yes, Mr Hallward." Jenny disappeared upstairs.

I stayed with Basil to give Jenny time to put the kettle on. I pitied her because Basil didn't seem to be in a good mood.

"Before you go up, could you give me a hand, James?" He set his briefcase down next to a desk in the corner of the showroom. "I have a few boxes in my car that need to be brought in."

I followed Basil down the path that led to the car park at the bottom of the overgrown garden and he called back over his shoulder. "The bloody posters aren't what I wanted! Goodness knows what went wrong. It's a simple enough job!"

While Basil spoke to Jenny, I waited in his office, sipping the tea Jenny had made me. I gloated over the changes in Basil's appearance, noting that he seemed more stressed these days. Over the last couple of years, he had lost the once youthful looks that seemed to attract the women. Deep lines etched his mouth and eyes and his once chiselled jawline was puffier now. Basil still had a full head of wavy dark brown hair and it showed no signs of going grey. Nowadays he now wore it cut short.

I knew the death of Martin Luther King wasn't the root cause of Basil's agitation, but neither were the problems with the posters. Out the window, which overlooked the rear of the building, I could just make out the newsagents through the gaps in the branches of the tree. I wondered whether the billboard outside the shop might now be reporting the assassination of King instead of the disappearance of another young woman.

"I really don't understand what the problem was, Jenny. A simple enough job to do!" Basil's voice boomed through the half-open door.

I had never before heard him lose his temper with Jenny. I moved closer to the door and listened. So softly spoken was

Jenny, I was unable to hear her replies clearly.

"Well, that's just not good enough." Basil thumped her desk. "If you're having any problems with sourcing the posters, I needed to know straightaway. I'm so disappointed with them. They're cheap and nasty!"

Jenny mumbled something about the company promising her they were of high— but Basil cut her off.

"Time is running out, Jenny and we needed at least..."

The telephone rang, cutting Basil off mid-flow.

The next voice I heard was Jenny.

"Hello, Hallward Gallery. Jenny Flood speaking, how can I help you?" Her voice conveyed no hint of what had just happened. "Yes, he's in today. Please hold on a moment, and I'll find out if he's free to speak to you."

"Who is it?" Basil demanded.

Jenny lowered her voice so I was unable to hear her answer. I glanced across Basil's desk. His telephone tempted me, but I fought back the urge to pick it up and listen in. I opened Basil's office door a little further and saw that Jenny's door was ajar. I waited, hoping to learn the identity of the caller. Jenny's door opened and Basil came out, his back towards me.

"It's a newspaper reporter, Mr Hallward."

"What? Why are they calling me?"

"Mr Hallward, don't you remember you asked me to get in contact with the editor? You wanted an article on Joseph Easter to help publicise his launch party."

"Oh yes, of course. Sorry, I've a lot on my mind. Right, I'll take that in my office. Thank you."

I grabbed the newspaper off Basil's desk and slumped into the chair. The headline that greeted me was the one I had seen on the newsagent's billboard.

Another Young Girl Missing!

No new leads' police report. Jackie Nolan's parents ask how many more families must suffer!

Basil entered and nodded in the direction of the phone. "I'll be with you in a moment, James."

"Okay," I mouthed, giving the newspaper a shake before turning a page.

Basil swung his chair around and faced the window. The view over the neglected garden was far more peaceful than the busy road. He rested his feet on the window ledge and leaned back.

"Hello, Basil Hallward speaking. I'm sorry to keep you waiting. Yes, I'm happy to answer your questions over the phone. I was expecting a reporter to come to my gallery with a photographer." Basil tapped his foot against the window glass.

"Yes, of course. I understand. Surely you would want to take some pictures of Easter with his work to illustrate your article." Basil's tone was sharp, I thought as I turned the page.

"Yes. He's a fairly new artist." Basil's foot tapped a little faster. "He's doing very well in America. Yes, he's a local boy so it would be, as you say, of local interest mainly. Look, I'm giving you the opportunity to interview the next big name on the British art scene. No, of course not, I wouldn't dream of telling you how to do your job. Yes, he's doing extremely well in America…"

Basil lowered his feet and sat forward. The muscles in his back twitched. If he didn't calm down, he would say something he would regret. "Yes, I know that, but…" His voice wavered, but he held fast. "Okay, yes, if you could. Of course, yes, but my secretary did explain all of this to your chief editor." He inhaled deeply and let his breath out slowly as he listened. "That's right. The exhibition launch is in three weeks, which is why we contacted you a month ago. Yes, I will pay for a two-page spread. Let me pass you back to my secretary." Basil swung his chair around. On seeing me watching him, he rolled his eyes and tapped his fingers impatiently on the desk.

"Yes, of course, she knows more about the numbers we're expecting to come. That I cannot say exactly but there will be an interesting cross-section of art lovers. My secretary has all the details. I'm looking forward to reading the piece. Yes, and thank you for your time, too. Have a good day." He jabbed a finger at the telephone keypad. After making sure Jenny had taken the call back, he slammed the receiver down.

"What a fucking moron!" Basil yanked his desk drawer open and pulling out two glasses, followed by a bottle of Johnnie Walker. After sloshing out a couple of drinks, he passed one over to me and then took a deep swallow of his. He stood and leant against the window, glass in hand. His anger was like a physical beast in the room. The muscles under the tight cut of his jacket tensed briefly.

I sipped my drink and waited. Basil hunched his shoulders. "I need more. There must be more." He placed his empty glass on his desk, and refilled it, before offering to top mine up.

"No thanks, I have enough." I covered my glass with my hand.

He nodded and dropped back into his seat. The air in the room shifted, and I knew somehow whatever came next, I wasn't going to like it. After recapping the bottle, Basil placed his glass directly in front of him and leant towards me.

It reminded me of waiting for mother. The air always buzzed with excitement and promise. You knew whatever happened next was going to be unforgettable. I lifted my glass and took a sip, watching Basil over the rim. I sensed his doubt. His look screamed his indecisiveness and radiated off him like heat from a bonfire.

"James…"

I just knew by the tone of his voice what he was about to ask.

"I know I've asked before but could you…" he rushed on. "I mean, would you allow me to… at least to show some of your mother's unknown works at Easter's launch?"

I folded the newspaper carefully and tossed it onto his desk. Was he crazy enough to believe I would allow him to use mother's paintings to bring the punters to Easter's launch! Did he have no faith in his golden boy? I swallowed my drink before standing.

"No, Basil you can't. I thought I'd made that clear to you the last time. You, more than most, should understand how much she suffered for her art. Let me reiterate. Nobody, not even me, will use her fame to advance their career."

"You're right. I am sorry, James." Basil leant back in his seat, glass in hand. "I shouldn't have asked you again." He nudged the newspaper with his fingertips, turning the headlines towards him. "I guess I'm a bit strung out at the moment." A pained expression crossed his face.

I placed both my hands on his desk and leant towards him. "I know it's none of my business, but I hope you don't mind me saying, Basil."

The tension in his face deepened and creased his forehead. He gave a slight nod.

"You were way out of order with Jenny. She's a good hard-working kid. You're bloody lucky to have her."

"Don't I know it?" He reached for the paper, with a flick of his wrist, he turned it over. I wondered if he was trying to create the illusion that he hadn't really read it, but I knew differently.

"If Jenny packs up and leaves, you'll only have yourself to blame." As I moved away from Basil's desk, he looked up.

"The blame is all mine and not Jenny's. That's what comes of cutting corners I should've listened to her in the first place." He tossed the paper aside.

"It's good to hear you appreciate her."

"I do. I allowed non-important things to cloud my judgement. And this isn't helping either." Basil picked up the newspaper and waved it at me before condemning it to the wastepaper basket.

"What's in the paper that's stressing you out?"

"Oh, never mind. Let's get back to business. How's the Cohen painting coming along? I hope it's finished because the client has been asking after it."

"It's getting there. It'll be ready this week."

"Ready as in dry enough to frame, James?"

"A done deal."

"Glad to hear something's going right. I won't keep you any longer, James. As you pass Jenny, please tell her I need to speak to her privately before we get any more interruptions."

Later in the week I received a phone call from Jenny asking about the Cohen painting.

"James, Basil wants it pronto."

"Is everything okay, Jenny?" I detected sadness in her voice.

"Oh, Basil isn't happy about Easter's article. It was published today."

"What's wrong with it?"

"After all the fuss he made, James, I think he got off lightly."

"What do you mean? The article was just a bit of marketing to spread the word, so what went wrong."

"Oh, you know what he's like, just can't go with the flow. Why do you think he leaves me to deal with such things? All he needed to do was agree to the first draft they sent him. No, he wanted more spice. His words, not mine, '*Call yourself reporters, well report and make it more interesting!*' So they did. Though, having said that, I too would like to know where they got their information. Do you want me to send you a copy, James? It makes for fascinating reading."

"No, it's all right. I'll pick up a copy when I bring the painting in."

Father never allowed daily newspapers into the house, so I stuck with this tradition of not having them. Father's biblical quote on such idle chatter, *no good comes from scandalmongers*, never stopped Mrs P from collecting the reviews of mother's exhibitions from all sorts of different magazines and newspapers.

"That'll be great, James." Jenny's temperament lightened. "Mr Cohen will be pleased. It's for his wife's birthday. I'll see you later then."

The drive into London helped to clear the cobwebs, giving me a chance to mull things over as I sped along with the windows down and the radio blaring. My most pressing problem was where I could find my next angel, but a nagging question from years ago had raised its head again. While in the process of overtaking a slow-moving car on a tight bend in the road, the question leapt into my thoughts, like an unsolved crossword puzzle you had given up on finding the last answer, but somehow your mind hadn't. Who had taken the photo of Candela and Basil on the night of the Hockley exhibition, and then a year later sent it into the newspaper office?

At the time, I would've placed my bet on Easter but I knew he never owned a camera, let alone had one with him on that evening. Of course one automatically assumed it was one of the press photographers at the exhibition, but it made no sense at all that they would've missed a golden opportunity to further their career when the police issued an appeal for any information. Surely any of the photographers there on that evening in 1963 were only interested in the celebrities rather than the rest of us. I hoped my early departure and lack of status meant I missed being photographed, but I also missed out on the drinks and drugs.

As I raced towards London, it occurred to me. Had the police searched the press photographers' photographs for Tommy Blackbird at that time? Maybe I was lucky and achieved what I had set out to do that night. Tommy was missing, but the police seemed to have overlooked him too.

Had Easter appeared in any of the photographs with Candela? And why hadn't the police made more of a fuss about Basil's involvement? Surely there was enough to link him to all the cases so far.

I parked up in the gallery car park and darted across the road to the newsagents. I was too early for Basil, so headed to St. Clair's bistro for a drink and a bite to eat before delivering the finished painting. In the bistro, towards the back I found a quiet spot and wiped the table down with a paper napkin before spreading the newspaper. I began to read the two-page spread about Easter as I waited for my order.

At the beginning of the article was what appeared to be a recent photograph of Joseph Easter standing solemnly beside one of his paintings. The caption beneath the photo stated he had just returned from a successful tour in America, but what caught my attention was a smaller picture further down the page.

Easter and Candela had their arms wrapped around each other. In the gap between their heads, in the background of the photo, clearly visible was Tommy Blackbird with his gappy grin. Where in hell had that photograph come from?

I read on. The article described Easter's heartbreak at the loss of his girlfriend five years ago after an argument at Hockley art exhibition. He told the reporter that the police had listed Candela Waterbrooks as being the first of five women who had mysteriously disappeared from the local area:

'Five years ago a young woman disappeared off the face of the earth with no explanation, and no one seems to care,' said the broken-hearted artist. 'Candela was my first love, my only real love. A day doesn't go by when I don't think about her and wonder what has become of her.'

When asked whether she might have just walked out on him wanting nothing more to do with him after their argument at the art exhibition, Easter wiped his eyes before answering.

'To this day I've remained in contact with her devastated parents. It's one thing to say she walked out on me, but her parents... never. They were always very close. She had sent them a letter two days before she went missing, saying she was coming home.'

Our reporter asked Easter about a photograph sent to our office anonymously a few years ago. It showed Candela Waterbrooks talking to Easter's agent, Basil Hallward, on the evening of the David Hockney Art Exhibition in 1963.

Stunned Easter said he was unable to comment any further on this revelation.

Our reporter then pushed him further, asking what his views were on the fact that the newspaper's sources revealed that the police had questioned his agent on several occasions to do with the disappearances of Candela and the other missing girls.

The artist stated that he was unaware that police had questioned Mr Hallward about his girlfriend, Ms Waterbrooks. Joseph Easter then would only answer questions about his up and coming exhibition at The Picton-Warlow Gallery'.

"Here you go, love." The waitress startled me as she set my order down. I thanked her and carried on reading, hoping she would take the hint, but she lingered. "It's shocking, isn't it?" She pointed at the paper. "I read that this morning. Such a sweet thing, too." She pulled a cloth from her pocket and wiped the table next to mine. "Her poor family. Fancy losing a loved one like that, and not know what 'appened to them."

The waitress's face was pleasant enough but was spoiled by her excessive use of make-up. Lumpy mascara clogged her lashes, while heavy black kohl lined her eyes. Added to this, her pencilled brows, heavily powdered face and blusher gave her a clown-like appearance. Though, the harsh lighting in the bistro could not rob her thick hair of its rich shades of natural brown. She had plaited it, then looped it up and pinned it at the back of her head under a nylon pink cap.

"Most of those girls who have disappeared come from around 'ere." She straightened up the condiments and then replenished the napkin holder.

"Sorry?" I noticed her nicotine-stained forefingers and thin pinched lips.

"Of course, the police never asked me about the other two that went missing." Once satisfied that the table was ready for the next customer, she faced me.

"Didn't they? I read somewhere that the police had issued an appeal for any information. I bet you hear all sorts of things that would've been of interest to them."

"You're right there, love." She peeked over her shoulder

towards the counter and leant towards me, giving me a whiff of her stale breath and cheap perfume.

"I knew Annie Linton as well as Candela. My friend, Dido, was a close friend of Jackie who went missing last year. Of course, we all knew Bella who disappeared four years ago. She was last seen leaving the bookshop, where she worked. For all I know, I could be next." The waitress wiped her eyes on a napkin.

"You'll be quite safe, I'm sure. Just take care when heading home late at night."

"What makes you say that? Is that when he takes them?"

"Why are you so sure it's a man?" I glanced down at the paper in hope she would take a hint.

"Of course it's a man." She waved the napkin at my paper. "It said in there that the police were questioning the owner of the art gallery, just down the road from here, Mr Hallward, but they freed him to do it again." She shrugged her shoulders and gave the table she had already cleaned another wipe. "Of course, they might not have enough evidence, I suppose." She wiped the table opposite mine, before adding more napkins to its holder. "Can't imagine why a woman would kidnap women. Then again, it takes all sorts, doesn't it? Perhaps you should ask them to look into the fact that it might be a woman."

"Why would they be interested in what I have to say?"

"You did say they were asking for information. Anyway, it'll sound better coming from you, than an uneducated woman. If they haven't caught the killer after all these years…"

"How can you be so sure they're dead?" I said, cutting her off.

"She wouldn't have let her parents worry so. Nor would've Annie or Jackie. Anyway, it's been nice chatting with you, mister."

I nodded and picked up my tea, swallowing it down in one gulp before wrapping my sandwich in a napkin and stuffing it into my pocket. By the time she was back at the counter, I was out the door. As it swung shut, the overhead bell rang.

Back at my car I tossed the newspaper onto the driver's seat before getting the carefully wrapped painting out of the boot. On entering the gallery showroom via the back door, I heard Basil's blaring voice. Only this time he was not shouting at his secretary. Jenny ushered me into her office and closed the door, something she rarely did. She took the painting from me and placed it into a large steel cabinet. On the carefully stacked shelves, I caught sight of Easter's work ready for his launch.

"What's upset him this time?"

"Can't you guess?" Jenny sighed. "It isn't him who's upset, James, its Easter."

"Ah, yes, I've just read the paper."

Jenny nodded. "So you'll understand why Easter wanted to see Basil. He didn't even wait for me to show him in, just pushed past. Not that it will resolve anything, just add closure I suppose."

"Does he blame Basil?"

"Not sure. There's just a lot of shouting. Mostly from Basil."

"If it all goes quiet, shall we call the police before we go in?"

Jenny laughed so sweetly it lightened the tension in the small room. "Let's hope it doesn't come to that. Anyway, I've work to do, so they can just get on with it. Basil wants me to make a few calls to find a model for Easter's launch night."

"A model. What sort of model?" I sat on the edge of her desk.

"The fashion model type rather than an art class type. It's to add a touch of glamour to the evening, according to Basil."

"That should be interesting."

"Not for me when I've got to deliver. Any suggestions? By the way, you'll be coming to the launch, won't you, James?"

I hesitated. Then realising Jenny, in her innocence, had just solved my problem.

"Please say you'll come, James," she pleaded. "Having a friend there wouldn't go amiss. It's been a tough assignment for me. I've been calling in favours left, right and centre, even begging my family and friends to come along just to make up the numbers."

"Gosh, it's that bad, is it? What, no celebrities?"

"Like who?" Jenny shook her head. "If I knew any I would've asked nicely, but I don't. That's up to Basil to ask them if he knows any. He's asked an American friend of his, but he's keeping that close to his chest."

"Really. So you've no idea who?"

"None," Jenny said, turning her head slightly as she raised her hand to her ear and cupped it.

"Does Basil have any idea how hard it's been for you to…?"

Jenny put her finger to her lips and cut me off. I turned to the door and listened. The shouting had ceased, but Basil and Easter were still engaged in using strong language and harsh tones.

"For a moment there, I thought they had killed each other," Jenny continued typing. "Anyway, at least they're talking. Hopefully, Easter will still want to go ahead with the exhibition."

"Why wouldn't he? You've put a lot of work into it."

"Just doing the job I'm paid to do."

"I'm sure Basil appreciates you."

Jenny's face brightened. "He's okay. Under normal circumstances he leaves me to get on with most things, but on this occasion, I could've done with some input from him."

"So what's his plan for the model when he finds her?"

"To stand in front of Easter's paintings with a glass in her hand, looking as though she's about to purchase it. He wants Easter's work to appeal to the New Age Hippies rather than his older clientele who seem to be drying up or dying off."

"So Basil realises he has to appeal to the younger generation."

"Yes, but he won't allow Easter to expand his style either. Like you he's fed up with painting the same old pictures."

"Why doesn't Easter tell him? He's in a far better position than I am, having a following in America."

"He might just be doing that now by the sounds of it."

Through Jenny's closed door, we heard raised voices again.

"Do you think I should break it up?" Jenny said, rising to her feet and coming around to my side of her desk. "I could put a call through, or knock at his door, with some lame excuse."

"What and spoil their fun?" I chuckled, enjoying our light-hearted banter. "Are you doing anything after work, Jenny?"

"Why?" Jenny moved back to her side of the desk.

"Please don't read anything into it, but I'd like to take you out for a meal."

"James, I…" Jenny frowned in puzzlement.

"Please hear me out first, Jen. I really enjoy your company, but this is work-related."

"Oh—well that's fine, I think…" She hesitated and for a moment I was sure I saw hurt in her eyes. "Please explain so there isn't any misunderstanding between us, James."

"Right, there's a girl who I think would make a suitable model for you, if that would help you out?"

"Great, but I get the feeling there's a catch."

"Isn't there always?" I said, shrugging my shoulders. I laughed. "You'll have to dine with me."

"Oh, is that all?" She tried to look disappointed but failed.

"I think it would be easier if you were to give her the once over as you know what Basil is looking for. And then, if she's suitable, you could speak to her on his behalf."

"Oh, so why not tell Basil and take him for a meal?"

I shook my head, trying to keep the humour out of my reply. "That's easier said than done, Jen. Especially when Basil is a red-blooded male, who practically eats his meat while it still has a pulse and the goddess in question works in a new alternative, healthy eating restaurant. An ideal place I think to exhibit some of Easter's paintings for the diners to enjoy. I can't imagine Basil enjoying dining out at a vegetarian restaurant."

She chuckled. "Never."

"So, will you join me?"

"Why not? It'll make for a very interesting evening. Both

in food and— company."

"Will you need to go home first?"

"No, I always keep a change of clothes here. 6.30 okay? Have you booked a table?"

"It's done."

"Really! You knew I would say yes!"

"Well, let's say I was hoping I wasn't going to be dining alone this evening."

The force of Basil's office door slamming against the wall reverberated around Jenny's office. It had us both out of our seats. Jenny opened her door just in time for us to hear Easter's parting shot.

"Find Tommy Blackbird, Mr Fucking Hallward, and then you'll find out what happened to Candela!"

Jenny glanced over her shoulder and mouthed something to me.

"Are you all right?"

She shook her head. "That name, Tommy Blackbird, now where have I heard it before?"

Below us, another door banged.

Chapter Nineteen

1968

"Tommy Blackbird." Jenny rolled each syllable around her mouth. "Where have I heard that name before?" She said more to herself than to me and leaned back in her chair, closing her eyes. The lines around them softened as her face took on a relaxed expression. Neither of us wanted to check on Basil, deciding to give him time to calm down.

I pulled a pen from my pocket while reaching for a sheet of paper off Jenny's desk. My thoughts transported me back to my studio. I stood before my easel, brush in hand. On a large, fresh canvas, the contours of Jenny's face appeared in confident lines. I roughly sketched the tilt of her head and the fragility of her neck, using the same backlighting that her office window had created. I added lustre to her hair, savoured the pearlescence of her creamy-brown skin and the moistness of her slightly parted lips.

Jenny's eyes snapped open and the image of her on the canvas faded. Pleased with my effort, I slipped the sketch into my pocket.

"Oh sorry, James. What must you think of me? I'm sure I'll remember later. Right, I think I'll go and see if Basil wants a word with you before you go."

"You are all right, aren't you?"

"Oh yes. I just hate it when I can't remember something. Perhaps, it's just an unusual name?"

"Hmm, maybe." I wanted her to forget, though I was curious to know how and when she had heard the name. "Do you think it's all over now Easter's walked out on Basil? The exhibition, that is—"

Before Jenny had the chance to answer, her office door swung open. Basil stormed in. "What the hell did that reporter think he was bloody well playing at, writing all that sodding crap? And where the hell did he get the photo from?" Deflated, he dropped into the chair next to the door, leaving me with nowhere to sit. The office now felt crowded, and I wanted to escape.

Basil sat wringing his hands. His washed-out expression gave me every reason to feel smug. It would only be a matter of time before his worst fears became a reality. Now that the local newspaper had told the world about his connection to the first missing girl, the big dailies would soon be hot on his tail with even more dirt they had raked up.

"So, Mr Hallward," Jenny said in her firm business voice. "I take it all plans are still the same?" Her hand rested on a stack of stamped addressed envelopes, she had just finished sealing.

"Of course. Why shouldn't they be? It's just a small misunderstanding. I'm sure you have plenty to get on with, Jenny."

"Yes, Mr Hallward." Jenny gathered up the envelopes and picked up her handbag. "I'm just popping out to the post office with these."

"Good. Don't be too long," Basil said before turning to me. "I take it you've brought in the Cohen painting, James?"

"Yes, Jenny has it."

"Good, good," Basil said as he led me through to his office.

Just as Basil gestured for me to take a seat, Jenny's phone began ringing. I wondered whether it was the police calling to ask him in for further questioning, or maybe a reporter from one of the largest newspaper offices. The phone rang unanswered.

Jenny's phone ceased ringing as I slumped into the leather easy chair. Basil wasn't in a hurry to talk as he slouched forward, his elbows resting on his imposing desk. He was an anxious man.

I leant back and made myself comfortable, the soft leather cushioned me. Why it had taken so long for the news of Jackie's disappearance to surface, I wondered. Surely old Bert would've known sooner that Jackie wasn't running the shop, unless he'd only just returned from his sister's.

"Basil old boy, what did you want to see me about?" I was impatient to get back to Suffolk and start preparing for my next quest. He remained lost in thought and rubbed at his tired eyes with his palms.

"B.a.s.i.l?" I drew his name out.

He blinked slowly at me. Was panic setting in now that the newspapers had named him? He knew as well as I did that others would point their fingers at him, saying he must be involved with the disappearance of other girls.

A sigh escaped Basil's dry lips. "I'm sorry. Oh God, I need to talk to someone. I feel I'm going insane, James."

"What's the matter?"

"I don't understand what's going on. Five girls have disappeared, and somehow I've been linked to them? Maybe our fine constabulary isn't as smart as we like to believe. Or maybe I'm just the unluckiest man on earth."

"You're unlucky."

His head snapped up. Under his eyes were dark rings. He wasn't sleeping well. "What the fuck are you implying, James?"

"Hey." I stood, angered by his tone. "Now listen to me. Just repeating what you just said. You're the one who needs to be careful, especially when you're talking to others who don't know you as well as I do."

He shook his head and ran his fingers through his hair as he regained his composure.

"I want you to come to Easter's exhibition, as my guest, James—and—" He paused, before adding, "and my friend, too."

I took my time answering. I wondered whether it was worth the risk. Would five years be enough to make a difference that Easter wouldn't recognise me? No, not me. Tommy Blackbird? It wasn't as though we spent a great deal of time together as both of us focused on our own careers. Tommy Blackbird had cropped his hair in the beatnik style with the ubiquitous goatee, and most of the time, he wore dark shades, too.

Easter spent most of his time locked in his studio, high on weed and other stuff, apart from the odd evenings. Then he would join the rest of the artists that lived at the squat as we all sat cross-legged at a low circular table, on scatter cushions, as we shared a meal in the dingy basement. Candela kept us updated on any art competitions or galleries on the lookout for new artists.

Of course there were things that time couldn't change about us, but I wondered whether Easter recognised the person after years of drugs and drink. Maybe it was just the name Tommy Blackbird that people recalled and not the person. After all, Jenny remembered it. Now, that was a puzzle. How?

"I really want you there." Basil cut into my thoughts.

"I'll come. Though I'm not sure if I'll stay all night."

"That's okay, I understand. I'm expecting someone so I shall have to leave early, as they need a lift from the airport to the exhibition. I'm waiting on a call from them at the moment to make the final arrangements. I'm glad you're coming. I must admit, I'm a little surprised you've agreed as I was sure you'd say no." Basil reached for the phone.

"Right." I felt he was dismissing me. As I reached the door, he said, "Oh, and thanks, James."

"For what?" I paused, my hand resting on the handle. "For saying I'll come to Easter's exhibition?"

"No…not just that, but for reminding me to think before opening my mouth."

The outer door buzzed, telling us that Jenny was back. Basil gestured for me to close his door as he spoke to someone on the phone.

As I passed Jenny's door, I stuck my head in. "I'll meet you down the road at the Railway Tavern, Jenny."

She looked up, a little surprised. "Oh, I thought we were going to—"

"We are. I'm just meeting you in the tavern's car park. Basil has just told me he's working late tonight, waiting on a call. I didn't think you'd want him to know we're meeting up."

"No, you're right. Yes, okay, I'll see you in…" she glanced at her watch. "In an hour's time, though I may be a little late. You know what he's like." She nodded in the direction of Basil's office.

By the time Jenny met me at the railway tavern she was a little flustered. "I'm so sorry, James. I thought he'd never let me go." She peered into a small mirror to check her already perfect make-up.

"Hey, no worries. You're only a little late. I planned to sit here all night waiting for you, if necessary." I laughed as we set off.

After a short journey I swung the car into a small car park at the back of a row of shops and restaurants. From the car park, a badly lit, flag-stoned alley took us onto a narrow street.

"I hope the restaurant isn't far, James. My tummy's rumbling."

"Not far now. About halfway up the street."

We could smell an amazing array of cooking aromas as we got closer. I realised that I had not eaten anything since breakfast as the uneaten sandwich was still in my pocket.

"Hmm, something smells good," Jenny said.

I retrieved the napkin-wrapped sandwich and disposed of it in a waste bin before opening the restaurant door. As I stepped back, allowing Jenny to pass, she said, "Leftover from lunch?"

"No, it was my lunch."

"I'm glad we're both hungry. Wow! This does look lovely. Hope the food is just as good as the décor, James."

The restaurant was larger than it looked from the outside. An intimate space though dimly lit.

"It's a popular place," Jenny said as we stood to wait for someone to show us to our table. "I love the wallpaper. Hessian, isn't it?"

“Yes,” I said, disinterested in the wall covering. My main concern was the lack of empty tables.

“It goes so well with the brown quarry tiled floor. I’m always on the lookout for ideas for when I get a place of my own.”

“All very rustic.” I commented while searching for something far more interesting than the décor.

“I wonder if the fireplace is original too.” Jenny took in the whole room now.

“It looks to be, especially with the red brick surround.”

“Oh…my…”

“Jen are you okay?” I sensed her unease, guessing she’d realised that it was mainly couples occupying the tables.

“A pleasant ambience, don’t you think? I wasn’t quite sure what to expect to be honest.”

Confusion flashed across Jenny’s face. “But I thought you’d already been here.”

I realised my mistake. Not sure what to say next as I couldn’t tell her I had been stalking the girl. “Oh, a friend told me about the place. After I had explained that I was on the lookout for a certain type of face for my next series of paintings. They told me to check out a girl who works here.”

“Really, what paintings would they be?” Her tone unnerved me.

“Something I’ve been working on that, unfortunately, Basil isn’t interested in.”

“Right, so you thought you’d bring me along to ask her to model for you, rather than you doing it?”

“Well you’re looking for a model too, aren’t you?”

“Two birds with one stone,” Jenny said with a chuckle.

“You could say that.” I grinned.

“You’ve done the right thing by asking me what with these disappearances, it would look better me asking, James.”

“Good Lord, Jenny. I never thought about that, but you’re right.” I nodded in the direction of a couple nearby. “The food looks good. Let’s hope we’re not kept waiting too long. I’m hungry.”

“Oh gosh, James. Me and my big mouth! That’s ruined the

ambience talking about a serial killer. It'll be the last time you'll invite me out."

Jenny's unexpected concern sent a rush of warmth through me. I found myself fighting the urge to sweep her into my arms and hold her tight. Aware Jenny was watching me, I smiled as unfamiliar words began to form in my head. I reached out about to take Jenny's hand, and opened my mouth not quite sure of what I was about to say when…

"Good evening. Do you have a booking?"

I turned. A striking young woman with sad holly-coloured eyes, peered at us from under a blunt blond fringe. All thoughts of Jenny dissolved. The weight of my brush heavy in my hand and sweeping strokes created lines on a fresh canvas as I transformed the beauty before me into my next angel.

"Err yes, the name's Ravencroft. A table for two."

"Mr Ravencroft, please come this way." With a swish of her long, orange and brown skirt the angel turned with elegant ease towards a small desk. As she leant forward to pick up a pencil, her low-cut peasant blouse revealed the milkiness of her skin around her neck. She ran her orange polished fingertips down the list of names. Halfway down, she crossed out my name with a single swipe of her pencil and picked up two menus. "My name's Flossie. I'm your waitress for the night. Please follow me."

As Jenny passed me, she winked and then addressed our waitress. "You're very busy in here tonight."

"Yes, it's good. So many lovely customers are returning along with a growing number of new ones. I guess the word is spreading."

"It's our first time," Jenny said. "A friend of James' recommended we try here."

"Then you're in for a treat. Will this table suit you?" she asked, stopping beside the fireplace.

Jenny gave a nod. "Thank you."

Once seated, Flossie handed us the menus. "I'll be back in a little while to take your orders."

As my angel moved away, Jenny touched my arm. "Gosh,

I do hope she's the one your friend was talking about, James?"

"I think she is, going by the description. Do you think she's what Basil is looking for?"

"Basil will love her. She's such an English Rose and those amazing green eyes. I'm so glad your friend suggested we come here, James. Let's hope she likes the idea."

We both focused on the menu, but I struggled to keep my mind on the food.

"I like the sound of toasted Israeli couscous with vegetables and fennel and celery slaw," Jenny said, breaking into my thoughts. "Though I'm not too sure about the fennel, but I'll give it a go. What about you, James?"

"Well the only thing I recognise is the vegetarian shepherd's pie. So that's my choice. Shall we have a bottle of white with it?"

"Please. Oh, here she comes."

Flossie took Jenny's order first and then turned to me. I continued to study the menu, giving Jenny a chance to ask our question.

"Flossie, may I ask you something?"

"Of course." Flossie's pencil hovered over her notepad.

"I work for an art gallery and we're looking for a model." Jenny offered a business card to the waitress.

"A model? What like Jean Shrimpton and Twiggy?" Flossie took the business card. '

Jenny lowered her voice. "Not fashion modelling. We're looking for a model to help launch a new artist."

Flossie handed the card back. "I'm sorry but I don't take my clothes off for anyone. Call it what you want—art, fashion, glamour— but nudity isn't something I'm interested in doing. Thank you for asking. Are you ready to order now, sir?"

Jenny looked at me, panic in her eyes. I gave a slight nod.

"Flossie, you misunderstood me. I work at a fine art gallery and Mr Ravencroft is one of our artists. He doesn't paint nudes but land and seascape. Mr Easter is another fine landscape painter, too."

"Like John Constable, you mean. I know his work. He's one of my dad's favourites. So what do you want a model for?" She took back the card.

"Come to the art gallery next Tuesday, and have a chat with my boss, Mr Hallward. He'll explain everything. I'll be there. You can bring someone along with you too."

"Can't you give me some idea now?"

"It's quite simple really. One of our artists is having a solo exhibition and we're looking for someone to mix with the clientele and talk about the paintings on offer."

"That sounds interesting. I'm studying modern art at college. That's why I work in the evening to pay my way."

"Then we've found just the person, Flossie. Mr Hallward is hoping to attract a younger generation into buying fine art."

"What time do you want me to call at—" she checked the name on the card, "Hallward Gallery?"

"10.00 next Tuesday?"

"That's ideal. My class doesn't start until an hour later. So Mr Ravencroft what can I interest you in?"

"Vegetarian shepherd's pie. Thank you, Flossie." I closed the menu and handed it back to her. Already my mind was busy planning the next step.

***

"Thank you for a successful evening, James," Jenny said, as I pulled into a layby at the top of her street.

"Are you sure you'll be okay walking from here?"

"I'll be fine. It's only a short walk."

"It isn't out of my way to drop you outside your house."

"After all that lovely food, it'll do me good to walk." She pushed the door open and picked up her bag. "The food was amazing."

"It was surprisingly good. And thank you for being such good company, too. We'll have to see if we were successful for Basil," I said, as she started to close the car door.

Jenny paused. "I'm sure she's just what Basil is looking

for, James. I shall let you know if we are successful with our choice. Bye for now."

I watched Jenny hurry along the street as I pulled away from the kerb, pleased to be heading back to Suffolk and knowing I'd found my number six.

***

The evening of Easter's launch could not come quick enough for me. I was tired of sketching out ideas and just wanted to start work on the next angel painting. It had almost been a year since I completed the fifth one.

The air in my studio was stifling. The glare from the freshly primed canvas standing on the easel was painful. It cried out for the arrival of my next muse so I could begin working. I opened the French windows and stepped out, hoping to catch a light breeze off the river.

Since our meal together, Jenny hadn't been in contact. I was impatient to know whether Flossie had taken up Basil's offer. If she hadn't then I wasn't sure what I would do next. Oh, her perfect sad eyes.

Father had told me how tiresome mother found men's compliments on the colour of her eyes.

"Why do they think they are being so original with their obsession? Why can't they see past the colour and into my soul, like you, Donald?"

"Green is a powerful colour. But in eyes it's mysterious, exotic and magical." He had told her. "What she had wanted from men," father told me, "was for them to admire her work, but instead they were obsessive about her eyes."

With my angels, I saw beyond the green of their eyes to the sadness of their souls, wanting them to be revered for their everlasting beauty, as I had captured for all to see.

Unable to wait any longer, I went down to the coolest part of the house the kitchen, to phone Jenny. "Hi, Jenny. Can you talk?"

"Hello, James. Basil doesn't have any commissions for you yet. I'm sorry."

"It's all right. Not looking for work. I've plenty of my own to do. The reason I've called is to speak to you personally. I wanted to say thank you so much for such a lovely evening."

"James, that's sweet of you. It was good." Her tone softened. "I've been meaning to let you know we were successful in our choice."

"So the girl turned up then?"

"Yes, about a week ago. She's just what we needed. So well informed and best of all she's familiar with Easter's work and loves it."

"Why didn't she mention that when we spoke to her?"

"She was a little flustered and didn't put his name to the work until she saw it."

"That's wonderful. I'm so pleased for you, Jenny."

"Anyway James, Basil is over the moon. I wanted to tell him that he might have met her sooner, if he hadn't viewed vegetarianism as a silly phase and not real food."

"It's going to be an interesting evening, Jenny." Through the window the clouds lifted along with my spirit. In the garden, the stone angel seemed to shine in the bright light.

"Hopefully an amazing one, too. There has been plenty of local interest. Thank goodness, I didn't have to call in favours from friends and family. James may I ask a favour from you on the night of the launch?"

"But of course."

"Would you be able to pick me up?"

"Er yes…"

"That's great. About 7.30? I'll need to be in early to make sure everything is ready. Having you there will be great. I won't feel out of my depth. Gosh, Basil's next client has arrived earlier than expected. Speak to you soon."

Chapter Twenty

1968

Yesterday, I found another one of mother's oil sketches was missing. I had uncovered its disappearance by accident, or maybe mother was letting me know. While on the balcony outside her studio, I was taking in the view of the river and broken trees in hope of inspiration. Something caught my attention, a trick of the light, maybe. I spun around expecting to see mother. I scrutinised the reflection in the French window. The image filled my mind. A burning desire to capture it sent me to fetch one of mother's old sketchpads from the drawer at the base of her drying rack. On pulling the drawer open I noticed a gap in the collection of her paintings still in the rack.

I flicked through the pages of a small leather-bound notebook. Mother had recorded each of the rack's numbers and details about the paintings within them. The book listed the title of the painting, where and when it was exhibited and if she had sold it and to whom. I located the details of the missing painting. How was it possible that Basil had taken it without me knowing?

Basil had paid me an unexpected visit the day before yesterday. Busy at work in my rooftop studio, I was only alerted to the arrival of a vehicle by the sound of a car door shutting. Normally, I heard the sound of tyres crunching on the gravel. I had just finished priming a new canvas and had stepped out onto the roof for some fresh air. From my eyrie, I looked down onto the top of someone's head. They stood beside the boot of their car.

Annoyed at finding someone on my property, I was about to shout down when something about their stance looked familiar. I grabbed a pair of binoculars and tried to see what they were doing when I realised it was Basil. The lid of the boot obscured my view. He disappeared from view. I lost sight of him as the chimneystack blocked my way. I thought about climbing onto the slates but decided against it. The sound of the side gate opening and closing told me he had gone around the side of the house.

I was about ready to go and confront him when he reappeared. Once again, he briefly rummaged about in his boot before closing and locking it. I tore downstairs. By the time I reached the main staircase, the front doorbell was ringing. On opening the door, I found Basil standing with a fixed grin, but without any warmth in his eyes.

"Hi James. You're at home," he said in a detached way, as though he regretted ringing the bell. "I wondered if you were at home. I didn't see any sign of your car. Hope I'm not disturbing you… if you have company." He brushed his fringe back from his eyes and added a little warmth to his smile.

"Yes, I'm here. Only just heard you ring."

"You weren't in…"

"In what?"

"Nothing."

"Do you want to come in?" I stepped back from the door. "Is it good news that's brought you out this way?"

Basil was casually dressed, instead of his normal suit and tie. He lingered in the hall instead of dashing to the drinks cabinet as per normal.

"Come through and I'll fix us both a drink." I opened a new bottle of Johnny Walker Blue and poured him a large one as he looked as though he needed it. Dark rings around his eyes and slight stubble on his chin made me wonder if he was having problems sleeping at night.

"Was I supposed to have a painting ready for you to pick up today?" I asked.

"No. I was in the area." Basil, lingering in the doorway,

reached into his jacket pocket. "A cheque. I owe you."

"Thanks." I handed him his drink, took the cheque, dropping it onto the table with the previous ones he had brought on other occasions.

"Shouldn't you bank them?" He nodded his disapproval at the pile of dust-covered cheques.

"Hmm, I suppose I'll get around to it sometime soon." I sipped my drink and sat in my father's chair as I waited for the whiskey to hit the spot. "Sit down," I said.

Basil moved over to the sofa and rested uneasily on the edge.

"So, Basil, what took you so long? I heard a car quite a while before you rang the bell."

His head shot up. "I had to check the boot. Something moved after hitting a blasted pothole in the track to your house. Goodness knows why your parents chose a place so far out from civilisation."

"Isolation. Mother craved it."

"It's certainly well hidden."

"Did you find it?"

"I've been here before..." Puzzlement swamped Basil's face as he tapped the side of his glass.

"I meant what was rattling in your boot."

"In my boot? Oh yeah." He gave me a tight-lipped smile and downed his drink in one. "Thanks for this." He raised his glass toast-style before setting it down next to the cheques. "I'd better get back to town. I'll see myself out, James."

I followed him out. He protested, apologising for disturbing my work, but I ignored him. As he opened the driver's door I placed a hand on the boot. The colour drained from his face.

"Are you all right?"

"It's the heat." He stared up at the house and a furrow creased his brow. "It's a big place for one person."

"It's my home."

"I guess." He gave a sharp nod, climbed into his car, and wound the window down. "I want to beat the traffic back into

London." He turned the key, and the car roared into life. "Bye James." The car shot forward, sending up a spray of gravel.

On returning to my studio I was unable to focus on what I had been doing. It was curious that Basil hadn't mentioned Easter's forthcoming exhibition, especially as he was keen that I came along. Was it my lack of enthusiasm for Easter' work that had put him off discussing it with me, I wondered.

What intrigued me the most was who had Basil visited in this area?

As I flicked through the notebook, I deliberated on how he was getting in. It wasn't as though I was leaving doors open. The police had found the place secure enough. The missing painting according to mother's record was called, *'Still Dreaming'*, an oil sketch for a much larger piece of work, also done in oils. According to the notebook, the finished piece of art had been part of mother's final exhibition, a major piece, exhibited in London before I was born.

The sketch, *'Still Dreaming',* showed spiralling blocks of colour, mainly in gold, reds and blues that cascaded over and around a central figure of a full-length naked woman. She stood with her hands clasped under her swollen belly while covering her modesty. Long dark hair fell around her shoulders and over her breasts. She carried her pregnancy high to symbolise a boy-child. Small, framed cartouches surrounded her, depicting symbols of matrimonial harmony, a band of gold, a house, beautiful garden, happy children at play, and a baby in a cot.

The notebook now showed me I was wrong in my belief that mother had painted it when she was expecting me. The date of the painting's creation was long before my date of birth. One of the cartouches showed a couple getting married. As a child I had examined the original finished painting carefully and thought the groom looked nothing like my father. When I questioned Father about it, he had told me, that the painting only symbolised the references mother was making and wasn't about her real life. I always believed mother wasn't very good at painting portraits. I tossed the notebook back into the drawer and slammed it shut, not wanting to question the nagging doubts that had slipped unwelcomed into my thoughts.

Jenny had spoken about Basil planning a trip to America shortly after Easter's launch. I wondered if that was how he got the paintings out of the country.

"He must have a buyer already lined up as he can't sell them on the open market," I said to mother's ghost. "But who was buying them? Whoever it is, is keeping quiet about their newly acquired works of art. Well, Basil your supply is about to dry up."

After hearing nothing from Basil, I pushed all thoughts of his theft aside, needing to focus on bringing my next angel home.

***

On the evening of the launch I drove down a leafy avenue of well-kept houses and pulled up outside a large Georgian house. Jenny's parents had done well for themselves I thought as I sat waiting. After a little while, I sounded the car's horn.

Jenny hurried down the path in the fading light. Something sparkled in her hair and off her arms. The car's interior lit up as she opened the door and got in.

"Sorry to keep you waiting James, especially after you were kind enough to pick me up this evening." Jenny seemed a little flushed as she laid a silver jacket and bag over her legs that were cased in fine silver tights. "Doreen said you're more than welcome to join us at her party after the launch."

"That's very kind of her. Will she be at the launch?"

"No, she's a friend of my mother's."

"Well, tell her thanks for the offer, but I need to get home. Jen, you do have a lift lined up to take you to Doreen's?"

"Yes, I do." She leaned out to pull the door shut and stopped halfway. "Oh dear. I seem to be caught on something."

I turned. "It's just your chain belt caught on the seat

fabric." I reached over and freed her.

"Thank you." She pulled the door shut.

"You look stunning, Jen. Pale mauve and silver really suit you. It must have taken you ages to weave those pearls into your hair."

"That's why I was late."

"It was worth it, Jen."

I put the car into gear and we moved off.

Easter's launch was taking place at the impressive Picton-Warlow Gallery. The gallery covered the ground floor of a large red and yellow-bricked Victorian detached house, with a gothic leaded-roof tower and arched windows. It stood on a corner of a busy road but set well back.

I drove through the ornate iron gates and stopped in front of the portico to allow Jenny out.

"I'll see you inside, James." I watched her running up a flight of stone steps and entering through the front door with its large stained-glass windows.

***

A few days earlier I had made a flying visit and found out that there was a second entrance into the grounds from a quieter backstreet. The gallery was once a family home before two wars diminished the need for such large estates. The owner, Peter Picton-Warlow, lived on site. He had decided it was worth landscaping the gardens in order to accommodate his growing clientele. The front garden had parking bays for his wealthiest clients, while the rear garden had further parking, plus easy access for delivery vans when the exhibits were changed.

I followed the signs to the area set aside for parking at the back and passed what looked to be an enclosed seating area at the far end of the garden. It was an ideal spot for garden parties, where people could share cigarettes, drinks and a chat.

I drove to a parking lot a few streets on where I had left

my replacement car, taking a serious gamble that Jenny wouldn't need a lift home. Though similar in colour, I had obtained a different model, hoping that it would be inconspicuous among the other cars, if she went into the garden.

The car park was relatively empty, and I parked in the darkest corner away from the back of the house but nearest the raised seating area. Three more cars also arrived, but they parked closer to the gallery.

I reversed into position, hoping no one would block my exit. As I climbed out, I saw Basil in a new E-Type Jaguar coming through the front gates. He parked in one of the bays at the front of the house. I waited for him to walk around the corner, hoping he would not spot me standing in the shadows of the pergola.

From where I stood, a flagstone path led past the parked cars. Two stone steps, flagged on either side by two large earthenware pots, took the visitors up onto a small lawn. In the centre was a small flagstone circle and a metal round table with four chairs under the pergola.

A line of mature oak trees obscured the view from the buildings behind, while on either side of the seating area, overgrown rhododendron bushes gave anyone in the small-enclosed garden complete privacy.

Basil reappeared at the side of the building. He stopped and turned as though looking for someone. I walked slowly down the path towards him, hoping to gage how close I could get to him before he became aware of me, but before I made it halfway down the path. He opened a side door and disappeared into the gallery. Pleased to know that the darkness of the garden concealed both my car and me from the house, I was ready to follow my plan.

I allowed a few minutes to pass before I entered the gallery. Inside I found a brightly lit hallway and the stripped pine floorboards made the place light and airy. Voices drifted towards me, so I followed them.

Jenny stood talking to three men and two women, none of whom I recognised. The carefully arranged exhibits covered the cream coloured wall and a series of movable screens that showed off Easter's paintings in the best possible light. In one of the alcoves, I found Flossie deep in conversation with a well-dressed man. Flossie's choice of modest attire was well chosen, but I was sure Basil found it rather uninteresting. She moved with grace in a long green flowing skirt that clung to her curvy hips and shapely legs and a dark green tight-fitted crop top to show off her bare midriff. In a similar style to Jenny's, she had piled her long blonde hair high on her head and had interwoven into it semi-precious stones.

Jenny appeared at Flossie's side and said something to her. The man shook Flossie's hand, at the same time he leant forward, and kissed her cheek. She giggled, putting her hand to her face before wandering over to chat with some new arrivals. A familiar raucous laugh echoed over the top of the screens, which caused Jenny to turn. On seeing me, she called, "Oh James" and gestured me over.

"Quite a few here, Jenny," I said, and nodded towards the man.

"James, at last, I get to introduce you two properly. James Ravencroft, this is Joseph Easter. While you two chat, I need to socialise. I'll be back soon."

"She's an angel," Easter said as we watched Jenny join another group. "When Basil told me you would be coming I was pleased. I've wanted to meet you, James."

I took the hand he offered me.

The man before me was unrecognisable from when I saw him at his first exhibition three years ago. His unkempt full beard and rat-tailed hair were gone. So too were the paint-spattered boots. His hair, now neatly cut, was greying at the temples. His whole demeanour shouted wealth and success from his black leather shoes, a dark blue fitted jacket, and narrow trousers, to the black Slim Jim leather tie worn with a white button-down collar shirt.

"I've been a great admirer of your work for some time now." Easter's grip was firm. "I've often seen it in Basil's office, and I can't understand why he hasn't given you an exhibition of your own."

"Really."

I picked up a glass of wine from a nearby table and took a sip of it. It tasted sharp and seemed more suited for cleaning my brushes in.

Easter held up his glass. "Basil hasn't exactly splashed out on expensive wine for the launch."

"Have you seen his new car?" It was the best I could come up with in answer to his remark.

"Yes. Love the colour. Dark blue is so moody. He even let me take it for a spin. It's only fair as he probably bought it with the commission he's made from me." Easter took a sip of his wine and I noticed a large gold ring sparkled on his little finger. It seemed hideous against the delicate wine glass.

I forced another sip of the wine down. It caught in my throat making me cough.

"God, it's not that bad." Easter held his glass up to the light. "Was there a piece of cork in it, mate?"

"I don't think so." I coughed again. Basil wasn't making enough money from Easter's sales to purchase such a fancy new car, more than likely from the deals made on selling mother's stolen paintings.

Jenny reappeared, glass in hand. Relief washed over me. "Jenny, where's Basil?" Before she could answer me, the booming voice and raucous laughter of Charles Jefferies cut through our conversation.

"He's upstairs introducing Mr Jefferies to the gallery owner." Jenny took a sip of her wine, pulled a face and set the glass down. On seeing me watching her, she chuckled and said, "Basil's choice, not mine."

"So, Jen, when does this party really get going?" Easter asked.

Jenny glanced at her wrist and twisted a slim, delicate silver watch to look at its face. "In half an hour the serious buyers will start to arrive."

"What?" Easter looked around the room.

"They always arrive later than what's on the invitations,

Mr Easter. Most don't like to be the first to arrive, preferring to walk into a crowded room."

"Surely it's better to arrive before it gets too crowded," Easter said.

"You and I might. But most come to be seen mixing with the right people."

"You're telling me that this isn't about my paintings? They come to see who else is here?" A flash of annoyance clouded Easter's calm features.

"Yep, I'm afraid so. They want to see who's buying your work before they will, afraid to miss out on being in Vogue."

"Unbelievable!" Easter drained his glass.

Once again, unable to stop myself from coughing, I held up the glass. "I'm sorry about that," I said.

"Oh, it looks as though someone else has arrived early." Jenny waved to a couple of women who had just come through the door. "Hello Mrs Norris. So glad you could come…"

I set the glass down and became aware of Easter eyeing me. "I think I'm going to see if I can have a quick word with Basil."

"Okay, but I think he's still upstairs," Easter said. "Is he holding back a cheque?"

"No—I just want to update him on a commission I'm working on."

"Right." He drew the word out still scrutinising me.

A feeling of unease twisted in my stomach. "The evening is starting to look very promising indeed. Filling up nicely."

"You remind me of someone. We've met before, haven't we?"

"In passing." I continued to watch the guests. "Quite a heated conversation Basil and you had the other day."

"Oh that." Easter looked around the room. "Has Basil laid on any food?"

I shrugged and then saw a bowl of nuts. "Nuts."

"What!"

"There's nuts." I crossed the room, picked up a bowl and gave them to him.

"Thanks." He scooped up a handful and munched them. After downing some more wine, he added. "The whole thing with the papers has really pissed me off. I don't want sympathy. I want answers. Did you read it?"

My mouth went dry. I looked up. Basil stood at the top of a spiral staircase, gesticulating wildly. I pointed at my chest, but he shook his head and pointed again. I then pointed at Easter and Basil nodded. "Looks like you're wanted."

Easter waved back. "I'll catch up with you later," he said, and handed me his glass and the bowl of nuts. "Thanks mate."

I set the glass and bowl down and headed off to find Jenny. She stood welcoming the new arrivals and handed out glasses of wine. Nearby Flossie chatted to the guests about one of Easter's larger paintings. Flossie's voice floated across to me as I watched the face of the men listening to her. She was explaining Easter's retelling of the rural landscape in oils. Over the heads of the growing number of art connoisseurs milling about with glasses in hand, I could see that Easter's work was more substantial than his previous soft, mixed media work.

"I'm more than certain we've met before," said the rasping voice in my ear. Years of smoking and alcohol abuse had given his voice the quality of sandpaper.

I turned. "As I said, apart from that chance meeting on the stairs at Hallward gallery, we haven't met before. Plus I live in Suffolk."

"Hmm, there's something—" Easter nodded.

"I don't buy dailies either. Too busy working, though Jenny did mention something about an article upsetting Basil the other day."

"Upsetting Basil," he scoffed. "So that's where her loyalties lie."

"That's a pretty unfair statement to make."

"You're right. She's on his payroll too. It always comes down to money in the end, doesn't it?" He placed the empty wine glass on a nearby table and went to join Jenny and Flossie. Easter slipped his arms around both of the girls' waists and hugged them into him.

"Well, my lovely ladies, let's get this party started. Where's the photographer? Where's my agent! Bring more wine! It's party time!"

Easter's eyes never left my face. They were cold and calculating. I felt something shift violently, the atmosphere, the tension I wasn't sure which. All I knew was I did not want to be there celebrating his success. Easter first kissed Flossie's cheek and then Jenny's. Flossie rested against his arm, her head tilted back to reveal the long sweep of her neck. Her lovely lips opened as she laughed along with Jenny. I drank in Flossie's details. The shapes, colours, and textures of her face, shoulders, and arms. I pulled out a notebook as a picture began to take on a physical form. I flicked over a couple of pages until I found a fresh sheet. I left the room to seek out a quiet space and began to sketch.

Chapter Twenty-One

1968

Finally, after five hours of endless chatter, I slipped outside and made my way to the raised terrace, away from the main house. Under a pergola, covered in climbing plants, I sat, breathing in the cool night air. Now, with some seclusion, I was able to watch the comings and goings.

Some of the older guests had drifted away as the evening had worn on, but the arrival of new guests meant the place was still heaving. The gallery owner did not allow smoking inside, so a small group of smokers, including Easter, gathered at the back of the house, where the French windows opened on a well-lit patio area.

Easter chatted animatedly with two young women. A leggy redhead hung on to his arm, her loud voice carried across the patio and lawn.

"I simply adore your work, Joe," she said, while pressing herself hard up against him.

I poured myself a glass of expensive wine from a bottle I had brought from home while watching the performance unfold. The quality of wine made my evening more pleasurable as I tucked into a bowl of peanuts I had taken from the gallery.

Easter acknowledged the redhead. "Thank you for saying so." He pulled his arm free while swapping his cigarette to his other hand, creating a barrier between himself and her. He seemed to try to involve her friend in the conversation, but the redhead moved to his other side, unperturbed by his lack of interest.

"Is it all right if my friend takes a picture of us together?" she asked.

Easter dropped his cigarette, grinding it hard with his heel before reluctantly moving closer to her. She took the opportunity to latch on to him again, slipped her arm around his waist and leaned her head on his broad chest. Flossie came out onto the patio behind them as the camera flashed. Her hair sparkled in its light. On seeing her, Easter disengaged himself from the girl and went over to where Flossie stood alone. He rested his hand on her shoulder as he leant in to exchange a few words. Flossie nodded and pointed into the gallery. Easter kissed her lightly on the cheek before turning to the girls.

"It has been lovely meeting you both," he said to the redhead and her friend. "But I am needed inside now."

The redhead said something to Flossie after Easter left. Flossie backed away from her.

The redhead stepped towards Flossie, raised her arm, and yelled, "You just stay away from him!" She grabbed her friend's hand and pulled her into the gallery.

Left alone, Flossie paced up and down the patio. For a moment I wondered if she had found the evening too stressful. Just as Flossie seemed to find the courage to go back in, Basil came out and closed the patio doors behind him. They stood chatting for a while. She seemed at ease with him. Basil walked with her around the side of the house, heading to his car. I thought for a moment that they were leaving together. Then they said their goodbyes. A few minutes later, the dark blue jag pulled out of the front gates.

As Flossie headed towards the French windows, I nearly called out to her, fearing a missed opportunity. In the end I said nothing, not wanting someone to recall seeing her talking to me after Basil had left. A shout within the gallery made Flossie pause at the door. She backed away and turned in my direction. I stepped into the shadows of the shrubs that surrounded the pergola. Flossie hurried along the garden path and came up the stone steps. On reaching the table where I had been sitting, she looked briefly over her shoulder and then sat down, facing the house. I remained out of sight, wanting to make sure that no one had followed her. She glanced towards the French windows again, then stood and moved to the next chair, seeming to check that she was out of sight. That's when it dawned on me. She was playing my game, but from whom or what? Flossie held my bottle of wine close to the flickering candle jar at the centre of the table. Unable to read the label, she gave the bottle a shake and uncorked it. She poured herself a large glass and took a deep gulp.

"Do you mind if I join you?"

"Oh, dear God, James, you gave me a start," she said, holding the glass to her chest.

"Sorry, but I can't bear to see someone drink alone."

"Thanks." She took another gulp of her drink.

"Are you okay?"

"Yes, I'm fine. Just—"

"What's wrong?"

"Oh, it's so stupid. A silly girl was getting jealous because I was doing my job…talking to Joseph Easter. I suppose it comes with being glamorous." She giggled.

"What a silly girl?"

"The leggy redhead with her—" She shook her head. "Hmm, now I remember why I stopped drinking." She wiped at her mouth. "That red head threatened me, James. I couldn't believe it. I'm only here to do a job. Nothing else."

"So what did you do to upset her?"

Flossie creased her brow. "Upset her by doing my job, I suppose. Gosh, this wine is strong. It's gone straight to my head."

"You were explaining about the redhead."

She leaned forward and put the glass down. "I was doing so well, avoiding drink. That's why I'm staying out here. Well, at least, until she's—gone. I think Easter was fed up with her— too." Her voice trailed off as her head dropped onto her arms, knocking the glass over.

"Flossie, are you all right?"

"What?" She tried to lift her head, but her eyes were

unfocused.

"Are you okay?" I moved the glass and candle jar away.

"Sorry… what…?" Her breathing became shallow.

I blew out the candle, picked up the bottle and two glasses, and pushed my way through the gap in the rhododendron bush to my car parked on the other side. I dumped the bottle and glasses in the passenger's foot-well and lifted the boot.

A glimpse at my watch told me Basil had only been gone for half an hour. I checked Flossie's pulse and breathing. Both were steady. With surprising ease, I pulled her up out of the chair and rested her over my shoulder. I swept the branches aside and pushed my way through the shrub.

The bottom of her skirt caught on the low branches. I tugged, but to no avail. I stepped forward, hoping the skirt would free itself and nearly tripped over the trailing part of the skirt. A movement to the right made me stop. I straightened up. Someone was heading in my direction. I stood motionless, taking shallow breaths as I waited, praying that I had added enough of the sleeping draught to the wine. A match flared and illuminated a man's face. He drew on his cigarette and then shook the match out before flicking it in my direction. Only the burning tip of the cigarette told me where he was.

He took a couple of steps forward and, for a split second, I thought he could see me or the light shining off Flossie's bejewelled head. He began to move towards the parked cars and my open boot. Flossie felt heavy on my shoulder and I desperately needed to shift my balance.

"Dan, where are you? You're wanted!" A voice rang out.

"All right, I'll be there," The smoker shouted over his shoulder. After a quick drag on his cigarette, he tossed it aside and strolled off in the direction of the patio. Then I heard the French window closing behind him.

I wrenched hard on Flossie's skirt. It gave with a satisfying rip. With my free hand I gathered up the trailing material, lifted her into the boot and rolled her onto her side. She moaned as I leant in and tucked the cushions around her. I pressed my fingertips against the side of her neck to check her pulse before closing the boot. I emptied the bottle and placed it with the glasses in the glove box.

Once I was satisfied, I returned to the party and mingled with the remaining guests, taking care not to be too chatty, but showing an interest in Easter's pictures. On the wall above one of Easter's largest paintings was a beautiful teak sunburst clock. When the photographer started snapping shots of the guests in front of the painting, I placed myself centre stage, smiling broadly, glass in hand next to Easter.

Soon the guests started to disperse, some collecting their belongings while others topped up their glasses before saying their goodbyes.

"I know you," a self-assured voice said behind me.

I spun around and came face to face with a rather elegant, elderly woman dressed in a lime green trouser suit. She stuck out a liver-spotted hand.

"Really?" I said, with a curt nod as I took her hand.

"Yes. My friend, Mabel, and I have a couple of your pictures. James Ravencroft isn't it?" She had a surprisingly firm handshake, her large, flashy gold rings digging into my flesh.

"Yes, indeed I am."

"I thought so. Now James—I can call you James?"

"Please do," I said, glancing towards the stairs, hoping to catch sight of Jenny.

"Can you tell me why Basil hasn't exhibited your fine work?" she asked.

"I don't know, Madam…" I said while trying to disengage my hand.

"Well, he jolly well should, you know. I'm sure there are others like us who would enjoy seeing more of your splendid land and seascapes in the one room."

"Thank you for saying so… Mrs Err?"

"Judy Norris. Of course, I knew your father, Donald." Her red lipstick had bled into the fine lines around her mouth giving her a vampish look as she chattered on.

Thoughts racing through my mind drowned out what she was saying as questions flooded in. How did she know my father? Had she known my mother too? Oh God, had she mentioned who my mother was to anyone else here. In my confusion by a sudden rush of vulnerability that made me focus on her red lips.

"Such a nice man. Mabel and I were only speaking about him the other day. We loved his services. So full of passion. Some even moved us to tears."

"My father's what?" I'd never seen nor heard of Mrs Norris or her friend Mabel before. As far as I knew, they had never been to the house. We never had visitors, apart from the gardener, his lad, Kelly and Mrs P. The only other people who came were the gallery staff to collect mother's paintings.

"His services. Mabel and I loved them. Your father was a brilliant speaker." She spoke slowly as though talking to a confused child."

"Oh, so you were part of his congregation." I wondered just how much more she and her friend knew about my family and checked to see if anyone else was within earshot.

"Of course, it was dreadful for him losing your mother so early in their marriage. Mabel and I believed he never fully recovered from that loss." She reached out and patted my arm. Her touch sent a chill through me. I jerked my arm away, praying she would not speak ill of the dead.

"I guess you never did either. It must be a blessing having your mother's wonderful talent. Mabel and I always said it must bring you closer to her, sharing such a gift. It's a shame Basil doesn't make more of the fact."

"And what fact is that, Mrs Norris?"

"Your mother's wonderful talent."

"I'm not my mother," I said a little too sharply.

Mrs Norris blinked rapidly; her hand went to her throat. "Please forgive me. Me and my big mouth. I hope I haven't upset you talking about your parents"

"No." I smiled, not because I wanted to show her no harm was done, but more to relax myself. "It's been a long time since I've met anyone who knew my family. As you know, I was very young when I lost my mother. Do you come from Suffolk?"

"Yes, many moons ago. Mabel and I were at school with Pauline Page. Well she wasn't Page then as she wasn't married."

"You went to school with Mrs P?"

"Yes, I know. Seems like a lifetime ago." She tilted her head to one side and cupping her white bouffant hair at the back of her neck. Her hair didn't seem to move, solid from too much hairspray, I guessed.

"Anyway, James, it's about time Mr Hallward let you exhibit your wonderful pictures. Is he about?" She glanced around the room. Not seeing him, she took hold of my arm. "I could demand on your behalf."

"That's very kind of you, Mrs Norris, but—"

"Jenny, my dear, where's Basil?" Mrs Norris yelled.

Jenny appeared from behind one of the screens, carrying a tray of dirty glasses.

"Hmm, I'm not sure." She set the tray down. "Have you checked upstairs, Mrs Norris? Oh, try asking Flossie. She was chatting to him a little while ago." Jenny picked up the tray and carried on with what she had been doing.

"Who's Flossie?" Mrs Norris squeezed my arm.

"The tall, young lady who was talking about the paintings when you first arrived and was dressed in green like you, but with jewels in her hair."

"Oh yes, a stunning woman I thought. We had quite a chat. Sometimes these launches can be so dull, but she was such a delight, very enthusiastic about the artist's work. You felt as though you were going on a journey of discovery with her. Do you know most people at these functions are here for all the wrong reasons?"

I shook my head.

"Art to them is about money, an investment. That's what destroyed your mother. What I see is a thing of beauty. I say get it out, put it on your wall and enjoy it. Life's too short." She squeezed my arm again. "If it makes you a bit of cash at the end of your life, fine, but if it doesn't, you've still had the enjoyment of a stunning piece of art. May I ask you a question about your mother?"

I tensed, wanting to brush her hand off my arm, but instead I nodded.

"I know you were only young when she died, but what happened to all of her unsold paintings?"

"What makes you think there was any?"

"Pauline used to speak about your mother. How busy she was, always painting. A studio full of amazing pieces."

My stomach tightened. So much for not gossiping, Mrs P. "Really."

"Well, Mabel and I could not afford to buy her work back then, so I was wondering if any were available to buy— a kind of memento of your mother and Pauline."

I removed her hand from my arm and stepped back. "It's been a pleasure speaking to you, Mrs Norris."

She gave a slight nod. "Your mother's paintings…" She was about to repeat the question.

"Sorry. None of mother's work survives. My father destroyed them in his grief."

Her hand flew to her mouth as tears formed in her eyes. "No, he never did—! How awful! All those valuable works of art destroyed…"

"His grief overwhelmed him. As you say, he never fully recovered."

"Mrs Norris, are you all right?" Jenny said, coming to join us. "Your husband has just arrived. He's waiting for you in the front car park. James, have you seen Flossie? I can't find her anywhere, and her friends are looking for her."

"No, sorry I haven't." I set my empty glass down.

"Okay. Maybe Easter knows. I'll ask him when he comes down from talking with Mr Picton-Warlow."

I joined the last stragglers as they left.

Chapter Twenty-Two

Stone Angels
The Seventh Painting
1969

I decided to take a break and scramble a couple of eggs after my stomach had reminded me that I had not eaten in a while. I laid my brushes down and stepped back from my seventh painting, pleased with my initial layout.

In the kitchen I made a mental note to check whether the sixth painting was dry enough to varnish. It was well over five months since I had finished it. I switched on the radio while I scrambled the eggs and hummed along with the music. The radio presenter's voice interrupted the song while I was eating. "We have some amazing breaking news this morning. I can confirm the first man has stepped onto the moon. A huge leap forward for humanity."

I poured a mug of tea and went out into Mrs P's herb garden. The early morning sun was doing its best to warm the courtyard where I sat. I caught glimpses of the fading moon when the low cloud occasionally broke. I'm not sure what I was expecting to see but thought there would be something to mark the occasion of humanity's first step on the moon's surface.

"Everything inside is made of stone." Dylan's words played in my head as I tipped the dregs of my tea onto the rosemary bush and placed the cup on the wall before strolling across the lawn toward the statue of St Mary. My parents' grave looked lovely as an array of small blue and white flowers tumbled over the rockery around the base of the statue. I walked on, following the path to the oldest part of the garden.

Here fragments of stone from the old church edged the lawns, flowerbeds and pathways. Nothing else grew out of the bare ground beneath the shady rhododendrons apart from a few remaining tombstones in what was once the old graveyard. One of these was the table top grave where Flossie and my other fallen angels now rested.

Back in my studio, I pulled the sixth angel painting from the drying rack and rested it on an easel. I gently tapped the rough surface where the paint was the thickest with my fingertips, checking to see if the paint was fully dry. My fingertips came away clean.

The backdrop for this particular painting showed a hazy sky, while in the far distance a band of white split the horizon. Fog drifted over the grey slate roofs of the houses and wound itself around towering spires, lead-covered steeples and chimney stacks with their swirling charcoal smoke. My angel stood in the foreground with her head lowered and her arms across her chest. Her gown hung in soft folds across her waist and emphasised her broad hips, as well as revealing a pair of shapely legs. Pleased with how I had depicted Flossie, I placed the painting back in the rack with the other five, satisfied it was dry enough to vanish.

My work in progress stood on a large studio easel. The seventh in my series. It captured the self-assurance that my goal was within reach. Every brushstroke echoed the sadness I saw around me.

On the canvas, among the towering chimney stacks, an angel stood in profile with her chin slightly raised, her eyes closed, and her lips parted. Tall and elegant, she was dressed in a grey shroud that covered the top of her head. It fell in soft folds over her shoulders and down the front of her body to pool at her feet. Her arms were outstretched, her hands resting one on top of the other as the shroud billowed out behind her, showing off the curves of her breasts, hips, thighs, and legs. On the backs of her hands, an owl rested, its feathers ruffled, and its wings lifted as though ready to take flight. The moon cast its silvery light over my abstract roofscape, causing the shadow of the angel and owl to take on the form of a raven in flight. I had hoped by adding another dimension to my painting, it would give the art connoisseurs something to theorise over while they discussed its true meaning.

Four months ago, by accident, I found my seventh angel. In truth, Basil had brought us together. After a phone call from Jenny, I had to deliver an urgent commission to his office to meet a client's deadline. On arriving at Hallward's Gallery, Jenny handed me an envelope. The note explained that Basil wanted me to meet him at the local library.

After parking the car near a bombed-out house, I walked the short distance via one of the many alleyways. On entering the dark wooden panelled library, I wondered if crossing the threshold into the underworld would've been much brighter. By the dimly lit front desk, I scanned the two rows of sloping desks with their high stools and individual reading lamps for Basil. There wasn't any sign of him among the people hunched over the free daily newspapers.

On the other side of the library, beyond the rows of bookcases, I saw a sign that read *'Archive'* and headed in that direction. Low wooden cabinets lined either side of a study area. At its centre was a row of microfiche readers. Basil sat facing a screen, while at his side a slim honey-blonde leant over the desk, her straight grey skirt strained across her slender hips as she pointed at something on the screen.

"Hello Basil." I came up behind them. The blonde straightened, and tugged the front of her tight-fitted jacket down.

"Great, James. You found us okay. I've something to show you." Excitement edged Basil's voice.

"Please, keep your voice down, sir," the woman said. "You're in a library. People are studying."

"Sorry…" Basil lowered his voice. "You must call me Basil, Jane. I'm sure we're going to see more of each other."

"Yes, sir." She gave a curt nod. "Do you need any more help, err… Basil?"

"No, I'll be fine for now. Before you go, let me introduce my friend, James Ravencroft. You know— the artist."

There was no flicker of recognition that she knew my name, or even cared.

"If you need me, or any further microfiches, I will be over at my desk, though I'm finishing early today as I need to catch a train. The other librarian can help you if need be."

"Going anywhere special?" Basil asked, though his interest remained fixed on the screen before him.

"I'm spending a few days with my mother. I haven't been home for a while, and it's her birthday. The family have ar…" Jane paused.

From between the bookcases, a large dowdy woman hobbled towards us. She leant against a cabinet and caught her breath. "Err… Miss," she puffed. "Could I have some assistance, please?" she asked, brusquely.

"Of course, madam."

"I'll see you later. Thank you for your help," Basil said as Jane and the woman walked away.

Something in the way Jane moved caught my attention. Her shoulders and head were erect, and her hair shone even in the harsh artificial light.

"It suddenly came to me last night," Basil said, tearing my thoughts away from Jane.

"Sorry, who came to you?"

He looked up. "Not who but what! I should've checked the papers to find out what the police wouldn't tell me. Do sit down, James."

I sat in the chair Jane had vacated, feeling her warmth.

"The press might be a pain in the butt," Basil said. "But you can always rely on the fact they love a good story, especially if it's a mystery. Every pressman's wet dream is a tale of kidnapped girls."

I twisted in my seat as the girl made her way back to her desk beside the main library door. Her stance was becoming so familiar to me along with the tilt of her head.

"For goodness' sake, James. Take your eyes off that girl and focus on what I'm saying."

"Right. Yes, of course. Great idea."

"Glad, you think so." Basil was looking at the screen again. "I've wasted too much time waiting for the police to sort this problem out. So instead of feeling so bloody helpless, I'm doing something constructive."

"Helpless?"

"For Christ's sake, James!" Basil oblivious to the reaction he had caused as all heads turned in our direction. He pointed to the screen. "I should've done this sooner, James."

"Done what?" I was impatient to get out of there.

"Is everything okay here?" Jane materialised beside us.

"Yes, everything's fine, thank you, Jane." Basil patted her hand as it rested on the desk next to him. She snatched her hand away.

"Please, could you keep your voices down?" she said, moving back to help the dowdy woman, who was now waving impatiently.

"Are you talking about those missing girls?" I asked, once Jane was out of earshot.

Basil lowered his voice. "Yes, James. It occurred to me if I could put together some sort of timeline that mapped their disappearances then maybe I could… I could…Oh, this is going to sound crazy." He ran his fingers through his hair. "I need to know, why me? Why it's happening to me."

"Now you want to play at being the detective?"

"I might as well as P.C. Plod and Co have no idea of the sort of hell I'm going through. I can't sit around waiting for my world to implode because of their inadequacies. I thought I might as well help myself."

"Good thinking." I was still watching Jane. She stood chatting to a colleague, but every now and then, she checked her watch. I knew she would be leaving soon. "What have you discovered so far?" I asked.

"Have I got your full attention, James?"

"Always." I shifted the chair around and leant my elbow on the desk to give myself a clearer view, not just the screen, but the entrance of the library.

Basil picked up his notebook and thumbed through some

pages. “I’ve started looking at all the daily papers from the beginning of 1963, making notes on any girls who had gone missing.” He turned a couple of pages. “The first girl reported missing was Candela Waterbrook aged 20 in 1964, but she had disappeared in 1963. The newspapers first reported her missing a year after the event.”

“And?”

“I couldn’t understand why the newspaper had waited a whole year before reporting her disappearance. If Candela had disappeared in 1964, a year after the art exhibition and when I first met you, I couldn’t have been the last person to see her alive, but unfortunately 1964 was when the press released the story.”

“What about the photograph of you talking to her?”

“Don’t remind me. If only there was a sighting of her in ’64 it would’ve cleared me.”

“So did you find out why the newspapers waited?”

“Apparently her parents contacted the newspapers on the anniversary of her disappearance. They were disappointed with the police making no progress.” He turned the handle on the reader and the screen revealed the next page of the microfiche. “That’s when I found what I was hoping for.”

“What was that?” I asked Basil while focusing on Jane. I checked my watch.

“There’s a sort of pattern— forming.” Basil moved to the next page.

“Really.”

“I cannot think why the police did not do the same. Though, I don’t suppose they would’ve revealed that to me.”

“Not if they have you down as a suspect.”

“Which they have…” His voice trailed off as he concentrated on the pages of the newspaper. “Anyway, I thought you might like to help me search.”

I bit my tongue, but knew I had to say something. “Basil, what about the two commissions you were chasing. I only came in today to deliver the one I had finished.” I leant back to see if Jane was still in the building. “I was hoping to get back to finish another one today.”

"Why didn't you explain that to Jenny instead of wasting your time coming here?"

"It's important not to let your client down, which was why I drove all the way from Suffolk this morning. Anyway, I wasn't expecting to find you in the library, playing detective. Couldn't you get Jenny to find the information you're wanting?"

"I'm not involving Jenny in this. Someone has a vendetta against me."

"Wow, Basil that's scary talk. What makes you think that?"

He focused on the screen. "I've upset someone. Any ideas, James?" He stared straight into my eyes and for a moment I thought he had read my mind.

I shook my head. "I don't know you well enough to know all your business dealings. Whose cookie jar have you been stealing from?"

"Stealing?" He snapped.

"Calm down, you'll have Jane over again. Remember people are studying." I patted his shoulder and noted he'd lost weight. Basil continued to run his fingertip down the page, scanning the headlines.

"It turns my stomach to think they're willing to kill, just to pin something on me."

"How do you know they are dead?"

He slumped back in his seat. "What in God's name are you implying, James? Of course, I don't fucking know if they are dead or alive?"

"Shh. I was just saying the girls are reported as missing."

"Yes."

"So you can't say one way or the other."

"No, James I can't." He snapped, causing heads to turn again. Basil ignored the shushing and said, "are you going to help me or not?"

I tucked the chair back under the desk and leant on its back. It gave me a clear view of the entrance. I hoped it was the only way out of the library for Jane. "I'm sorry if I don't seem very helpful, Basil, but I'm sure you would prefer me to put the clients first."

"Yes, you're right." He lowered his voice.

"I'll help as soon as the paintings are finished, I promise. Let me know how you get on with your research." I stepped back just in time to see Jane open the door, wave goodbye to her colleague and leave.

"I'd better get going if I'm going to beat the traffic, Basil."

With an aggressive flick of his wrist he dismissed me. I hurried after Jane, keeping her just in view. I prayed that to save time she would turn right into the narrow alleyway the one I had used coming to the library.

Just as she did so I reached in my jacket pocket and felt for the familiar box that held my syringe.

Chapter Twenty-Three

1969

I was walking through to the hall, after having a bite to eat in the kitchen, when the phone rang. For a moment, I considered not answering it.

"Thank God, James. I thought you weren't going to pick up."

"Basil, is that you?" He sounded distraught.

"For Christ's sake, James, you know it's me. Stop arsing around. I'm not in the mood for it—"

"Righty-ho, what's the problem?"

"Another bloody girl is missing! Some sodding woman gets herself lost and the police are questioning me! It's beyond a joke. I'll make them pay, whoever they are. I've got a lawyer now," he shouted down the phone.

"Calm down or you'll give yourself a heart attack. What's happened this time?" I leaned against the wall.

"I'm glad I can talk to you, James. They're trying to link two more missing girls to me."

"Two?"

"Yes."

"But—"

"But nothing, James," Basil interrupted. "Remember when we met in the library—"

"Hmm…" I wondered how the police had realised so quickly that Jane was missing. "But Basil, how have they traced her disappearance back to you? Didn't she say something about travelling to see her mother?"

"James, I didn't say anything about who the girl was, so

how do you know it was Jane?"

My legs gave way and I dropped onto the hall chair. "You said the library. She was the only person who spoke to you while I was there."

"That's right. Though, it was you who couldn't take your eyes off her. Unfortunately, on Jane's last day at work, good old muggins here had his name booked in for the reader. And, get this, James, Flossie Nightingale, the girl we hired for Easter's launch is also missing."

"What? Flossie is missing?"

"Yes, can you believe it? Of course the police sodding well believe I am their man. Most of yesterday they questioned me, wanted to know why I had ordered the newspapers on microfiche for the years linked to the missing girls. They jumped around, making waves, with me on their radar. Makes you bloody laugh, doesn't it," he barked.

"I suppose." It made no sense to me how the police were able to make a link to Basil. There were other people in the library. Though in all fairness he was already on their radar, so when his name popped up bingo. Full house.

"She left just before you."

"Did she?"

"I saw you leave after her. I got up to get another microfiche."

"It was quite a while ago." I ran my hand through my hair. That was bad luck. "The girl must have spoken to others on the way to catch her train. At least at the station, when she bought a ticket."

"That's a good point." Basil's voice lightened. "I'm glad for the chat. It's like we've been going through this together for years."

Have we? I kept quiet as he rattled on.

"Not being believed is horrible. Imagine my frustration at being their only suspect. It's bloody hopeless. They don't listen to me." Basil's words tumbled. "God, they might've found the real kidnapper by now. I tried explaining my reason for being in the library. Well, you can imagine the response I got. I told them I was searching for anything that they might have overlooked. *'What Mr Hallward? Don't you think we're doing a good enough job,' said old P.C. Plod. Well, that's a new one on us, a suspect actually helping us with our enquiries.'* Then they bloody well laughed." Basil enunciated each word of that final sentence, filling every syllable with heartfelt loathing. He pressed on, grinding the words between his teeth.

"For a moment I thought they might piss themselves. Bloody humiliating, James. Ever since the publication of that article, I've felt that others are judging me, finding me guilty. Now even Jenny gives me that look. You know, the one that says, '*you must be guilty otherwise the police wouldn't be questioning you*'. It's driving me bloody crazy and I feel like I'm living on the edge of..."

"Despair?" I offered.

"Don't joke, James. It's not at all funny. I thought you would be more understanding."

"Sorry, of course it must be very difficult for you, Basil. Surely if they had enough evidence, they would've arrested you long ago." I was just as annoyed as Basil with the lack of progress, believing he would have been behind bars by now or at least ruined.

"You're not making me feel any better, James. They've no evidence because I haven't done anything to any of these girls! By now they should've started looking in a different direction. Every time the newspaper reports a missing dog or cat, I want to phone my local police station and say '*It ain't me you're looking for*'. Fucking years I've had to put up with this. Every time the phone rings, my stomach flips. Now I've started to lose clients."

"You're overreacting, Basil." I let an edge of impatience creep into my voice.

"I wouldn't laugh too much, James, because soon I won't have the money to promote your paintings, let alone think about exhibiting your work." He paused. Then there was the sound of a bottle hitting a glass. After a moment he continued. "Anyway, enough of that, James. How's my next commission coming on?"

“Fine. Was your client happy with the last one?”

“Yes, of course they were. Your work sells well. The client wants another commission from you. I was hoping to chat with you last night before Cleo’s exhibition opened. Why didn’t you come?”

“But I did. Though I must admit, I was late getting there. Your latest prodigy is a little darling. Her work is brilliant.”

“She is, isn’t she? Not much to look at and quite lacking in personality, but her art is amazing. So much depth and raw emotion. I’m sure with my guidance I can find a market for it.”

“You’ve given Cleo free-range, or is she painting to order like me?” The words were out before I could stop myself.

“Please, James, don’t start! I know you’re pissed off by me allowing Easter to exhibit his work alone last year. I’m sure you’ve heard what a great success it’s been.”

I hadn’t, but I wasn’t about to tell Basil.

He went on. “At least something positive came out of the evening. Easter has settled well in America, so his agent tells me. Made quite a name for himself there.”

“Hasn’t he been in contact with you?” I began to pace the hall as far as the telephone cable would let me. I didn’t give a shit whether Easter was making a success of it or not.

“Too busy I suppose. Chuck Sparks is his agent. It’s a shame you missed him at Easter’s launch. I did try to find you, but Chuck couldn’t wait any longer as he had another event that evening before Easter, Chuck and I flew out.”

Whether he was expecting me to comment or not I wasn’t sure. I knew when he was trying to butter me up. Having sweet little Cleo step into Easter’s shoes didn’t piss me off. I was used to Basil’s betrayal. The one thing I had noticed recently was a sudden change in Basil’s demeanour. Apart from the stress of the cops breathing down his neck, he had an air of resilience about him. When Jenny introduced me to Cleo at the exhibition, I saw a hidden intelligence behind her owl-framed glasses. She was not the gullible type to fall for Basil’s charms. I saw someone who was far more observant than she let on and who, like me, learnt to express themselves through their work.

I have learnt to recognise the sort of girl Basil favoured. They were the brainless beauties that clung to his arm and knew when to giggle and smile reassuringly up at him. There had been a noticeable lack of giggling beauties following him around for quite a while, but I thought nothing more of it until a couple of weeks ago. I had phoned his office to find out what was the best time to catch him when Jenny told me the astonishing news.

"What time are you expecting Basil in today?" I asked while I stood in my kitchen fixing myself breakfast.

"Good question, James. Anytime would be nice," Jenny said with a laugh, though it might have been a hint of sarcasm.

"Sorry— is Basil having a lie in then?"

"Your guess is as good as mine. Don't think he's resting, though. I really don't blame him for taking time out. He's a bit strung up about something. From what I can make out, he has a lot of crap going on in his life."

"What do you mean, Jenny?"

"Something other than business, James."

"Are you saying he's— got someone special in his life rather than those giggling beauties?" This was not what I wanted to hear.

"Oh, James. Why the surprise?" Jenny's voice was almost drowned out by a truck that clattered past the gallery. "He's a great catch. I cannot believe he's been a bachelor for so long and have often wondered why."

"I guess he's never found one to win his heart." I hoped Jenny would say more about the woman.

"I think Basil has finally realised that there is nothing quite like having a woman to go home to after a busy day," Jenny said, as the familiar sounds of her winding a sheet of paper into her typewriter echoed down the phone.

"How can you be so sure he has?" I didn't need this now. Three more angels would complete my set of ten.

"When a man's in love, it's easy to spot. I think it's wonderful. He's not like you, James."

"Not like me…?"

"Creative. Arty types need solitude and isolation to be at their best."

"I see what you mean. Any clues as to who she might be?" I turned from the window and filled the kettle one-handed as the receiver echoed with the sound of Jenny clicking a few keys.

"Not yet, but before long. I'll be running around collecting gifts, booking tables, picking up his dry cleaning and the rest of the things we secretaries have to do for our bosses. I'll give you a ring when I've set up a meeting for you with Basil. Sorry, must go, James. A call's coming in on the other line. Bye."

***

Of course, Jenny never got back to me. Why should she? Now I stood in my hall with Basil waffling on with the same poor excuses about not allowing me a solo exhibition, I wondered if his new love was Cleo.

"So where did you find Cleo, Basil?" I rested one foot on the hall chair as I formulated a way of finding out more about his mystery woman.

"Easter told me about her before leaving for America. She was exhibiting at a local open-air exhibition. I went along, not expecting much but was blown away by the originality of her work."

"Really? Well last night's punters didn't see what you saw. Weren't you disappointed by the lack of red stickers, old boy?" I added a hint of sarcasm that Basil didn't pick up on.

"Oh, God! I haven't been into the office yet."

"You're not there? So where are you?"

"None of your business."

"Okay. Sorry I asked." I could not hear any background noise that would give his location away. Just hollowness.

"So what are your views of her work, then?" His dispirited tone told me all.

"Don't get me wrong, Basil. It's good, but I don't think the buying public gets it. Pictures of unmade beds won't appeal to housewives when they see them every day. Just imagine you're a housewife. Would you want a painting of an unmade bed hanging on your wall reminding you every day to get on with the housework?"

"But it's the aftermath of lovemaking, Cleo explained."

"Really?"

"For goodness' sake, James, I know you live in the outback of nowhere, but you must be aware of the Free Love movement. Ever since women got the Pill, it's been about their rights to express themselves and their sexuality. Cleo said it shows that they are more than a domestic sex slave."

"I see. To me her work lacked any real focus."

"What! You mean in their execution?"

"I'm not questioning her ability as an artist. I'm just saying the paintings have no soul. They're just a concept. You understand its meaning because the artist has explained it to you. The viewer sees only an unmade bed so may not '*get it'*."

"But the title explained it all. '*Aftermath of Free Love*.'"

"That's the thing about titles…" I recalled the ambiguity of mother's own. "That's Cleo's viewpoint. Wild sex and no forethought, I suppose. At the exhibition last night, all her paintings had the same message. Let me explain. Yes, they were beautiful in a romantic way, with their ornate balconies and sweeping muslin curtains that surrounded an open French window and with their wonderful views across a series of romantic landscapes, but the paintings lacked any signs that a man has entered or even left the scene. All the viewer sees is just piles of discarded women's clothes on the floor."

"Cleo explained that the clothes symbolised how women are discarding their old ways. Like a caterpillar shedding its skin. That's why she put a butterfly in every painting."

"Hmm, but this isn't what the punters saw last night. All it depicts is an untidy woman living the high life with servants to clean up after her. Most women's lives are full of screaming kids, and domestic chores in between quick romps in their beds. I bet the husbands bugger off to the pub for the evening while their wives catch up with household chores."

"Fuck it! I see your point. I've signed her into a contract for more of the bloody stuff."

"Hey, don't be so hard on yourself, or her. If you want to appeal to the masses, you have to see it from their point of view."

"But you've made a valid point. I didn't think along those lines. Right, I have to go now. I'll catch you again soon."

No sooner had I put the phone down on Basil a car swung round on the drive. "Who the bloody hell is that?" I crossed to the door, and hesitated, before it, my hand resting on the lock. I didn't need to answer it. It wasn't my agent, so I turned and hurried up the stairs, ready to start adding the finishing touches to the seventh painting. Whoever it was, I hoped they wouldn't lean on the bell for too long.

Halfway up the second flight of stairs I caught a glimpse of the car, through the landing window. Two familiar men sat talking. My heart sunk these visitors wouldn't leave if I didn't answer the door. Hastily I descended. Through the frosted glass, one of the silhouettes raised a hand to the doorbell, and I knew I was right not to ignore them.

Chapter Twenty-Four

Stone Angels
The Eighth Painting
1970

On stepping away from the easel, I stretched, glad to be finished. I laid my brushes and palette down and dropped my cleaning rag on top of them. Every brushstroke sang in harmony, making my angel shine in all her dark glory. I had placed her at the centre of a cubist background of blue, browns and soft greys. Seven abstract statues stared vacantly at the viewer. Each face had a mask-like appearance with their features etched in profile and their eyes placed together on the same side. Like Macbeth's witches, they all looked in the same direction.

My angel was in the centre of the painting. It was the only figure in perspective to represent the single-mindedness of my mother. A garland of ivy held a shroud that covered her head and flowed down the full length of her body. Through the veil, the angel's eyes were downcast. Her arms hung weakly at her side and her cold lips were slightly parted as though a final sigh rested on them. At her feet, a black dog sat on its haunches.

As I placed the painting in the drying rack along with the others, I wondered if it was possible to create a living statue. I began to clean my brushes and realised just how tired and hungry I was after working through the night. I caught a whiff of stale body odour and ran a hand through my matted hair.

On entering the dimly lit bedroom I caught my foot on

something, fell forward and only just managed to catch my balance. With caution I made it to the window and drew back the curtains. I found I was standing in a pigsty. Dirty bed linen along with discarded clothes were strewn across the floor. After months of focusing all my energy on my work, I had ignored mundane things like housework. I stripped and took a shower.

I should've taken Mrs P's advice and hired a cleaner, though the idea of placing an ad in the local paper unnerved me. Mrs P wasn't fond of hiring local people and often stated. '*A wagging tongue from the village would only lead to trouble.*' Curiosity would get the better of anyone I employed, and I would soon be known as the crazy artist that lived down the lane.

After showering I dressed in my oldest and tattiest clothes and returned to my studio to tackle the small problem of the disposal of Phoebe Browning. She hung from the ceiling in the same way a spider discards a fly once all the goodness was sucked out of it. Her waist-length hair hung dull and lifeless making it harder for me to see what had first attracted me to her Gone were the same beautiful hollowness in her green eyes, like mother.

I sat at my desk, pencil in hand, and sketched out the image before me while I planned how I was going to encase her body in concrete.

***

Eight months ago, I had become a little desperate as to where I would find my next muse, but fate had kindly stepped in. I had completed another commission and was delivering it to the gallery. I was halfway up the stairs when a young woman emerged out of Jenny's office and came hurtling down the stairs. I threw myself against the wall, hugging the painting to me, in fear we would both land at the bottom of the stairs in an untidy heap.

"So sorry. I was in a world of my own," the beauty gasped while pushing her long copper-coloured hair behind her ear.

A slight smile played on her lips as she adjusted the strap of her shoulder bag and continued past me.

For a spilt-second I couldn't speak. In her beguiling eyes I recognised the all too familiar emptiness. Her honesty and sincerity in the few words she uttered had silenced me. I hurried after her, but by the time I reached the high street, she had disappeared among the crowds.

A month or so later I spotted her at Cleo Anderson's exhibition. She leaned against a wall, glass in hand, surveying the crowds of art connoisseurs. It surprised me that no one spoke to her. It was as if she seemed invisible to all around her, but me. I had wanted to ask Jenny if she knew who she was but thought better of it. I didn't want to draw attention to the fact I had shown an interest in her. When the time came seizing Phoebe Browning was far easier than I had expected.

After finishing the sketch, I made a list of things I needed for my project. A quick wander around the outbuildings delivered some positive results as I managed to find many of the items I needed.

In one of the stables I reconnected the electricity. On entering its dark space, I discovered it had become a dumping ground for unwanted items from the house since father fell ill. I ran my hand up and down the wall just inside the door until I found the light switch. The bulb crackled as it came on. Once settled, it revealed before me a collection of old paint cans, a motley collection of bicycles, odd bits of damaged furniture, boxes of jam jars, and newspapers.

I hauled the unwanted clutter out and dumped it in the next stable along. I thought about the obnoxious bastards, D S. Heythorp and his sidekick Wicklow, and my missing paintings as I worked.

***

Late last year their unannounced arrival at my home caught me at a bad time. On that particular morning Basil had already interrupted me, so the last thing I wanted was the police appearing on my doorstep, but there they were like a couple of annoying fleas. Desperate for a drink after Basil had pissed me off, I showed them into the drawing room, knowing if they were going to delay me further in my work, I might as well be comfortable. Wicklow already had his notebook out as he surveyed the room. I wondered if it was something he automatically did.

"Would either of you like a drink?" I had offered half-heartily, knowing they would both refuse. After pouring myself a large one, I gestured for them to take a seat.

I dropped into my father's chair while Wicklow took his usual stance and positioned himself away from Heythorp. He stood in the corner of the room just on the outskirts of my peripheral vision. Much to my annoyance, I found I had to turn away from Heythorp to keep an eye on him. On a previous visit they had given me a lot of shit about my security and mother's missing paintings.

Unfortunately, unbeknown to me at the time, Wicklow had the proof I needed about mother's disappearing paintings. He was the last person to see them before they vanished. I sipped my drink and waited.

During their previous visit I had let slip that I suspected my agent had taken mother's paintings. Their reaction had surprised me. They wanted to know if I could enlighten them on Basil's whereabouts on certain days over the last six years.

"Yes, I'm sure I can. I'd been making notes. Most of the paintings' disappearances coincided with my agent's visits as he wanted to ensure that I could deliver the commissions he had ordered. He wanted updates before he flew out to America."

"But surely your agent has rights over all your work?" Heythorp had asked.

"Not my mother's paintings he doesn't!"

"So all the missing pieces are your mother's works, then?" Wicklow had asked while studying mother's sketches father had framed years ago. Though his eyes wandered to the semi-nude portrait of mother that hung over the fireplace. He had shown a keenness for the painting since his first visit

"Mr Ravencroft, the last time we visited," Heythorp finally opened the conversation as I sat nursing my glass, "you told us about your mother's disappearing pictures. How can you be so sure it's him?" He leaned forward, his notebook resting on his knee.

I swirled the whiskey around in my glass before answering. If they didn't believe me previously, why should I help them with their enquiries now? My expression must have said all that I was thinking as Heythorp stated, "I'm not questioning you, Mr Ravencroft. But as police officers we need evidence."

"Look." I had slammed my glass down, and splashed whiskey over my hand. "If I show you something, you'll have your evidence."

"Show us," Heythorp said.

They followed me up the stairs to mother's studio. Of course, Wicklow and Heythorp had been there before only this time it was on my terms.

"Your mother's studio." Wicklow's tone of voice edged with excitement.

"Still have all your mother's gowns, I see," Heythorp commented, though it was more of a statement than a question. He hovered in the doorway as though a little hesitant about entering this time. Previously he had burst in and made stinging remarks about my sexuality, saying the gowns suggested I was a cross-dresser.

"No reason for me to dispose of them." I tugged on a drawer beneath one of the drying racks. "A house of this size has plenty of room to store all my parents' belongings." On opening the drawer, I slid my hand under a pile of drawings until my fingertips found what I needed.

Heythorp moved past mother's dressing room and stood beside the French window. He scanned the room, with its collection of paintings that leant against the walls and filled two racks along another wall. At the centre of the room, on a raised platform, was mother's large gothic bed, made up ready for her return, the cover too fresh and dust free.

"Do you have a cleaner?"

"No, I do it myself when I have time. I paint here, too. The light is always good."

Heythorp ran a finger along the edge of a cabinet where I had laid out my paints in the same way she had. Wicklow scrutinised something on mother's bookshelf, and then with the tip of his pencil moved it. On seeing me observing him, he had straightened.

I found mother's book and pulled it out. "You need to understand that she kept a detailed account of all the works she sold. She never gave anything away. Every picture Mother painted, drew or created, no matter how small was numbered and catalogued in here." I waved the notebook as if to emphasise its importance. "I've checked. They're no longer in the house."

Heythorp gave a brisk nod, and then picked up one of the paintings. He turned it and his eyebrows lifted, as though unsure of what he was looking at it. "These are valuable." He set it down again.

"Yes. If you're wondering if I've sold them, then the answer is no. My parents left me well off. Also, I have a steady income from my own work."

I passed mother's notebook to Wicklow. He eagerly flicked through the pages. Every now and again he would stop and make a few notes in his own book. "Are those the missing ones you've marked and dated?"

"Yes, that's right."

"They tally with dates we have for when Mr Hallward was out of the country."

"So is that evidence?"

"Not enough. We need to catch him leaving the country with a painting." Wicklow held out mother's notebook to me. "Your mother certainly kept a detailed record."

"She couldn't bear being parted from her creations. As you can see, she coded them as well as their titles."

"You would need a code breaker to work it out." Wicklow said with a grin.

"Not if you knew mother. The code tally with the date of

creation, the numbers on the drying racks and their log number in the book. She did it so no one could make copies."

"Your mother was paranoid?"

"Mistrust seemed to be part of her nature. She felt people were too greedy and judgmental. It's why she sold so few. She made buyers sign a contract to say that, if they decided to sell her work on, she had the right to buy it back at their original price."

"Were any of the pictures taken from here?" Heythorp had asked.

"Yes, and four small framed sketches off the walls downstairs. Most of the rooms in the house had some of her work on display. I'm really not…"

"If I recall," Heythorp interrupted. "We spoke to you about security a few years back."

"That's my point. There's no way anyone could have broken in. *It's an inside job*. Nobody other than me lives or works inside this house."

"Hired help? Your lawns look immaculate," Wicklow said, pointing through the French windows.

"That's old Bill's handy work, but he doesn't enter the house. If he needs to ask me anything, he telephones. I leave his wages in the potting shed every Friday. The only time we speak is if he sees me in the garden."

"Right." Heythorp enunciated the word, drawing it out.

"I'm sure if someone had broken in, old Bill would've said something."

I stepped out onto the balcony and Heythorp joined me. We peered down into the garden.

"If someone was to break in, there would be damage to the garden. Old Bill's very proud of his work. Footprints all over his neat borders wouldn't go unnoticed."

"Yes, your point is noted, though we would need to chat with him." Heythorp entered the studio before me. By the time I closed the door behind me, Wicklow had drawn one of mother's painting out from the rack.

"Jane Maedere was a prolific painter."

"She was. Having Mrs P allowed her to focus all her

energies in one direction."

"Mrs P… your housekeeper?" Heythorp asked.

"Yes. She more or less ran everything."

"Must've been lonely for you, a child in the house full of adults." Heythorp looked around.

I wasn't sure whether he was expecting me to answer, but then to my relief, he changed the subject, sending the ghosts back into the shadows.

"It's easy to see if someone has been in here." He pointed to a stack at the back of the room. "With the amount of dust covering those paintings."

"Yes, if you look here." I showed him the clear imprint of a hand on the back of mother's painting. "There's a nick in the top of Basil's little finger on his left hand."

"Yes, we saw he had a damaged hand," Wicklow said. "Though you could've easily shown him the painting."

"So you're saying it's no proof at all?"

"Look, Mr Ravencroft, we're not your enemy. Since we last met, I've acquired some new duties." Pride shone in his eyes. "I'm now part of a new branch of the police force. We investigate stolen works of art. We can start looking into the loss of your paintings, but you'll need to fill out a report. Do you have any photographs of the missing works? If you do, we can add them to our database."

"Photographs? A few of her earlier works appeared in old magazine articles. There might be a few in the background of family snaps. Mother focused more on painting than taking snaps of her finished works."

"It's worth checking in family albums. We can enlarge the paintings from the main shot." Heythorp headed for the door.

"I'll need to buy a new camera. Once I've taken shots of the remaining pictures, if any more go missing, I can send you a copy." I followed Wicklow.

"Much obliged. We'll let you get back to work…" Heythorp paused, his hand resting on the banister as he reached the head of the stairs. "I take it that's your studio now?" He raised one eyebrow in a questioning slant as I came towards him.

"Yes. I'm busy working on another commission."

"Hmm…" His eyes narrowed as he pursed his lips in thought. "Why is there only one painting of your own in the studio?"

The hair on the back of my neck rose.

He sighed, a fleeting wry smile crossing his lip. "I guess you sell your work regularly. There doesn't seem to be much in the house either." He descended, with Wicklow following next. I hung back, looking towards the studio. On the first landing, Heythorp handed me a card over his shoulder. "Here's my number. You'll come straight through to me if you want to file a report. Let us know if any more pieces go missing. We can check for fingerprints. Other investigations have led us to believe that there's a syndicate at work in this country. They're stealing to order for overseas collectors."

"Only Basil knows I have this collection."

At the bottom of the stairs Wicklow turned as I came down to join them. "Don't quote us, Mr Ravencroft." Wicklow had dropped my first name, his tone sharper. "We'll deny making such a statement."

"But you said you're investigating art thefts?"

"No. We came to question you about Basil Hallward's connection to the disappearance of six young women over the last six years. You're the one making allegations against him in connection with missing paintings. Until you have sent in your details and we've opened an investigation, we can't make any further comments. Thank you for your time, Mr Ravencroft. Good day."

***

After shifting the last dusty box, I rubbed my hands down my trousers and surveyed the empty workshop. My stomach churned at Heythorp's last comment about my lack of completed paintings and sketches in the mother's studio. For days afterwards it had worried me. Had Basil been so focused on mother's paintings that he hadn't commented on my lack of work, sketches or drawings? If he had just mentioned it once, I would've set the stage better.

Clearing my thoughts, I focused on the disposal of my last angel ready to begin hunting for my eighth one.

I set to work on my new project enthusiastically, never having worked in three dimensions before. I just hoped that Old Bill hadn't noticed that his chicken wire had gone missing. I laid the tools out on the bench along with a pair of thick gloves. I had already practiced on a dead rat I found at the back of the workshop while shifting the boxes. I used a pair of wire cutters to cut a large square of chicken wire. Then I bent it around the rat's body shaping it as I went. It was impossible to wear the gloves as I worked. The wire caught the fabric too often, leaving a finger of the glove trapped as I pulled my hand free after trying to bend the wire into the shape I wanted.

I soon discarded the gloves. The wire dug into my hands and fingertips like sharp needles. The pain increased my sense of pleasure, but soon beads of blood pooled on the surface of my arms and scarlet rivulets ran down my fingers. Without wanting to stop to wipe the blood away, I licked my skin. The metal taste of blood left a horrid taste in my mouth, and I spat it out.

Once pleased with the overall shape of the rat, I placed it in a seated position, resting on its tail and with its front legs up as though it was sniffing the air for danger. I tweaked the wire cage that held the rat with pliers, bending the wire until I was happy with the finished sculpture and then, nailed it into place on a board. After mixing some concrete, I began to mould it over the wire frame with a small spatula. Starting from the rat's tail, I built up the layers and soon discovered that I could give texture to its surface.

In one of the toolboxes I found a small wire brush once used for cleaning spark plugs. Brushing the surface of the wet concrete brought the rat to life by giving it the texture of fur. I shaped its features by extending its nose. Then I pushed the tip of a pencil into the wet concrete to mark the eyes. Once he was complete, I left it to dry.

A noise outside the door caught my attention. A figure

moved across the doorway. I shielded my eyes and asked. “Hello. Can I help?”

“Sorry to disturb you, Mr Ravencroft. It’s just me dad saw you working over here. He’d like to speak to you about something.”

“Tell your father I’ll be with him in a moment, Carl.”

“Righty-ho.” The gardener’s lad disappeared from view.

I pulled the doors shut, turned the key and slipped it onto my key ring before following Carl into the garden via the side gate.

Old Bill was busy digging a flower bed. His broad back rippled with strength as he turned the soil. He was a tall man in his late forties, with a weather-beaten face and a head of thick blond hair. His son, a shorter, thinner version, tapped his father’s arm. Old Bill stabbed his fork hard into the lawn and rested his arm on its handle as I strolled towards him.

“Ah-ha, Mr Ravencroft…” He doffed his cap and I recalled his father, Bill doing the same. “There’s something not quite right about the old grave.” He pointed to the far side of the garden.

The muscles in my face tightened. “Bill, I thought I told you that the stone angel was unsafe. Neither you nor your son should be working anywhere near it. At least not until I get someone to undertake the repairs.”

“Aye, ah know what you said, Mr Ravencroft. But it’s not the angel.”

“I’m more than happy to tidy that area myself, Bill. I know how hard you work to keep the grounds looking pristine.”

“Ah know. It’s them graves in the bushes over there.” He nodded in the direction of the rhododendrons.

I swallowed. My temper started to rise. Why couldn’t Old Bill follow such a simple instruction? His father had worked for my family and now he worked for me. He knew his job inside out. To keep the front gardens tidy. Its gravel drive free from weeds, the lawn cut, shrubbery pruned, and spring bulbs planted. The boy just had to rake the gravel. Order ruled my life. Mrs P understood, *Everything in its place and a place for everything.*

"Aye ah know you told us, Mr Ravencroft. And as ah said to me boy, they aren't our problem. What it is sir, is them flies."

"What flies?"

"Them that swarm around the old grave. Those that are buried there, are no more than dust now. Ah reckon that an old fox or brock crawled in and died, but ah can't rightly see how it got in there meself."

"Please, Bill. I'm too busy to worry about it now. If you're right and it's an old badger, then God bless it. It's died in the right place. Thanks for letting me know."

"Mr Ravencroft, it ain't any of my business, but something ain't right. Ah'm telling you. There ain't any way they can get in."

"I couldn't care less, Bill. If you don't mind, I've work to do. And so have you! Please stay away from the angel and graves." I turned on my heels and headed back to the house.

From the attic landing I watched Old Bill and his son. Unable to move Phoebe Browning out to the stable, I took her body through to the windowless room, undressed her and then wrapped her body in a sheet.

Once the gardener and his son were busy at the front of the house, Carl raking the gravel, while Old Bill was busy cutting back the overgrown shrubs around the gateway. I left the house via the kitchen garden and nipped round to the potting shed. Three wheelbarrows stood beside the compost heap.

I took the closest one and hurried back to the house. As I approached the kitchen garden, I heard Carl coming towards me. Not knowing how I was going to explain my need for a wheelbarrow, I headed towards the French windows.

As I approached a baby bird flapped at the base of the door. It didn't surprise me; the wisteria covering the wall above the door and beneath the stone balcony was full of nests. I went to investigate, hoping to be able to return it to its nest. To my surprise, it was not a flapping bird at all, but the drawing room curtain wedged under the door. I pushed the handle down, expecting to find it locked, but it opened easily. I drew the curtains aside, pushed the wheelbarrow in, moving some furniture away from the door.

On locking the door properly this time, I pocketed the key, and realised it was Basil's point of entry.

It had been nearly nine months since I had last seen the police, but still they hadn't arrested Basil. Just before last Christmas, Basil had turned up unexpectedly with his normal excuse about being in the area. He had even mentioned something about having made a personal delivery of a painting to an important client. I had invited him in for a seasonal drink and, in the drawing room, he had handed me a card and a cheque for my percentage of the sales made in the previous year. He had left soon after bringing me up to date on Easter's continuing success in America.

If Wicklow was right, Basil would soon be tempted to steal more paintings. I decided to see just how much of an expert Basil was by adding an extra line of code to mother's original.

In the back of her notebook was a series of letters, words and numbers. I added a few extra letters and numbers to some of the easy to reach smaller pieces of mother's framed works. I was certain that if Basil's buyer was a true art connoisseur, they would have no problem in deciphering my message, and would know that Basil had illegally obtained the works. I hoped there might be a chance to find out who had them, and a way of getting them back.

By the end of the month, Basil had taken the bait.

Before heading upstairs to bring the body down, I made sure the wheelbarrow was out of sight of the French windows. On the landing I paused to look out the window. Old Bill and his son were busy working on the far side of the garden. It was a risk moving Phoebe in the daytime, but the sooner I could get rid of her body, the sooner I could start planning my next painting. I placed Phoebe in the wheelbarrow and covered her with some old blankets,

After the problem with flies I could not afford to add Phoebe to the tomb with the others, so I spent the remainder of the day repeating what I had done with the rat on her body.

I shaped the wet concrete, adding texture and features. I delicately carved in a long flowing shroud that covered the statue's head and flowed like water over her body, emphasizing the shape of her breasts. Around her head a garland of concrete ivy held a veil beneath the shroud in place. Her features, closed eyes and slightly parted lips, were visible, beneath her veil.

A week later I was ready to tackle the problem of getting her into the van. It was slow progress but, with the help of a sack barrow, I was able to move her by myself. I drove into London, to a bomb-damaged church not far from Basil's office.

On many occasions I had walked through its overgrown graveyard as I followed one of the many footpaths around the area. At the rear of the church there was an ideal parking place for the van. Overgrown shrubs hid it from view.

Three hours later, after working up a sweat and nearly crushing my thumb, I managed to get her in to a crypt. Once settled into her final resting place, among the dusty remains of church's nobility, I placed a row of candles at her feet. Pleased with the results, I left the way I had entered through the boarded-up church widow after bolting the main door.

As I headed home, I began to focus on my next hunt.

Chapter Twenty-Five

Stone Angels
The Ninth Painting
1971

As the car swung around on the drive sending up a spray of gravel, I covered my painting with a damp cloth. By the time I reached the second landing, the doorbell had rung twice. I opened the door and Detective Sergeant Heythorp stepped inside before I had the chance to invite him in.

"So you're in, Mr Ravencroft. So glad we didn't have a wasted journey." The difference in Heythorp's appearance in just over a year shocked me. His hair was almost pure white now, but he hadn't lost the fire in his cold blue eyes.

"So good to see you, too, I think."

He moved towards the drawing room while I kept my hand firmly on the door handle.

"Well that all depends on you, sir," a second voice said. "If you want to turn a simple situation into a difficult one, Mr Ravencroft, by all means feel free."

I swung around to find Wicklow standing in the doorway.

"We just want a little chat, but if you would rather take a ride to our place." He winked as he passed me. I closed the door before joining them in the drawing room.

Time had changed Wicklow too. Shades of grey hair touched his temples, while deep lines etched his eyes and lips. The new job kept him at his desk too long, or maybe he spent too much time after work down the local with his mates, as he now carried extra weight.

"It must be a full twelve months since you last darkened my door." I unlocked the French windows and threw the doors open allowing the smell of the freshly cut grass in before crossing to the drinks cabinet.

"I do hope it's a social call. Gentlemen please, you'll join me." I proffered a bottle of Johnny Walker Blue.

They shook their heads. "Sorry," Heythorp said. "I'm afraid we can't join you. Once again, we're here on official business. Please take a seat." He gestured towards my father's easy chair.

"Shouldn't it be me saying that to you?" I filled a glass to the brim.

He nodded. "We just need to ask you a few questions."

I dropped onto the nearest sofa and leant back. The room filled with an air of awkwardness, Heythorp stood looking down at me. I sipped my drink, happy to keep them waiting until I finally gestured for them to sit, with a quick flick of my wrist.

Wicklow remained standing, like a returning lover his attention moved to mother's portrait above the fireplace.

Heythorp coughed, "James…"

I gave a curt nod.

"Right." He relaxed into father's chair, seeming almost to take on father's stance, the way he did when he was about to lecture me on my bad behaviour. "I'm curious to know about an incident that happened at your school in 1951."

"What? 1951?" I nearly spilt my drink as I sat upright. "I can barely remember what I was doing two years ago let alone back then."

"It's important." He flicked through his notebook.

"For who?" I leaned forward.

"Our investigation," Wicklow added.

"What investigation?" I looked over my shoulder.

"Please just answer the question, James," Heythorp said.

I leant back in my seat and took a deep swallow of my drink.

"Mr Ravencroft?" Heythorp's tone was gravelly. From years of smoking and drinking, I guessed.

"What do you want to know?"

"An incident at your school in 1951 and why your name

popped up."

"My name popped up because I was a boarder at the school, along with hundreds of other names, too."

"The incident we're interested in happened during the school holidays when only a small number of people were present."

I sipped my drink and waited.

"It's interesting that your name came up."

I leaned forward. "My mother had died. My father was a very ill man, being cared for by our housekeeper. I was staying at the school during the holiday in 1951."

Wicklow checked his notebook, flicking a few pages. "It's odd that a teacher disappears, and lo and behold your name appears in connection with hers."

"Oh, Miss Dearborn. A strange case."

"You remember the incident?" Wicklow asked with a hint of sarcasm.

"It would've been obtuse of me not to, don't you think? She was my art teacher. It happened not long after I lost my mother. I'm sure it made an impact on all my classmates and the teachers, too. Have you asked any of them?"

"We spoke to Phillip Jones. He recalls that you were one of her favourites. Is it true that she held you back after class?" Wicklow asked.

"Phillip Jones—That's a name from the past. A classroom bully and a fool. At last, he has his claim to fame. Nasty boy. Very fond of telling me that mother killed herself because of me."

"What happened in these *after class activities*?" Heythorp emphasised the last few words with an air of smuttiness.

"He shared that information with you? It's only taken nineteen years for someone to ask the question no-one wanted to ask at the time. Maybe you should be asking Jonesy why he didn't speak out about Miss Dearborn's *after class activities* back then."

"We're asking you," Wicklow said.

I ignored his remark. "It's odd Detective Heythorp that it's only now Jonesy has spoken out. If he had done so back then,

Miss Dearborn's behaviour might've become known sooner. Maybe the school didn't want to acknowledge that Miss Dearborn was a child molester."

"Was she?" Wicklow's eyes remained on me. As he addressed his next comment to Heythorp. "Just can't believe it, Sarge. Rich kids have all the privileges; private education, money and a gorgeous young woman with the hots for them. She was willing to help them into manhood, and they complained about it. The real tragedy is that you didn't get your jollies away, while you could."

Heythorp said nothing.

"I wasn't there for her sort of education. My father expected high grades from me. You might've enjoyed the attention of an older woman, as many of the boys did. Oh, and you do know she wasn't just interested in grubby little schoolboys. Have you questioned some of the teachers, D.C. Wicklow?"

"We plan to, but for now we're interested in what you can tell us."

"And what would that be?"

"For a start, what happened to Miss Dearborn?"

"I've no idea. I tried to keep out of her way as much as possible. You know the sort of thing, sitting at the back of the class, not being on my own when she was about."

"Was there a reason you didn't take up her offer?"

"What do you mean by — offer?"

"You didn't like her unwanted attention?"

"Of course not. It was unseemly…" I let my words trail off.

"Most boys in your class saw it as a rite of passage."

"Is that what Jonesy said? Ha, just the sort of thing he would say."

"Did she have sex with other boys in your class?"

I crossed to the drinks cabinet, giving myself time to think as I poured another glass. "If you're asking me if I saw her having sex with any of the boys in my class. No, I did not. If you're asking me if there were rumours, then yes, plenty." I sat on the edge of the sofa and took a sip. "Of course, your star witness, Jonesy, mostly started the rumours. He liked to exaggerate his involvement with Miss Dearborn. The first-year students loved his lusty stories during their long first lonely nights away from home. Peeping Tom Jonesy had plenty of tall tales about how he had watched her undressing, taking a shower, swimming naked in the lake with married male teachers etc… I could go on. Oh, I don't suppose he mentioned how he supplied filthy magazines to the boys to drool over. Quite an entrepreneur Jonesy was back then. To be honest, I'm more than happy to forget about the sound of schoolboys masturbating late into the night after lights out."

Wicklow laughed. "Oh, and you're saying, what? You didn't masturbate?"

"Are you suggesting I'm abnormal for not wanting to have sex with a woman old enough to be my mother?" I glared in his direction. Wicklow stood in a small alcove in the far corner of the room and had his back to me. His shoulders hunched forward as he examined first one group of mother's sketches before moving onto the second group. The small framed drawings and sketches were a detailed study mother had made for one of her larger pieces. I wondered whether he had not heard or was just ignoring me.

He straightened, pulled a slim black notebook from his pocket and flicked over a few pages.

"Is there something wrong?" I set my glass down.

Heythorp turned in his seat, a concerned look on his face.

"Last time we came you had four other pictures hanging here." Wicklow pointed at the wall.

"What!"

"Here." Wicklow tapped the wall, not touching the frames.

"I haven't changed them." I moved to his side. "I don't believe it." I snatched an empty frame from the wall. "The bastard."

"You're talking about your agent?" Wicklow asked.

"Yes. Clever of Basil *bloody* Hallward to leave the frames. I don't use this room much. I spend most of my time painting. I pour myself a drink and then go upstairs to paint."

"When did he last pay you a visit?"

"About Christmas time. He made an unexpected visit. He brought me a card and a cheque, my earnings for the year." I lifted my head, pointed to the four faded rectangular patches on the opposite wall. "He had those four too. I hadn't realised he'd been back for more. I should've checked the frames more closely. Tucked away in the corner they aren't so noticeable."

"You didn't think to report it."

"Yes. But I wanted to catch him red-handed."

"You're making a serious claim, yet you failed to report a theft of four valuable sketches."

"I'm aware of how it may seem to you. The last thing I want is to draw attention to the rest of my mother's collection."

"The paintings are valuable?"

"I'm not interested in their monetary value. They belonged to my mother. That's the only value they have to me, but you wouldn't understand that."

"We understand. What I'm trying to comprehend is how your agent came to know about your huge collection. You said no one came to your house. Yet you allow your agent in."

I laughed and went to fetch my glass. "He's an art agent and recognised her work straightaway. He suggested marketing her works, alongside mine, but I wouldn't allow it. Then he wanted to market me as the son of— again, I said no."

"You're suggesting he took your rejection badly?"

I shrugged and returned to my seat. "At first, he seemed okay, still interested in marketing my paintings. He's making a good profit without exploiting my mother's name. Soon I realised he was promoting other artists over me, by allowing them to have solo exhibitions. All I got were empty promises."

"If your exhibition was to be successful, would you go it alone?" Heythorp leaned forward in father's chair.

"I guess I would. Easter left Basil's agency and is now in America."

"So it's a case of him barring your route to success. It would piss me off." Wicklow glanced at his superior.

"You think I'm setting my agent up because I'm pissed off with him." I downed my drink in one, went to the drinks cabinet, sloshed more whiskey into the glass and slammed the bottle back into the cupboard.

"You'd be amazed by how many fraudulent claims we come across in our line of work." Heythorp softened his tone.

"That's what you think I'm doing?"

"No, but with a huge growth in the number of art thefts we are well aware of the growing market as most stolen paintings disappear into someone's private collection." Heythorp looked at the remaining pictures. "Hayden, if James is right, why did he select those pictures over these ones? Are they all of equal value?"

"Difficult to say, Sarge. Jane Elspeth Maedere's work is sought after by all great collectors. A small piece like this..." He pointed to a framed sketch of a woman's hand. "I guess at least a quarter of a million easily, maybe even more on a good day."

"That's a bit of a wild guess for something like that. Dear God. It looks unfinished."

"They're sketches, Sarge." Wicklow grinned, flashing white teeth. "Please forgive him, James. He's a philistine."

"Can't see what all the fuss is about meself." Heythorp shook his head.

"I won't be making an insurance claim, because they're not insured."

"Well, that's very imprudent of you, Mr Ravencroft."

"You can't make your mind up. If I had insured them, I'm making a false claim. Now, I'm a fool for not doing so. All I want is their return. Mother was exploited while she was alive, now she's being exploited in death too."

"Okay." Heythorp moved back in his seat. "What can you tell us about your agent's trips to America?"

"In what way?"

"Why does he go so regularly?"

"Through his contact there he has access to the American

market and beyond. That's where he first encountered mother's work and became infatuated with her."

"So he's an art collector? Stolen works maybe, or just a dealer in stolen works." Wicklow's eyes sparkled as he pondered.

"A possibility." I glanced out of the window. Old Bill was pushing a wheelbarrow towards the rhododendrons. I fought back the urge to storm across the lawn and ask him what he was doing.

"So Mr Ravencroft, you're saying you didn't…"

Aware that Wicklow was talking to me, I turned.

"…a clever man, like you."

"These collectors are at a disadvantage. They can't exhibit their collections if their works are stolen."

"It's possession they're interested in. Owning something no one else has. What's so wrong with sharing your mother's art?"

"Having my own career and not living off my mother's fame. That's why I use my father's name."

"Surely it would be a blessing."

"Dear God! You're just like everyone else. If you have either rich or clever parents, people say the same."

"So your agent only found out later, who your mother was?" Heythorp asked.

"Yes."

"Refresh our memory to how you met. You live here, in isolation, and Basil is a Londoner," Wicklow said, flicking through his notebook.

"At the launch of David Hockney in '63. The evening was very noisy so we exchanged details by writing our addresses down. I then met him at his office."

Heythorp's eyes widened and he gave a sharp nod in Wicklow's direction. I ignored it and carried on. "The following year he turned up here unexpectedly. That's when he discovered who my mother was."

Heythorp straightened in his seat. "Mr Ravencroft, why did you fail to mention that you were at the Hockney exhibition in 1963?"

My stomach nosedived. Too much whiskey had loosened my tongue.

"Were you living in London at the time?" he persisted.

"Yes, in some ropey old squat and lasted about three months. With some other artists all dreaming of fame and fortune. It was the first time I had to support myself. My parents were both dead—" I rambled and only stopped when I saw Heythorp exchange looks with Wicklow.

"A squat. Whereabouts was it?"

"Cartwright Gardens, Holborn." I didn't hesitate, knowing it was long gone, along with the other artists.

"Why haven't you ever come forward when an appeal went out for any information on a missing artist, Tommy Blackbird, and a young woman named Candela Waterbrook? They were at the same squat as you."

"Sorry—not familiar with those names. After I met Basil at the gallery, I left London, Detective Heythorp."

"You were seven when you lost your mother," Wicklow broke in.

His question threw me. "Yes. But what has that to do with Basil's theft?"

"It's why you feel passionate about your mother's work."

"Is that a crime?"

"You would be surprised what we come across." Heythorp leant forward. "Some would even sell their parents' hearts, if they thought they could make a bob or two. Nothing's sacred these days."

I looked into my glass. It was empty. Another one would loosen my tongue further. I crossed to the French window and drew in a couple of deep breaths trying to clear my head "My agent has the same driving force as me, but unlike Basil I wasn't about to exploit my mother to the highest bidder, just to be the best, nor am I willing to help Mr Hallward to fulfil his dreams."

"His dreams?" Heythorp asked.

I leant against the doorframe. "A renowned international art agent, and ultimately the art dealer, who discovered a major missing art collection."

“Two strings to one bow. Nice.” Wicklow said. “Who’s his American contact? Do you have a name?”

“Someone called Sparks.”

“That’s a start, I suppose,” Heythorp said in a dismissive way. “Sparks.” He repeated as though storing it to memory. “This *Sparks*— is there anything more you can tell us?’

The silence of the garden was shattered as the sound of Old Bill’s ride-on lawn mower started up.

“Look, this will sound as though I’m an eavesdropper, but I once overheard Basil in conversation with his American counterpart. What he said pissed me off. It served me right for listening in…”

“What did you hear?” Heythorp cut me off.

“I’d been on his books for seven years and he took on Easter and allowed him to have his own exhibition. So when I heard my name mentioned, I listened in on his secretary’s extension. Basil and the Sparks person have joined forces and gone into partnership. Sparks is definitely some sort of big name in the American art world. That’s all I can really tell you.”

“Who is Easter?” Heythorp began to pace about, and I suspected that’s how he did all his best thinking.

“Joseph Easter.” The name was out before I could stop myself.

“Small world.” Heythorp scribbled something in his notebook. “There can’t be many with that name. He’s the artist that lived in Cartwright Gardens, Holborn in 1963, too.”

“I wouldn’t know.” Old Bill cruised across the lawn making sweeping strokes. As he came towards the house the sound got louder and then it faded as he moved away, leaving only the smell of the grass.

“At least we have this Sparks person to investigate for the time being. What sort of sizes are the missing paintings?” He nodded in the direction of the painting above the fireplace. “Bigger or smaller than that one?”

“None that size. I’m sure I would’ve noticed sooner if something as large as that disappeared. Most are small pictures."

"The sort of size to fit easily into a suitcase?" Wicklow asked.

"Yes."

Heythorp moved towards the front door with Wicklow trailing behind, still looking at mother's paintings that hung in the hall.

"You seem quite taken by my mother's work."

"A fascinating woman. Her work's a delight when you have an enquiring mind like mine, Mr Ravencroft." With that, he walked out the front the door into brilliant sunshine.

"I'm sorry about my colleague." Heythorp turned to face me. "He gets quite attached to the pieces of art. I cannot understand it myself, but then I'm rather a philistine as my colleague has told you. The only stuff I enjoy is the sort my kids do. If you understand what I mean, nice and simple, nothing too taxing for the brain. Anyway, it has been nice meeting you again. I hope we haven't disturbed you too much."

As I followed Heythorp out, I heard voices. Wicklow was talking to the gardener and his son.

Heythorp followed my gaze.

"So that's your gardener?"

I nodded. "Bill Jarman and his son."

"Have they worked for you long?"

"For nearly twenty years. Bill's father worked for my parents. Why?" I wasn't really focusing on what Heythorp was saying. Bill was pointing and Wicklow was following his direction.

"Wicklow is quite a keen gardener, too," Heythorp said.

"Really," I muttered as Wicklow and old Bill walked across the lawn to the fence.

"Of course, it probably doesn't mean anything. But if we don't follow up on tip-offs, we get all sorts of complaints." Heythorp pulled out a packet of cigarettes and lit one up.

"Sorry." I turned to him.

"It's like my old dad used to say." He let out a puff of smoke before continuing. "We're damned if we do, and damned if we don't. It doesn't do to waste any new information, we get. That's why we had to come and speak to you."

"Then explain to me the connection between the death of an art teacher in 1951 and my missing paintings?"

"Well, Mr Ravencroft you need to understand it from my point of view. My gut feeling won't go away. It has a nasty habit of creating a link between all sorts of unconnected pieces in my head." Heythorp tapped the side of his head with his thumb while holding the cigarette. "I can't just let go. I have to make sense of it all. At the moment there's no real picture yet."

"Mrs Norris has spoken to you," I muttered under my breath.

Heythorp drew on his cigarette, gave a noncommittal nod and crossed the lawn to join his partner. I waited a moment before joining them.

"Good afternoon, Mr Ravencroft," my gardener said, touching his cap.

"Is there a problem, Bill?"

"No, sir." He nodded his goodbyes to the two detectives before pushing his wheelbarrow around the corner.

As the two police officers and I walked over to their car, Heythorp said, "Oh James something else that's just come to mind. You were at the launch of Joseph Easter's art exhibition last year, weren't you?"

"Yes, why?" I stopped in mid-stride.

"Didn't anyone question you?" Heythorp stopped too.

"About what?"

"A young woman employed by Basil Hallward. She disappeared. You must have heard about it."

I shook my head. "You see where I live. I don't have the dailies delivered, nor do I have a telly. Are you questioning me about her disappearance?"

"Eight women have vanished without a trace. We're asking anyone who has any connection to them, no matter how slight, if they remember anything out of the norm. You were there at Easter's launch party before Hallward went to

America. Do you remember anything?"

"That's nearly a year ago—"

"I know, but any little thing could help trigger someone else's memory. So see if something comes to mind and if it does, please give us a ring." Heythorp gave me another one of his cards. "Any little thing could make a huge difference."

I gave a curt nod as they said their goodbyes and climbed into their car.

Once they were out of sight, I closed the door and went through to the drinks cabinet. I poured another whiskey and carried it up to mother's studio where I lay down on her bed.

Chapter Twenty-Six

Roofscapes
1971

As I swung the car into the road that led to Hallward Gallery car park, I caught sight of the headline emblazoned across the newsagent's stand.

'*Grim discovery found in a derelict church*!'

My breath left me, as my mind could not process what I had read. Suddenly aware of a blaring horn, I looked in its direction. Something large and dark green was bearing down on me. I accelerated hard and shot across the road out of the path of an oncoming lorry straight into the car park, narrowly missing Basil's car and another one parked at an odd angle across the space I normally used.

My heart raced as I rested my head against the steering wheel, allowing the tension in my back and shoulders to ease. After a few moments, I climbed out and was surprised to find I was shaking. I took a few deep breaths unable to comprehend the shock, not the fact I was nearly killed, but the discovery of the eighth angel.

Part of me wanted to dash across the road to buy a newspaper, but reason forbade me. Now was not a good time to change my behaviour. I paced the car park trying to convince myself that it was impossible for anyone to identify her as the concrete had set. The headline shouted at me, *'Come buy me. Then you'll know!'*

I aimed a sharp kick at a car tyre while marvelling at my

own stupidity. If only I had kept them altogether, this wouldn't have happened. After convincing myself I had nothing to fear, I pushed open the gate into an overgrown garden and followed the flagstone path. The headline stated, *'Grim Discovery Found in a Derelict Church,'* which could mean anything, I reasoned. From an unexploded bomb, to the remains of people who had been sheltering from the blitz that had lain undiscovered until now.

As I climbed the stairs to Jenny's office, the sound of crying confused me. Jenny sat weeping into a hanky as I entered her office. Along the corridor loud voices boomed from Basil's office. For once, the raised voice didn't belong to Basil, but to an unknown woman.

"Jenny, what's going on?" I whispered, which seemed a stupid thing to do with hindsight, as neither Basil nor the woman would've heard me.

"It's too awful. Just too awful. The poor girl," Jenny sobbed into her handkerchief.

"What's the matter? Who's shouting at Basil?"

Jenny looked up, her eyes red-rimmed. "Oh James," she said, as though only just realising I had spoken to her. After dabbing at her nose, she continued. "Cleo's here with her mother. They're blaming Basil for Phoebe Browning's death."

"What? They found Cleo's missing friend?"

"Haven't you heard? She was… encased in concrete. It's been on the radio and the television since the story broke."

"I've been busy. Did you say she was encased in concrete?"

"Yes." She blew her nose. "Was there something you wanted?"

"I've just popped in with the commission Basil has been hounding me for."

"Of course, the commission. I'd forgotten all about it." She shook her head. "Where is it?"

"I'll fetch it from the boot of my car. Only another car was in my normal parking space."

"That'll be Mrs Anderson." Tears ran down Jenny's

cheeks. “I’m sorry, James. I know she’s been missing awhile, but you kind of hope that she’ll turn up safe. I guess this means Flossie is… is…” Her voice broke. She wiped at her eyes and gulped in air until her body stopped shaking. “Poor Flossie. She must be encased in concrete too.”

“Please don’t upset yourself.”

“I can’t help it.” Her lips began to tremble again. “I just feel…responsible in some small way. I persuaded Flossie to work for us.” She dabbed at her eyes with the soggy hanky.

“Then we’re all to blame. Basil for suggesting he wanted a model, me for taking you to the restaurant where she worked, and also my friend for telling me to go there in the first place. Jenny, it’s just all a coincidence. None of us is really to blame.”

Something in Jenny’s expression told me a thought had crossed her mind. As her features relaxed, she nodded in the direction of the shouting, “I think I better make us some tea.”

She leaned over her chair, pulled a folded newspaper out of her bag and thrust it into my hand. “Read this.” Jenny crossed the landing to the small kitchenette as I unfolded the paper. The front-page bold headline spelt out my downfall.

‘*Horror found in disused Church!*’

Police confirm that the grim discovery made two weeks ago in the war-damaged church of St Sithes was the body of 26-year-old Phoebe Browning who had been missing for over a year. Phoebe’s body was uncovered while the site was being prepared for much-needed housing. Two labourers working on behalf of the church, along with a priest, Father Philip who was overseeing the decommissioning of the building and the removal of its historical fittings and tombs, made the awful discovery in the crypt.

With only three torches between them in the semi-darkness, they found a statue of a young woman instead of the expected church relics.

Father Philip told our reporter, ‘Even though St Sithes is the patron saint of serving maids, he had not expected to find a statue of this kind in the crypt as there was no mention of it on his list,'

'Father Philip had prayed for the strength of mind for her family and that of his two co-workers as they all suffered a nasty shock while trying to move the statue.' He said, 'As we tried to lift it part of the arm crumbled away, exposing rotten flesh, bone, and matted material. The smell was indescribable. In our shock, we dropped the statue. It crashed against one of the stone tombs and broke open. Never have I seen anything like it. Who could do such a thing?'

When asked if he knew how Phoebe Browning died, Father Philip said, 'The police are still investigating, and the church has been cordoned off to stop sightseers. I don't know which is worse, the discovery of the poor girl or the ghoulishness of people who want to see the place where she died.'

Our reporter asked for his views on whether Phoebe's death had any links to witchcraft after someone reported to the newspaper that the statue was found within a circle of candles, and on the walls were a series of strange symbols, but Father Philip refused to comment any further. What he did say was that the police would make a statement once they had finished their investigation.

With my elbows resting on the table, I sat with my head in my hands. My mind began to turn everything over. It was only when Jenny placed a cup in front of me that I was aware of her return.

"It's awful, isn't it?" She closed the door. The shouting became no more than a strangled, muffled sound. Once seated, she continued. "What that poor girl must have suffered is beyond belief."

I sipped my drink while puzzling over how it was possible for them to know that it was Phoebe. Surely the quicklime in the cement would've dissolved her features. Jenny leant forward on her elbows, nursing her cup.

"Sorry, what were you saying, Jenny?"

"I said it must've been shocking for her family." She lifted her cup, testing the heat of the liquid against her lips before taking a sip. Jenny's expression was more than just sadness for a girl she hadn't really known.

"It's a lot to take in." I laid the newspaper down. "Are you all right, Jenny?"

"Yes… well, no. I can't help but think there's some sort of ghastly coincidence that links us to what's happened to these girls."

"These girls? What do you mean?"

"The missing girls, James." Her eyes widened.

"Yes, but… there's no *'us'* about it!"

"Oh, but there is, James." She tapped the newspaper with her long pink nails. "Phoebe Browning isn't the first to go missing in this area. There've been others; even the newspaper has stated that."

"But what's that got to do with us?"

She shrugged and sipped her drink. I sensed her unanswered questions and knew she was trying to put her thoughts into words.

"Well?" I prompted.

"Something's just not right. And I'm not the only one who thinks so. That's what they're arguing about in there." She pointed in the direction of Basil's office.

My chest tightened as I glanced towards Jenny's closed door.

"Don't give me that look, James," she said as I turned to her. "You know there have been others. You must be aware that Basil has been questioned every time another one goes missing."

I gave a non-committal shrug. "As I've said before, I live…"

"Yes, don't I know it…" she interrupted, with a bitter tone. "You live in the wilds of Suffolk, but I know for a fact that the police have spoken to you about Basil, so don't pretend you don't know."

"Okay, you're right. But he hasn't really confided in me. You know what he's like and he doesn't want you getting caught up in all of this."

"In what?"

"A vendetta against him."

"A vendetta?"

"Please don't let on I've told you." I studied my fingernails and then met her gaze. "He has some crazy notion that you might land up on their hit list."

Jenny picked up the newspaper. "That's crazy on so many levels." She pointed at the article. "What has a young woman encased in concrete have to do with a vendetta against Basil? We're an art gallery and this is London, not Italy."

"I know, Jen."

"All the artists on our books get a good price for their work." Jenny folded the newspaper and dropped it into her bag. "I've never received any complaints from clients. The gallery hasn't received any threatening calls."

"You know more than I do about Basil and this gallery."

"A possible link between the women and us is more about the gallery's location. From what I've read, all the women worked in this area, but apart from that it's very random." Jenny took a sip of her drink. "It's sweet that Basil worries about me, but I'm not at risk. I can't believe that Basil hasn't noticed that all the missing girls are white."

"I think Basil was concerned about why he was being singled out, and that they might go after you too. I'm glad it isn't worrying you personally."

"You're wrong. I am worried. Eight girls go missing and one's found encased in concrete. It's bloody serious. I might be black but I'm a woman first. Anyway, if they're linking Basil to these women, then I must be a suspect too because I knew most of them in one way or another through work."

"Okay, I get your point. It's nothing more than coincidence; you must see that, Jenny."

She pulled a file off the shelf behind her and laid it open on the desk beside her typewriter. "I've been collecting these." She thumbed through the newspaper cuttings and then held each little paper-clipped bundle up in turn. In the file box, I noticed a small notebook too.

"I don't see it as a coincidence. Why has Basil been singled out? What is his link to the girls? Remember, I know his movements more than others do." She paused and unclipped one of the bundles.

I waited for her to go on.

"Something has been nagging at me. And, for the life of me, I can't put my finger on it." She leaned forward and rubbed her left temple. "The answer must lie with us somehow… Oh, never mind. Ignore me, James." She gathered up the bundle and dropped them into the file before picking up her cup. "I'm not sure what I mean. I guess I'm in shock, but there's one thing I know for sure. Basil isn't connected with this girl's death."

"I agree with you, Jenny. But it isn't us he has to convince."

She slammed her cup down, splashing some tea on the papers in front of her. "I know for sure this time, because I made arrangements for his weekend away with Nancy."

"Nancy?"

"Yes, Nancy Windgate. They've been together for a year now."

"Why didn't you tell me, Jenny?"

"Tell you? Why should I tell you, Mr Ravencroft? It isn't my place to tell you about my boss's personal arrangements." She gathered up our cups, and opened her office door. The argument still raged as Jenny crossed the landing. I closed my eyes and saw the dark green lorry bearing down on me. Had it been a warning? I decided the best thing was to keep Jenny on my side. When she returned, I tried to inject a little humour into my tone. "I'm sorry, you're right. Of course, your loyalty is to your boss first."

"I'm glad you understand. Hello they've gone quiet. Sounds like peace has returned." She looked towards her door. "At last, they've stopped shouting at one another."

A loud thud as a door struck the wall, followed by heavy footsteps hurrying down the stairs, told us the shouting was over, but happiness hadn't been restored. Jenny's office door flew open and Basil appeared. His face flushed and his cheeks puffy.

"Jen, please hold my… Oh, James, you are here! Could I speak to you, err now? Jenny, I won't be speaking to anyone and I mean anyone. If *they* ask say I'm on my way home as far as you know."

"But what if I'm asked what time you left?"

Basil checked his watch. "Say one o'clock."

"I have to tell the police the truth, Mr Hallward."

"I know you do, Jenny. I just can't be dealing with them. Not now and not today. Any other day I wouldn't ask it of you. If you want, take the rest of the day off…" He paused. "Yes, that's it, please just go home now, and come back afresh tomorrow. I'll still pay you for the whole day. As soon as I've had a chat with James, I'm going to see my solicitor."

Jenny smiled briefly. "Thank you, Mr Hallward. It's very kind of you, but I would rather get on with my work. What with Cleo's next exhibition coming up soon, there's…"

"Forget it, Jenny. She's just withdrawn her work. That's what the shouting was about."

"What! But I've put in so much time…" Jenny's voice died away when she saw Basil's stricken face.

"Yes, I know, but there's nothing we can do about it. My main concern is how it makes the gallery look. With all these accusations floating about, the last thing we needed was her pulling out. I tried reasoning with her. To get her to understand I've played no part in any of this. I'm just too angry to deal with the police today. Tomorrow I'll be fine."

Jenny nodded. "Okay, Mr Hallward. I have a few other errands I can be getting on with outside of the office. I'll take my keys with me, so I can let myself back in after you've gone."

"Thank you," Basil said.

"Mr Hallward would you like me to make you a cup of tea before I go?" she asked, while switching the phone over to the answering machine.

"That would be great, thank you."

We went through to his office. Basil sat down with a heavy thud as though all the fight had left him. On his desk, I noticed a large grey box folder. Written on the label was

was '*Private Information*' in Basil's distinct handwriting.

I took the chair opposite him. Basil picked up the folder and placed it on a shelf behind him. I wanted to ask what progress he had made in his research into the girls' disappearances, but after reading the newspaper article, I decided against it. With both Jenny and him absorbed in hunting for answers the less, I said the better.

Basil leaned forward in his chair, his eyes scanning my face. "I need… err, I was wondering if you would be interested in filling Cleo's shoes."

"Sorry?"

"I know it's short notice, but you are my only hope. I was thinking we could put together an exhibition using your landscape pictures."

I paced the floor.

"Please, James…"

I faced him. "Am I your last resort?"

Basil stood. "I'm not in the mood for dealing with hurt egos. I've been calling in favours all morning after Cleo phoned me first thing. I asked her to drop by to see if I could talk her out of it, but as you heard, she wasn't about to change her mind."

I sat down.

Basil did the same. "I can't tell you how embarrassed I feel. Just knowing that young woman was too scared even to come on her own to talk to me about what has happened."

"I'm sure you are."

"Anyway, we won't dwell on that now. I've made some enquiries and know a few clients who have bought your work in the past, who are willing to loan us their paintings."

"You're giving me my own exhibition?"

"Yes, but I'm hoping that you can provide some new pieces of works, too. Do you have some we can sell on the evening?"

I smiled. "One or two. When is it for?"

"You've a couple of months' grace. Three at the most, James." A physical weight seemed to lift from his features. "Thank you, James" He began to shuffle papers around on his desk as though he was avoiding eye contact with me. Then he drew in a deep breath and cleared his throat. "Also, would it be possible… Well, more of a favour, if…" he hesitated and then made eye contact with me. "I know I've asked before, but…"

It was too much to expect. He still wanted the son of Jane Elspeth Maedere.

"It would be of great help. You do understand, don't you?"

I shook my head as the twitching of a muscle in my temple began. "Is this blackmail, Basil? If I say no, I don't get an exhibition?"

"Not at all, James. I was just asking."

"You're implying that you have no faith in my work." I stood ready to leave.

"You know that's not true, James." Panic edged Basil's voice. "You're an unknown, and you're not even using her name."

"That's not true, Basil." I placed my hands squarely on his desk and leaned in. "Not according to Mrs Norris."

"Mrs Norris?" Basil leaned back in his chair. His skin looked sallow, and his hair had lost its shine. "She's one of my best clients along with a few of her friends. I wasn't aware you knew her."

"We met at Easter's launch. Actually, she asked me why you hadn't allowed me to have a solo exhibition yet." I straightened up as Basil leant forward.

"Really. So that's why she nearly bit my arm off when I asked if she would be interested in allowing her paintings to be part of the exhibition. Mrs Norris can be very persuasive when it comes to getting what she wants. If we get her on-board then she'll persuade all her rich friends to come along to the event. Well, my lad, Cleo pulling out has done us both a favour. It might even be the making of us both, too."

"How many paintings do you want?" I dropped back into my seat.

"Five." He leaned back in his chair, which engulfed him.

"Five hmm?" I knew I had already completed three. Not to my usual high standard as I had grown bored with painting land and seascapes. The paintings were good enough for people like Mrs Norris and her friends who were only interested in the monetary value of art. “Yes, I can fulfil your order.”

“I knew I could rely on you. Deliver the paintings on time, and if this exhibition is successful then we’ll talk about you having a solo one next year.”

“A whole new body of work, Basil?”

“Something to consider. But for now, let’s see what happens on the evening. If you have a picture for me, please leave it with Jenny. I’ve got a few things I need to sort out before heading home.”

“To Nancy,” I added with a smirk.

“How do you…” He stopped himself.

“Why the big secret? I’m happy for you, Basil.”

“There’s no big secret, James. I just don’t mix business with pleasure. It’s the way I’ve always been.”

I was heading for the door when Basil said, “Thank you, James.” Though this time I was not sure what it was he was thanking me for.

Chapter Twenty-Seven

Stone Angels
The Ninth Painting
1971

I suppose I should've been grateful that the police had not arrested him before the exhibition. Otherwise I would've missed the opportunity to launch my long-awaited career. I wanted it to be my *first* solo exhibition, but I had to satisfy myself with the fact that the main body of the work was mine.

Basil suggested he would fill the two smaller areas before the main hall with a selection of works done by his other artists, as it was such a large venue. He called them a taster that led the viewers into the main exhibition. Still, it was a chance to show off my back catalogue, plus a few new paintings.

I hadn't realised the underlying pressure I was suffering until early one morning two days prior to the exhibition. I woke with a start and found myself cocooned in damp sheets and unable to rise from the bed. Panic washed over me as I relived every painful second of a vivid nightmare in which I was naked, with my back to my paintings, facing the connoisseurs gathered at the launch of my solo exhibition. The unfamiliar faces pointed and jeered at me as I tried to shield my work from their cruel criticism.

A cold sensation ran down my back as I became aware that the crowd was now pointing at my feet. The paint I had so meticulously placed, brushstroke by brushstroke, had bubbled up and cascaded in a stream of colours. Blues, reds and yellows blended into a dark, muddy pool as though paint had melted off the canvases.

My body shook as the paint ebbed between the gaps in the floorboards. It pulled at my ankles and feet until I toppled over. With flailing arms, I tried to escape the tide of paint that swept me along past the jeering crowd. I clawed at the floorboards but there was nothing to grab onto as the paint slipped through my fingers. The chortling connoisseurs ignored my cries for help as they all raised their glasses in a toast to the disappearing art. The sound of their laughter grew deafening as they merged into a single figure that rose up out of swirling paint. It towered above me in a familiar form—my mother.

She leaned forward, offered me her hand giving me hope of rescue. Stuck between the floorboards, I reached for her, begging to be saved. Without warning, her face began to melt. Her mouth became a black cavern that folded back over her head. As it did so it spat out all the insults she had screamed at me as a child.

"How dare you think you're better than me?"

"Who do you think you are, you stupid boy?"

I wrapped my arms around my head and allowed the paint to swallow me up.

I shook myself free from the sheets and sprang off the bed. Naked and still shaking, I padded through to the bathroom and took a shower. The water washed the sweat along with the remaining threads of my awful dream. Refreshed and dressed, I went to my studio. The eighth Stone Angel rested on an easel. I was on target to complete my collection, just two more to go.

Though I was eager to show Basil, I held back. The timing had to be right. I knew that once he viewed the first few paintings, adding to the series would be impossible. My thoughts wandered to the discovery in the church. Maybe I shouldn't have been so hasty, but I needed my ten.

I pushed the finished picture into the rack and turned my concentration to finish the much-needed pictures for the exhibition. Once completed, my hunt could begin for my next angel. In mother's studio, I worked swiftly on the land and seascapes needed for the exhibition though my mind kept churning over my disturbing nightmare. I mixed Cadmium red, yellow Ochre, and Titanium white together ready to add to a sunset I had been working on. It occurred to me then that the dream explained the anxieties mother had suffered, too.

Did I have the same fears?

I added small dabs of colour to my painting and became so absorbed in what I was doing that it took a while for me to realise the phone was ringing.

"Hello. Yes?"

"James, my dear boy. I've some great news."

"Really?" I wedged the receiver in the crook of my neck, as I continued mixing the colours.

"Yes. It's something to get your creative juices flowing."

"That's good." My neck began to ache as I tried to add more paint to the canvas.

"I've just finished chatting with a new client. They've commissioned a painting of Dunwich, Suffolk."

"What? Not another fucking commission for that damn place!" I threw my palette down and placed the receiver to my ear properly while stretching my neck. "Good God, Basil. How many sodding paintings can an artist paint of a place that does not exist anymore? I've even done it in every type of weather too."

"Now don't disappoint me."

Pleased he could take my anger so light-heartedly, I knew it was a sign that he was making progress with getting the arrangements sorted for the exhibition. I was confident that soon my career would be on the up, while his would soon crash and burn.

"Basil, I'm really busy. I'm working on the pictures you specified for the exhibition."

"Listen. The client doesn't want Dunwich as it looks now, but your interpretation of its past. You have free rein over that. Their only request is that it's in your own unique style."

"At last. Can I have that in writing, Basil, just in case

they're not satisfied?" My temper was abating.

"If you must. I'll draw up a contract if it makes you happy."

"Thanks. Though I'm excited about having free rein on the painting I create."

"I thought you might. The client has given us permission to use it in your up and coming exhibition. It'll be the star piece."

"Then I better get started on it right away." I replaced the receiver, picked up my palette and stepped back from the easel. "Hmm. I was happy that I could even make a sunset look as sombre as the rest of my work."

***

I drove to Basil's office to sign the contract he had drawn up. Before returning for home, I took the opportunity to visit the library near the gallery hoping to find some history books on Dunwich.

I had visited the location of the medieval port many times, but nothing of it remained. What I needed was a historical account of how life was in Dunwich in hope that it would inspire me to create a new interpretation of the well-worn subject. Not finding anything suitable, the librarian recommended I tried a second-hand bookshop a few streets away. The shop bell rang as I stepped into Starlight's bookshop. Lighter and brighter than the library, the rows of books stood on lined pine shelves around the shop. Crisp white labels marked each section of the shop, allowing customers to find what they wanted easily. I breathed in the musty air, glad it still contained the all too familiar odour of old books. A mix of countless lives lived in the pungent scent of curiosity, wood shavings and mothballs. As I pondered whether what I needed came under travel or history, a door behind the counter opened. A young woman wearing a turban in shades of gold and russet emerged carrying a pile of novels. As she set the books down on the counter, she caught sight of me.

"Oh, hello. Can I help you?"

She had high pale cheekbones. The fullness of her pink lips held the hint of a smile that I could imagine some men would adore, but for me, what held my attention was the sadness in her dark green eyes. I closed the book I was holding and placed it back on the shelf.

"I hope so. I tried the library first with no luck. The librarian suggested I tried here. I'm on a quest."

"How exciting." She moved the books to one side and opened the counter. She was dressed in a full-length skirt that matched her turban, and a soft brown fitted blouse. "What are you looking for?"

"The history of a place called Dunwich. It's in—"

"Suffolk," she interrupted. "A very interesting medieval town on the East Anglian coast."

"So you've heard of it?"

"I know it well. Follow me." She led me to the back of the shop. "My father originally came from there."

"From Dunwich?"

"Not the part that's under the water. I meant what's left of it on the shore. Here we are." She gestured to a larger bookcase. The top half had a glass front. "The door's unlocked. Please help yourself to any book that takes your interest."

"Thank you." I ran my finger along the spines of the books.

"My father was a terrible hoarder. It's why I have a wide selection about that area of the country. What's your interest in the place?"

"I've been commissioned to paint a scene showing the last moments of the town's life as the storm hit."

"You're an artist then."

"Yes." As I hunted along the rows of old books, her sickly-sweet perfume overwhelmed me with the stench of lilies reminding me of decay and death. I focused on the books. In among the larger books, I found a small blue nondescript book, *The Story of Lost England,* by Beckles Willson. I opened it to the index. After running my finger down the list,

I turned to the page I needed.

A verse leapt out at me. *'Nor will they coldly turn away, because my verse shall tell a story of the fearful day when mighty Dunwich fell'.*

From my pocket I pulled out my sketchpad and began to draw a thumbnail sketch, an impression. Black storm clouds rose high in the night sky blocking out the stars. The sea broke through the defences, while forked lighting seemed to announce the end of the world.

I closed my sketchpad, ready to pull out another book when I became aware of the girl peering over my shoulder. I wanted to focus completely on the Dunwich painting, but the smell of her perfume distracted me.

I moved my finger onto the next book. My mind told mc that she could be my number nine as I selected the next book.

'S*he's not the one!'* I told myself while fighting to concentrate on my Dunwich painting. Time was getting short *'Yes but her eyes... they are enticing.'*

I glanced at her discreetly. Everything was so wrong about her. Nothing about her could spark my imagination. Too short in stature, her breasts too heavy, too much weight on her arms and, no doubt, her ankles too. What I could see of her hair from the tufts poking out from under her turban was bleached blonde something that I didn't find attractive.

The shop bell tinkled.

"Oh, another customer. If you need any more help, just call—hmm." The girl twisted a tuft of hair near her left ear, where a large hoop earring hung.

"Tommy," I said, straightening up.

"Tommy," she repeated my name, enunciating it carefully. The lines around her eyes crinkled as a broad smile lit up her face. It was then that I saw something special. The strength of her jawline and her high cheeks were very attractive. Something I could work with. As she hurried away, hips swinging, I focused on the Dunwich project and hastily selected another book.

I sat on a stool with a pile of the most interesting books resting on an empty shelf. After deciding which one gave me the best insight into what the medieval town looked like, I took them to the counter.

The young woman was busy pricing a pile of paperbacks. She tossed one or two that were either tatty or torn into a large wooden crate that stood to one side of the counter.

"Did you find what you were looking for?" she asked, laying her pen down.

"These look helpful." I placed them before her.

As she wrote the prices down on a piece of paper, she said, "Your accent sounds as though you come from that part of the world. Why didn't you just pop into the museum there and ask?"

"It isn't really a museum as such. Nothing as grand as the British Museum. It's more a shed in someone's garden. Anyway, I was staying in town over the weekend, so I popped into the library, thinking I might find want I needed there, but with luck, your shop has it all." I gestured to the books. "Now, I can get started on my next commission as soon as I get home."

She smiled and her face lit up in a way I had not expected. "I'm so glad I could help." She blushed as she pushed the books towards me.

"Thank you." I reached for them, allowing my fingers to brush the side of her hands.

She didn't pull her hands away but held my gaze and I recognised her neediness.

"I—was wondering." I reached into my jacket pocket for my wallet. "Are you free for a drink tonight?"

Her smile broadened and excitement filled her eyes. "Oh gosh. Are you asking me for a date?"

"If you're free." I pulled out the cash and paid for the books.

"Oh yes, I am. Wow, it's been a long time since someone asked me out."

"Has it?" I frowned.

"That makes me sound like such a loser, doesn't it?" She pulled a bag out from under the counter.

"Not at all. Obviously, no-one has noticed the real beauty

within you."

She blushed again, adding even more colour to her cheeks. "Do you need a bag," she stammered.

"Yes, that would be helpful."

"What… what time would you like to meet up?" She stumbled over her words as she dropped the books into the bags.

"Well." I didn't want her to have time to tell anyone else. "What time do you finish here?"

***

I couldn't believe my luck with number nine, especially with the recent discovery of Phoebe Browning's body. Jenny told me that the papers had reprinted details of the other seven missing girls, along with speculation over their disappearance. Stella from Starlight bookshop, however, seemed more than happy to climb into a car with a total stranger.

She chatted easily about herself as we drove towards Epping while glancing out of the window every now and again. She seemed to be unconcerned about where I was taking her. I turned into a busy Theydon Oak pub leafy car park at Coopersale.

Stella looked around excitedly. "I've always wanted to come here. I've heard it has quite a reputation. Some famous singers have been here," she said, as I drove to the quietest spot in among the trees.

"Have they?" I reached into my pocket.

"Haven't you ever been here before?" She grasped the door handle.

"Hang on a minute."

She turned towards me, her lips parted as though she was about to ask a question. I smiled and leaned towards her, placing my arm around her neck. She leant in to receive my kiss and closed her eyes. I rammed the syringe into her leg. Her eyes sprung open in surprise, as she tried to struggle and pushed hard against my chest. I pressed my lips firmly against hers as I held her tight to me.

When at last her body relaxed, I propped her upright and checked that she was completely subdued. I reached behind her seat and pulled out a set of harnesses to strap her in, before laying a blanket across her shoulders. Satisfied she looked natural and her breathing was steady, I slipped the car into gear and pulled out of the car park and headed home to begin work on my next angel.

***

On the evening of my launch, the Dunwich painting, *'The Final Hours'* covered the far end wall of the gallery. It caught the eye of everyone who entered. I was thrilled to discover it received the most comments and requests for purchase.

"Spectacular, James!" Basil raised his glass to it. "If only I had a hundred such paintings, I would be a wealthy, happy man."

"Has the evening exceeded your expectations?" I sounded, even to myself, like a needy child again trying to please the adult in the room.

"Far more, James. I'm ecstatic. The evening has brought more wealthy clients to our list. A few more exhibits like this and the art world won't know what's hit it. I for one will raise a glass to that and sleep well tonight."

***

I admired the completed ninth painting in my *Stone Angels* series and was happy with the result, although Stella Cavendish hadn't been an ideal model. My desperation had got the better of me. By encapsulating elements of her, the sadness in her eyes, the shape of her jawline, and the unsaid question on her lips in the central figure of the painting had worked well I thought. I had made my angel taller than in real life and she stared down on the rushing citizens and traffic far below.

It seemed unbelievable that seven years had passed since

Basil suggested I painted something urban and I was curious to see what his thoughts were about my interpretation of the word *urban.* I decided the time was right to risk showing him my true capability, believing it might even spur him in to finding a bigger venue for my solo show.

The opportunity came three weeks later when I received a phone call from Basil. I had been busy sorting out a canvas ready for my tenth angel. It was to be the largest one possible, as she was to be my statement piece—the ultimate angel, my morning star. I had just finished stretching the canvas, ready to prime it when the phone rang.

"Ah James. So glad you're home. Not busy are you?"

"As always, old boy. But I've time for you."

"So glad. I've been meaning to call you about your next project. I'm in the area and was wondering if I could pop in."

"By all means. Feel free."

"I'm just finishing a wonderful pub lunch. Half an hour, if that's okay?"

"That's fine. See you soon." The receiver buzzed in my hand. *Just had a wonderful pub lunch.* So Nancy lived locally to me and was possibly one of his wealthy clients. "You old dog, Basil." I put the receiver down.

I decided not to show him all the paintings at once and set the first angel on an easel facing the drawing-room door. I wanted to catch Basil's initial reaction on entering the room.

While I waited for his arrival, I experimented by sitting in a different place around the room. Once I had found the best angle to view his expression, I readjusted the furniture slightly so I could sit comfortably. I poured a drink, too anxious to think about food and sat back in father's chair. As the drink settled my nerves and warmed my gut the weight of the glass in my hand became the brush that made the first stroke on the naked canvas seven years ago. I relieved every emotion and was satisfied that the first angel still conveyed all I wanted it to say.

I sipped my drink and surveyed the room and then got up to close the curtains to soften the light in the room. It made the corner where the painting stood seem too dark. Next I switched on the lights, but they caused a glare on the painting. I reopened the curtains and switched the lights off before settling once more into father's chair and tried to imagine what Basil's thoughts might be on seeing the painting.

Would he take in the fine brushstrokes that held the light and darkness together? The way one foreshadowed the other to give life to the picture. Would he appreciate the strength in the form of the figure? The way it towered over the cityscape, reflecting its sense of isolation?

The figure's appearance seemed to be statuesque as though carved in stone. Its pallid skin looked stretched, adding to the hollowness of her eyes and cheeks that gave depth to her jawline and the lines around her mouth. The gown wrapped around her legs gave her a classical Grecian look, as it held her up, trapping her into position on the edge of the roof.

I had finally finished the ninth painting six months ago and in that time, Basil's interest in me had grown. Oddly enough, his pilfering had stopped, too, but that might have been because he no longer made unscheduled trips to the States. Maybe Basil didn't want to risk losing the new woman in his life.

One thing was for sure—his business had suffered because of the police harassment as he called it. Not that any of this mattered to me I was just glad to have him focusing on my work after all these years.

The doorbell rung twice before I got up to answer the door.

"James, I hope you don't mind, but I—"

"Basil, come through, and have a drink, old boy," I said over my shoulder, as I took my place beside the drinks cabinet, with a glass in each hand, waiting for him to enter.

"That's good of you. I could do with— Oh my God!" He crossed to the alcove. "When… How… Dear God, James, why haven't you shown me this before!"

He drank in the first angel and satisfaction washed over me. All my efforts to wear him down began to reap the rewards I had hoped for, but there was no pleasure in the loss of mother's paintings.

Two days later I received a phone call from Jenny requesting that I join Basil at his office to discuss plans for a major exhibition.

***

Leaving Halghetree Rectory early, I raced along the A12 to avoid the build-up of traffic trying to get into London. Bored with my own company, I switched on the radio. After humming along with the latest number one, the music faded as the DJ handed over to the news station.

"We've received the latest update on the disappearance of the owner of Starlight bookshops last seen six months ago."

I leant over to retune the radio onto another station as I didn't want to hear an update when a flash of blue appeared in my wing mirror. I grabbed the steering wheel with both hands and slammed on my brakes fighting to keep the car under control, while cursing the driver's parentage as he shot across in front of me.

On the radio the newscaster announced that the police had confirmed the body found encased in concrete was that of Phoebe Browning, one of the missing eight. He continued.

'Our reporter has briefly spoken to her family. Understandably they are deeply shocked over the circumstances of their daughter's death. The Brownings stated that just knowing they are able to lay their daughter to rest in their local church gives them comfort. They hope that some good will come out of their loss, believing her discovery will help track down the killer and reunite the other seven missing women with their loved ones too.'

I switched off the radio. The road ahead into London was congested and for once, I was glad as it gave me time to think.

Chapter Twenty-Eight

Exhibition
Stone Angels by Ravencroft
1972

"Oh my dear God, James, you must paint more of these. She's amazing! I want the world to see this as soon as possible. Please tell me you have more of these stashed away?" Basil's reaction to my painting late last year was more than I could've wished for, but his enthusiasm waned for the title *'Roofscapes.'* It worried me that he might not fully understand my concept, or even what I wanted the paintings to represent.

"I think *'Stone Angel'* has a better ring to it than *'Roofscapes'*. I mean the painting isn't focused on the roofs, is it James?" He looked over his shoulder at me. "Don't you think so?"

I shook my head, thrown by the abruptness of his question. "They are trapped between worlds, above us, but not in heaven." I tried to explain. "I've been busy sketching an idea for another one."

His brows lifted.

I paused. Conscious of his excitement feeding into my own, I fought not to say more but a flick of his wrist stopped me.

"You're an artist, so I understand your point of view, but from my point of view it's all about the selling." He leaned into the painting, scanning every part of it with a critical eye.

"She's a stunner. How long do you reckon you'll need to complete enough for an exhibition?"

I had tried to add up how long it had taken me to paint them, still regretting the fact I had not found my number ten.

"I'm sorry," Basil stammered as he straightened a concerned look on his drawn face. "That's thoughtless of me. You can't just chuck paint at a canvas, so forget it, I can wait." He drained his glass. "Take as long as you need to create more masterpieces. If I may make a suggestion… say in about twelve months from now."

I reached for my glass.

"That's not written in stone. I just need some sort of timeline to work with so I can start making advanced bookings for the best possible venues as soon as I can."

"A major exhibition?" My hands trembled as the needy child raised its head again.

"Yes, dear boy, of course. Our beauty needs the finest audience we can find to appreciate her true value. She's outstanding." He crossed to the drinks cabinet and poured himself a drink without asking. After taking a couple of swallows, he continued. "I might be wrong in saying this, James, but you can't even compare your work to your mother's—"

"What! Do you mean it?" I interrupted him. My legs went beneath me, and I dropped into my father's chair.

"Your brushwork is far superior."

"Basil—what are you saying? I… don't know how to… You've never… said, or encouraged… me…" My words tumbled over themselves.

He smiled and poured himself another drink. "Don't say you've misunderstood me all these years. Okay, so I could've pushed you as hard as I did Easter, but I didn't like to. Believe me when I tell you I've always known you had it in you. I just had to let it come out naturally."

My mouth opened to protest but he raised his hand to silence me.

"You need to understand, I never wanted to see you destroyed in the same way as your mother. You do see that, don't you?"

Basil brought the bottle with him and came and sat on the

sofa in front of me.

I put my head in my hands. What had I done? I glanced towards my painting. Candela wept tears of blood for me in her silent beauty.

"James, are you all right? You've gone very pale."

"I'm fine. Just need some air." I crossed to the French windows and threw them open. "Just a little overwhelmed, I guess."

After a light shower of rain, everything in the garden glistened. The grave marker, the stone angel seemed overshadowed by a lingering dark cloud as the sun broke free.

Basil invaded my thoughts. "Right, let's not dwell on the past. You get as many paintings done as you can over the next twelve months. All up to this high standard please. Then, give me a call as soon as you're ready. I'll sort out everything at my end."

He headed towards the front door and I followed. On reaching it, he said, "If you need any money for paints, canvases, brushes, or food, please let me know. Can't have you starving for your art, can we?"

I laughed. "The only thing I need is time, and you can't buy that."

A smile played on his lips but there was no humour in his eyes. "No, you can't. But you can serve time. This business with the missing girls might have me serving time, and that will ruin the both of us."

After waving Basil off, I returned to the drawing room and lifted a glass to Candela. Without my angels there would be no paintings, without Basil no exhibition. In twelve months my journey's end would be in sight and my career would truly begin. But now I needed to fill my time. I could've begun working on my tenth angel painting for the exhibition, but that meant I needed a muse. Of course, for that I needed to go hunting and that was far too risky just now.

So I set to work making sure everything was ready, from paints, brushes and other materials. With a mop and a bucket of hot water, I washed the floor and every corner before climbing a ladder to wash down the walls with detergent. Next was the guest bedroom. I stripped the cot bed and washed the bedding. I washed the floor and walls leaving no trace of my past guests. By the time it was finished, the room smelt of pine, and the cot bed was made up with clean sheets and blankets.

Over the next few months I worked my way through the rest of the house. Every room was cleaned to Mrs P's high standard, from soft furnishings to dusting high shelves. I felt exhausted, but strangely exhilarated, and I knew that Mrs P would be proud to see everything shining.

I was tempted to phone Jenny to ask whether the police had contacted Basil, but as soon as she heard my voice on the phone, she put me straight through to her boss. In the end, I decided, maybe it was a blessing. Even though Basil was enthusiastic about my work, I knew not to trust him. The draw of instant fame for him from the discovery of mother's vast collection of work would be too much. I decided to use my time to record her paintings and drawings.

I made a pot of tea and took some biscuits with me up to mother's studio. Starting with her large desk, and in the order in which she had stored her work, I begun to record everything. Through the camera lens, the hidden meaning within the detailed sketches to some of her larger pieces of works slowly revealed themselves to me. Page by page, sheet by sheet her life slowly unravelled itself as her work became darker and more disturbing.

Most sketches showed a figure of a naked woman with long black hair. She stood in some pictures with her back to the viewer, whereas in others she crouched. Sometimes she was alone, but in others she was a ghostly figure hovering somewhere in the background. A tale of an abandoned woman losing her grip on sanity.

As I went to close the last drawer, it stopped short. I tried kicking it, but still it wouldn't budge. After checking that none of the sketchpads had blocked it and were all lying flat, I pulled the drawer out again. On my knees I peered into the drawer space. Wedged at the back was a screwed-up piece of paper. I used the handle of mother's longest paintbrush and managed to dislodge it.

I laid the crumbled paper on the desk and with the side of my hand, I flattened it out. The letter wasn't one of love, but an end of an affair.

My darling Jane,

Dear girl, please, I must end this foolishness. You need to understand there's no 'us'. There never was, nor can there ever be! It was wrong and unforgivable on my part. I should never have allowed it to happen. I take the full blame. You are as always sweet and charming, but from now, our relationship is purely a business one.

I have been nothing but honest with you, Jane. I love my wife dearly and my family mean the world to me. You have your husband and a baby on the way, so please think of them.

I'm returning home soon, so this will be my last contact with you and about the matter in hand. I must reiterate that our relationship has never been anything other than a business one.

Yours,

CS

After reading through it twice I realised mother had betrayed father. The letter, undated gave no clues to when or how mother had received it. No return address anywhere, just the initials CS.

I folded the letter in half, returning it to the drawer. Just as I was about to shut it, I pulled out the letter again and re-read the linc, '*You have your husband and a baby on the way now, so please think of them'*. Had the affair ended because of me? Was I the cause of her depression? Had her lover meant more to her than father and me?

I tore the letter to pieces and dropped them into the drawer before slamming it shut. I crossed to the drying rack and pulled out a couple of the larger pictures and laid them on her desk.

Both paintings showed a figure of a woman standing

alone. In one, she stood with a cloth cascading in folds from one shoulder to the floor, covering her breasts and waist. Her thick, curly hair crowned her head halo-like giving the painting a religious feel. In the larger of the two pictures, the viewer looked down on her from above. It showed her suspended in the air, nailed to a cross and crucified, her arms outstretched, head lowered.

Too many thoughts crowded my head as I returned the paintings to their rack. I gathered up the rolls of films and headed to the garage. As I drove to the chemist to develop the films, I thought about father and how hard it must have been on him. Had he forgiven her for her indiscretion?

After wasting six months pottering around the house, doing nothing but sleeping, cleaning and sketching ideas for my tenth angel, I needed something more to focus on.

"Hi, Jen. Is Basil available?"

"Yes, of course. I'll put you through."

"Hello, James. I hope everything is okay."

"Are nine paintings enough for the exhibition, Basil?"

"Nine! That's brilliant work, James!" he shouted down the phone. "I'm free tomorrow afternoon. I have a client to see in the morning. May I swing by, and take a look, if that's okay with you."

"Yes, of course."

In my eagerness to be ready for Basil's arrival, I brought all nine pictures down to the drawing room. I stood in the doorway trying to decide how to display them to make the best impression. Once I was certain I had them set up right, I went up to my rooftop studio to watch for Basil's car twist its way down the lane. On opening the door, Basil burst into the hall.

"What a morning, James!" Basil's voice was edged with relief. "It's been unbelievable. I thought I would never get here." He headed straight for the drawing room before I had a chance to invite him in.

I followed close on his heels and found him pivoting on the balls of his feet, taking in my collection of angels in one sweep of the room.

"Oh Lord, they are so beautiful. So dark, James! I've never seen anything like these before."

I broke open a new bottle and selected two lead crystal glasses, freshly polished and poured us both a drink. Basil was so in awe of the paintings. He didn't even seem to notice when I pushed the glass into his hand. After taking a couple of sips, he removed the paintings from the sofa and stood them against the legs of the easels before sitting. He reclaimed his drink and leant towards me.

"The way I see it, James," he enthused. "If Kasmin Gallery can launch David Hockney to stardom then it can do the same for you. I reckon we can put together an exhibition within three months. I've been putting feelers out and the feedback I've been receiving is all-good. Your work will be the talk of the town. I just need to hear back from Kas first."

"How long will that take?"

"Don't be too impatient. May I take them with me?" He gestured to the angels. My expression must have spoken volumes because he added, "I'll take good care of them. They will be under lock and key until the exhibition, James."

The tingling started in my legs as my stomach churned. Echoes of mother's fears flooded me as I watched Basil carefully wrap each of the nine paintings in some old blankets I had found in the coat cupboard. I gave him the cushions stored there, too.

"Use these for added protection." I passed them one at a time until he had enough.

"These are great. Thank you." He edged the boot with them. "I'm a lot happier to know the paintings are well padded. You never know when an idiot is going to pull out in front of you." Basil laid the paintings on top of each other with a thin board between them. Once packed, he closed the lid. "I'll bring the cushions back next time I'm over."

With more days to waste while waiting to hear back from Basil boredom drove me to seek solace in my studio. But I found it hard to stay focused. After hours of working and reworking an idea, hunger drove me to raid the kitchen cupboards. I had just put together a cheese and tomato sandwich when the phone rang.

"Oh James, I've been trying to get hold of you all day!"

"Sorry, Jenny. I locked myself in my studio to stay focused."

"I guessed that's what you would do. Anyway, I've something to tell you that will make all your hard work worth it. Forgive me for letting the cat out of the bag, but Mr Hallward has only gone and done it!"

"Given you a pay rise!" I laughed. "Great news, Jenny. Do we hit the town to celebrate?"

"Would you, if I asked?"

I detected an air of caution in her voice. I never wanted Jenny to feel I had betrayed her trust. "I would be more than happy to celebrate your good news."

"Thank you. James. I haven't just got you out of bed?"

"No. I was just fixing a bite to eat before bed. Basil hasn't got you working late again, has he?"

"Of course, but it's okay. I need the money. I'm helping my parents to buy a smaller house somewhere nice in the country."

"What about where they live now?"

"They're converting it into flats for my brother and me. The extra money comes in handy. But the reason I called—" She paused.

"Jenny—"

"I shouldn't be telling you, but I'm just so excited, James."

"What is it?"

"Promise you'll act all surprised or whatever it is you do when you hear good news. I've just overheard Basil on the phone."

"Jen…" I bit into my sandwich as the sound of a door shutting echoed down the receiver moments before Jenny came back on the line.

"Basil has done it. He got you the top venue for your major exhibition."

"That's brilliant news."

“He’s really going to town. A sample of the poster has already arrived. He’s calling it, ‘*Stone Angels*’. I was under the impression they were called ‘Roofthingys’ or something like that. Urban-scapes. Anyway, he’s almost bouncing off the walls with excitement.”

“The word you were looking for was ‘*Roofscapes*’, Jen.”

“Roofscapes, I love that! It’s a shame Mr Hallward has changed it. Are you okay with it?”

“Yes, of course. He wanted to change the title. Never mind, as long as the exhibition goes ahead, I’ll be happy. I’ve only done nine, but Basil feels that’s enough.”

“Very intriguing. What a shame you haven’t finished the whole series.”

“It’s just one of those things. I wanted ten to keep the balance.” I pulled the kitchen stool with my foot so I could sit and nibble my sandwich while Jenny chattered on.

“Is that what you were working on when I called?”

“Yes, just putting together a few ideas.”

“Maybe you can use it in the next one. Mr Hallward has been in negotiations with his American partner, Mr Sparks. It sounded as if he’s coming over to see your work for himself. Oh, James, I’m going before I say anything more. I’m just so pleased for you.”

“Thanks for letting me know.”

“I’ll make sure you have the best exhibition ever. I can’t wait to see the pictures. They sound fascinating.”

“So you’ll be organising it then?”

“Yes, as always. Basil tells me who to invite, and roughly what he wants while I do all the legwork.” She chuckled. “He’s taking more of an interest, this time, so I won’t feel cheated when he takes all the credit if it goes well. If not, then it’ll be down to me as usual, I guess.”

“Just like Basil. Have you met Mr Sparks before?”

“No, not really. He did make a flying visit to Easter’s first exhibition, if you remember, but remained upstairs talking business with the gallery owner. I’ve only spoken to him on the phone. Well, I say spoken, but only in the business sense, not chatty like us. He sounds nice. You know, polite and caring. Gosh, is that the time? I'd better go, otherwise, my parents will worry that something has happened to me. My father gets nervous since those girls vanished."

"Jen, I don't think you have anything to worry about."

"Why, because they're all beautiful white girls?"

"What are you implying, Jen?"

She gave a humourless laugh. "I know you're stuck out in the middle of nowhere without a TV and newspapers. Well, I'll tell you. Like your paintings, our killer/kidnapper is up to number nine. My father, an avid reader, likes to keep abreast of things, especially local news. He's always telling me to be extra vigilant at night."

"So you should, Jenny. You're such a smart young lady. None of us would want anything to happen to you."

"Thank you." She sounded a little embarrassed but went on. "I'm sure Mr Hallward will call you soon, so remember to act all surprised, won't you."

"Of course. It's our little secret. Be careful and give my best wishes to your parents."

Chapter Twenty-Nine

Stone Angels
The Tenth Painting
1972

The gallery was just as I remembered it; bright, light, and airy. From the loft space, I gazed down on two young women who were busy hanging my paintings. Behind me, Basil chatted with the owner, John Kasmin.

We had arrived early in the morning. I followed Basil up the stairs to Kasmin's office. As I glanced over the rails, the two picture hangers were shifting the gallery's display panels into place ready for the next exhibition. The uniform they both wore was dove grey trouser suits and purple blouses. As I observed them, I recognised their individual personalities through their body language. Most people do not realise just how much a creative mind can learn about others from their gestures, posture, and mannerisms.

The fiery redhead was shorter and slightly heavier built than her colleague. Her bubbly personality floated up to me in her giggly voice as she chatted with her colleague. The one that intrigued me the most carried her height and slenderness with ease. She seemed calculating and far quieter than the redhead.

I had lost interest in what Basil and John were saying as all my attention was on her. She squatted before one of the paintings like a worshipper in the presence of a deity, as it stood propped up against the wall. With ease, she rose up and stepped back, her head tilting from one side to the other, before hastily scribbling something down.

Curiosity demanded that I rush down and snatch the clipboard from her to read what she had written, but I held back. I knew I was being oversensitive, and that girl was just doing her job.

Back in the 60s, Candela had explained what being a picture hanger entailed. Most galleries liked to have a theme when putting an exhibition together, though sometimes the title might seem unconnected to the paintings themselves.

"There's an exact science to showing off art," Candela said. "It's so much more than simply placing a picture on a hook. It's all about the importance of getting the lighting right for each piece, to allow the viewer to see each one at its best, and to give it the chance to secure a sale."

The picture hanger I was watching was precise in her movements, as though she never wasted her energy on anything. I understood what she wanted, maybe needed. She was trying to get up close and personal with me the artist, to interpret and clarify the significance of each of the paintings. Then she disappeared from view, leaving the paintings abandoned.

On seeing my angels neglected in such a careless manner, I gripped the rail as the tingling raced up my legs. I leant over the rail to see where she had gone. After a couple of minutes, I heard voices and she reappeared with her colleague carrying another painting. After setting it down, her colleague left again. The dark-haired girl went to a bag that was hanging on the back of a chair, and pulled out a sheet of paper. She unfolded it and held it up to my paintings one at a time. After a few minutes she returned it to her bag.

"James."

Startled, I turned to find Basil standing behind me.

"John and I need to sign some paperwork. I won't be long and then we can go for something to eat."

"Oh okay. Is there anything I need to sign?"

"No, no all's fine. Why don't you go down and join Tina and Jude?"

"Tina and Jude?"

"Yes, down there." He pointed. "You've been eyeing them

while I've been sorting out your next venue."

"My next venue? But— you don't know whether this one will be a success."

"Have more faith in your work. John is very impressed and wants to exhibit your work in his New York gallery, too."

"Wow. Thank you, Basil."

"Look, I won't be long. Go and chat to the girls. I'm sure they'll be excited to meet you. Check what they've done, too. Don't forget they'll value your input if you're not satisfied. After all, it's your exhibition." He gave me a reassuring pat on my shoulder. "If you want to change anything, just say so."

"I would be interested in their feedback. After all, they've seen many exhibitions." I headed towards the stairs.

On the gallery floor, a series of movable panels created a sort of maze as the picture hangers had divided the gallery space into a series of smaller enclosed spaces. Each one of these displayed a single painting. Stark white walls and ceiling along with a pine floor helped to reflect light onto the pictures. The maze-like route ensured that the viewer saw each individual painting as a single entity. The lights, fixed onto metal runners, crisscrossed the ceiling at various spots, allowing the picture hangers to move them into the best position to highlight the paintings.

I followed the maze. On seeing the first picture I was stunned. It hung in a pool of bright white light. Candela's wide blood-shot eyes glared down at me from behind streaked black make-up. Others viewing the grisaille-style painting would only see a stone-faced angel, not the bloodless, blue-lipped girl I saw.

She stood high above the rush of humanity, silhouetted against the dark roofscape. The streetlight illuminated her pallid features, adding an unearthly beauty to her stony face.

To my surprise, I found that the picture hangers seemed to have hung the paintings in the correct order, even though I hadn't dated them. As I rounded the next panel, I found the fiery redhead balancing precariously on a low stepladder, while clutching one end of my seventh painting. As she began to topple backwards, I rushed forward, snatching the end of the painting from her grasp leaving her to fall backwards onto the floor with a thud.

The other hanger held on grimly to her end. I lifted the picture into place. That's when I noticed the brilliance of her stunning green eyes.

Once I was certain my painting was secure, I left them to get on with their work. I saw my mistake in selecting Stella as my number nine. With all pictures in situ, her size was unimportant, but something was not quite right about her. It is easy for the uncreative to say that a model's size and shape has no bearing on an artist's work because they create a fantasy, but what they don't understand is the artist's need for inspiration.

Stella was an important element in my creation, a muse incarnate. Her individuality gave life to the essence of the figure on the canvas. I tried to recall what had attracted me to her in the first place, but couldn't. My earlier paintings still pleased me. I couldn't afford to allow my final masterpiece to let me down.

"James, is everything all right?" Basil appeared at my side.

"Yes." I needed to stay focused on savouring the rewards of my labour.

***

On the evening of my launch, my stress levels must have been on a par with mother's as I rocked gently back and forth on the balls of my feet, watching the guests beginning to arrive.

"You're okay, aren't you?" Basil enquired, snatching a couple of glasses of wine from the tray of a passing young waitress. She smiled at us, but Basil didn't notice her.

"I'm fine." I took the glass he offered. Once he seemed satisfied that I was okay, he turned and scanned the room. I wondered if he was as nervous as I felt.

I noticed the meet and greeters looked exceedingly uncomfortable dressed in short black tutu skirts, frilly white low-cut blouses, and long white socks. Their make-up gave them a clown-like look with pink cheeks, black kohl-lined eyes and red lips and nails. What the link was between my paintings and what the girls were wearing, I had no idea. It took me a moment to realise that they were the two picture hangers from this morning.

No longer dressed in their smart uniform, they struggled to keep a pleasant smile on their faces. Whenever a new guest arrived, the photographers insisted they had a photo taken with the girls. The word *hookers* floated across my mind. I wanted to ask Basil whose crazy idea it had been to force the two girls to dress in such a way.

"A little uptight, I'm guessing." Basil broke into my thoughts.

"I am." I sipped my drink, the girls forgotten.

"Relax and enjoy the evening, James. It's your time to shine," Basil said, downing his wine in one, before facing me. "You really need to chill out. At least look as though you're enjoying yourself. Start mingling. These punters are here to buy your fabulous work, so smile and just get selling." He took a sharp intake of breath before carrying on. "Even if it means you have to sell your soul, but get the punters to buy, buy, buy!"

"You make it sound so callous."

"You have a problem with that, James?" He grabbed another drink as the waitress passed with a fresh tray. "Good God, James. You sound like your mother."

"You never knew my mother."

"You're right there. But I understood her well enough to know what destroyed her in the end."

"And that was what?"

"High ideals." He gave a raucous laugh. "Art isn't about decorative things hanging on the wall. It's about what the collectors are willing to pay for unique pieces." He pointed a long finger at me. "Are you so naïve? It's all about making money. Just like you, I want to make a name for myself to become a major player in the international art world."

"So I'm just a stepping stone to you?" He might as well have slapped me across the face.

"Oh, do come on, James. It's mutual. And you aren't using me? We benefit each other. Easter didn't have a problem with selling his soul. Though I should've guessed, you'd have morals. Not using your mother's name where others would've gladly taken the straight route to stardom."

"And that makes me a bad person?"

"No, just stupid. Jane Elspeth Maedere was obsessive. That's what destroyed her in the end."

"That's what you think. An insatiable need to create things of beauty makes you stupid?" I scanned the clients, glass in hand trying to understand what my paintings were telling them, completely oblivious to the waitresses moving around them handing out drinks and nibbles.

"Not at all! You have to keep everything in perspective. Having some crazy notion that the masses have the right to be able to purchase your work is ludicrous. Your mother thought by keeping her prices down that Joe Public would rush to buy them, but it backfired."

"Really? Is that what happened?"

"Joe Public is just as greedy as everyone else." He chortled and took a gulp of his drink. "They bought them all right, but sold them on. As they say, money talks, so much for Mr & Mrs Public appreciating art for its own sake. Just like everyone else, they understand the value of money far better. The loss of control over was what your mother couldn't cope with. That's why you need us agents to market your work and get you the best deal. Without us, you're nothing. Go and introduce yourself to anyone who's showing a serious interest in your work, and sell both it and you."

Basil gestured to a tall, elegant woman who had just entered the gallery. Once he had caught her attention, she waved back to him. Without another word, he left me. I watched him as he made his way over to her. She introduced Basil to another man.

I wasn't on my own for long as Mrs Judy Norris moved

towards me with a tall, wiry woman in tow.

"Hello James. Let me introduce you to my friend, Mabel."

"Hello, Mabel." I offered her my hand.

Mabel gave a sharp nod but remained tight-lipped, not even taking my hand.

"What an amazing collection of paintings," Mrs Norris said. "I've never seen anything like it before. They seemed almost alive but carved in stone."

"The style is known as *Grisaille*. It imitates sculpture. I'm so glad you like them, Mrs Norris." I took a sip of wine. The wine was good, but I needed something stronger.

The growing chatter in the gallery almost drowned out Mrs Norris as she nattered on. I nodded, not really listening. I took in the atmosphere. Out of the corner of my eye, I noticed Mabel scrutinising me. I beamed at her and got no reaction back.

Eager to get away from Mrs Norris and her less charming friend, I said, "Well, it's been lovely seeing you again, Mrs Norris but I must—"

"Please James." She rested her hand on my arm. "Call me Judy."

"Right, Judy it is then. I hope you both enjoy the exhibition. It's been nice meeting you too Mabel."

"You don't have your mother's eyes, do you? Jane had amazing green eyes, whereas Donald's were brown—" Mabel said in a rush. "When I looked into Jane's eyes— they were empty, cold, and almost dead. It saddened me that Donald had so much love to give, but wasted it on her, after I had spent years desperately staring into his beautiful, but sad lonely eyes—"

I couldn't speak. I tried to process what Mabel was saying.

"Hush, Mabel," Mrs Norris said loudly, startling her friend into silence. "The lad doesn't need to know about an old woman's fantasy."

"I was just saying it's odd that his eyes should be so blue — that's all."

Judy smiled up at me, "We'll catch up with you later, James." She tugged at her friend's arm. As they walked away,

Mrs Norris chastised Mabel. "the boy doesn't need to know."

The words echoed in my head as I moved among the crowd. I tried to relax by milling with connoisseurs, smiling, and laughing while answering their questions. They raised their glasses and toasted my talent.

For some unknown reason I glanced up. Basil stood in the loft space from where I had been watching the picture hangers put together my exhibition. Basil was not alone. He stood next to a slender and older man who was dressed in a dark suit. Something in the man's demeanour reminded me of a Native American. His long jet-black hair showed signs of grey around the temples. As Basil raised his glass in my direction, it occurred to me that the man might be Basil's American partner, and Easter's agent, Chuck Sparks.

"Excuse me," a timid voice at my side said.

I turned to find Jude, the picture hanger, holding out a pen and a catalogue. "Please could you sign this for me, Mr Ravencroft?"

"I'd be delighted to. But wouldn't you rather buy a painting?" I asked with a wink.

"Gosh, I'd love to. But my wages wouldn't even buy the frame. Your paintings are amazing, so dark."

"You think so?"

"Oh yes, quite romantic in a dreamy sort of way. I love them," she said coyly.

"Right. It's Jude, isn't it?"

"Oh yes, I'm Jude."

I signed the catalogue and handed it back to her, just as her friend appeared in a doorway to one side of the display panels. "Jude! Please! I need your help," she said, brusquely.

I smiled at her, hoping to get a positive reaction, but something in her eyes told me to back off.

"Sorry," Jude said. "I must go. Thank you for signing this." She waved the catalogue at me.

"Your friend Tina seems upset?"

"Not so much upset, more stressed about this evening mainly."

"From the comments I've heard so far, the evening has been a success."

"Oh, thank you. I shall tell her." She flashed her eyelashes at me as she hobbled away, her high heels echoed off the wooden floor.

My impatience grew. The evening seemed to go on forever. I avoided drinking too much, knowing I needed a clear head. I made sure I did not stay talking long in the one place fearing I would miss seeing Tina leave. I engaged in mind-numbing chatter while discreetly following her around the gallery. Basil had tried to persuade me to leave my car at his gallery and travel into the city centre with him, but knowing I needed to find my number ten I had declined, giving myself one less hurdle to cross.

"James…"

"Oh, hi Jen. Sorry, I was miles away."

"Sorry." She raised her voice over the babble and leant in close, so close I could feel her breath on my cheek. "I've just been chatting with Basil. He's very pleased with how things are going, and so should you be, too. The evening is a roaring success. You won't believe the numbers of bids that are coming in. It's amazing!"

"What bids?" I was puzzled.

"Oh, didn't Basil explain? He decided to set a starting price, rather than just sell at a fixed price. It is down to the clientele to name what they are willing to pay over the top in a sealed bid. That way no one knows who's bid what."

"I see. The highest price gets it."

"Yes."

"And Basil takes his commission from that."

"Of course," Jenny said, as though I should've been aware that sort of thing happened.

I nodded in Tina's direction. "That couple look as though they are willing to buy three."

"You should be pleased. Isn't this what you've always wanted?"

Was it what I had always wanted? Suddenly it all became a little less important. Was I my mother's son the artist or my father's son chasing butterflies as my object of desire switched to Tina. What was the importance in the creation of art?

Elements of my final painting evolved in my mind. The slightest movement of Tina's head, the way she raised her slim, delicate hand towards the large canvas and gestured, flooded me with excitement. I wanted to be alone with her, in a room that smelt of paint, to feel the darkness envelop me as I lifted a paint-filled brush to mark the canvas for the first time.

Jenny's voice broke the spell. Something she was saying made my skin crawl. "Sorry, you were saying something I didn't quite hear."

"Yes, I have a friend who worked here in the 60s. Amazing stories she has told me about this place…" Jenny paused momentarily, her chain of thought interrupted as she looked curiously at the ninth painting. Something flickered across her face. She shook her head and gave a faint smile.

"Anyway, Mr. Hallward tells me that Mr Kasmin wants to move the exhibition to his other gallery before the clientele take ownership of their paintings."

"Yeah, he told me the same…"

Jenny stepped back to get a better view of the ninth painting. Her gaze was unwavering, causing her brow to knit. "Quite a moving subject James, the way you've caught such sadness in her eyes, such desolation. It makes you want to cry for her. These are such very powerful pieces. They kind of remind me of the missing girls."

"In what way?" I wanted to know more, but at the same time, I wanted Jenny to stop talking.

"Oh, their families' sadness. I guess that's your inspiration. I suppose after reading about their disappearances in the paper." Her eyes never left my face.

I nodded.

"My friend. Well, she's more my mother's friend. She has an amazing collection of photographs taken during her wild youth. She's such an interesting person. Anyway, I knew I had heard the name of Tommy Blackbird before, but just couldn't remember where. You know, he's that missing artist from 1963. It wasn't in the paper that the police were looking for him."

I said nothing, but continued to stare at Jenny's lips as though lip reading because of the noise.

"They have been to see Basil again."

"Have they?" I sipped another glass of wine.

"Something to do with new information, I believe."

"What information?"

"No idea. Nine go missing here, and they get new information from America. So I can't tell you what."

"Can't or won't?" Suddenly I'm in mother's dressing room with my hands around something soft, desperate to stop the voices.

"Can't," she said, with a hint of a smile. "I'm not privy to all Basil's secrets. Sorry."

Jenny's attention wandered back to the paintings. "You're an amazing artist, James. A little too dark for my taste though. Did it really take you six months to paint all nine paintings?"

There it was again. A coldness from my gut reached for my brain. The question threw me, especially coming from someone I thought I knew. I stuttered, "Are you… questioning… my ability, Jen?"

"It's just you had all the commissions to paint, too." With a sweep of her hand, she gestured to the paintings. "A lot of thought has gone into these works. They're so different from your 'Of Land and Seascapes' series. These are almost portraits in their execution. On the day we went to see Flossie to ask her to model for Basil, you spoke about needing a model too. It seemed strange to me at the time, that's all," Jenny said, with a smile, but this time there was no warmth. She glanced over her shoulder. "Oh dear, Mr Hallward needs me. Must get back to work."

As Jenny walked away, I knew my time was limited.

***

"Please don't hurt me," she said, her voice was barely a whisper, drowned out by the sound of the heavy traffic racing past us. I guided her to the alleyway. Her weight against my arm made it difficult for me to keep her upright. She kept slipping from my grip, her legs refusing to respond to her commands.

Once clear of the main road, I picked her up and carried her back to my car.

"You're my number ten," I told her, aware she could no longer hear me. I lowered her into the boot. It was a risk taking her so soon after my first exhibition, but there was no other choice. I saw the coldness in her eyes and nothing else mattered.

Waiting in the shadows for her was so beautiful. The air buzzed with pure tension. Basil had shouted his goodbyes to his clients as they went their separate ways after the exhibition. Tina had followed soon after. I had made sure a large number of people had seen me leave.

The endgame was insight as I lowered Tina into the boot and tucked the cushions around her. I brushed her hair away from her face, and checked her breathing, before lowering the boot lid with a satisfying click

Once out in the flow of traffic leaving London, I felt the tension gone and my mind clear. All nine of my angels had left me and now I was returning to an empty studio. I glanced in my rear-view mirror and moved over into the fast lane. I hoped Tina Whiteoaks was strong enough like each of my other angels. Their hearts had beaten right up until the last brushstroke had completed their image.

Rain and wind raced after us on the A12. By the time we arrived back at the rectory, it was too late to start work. I carried the sleeping Tina to the lift and took her straight to my guest bedroom. Once she was comfortable, I switched off the light, knowing the drug I had given her would help her to sleep until morning.

I crawled into mother's bed, dog-tired, but unable to sleep. Outside the wind grew in strength. It battered against the windows and moaned and groaned its way around the dead oak trees. On gathering its forces, it raced around the chimneypots. Sleep wasn't going to come easily to me. I shifted uncomfortably in bed my mind not settling. I needed to be fresh in the morning if I was going to create my *piece de resistance.*

Moments later, an almighty crash of thunder rolled across the sky, startling me out of my sleep as the house shook.

I woke feeling as cold and grey as the early morning. By the time I arrived in my studio ready to start work my spirit still had not lifted. I opened the French windows and stepped out onto the roof. A chilling sight greeted me. The three dead trees that had inspired mother lay smashed and broken, felled by the overnight storm. I was glad she had not witnessed it. To her it would've been the ultimate sign to self-destruction. For me, it was the end of an era.

Once my last angel was in place, I selected the right brush, picked up the palette, and closed my eyes. I drew in a deep breath; the smell of the paints and linseed oil began their magic. Mother stepped out of the shadows; her eyes bright with rage. I opened my eyes and selected the first colour. The brush caressed the paint before I lifted it to the canvas, and Tina and I became one.

Chapter Thirty

1972

I pulled the collar of my denim jacket up against the cold as I stood leaning against the parapet. I was glad to be out in the fresh, crisp air after days of working long hours on the final painting. The shotgun-grey sky reflected my grief as I surveyed the garden below. The light falling snow was trying its best to cover the damage caused by the storm ten days ago. The skeletons of the old oak trees had suffered.

All that remained were their splintered trunks which marked their place beside the river. Some of their shattered branches lay scattered across the lawn. The swirling, rushing of the black waters from the river when it broke its banks had swept the rest away. What broke my heart the most was to discover the shattered remains of the old statue laying among the broken gravestones. St Mary had finally toppled from her plinth.

My latest creation rested on the easel. Its paint was still tacky, but I was pleased with the result. The last of ten was suspended above the inattentive city, floating crucified for all to see. Her head rested on her chest as she struggled to support the weight of her body. Nails held her hands outstretched. Her feet rested on a small block of wood as she bent her knees in an effort to lift her body up to free herself from the agony of her aching arms and damaged hands. Her face lined with anguish that radiated from her clenched mouth. Blood from her crown of thorns ran, along with tears, down her cheeks.

The multi-coloured lights marked the beginning of the

twelve days of Christmas shone from the rain-soaked streets below. While a frenzy of people hurried to complete their shopping before the big day oblivious to the crucifixion above their heads.

The incessant ringing of the phone had disturbed my tranquillity, but I had not answered it during my marathon painting session. I had already dismissed Old Bill after receiving an unexpected visit from him.

I found him wrapped against the cold in a mud-spattered army trench coat, wellington boots, a grey woollen hat pulled tight over his domed head, and with a scarf around his neck. He was pushing a wheelbarrow around the garden gathering up debris a day after the storm.

"What are you doing here?" I confronted him as he came towards me.

"Ah, Mr Ravencroft. T'was a bad storm last night."

"Please just go and enjoy your Christmas holiday, Bill." I held my temper.

"Thee can't just leave it like this." He gestured to the shattered branches, fallen trees, uprooted shrubs, and broken trellising.

"Yes, you can. I'm asking you to. Please just go!"

"Look, Mr Ravencroft. Ah sorry if ah've disturb thee. Ah can've the job done in no time at all, then Ah shall be gone." He gathered up more broken branches and dropped them into the barrow.

"No! I don't need you anymore." I snatched the wheelbarrow from his grasp. "Please go! And forget about coming back."

His jaw dropped as he gasped. He shook his head, unsure about what had just happened. Without another word, he turned on his heels and walked away. As I watched him go, shoulders hunched against the cold, I knew I had done the wrong thing. Lack of sleep and good food had taken its toll. For ten days, I had wanted nothing more than to finish the painting.

Tina had amazed me with her endurance, but then again, I

shouldn't have been surprised. My fourth angel had been equally resilient. By the time I had completed the painting and lowered her to the floor, I thought she had left me, but to my astonishment, I found she had a pulse.

I returned her to the cot bed and pushed it through to the antechamber. I made her as comfortable as possible. As I swept her hair away from her eyes, my fingertips brushed her skin. There was no warmth, just clammy to the touch. I pressed a moistened cloth to her cracked lips allowing some water to wet her mouth, but she showed no signs of being aware of me as her eyes remained shut.

I turned her onto her side and covered her in a thick blanket though the room was warm. I placed a plastic beaker of water at her bedside within her reach, should she regain consciousness before I could check on her again.

***

Once I had had a shower and had a bite to eat, I headed to mother's studio to hunt among her rack of unused canvases, hoping to find a good-sized one to inspire me.

After finding most of the canvases were either too small or slightly damaged, I pulled on the last one in the rack, but it would not budge. I grasped the canvas by its top and bent forward, looking down between the gaps to see what held it in place.

Something brown and off-white held the canvas-frame in the rack. Using the handle of a paintbrush, I forced the brown object down as I pulled the canvas towards me. It sprung free. I reached in and plucked the crushed thing out. It was a tiny leather-bound notebook. The double-sided book had an address section on one side and a journal on the other. I flicked through the addresses, noting most were in America, though a few were galleries in London. I turned it over and read the notes. In the silence of her studio, mother's voice echoed in my mind as I read the tiny, well-formed, neat writing. The date the journal began was only five months after my parents had married.

October 1936, 'I'm so excited. After receiving a telephone call late last night, today I'm travelling to London to meet Chuck. It has been such a long time since I last saw him, my darling American agent. To look into his blue, blue eyes again will feel like gazing into heaven and seeing only diamonds.'

The name threw me for a moment. Then I realised, Basil once told me that Chuck Sparks was Mother's American agent. He also implied that their relationship had been a brief business one when she had been exhibiting abroad

I read the journal again, making sure I fully understood. According to Mother, their encounter in London had been much more than just talking about her next exhibition. I slumped against her desk allowing the details of both the letter, I had found earlier and the journal entry, to sink in.

The phone rang. I reached for it without thinking, and said, "Hello?"

"Oh, hello. Is that James Ravencroft?" asked an American voice.

"Speaking."

"Hello, I'm Tom Quinn."

"Yes, what can I do for you, Mr Quinn?"

"I'm hoping you'll be willing to deal with me, rather than going through Hallward and Sparks Ltd."

"Sorry, who are you?"

"Quinn, I'm a fine art dealer in New York. It's a lot better when you miss out the middleman, do you not think, Mr Ravencroft?"

"Sorry, were you at my exhibition the other day?"

"No sir. I think we have crossed lines. You see, I've been led to believe you have a fine collection of Jane Elspeth Maedere for sale."

I slammed the phone down and tore it from the wall. After all, mother had suffered, and still Basil and her agent were out to make money from her. I pulled out *'The Lost Moment'* painting, and for the first time, I understood what she had wanted.

It wasn't just about her art being rejected that pushed her over the precipice. All she had ever wanted was a simple family life, with her husband and child, but the pressure of fame had robbed her, stealing her love from me too.

I yanked open the desk drawers and began to toss everything out. Then I crossed to the balcony and threw her sketchpads, drawings, and paintings over. They drifted down adding weight to the flurry of the falling snow. Once everything created by her was in the garden, I hurried downstairs.

I dashed along the path to the back of Bill's potting shed to fetch a wheelbarrow and a straw bale. I began to fill the wheelbarrow with mother's artwork and carted it to the centre of the lawn where I had placed the bale. Using the bale as the heart of the bonfire, I added paper and the debris from the storm.

As daylight faded and the temperature dropped, I slipped on father's old trench coat.

The rectory seemed to reflect what I was about to do. A blaze of burning lights in the house marked my desperation to hunt out every remaining piece of mother's work. Even my studio lights shone into the night sky like a lighthouse guiding ships safely home.

I took a match from its box and struck it. As it burst into life, I thought I saw a shadow move across mother's balcony window. With a flick of my wrist, I tossed the match onto the white-spirit soaked straw.

Nothing happened.

Then, with a whoosh the bonfire ignited. The flames grew steadily. Like hungry tongues they licked at the sheaves of papers until finally taking hold and reducing them to ash. As wisps of ash-filled smoke rose into the night sky mixing with the snow flurry, I added the paintings. At first I removed them from their frames, but as the heat grew, everything burnt more easily so I tossed on the lot. The racing flames heated the paint, making it bubble up and add fuel to the fire. As the paintings blistered and melted, I imagined hearing Basil's outrage and disgust. "Your mother wouldn't have wanted this!"

How wrong was he! I was doing the right thing.

November 1936. Agents are liars and cheats only interested in making money and a name for themselves. I wish I hadn't made that trip to London to see Chuck. How could I have believed in him over Donald?

My darling Donald is too kind, too gentle and far too trusting of me. I betrayed him, his love, and belief in me. All I've wanted, I've lost.

Donald said 'God can see within the hearts and souls of all men and know the truth, which resides there.' This means Donald's God knows what I have done. Donald says he forgives, but I cannot have a clear conscious, knowing that the God Donald loves so much, will always judge me.

***

Too lost in what I was doing, I didn't hear the faint sound of sirens. By the time I heard the sound of squealing tyres above the sounds of crackling wood and splintering glass, I thought some concerned neighbour a field over must have reported seeing a fire at the rectory.

I tossed the last few paintings onto the hungry fire, satisfied that the fire brigade had a wasted journey.

A shout echoed through the smoky haze as a figure came running towards me, arms flailing as their feet slipped on the icy grass. On catching their balance, they seemed to realise they could make better progress by moving slowly. Once the figure came within shouting distance, I recognised the voice.

"What the fuck are you doing? Christ! No. Don't!" Basil screamed and rushed round to where I stood.

He was too late.

I released my grip on the last painting and stepped back. The canvas twisted and buckled under the white heat. *'Eve was as perfect as the apple until her destruction,'* melted as the greedy flames incinerated her and her worm in seconds.

"Jesus Christ, man! Why? Why the fuck? Why?" Basil

sobbed as he scooped up a handful of snow and tossing it onto the flames. It hissed but the fire carried on burning.

I strolled towards the house leaving Basil to his futile task. Halfway across the lawn, I halted. The garden seemed to erupt with running men. A man stood by the kitchen door yelling his orders.

I recognised the voice. Not the fire brigade after all, but my good friends P.C. Plod and Co. The men divided into two groups. Four of them carrying torches headed in the direction of the outbuildings while the rest entered the house. As I entered the kitchen, I came face to face with Heythorp, and another bobby I had not seen before. Heythorp seemed just as surprised at seeing me as I did him.

Dishevelled and unshaven, a muscle below Heythorp's right eye twitched nervously. His mouth tightened before he spoke. "Where is she, Ravencroft?"

"Ah, Heythorp. How lovely to see you." I slipped off father's coat and hung it in the coat cupboard. "You've certainly brought a party with you this time. But you've entered my house without consent."

"Forget about the niceties, Ravencroft." Heythorp jabbed a finger in my direction. "This time we have a warrant, so we're well within the law to search your house. But you're within your rights to watch us and make certain everything is above board. Now answer my question. Where is she?"

"Who?"

Above our heads a door banged, followed by heavy footfalls on the stairs. I met Heythorp's hard stare. "It sounds as though you've started without me."

"Where's Tina Whiteoaks?" He demanded his voice even, but his face was taut with rage as his nostrils flared.

"Who…?"

"Don't play dumb, James. You know who!"

At the sound of Basil's voice, I spun around.

Basil was unrecognisable. Smoke-blackened and flush faced, he stood ungroomed and unshaven. The knees on his creased suit were wet and stained. With bulging eyes, he yelled, "you bastard James! All these fucking years, and it was you all along."

"Yes, it was me. Someone had to inform the police about your thieving. What was so difficult about the word NO?"

"What the hell are you talking about Ravencroft? You little shit! You set me up for murder. All these years I've had that hanging over my head. I could kill you right now!" He rushed towards me, fists flailing.

Heythorp stepped in front. "Mr Hallward, we don't have time for your gripes."

"Do you know what this little sod's done? He's burnt all her paintings."

"I don't give a fuck, Hallward! It's the girl that concerns me. Not fucking paintings! Where is she, Ravencroft?"

"What girl?"

Heythorp grabbed the collar of my jacket, slamming me against the cupboards. "Right you little shit, stop playing games! We know she's here somewhere, so either tell us where, or we tear the place apart."

I shoved his hands away. "Back off!" I straightened my jacket. "I'll get you for assault!"

"Really, Ravencroft." Heythorp snarled as he leant in, squaring up to me. "I think you've just confessed to murder. I have witnesses too, right?"

"That's what I heard, Sarge," said a fresh-faced bobby.

"What murder? I've no idea what you're talking about!"

"You think I'm some dull-wit, don't you, you little jumped up shit?" Heythorp's lips narrowed to black lines.

"I haven't seen a warrant yet. I thought you were here because of that thieving bastard!" I pointed at Basil.

Heythorp shook his head. "No, we fucking ain't. We're here for the girl! So where is she?"

"I've no idea who you're talking about."

"You know full well, James." Basil snarled. "We saw you follow her up the road after your exhibition. My American friend and I drove past you."

Heythorp turned on Basil. "Will you shut up, sir, and allow us to do our job? You've no rights to be here."

"And you believe him, the thieving bastard?" I said.

"As you're not going to answer my question, sir. I shall take matters into my own hands." Heythorp stepped back from me, his face rigid. "George—" He addressed the fresh-faced bobby.

Wicklow appeared in the doorway to the hall. "Sarge—!" On seeing me, he said, "Well, there you are, Mr Ravencroft. You've finally surfaced then. We thought you might miss all our fun when you didn't answer the front door."

"Any luck, Hayden?" Heythorp asked.

"I need a word, Sarge." Wicklow kept his eyes on me.

"Did you check the cellar?"

"Yes, Sarge. It's all clear. But get this. The fucking roof is lit up like a Christmas tree. I told you, Sarge, there's another room up there. The lads and I are sure we've just heard banging coming from the attic."

Heythorp's face was a mask of control as he addressed the room. "Right lads. This is it! Time to take the place apart, Wicklow—"

"Yes, Sarge?"

"I've told you I don't know,"

"Really, Ravencroft. Just spill the beans. Sarge and I know this house is full of little hidey-holes, so show us the one upstairs." He grabbed my arm and hauled me out of the kitchen.

I kicked out, but Heythorp grabbed my other arm.

"I'm glad you're being cooperative, Mr Ravencroft." Heythorp turned to Basil. "You! Stay here!"

"But—"

"George, don't let him out of your sight. Do you understand?"

The bobby nodded.

"Oh, and when Andy and the other lads have finished searching the outbuildings, get them to guard the exits. Take Mr Hallward through to the kitchen. If he needs a slash, take him into the garden. But whatever you do, keep him in sight."

As they dragged me into the hall, I heard Basil complaining about his treatment. "For fuck's sake, let me go!

I can walk on my own," I demanded as they marched me up the stairs between them. On reaching the landing, I saw two more Bobbies appear from mother's studio.

"Any luck boys?" Heythorp asked.

"All the rooms on this floor are clear, Sarge. The noises from above aren't so distinct now. We've had a good look but can't find any access to the floor above."

Heythorp yanked my arm back and got in my face again. "You're pissing me off, Ravencroft!" He spat the words in my face. "Bet you think it's hilarious making us look like a bunch of bloody incompetents. If you don't want to suffer some real police brutality, you better tell us what we need to know!"

I said nothing.

"Wicklow, time to get the party started. No one will hear Ravencroft's screams when he has a little accident."

"Not out here. The next house is miles away."

"Right, Mike. Take your men and start stripping the wooden panelling off the wall. Go through the place like a dose of salts. Do whatever you need to do. She's here somewhere."

A loud crash made everyone look upwards.

"Jesus Christ, No! She's in the main studio. If she's touched the painting, I'll—" I jerked my arms free, bolted down the corridor. I slammed my hand against the wall.

A panel popped open. I dashed up the steps two at a time, but before the second safety door had a chance to close, I heard Heythorp shout. "I can't hold it. Jam it with something."

"Bloody hell, I just fucking knew it!" Wicklow exclaimed. "If he had one, why not others."

In the centre of the studio, bathed in bright light, Tina lay spread-eagled on her back covered by a white silk gown, the contours of her body clearly visible. To one side of her, my large studio easel lay on its back, too, while the painting rested against a chest of drawers undamaged. It had skidded across the floor when the easel fell. Luckily, landed paint side up.

I dived across the room and snatched up my precious painting. I slid it into the drying rack out of sight among the other 'Of Land and Sea' paintings. I moved away from the rack, just as the sound of pounding feet came up the stairs.

Wicklow burst into the studio, hunched with his legs apart and feet firmly planted. He held his arms bent at the elbows as though ready to tackle an escaped animal. As Heythorp's head appeared at the top of the stairs, I lifted my hands in a defensive stance, bracing myself for their violence.

Tina moaned.

Wicklow dropped to his knees and gently pressed his hand against her shoulder. "Tina Whiteoaks, it's okay, love. You're in good hands now." He lifted his black eyes to me as he shouted into his radio. "We'll need a doctor. Now!"

"You can count yourself fucking lucky, Ravencroft," Heythorp said, as the studio filled with his lads. "If she dies, you'll be charged with murder. Mike, get a full set of Ravencroft's dabs for elimination purposes. Send up two of the lads so we can start dusting the whole place— you never know what else we might find. Get someone to read him his rights. Then, get him out of here. Now! We'll continue this at the station, Ravencroft."

Chapter Thirty-One

1972

I had been waiting for nearly ten hours for police to track down a solicitor so they could question me further. Mr Bennett, father's solicitor, had passed away years ago, but I had no idea whether his son had taken over the practice or not. I wondered if the police had interviewed Lydia and Robert, my half-siblings.

No, of course they were no longer my half-siblings. Maybe they already knew about mother and her indiscretion. It would explain why they never really treated me like a kid brother who needed their support. The last time we had spoken was just before the reading of father's Will. Sorry, Donald Ravencroft's Will, the man I once called my father. Lydia and Robert's mother had left them both comfortably well off, so I never saw nor heard from either one of them again, once their father's solicitor settled the Ravencroft's estate.

My arse ached from sitting on a hard chair. In an effort to get more comfortable, I stretched my legs. I would've preferred to pace the room, but they had chained me to the table. So far, Heythorp had only given me one toilet break and a cup of disgustingly bright orange-coloured tea in the time I had been waiting. After taking a sip of it, I pushed it aside.

I glanced up at the grubby ceiling tiles and began to count them. The dull grey walls seemed to close in, making me more aware that my future would be a lot less colourful. Halfway through counting the tiles for the second time the door opened. It crashed against the wall with a bang. Heythorp entered carrying a large brown folder under his arm, instead of a solicitor. Without a word, he dropped the folder onto the table causing the film on the tea to ripple as he took the seat opposite.

I waited for him to speak. He didn't even bother to make eye contact with me but just flicked the folder open, took out some sheaves of paper. After scanning a couple of sheets, he leant back in his chair and began to read.

The disturbance of the fine film on the top of the teacup made me recall ripples of a different kind. A long-ago school summer holiday when I had woken early and jumped out of bed. On drawing back the dormitory curtains, I was greeted with a cloudless blue sky. Not wishing to miss the perfect light, I had dressed quickly eager to finish my painting of the priory.

The happiness I had felt in the morning was shattered as I sat soaked through, panting and trembling uncontrollably in the hot sunshine. Beside me, my painting lay destroyed on an upturned easel. I hugged my knees to my chest and scanned the lake waiting for Miss Dearborn, but all that broke the surface was a string of bubbles. Then nothing, but stillness.

The water betrayed nothing of what had happened moments before. One moment Miss Dearborn stood naked before me, tormenting me with her filthy words. The next there was a splash.

The water chilliness hit me with a paralysing force, stealing my body heat as a weight around my waist thrashing wildly as it dragged me down. The pressure on my chest forced my lungs to burn as if on fire, while dirty water tried to seep between my lips. An explosion of air bubbles escaped from me when I saw what was weighing me down.

Through the murky water, a pair of wide, vacant eyes in a pale stony face stared up. The ghost of my long-dead mother was coming for me with arms outstretched. At its centre of her face, her mouth screamed inaudibly for her revenge. A tangled mass of black hair rippled tentacle-like stretching towards me. Its fine tendrils brushed against my body and face. A sense of anguish raced through me. I struggled to free myself before my muscles weakened. I tugged at the fingers which dug into my flesh as the darkness threatened to swallow me whole. My head pounded as my mind screamed for oxygen. With inexplicable strength, I kicked out, twisting my body at the same time. My heart hammered against my ribs as I reached towards the flickering light.

On breaking the surface, I gulped in air as the brightness of the sun blinded me. Once my lungs allowed me to, I swam to the shore. I lay on my back panting. The pain in my chest was unbearable. As my breathing eased, I sat up expecting to see Miss Dearborn sprawled in the sunshine beside me.

I couldn't say for sure how long I sat scanning the surface of the lake, but once the sun had lost its heat, I gathered up my belongings and left. Miss Dearborn robbed me of my innocence and left a dark shadow in its place.

Heythorp's face revealed nothing of what he was reading. He had questioned me about Miss Dearborn years ago after including her name in the list of missing women, but she had no rights to be there. She wasn't one of my angels, nor was Mrs Loring.

I had locked away the events of that fateful day. To be quite honest, I never really believed it had happened. As far as I was aware, no one else knew. At the time, no one came forward with any information as to what had happened to her. As for Jonesy, what did he know?

That summer he had gone home for the holidays. After the school break, life at the priory had carried on as normal, apart from having a new art teacher. Later in the year, news of the lady in the lake surfaced, when an article in the local newspaper recorded Miss Dearborn's death as being by misadventure, as she was well known for wild water swimming.

Heythorp called out. "Come in!" when a sharp knock at the door disturbed his peace.

I looked up expectantly and Wicklow entered, carrying two mugs, with an envelope tucked under his arm. After placing the mugs on the table he took the empty seat next to his boss, laying the envelope beside the documents Heythorp had already read.

No words passed between them. Heythorp continued to thumb through the report, examining each sheet before placing it face down with the rest. Wicklow lifted his cup and took a nervous sip, testing the heat of the liquid against his lips. Finally, Heythorp leaned forward. His eyes held a bleak expression, one I recognised, but couldn't read.

I held my tongue and waited for him.

Heythorp and Wicklow looked shattered. Neither looked as though they had grabbed any sleep in the time I had been waiting. Both of them had dark circles beneath their eyes and stubble. After taking a sip of his drink, Heythorp coughed, cleared his throat, and then took another sip. On lowering his cup, he patted the pile of papers and said, "You need to understand the state of play. Do you remember me telling you about my gut feeling?"

I didn't respond, knowing there was no point.

"Well, let me remind you. Last year was the third time we had visited your home. Remember how we stood outside chatting while my colleague here." He gestured to Wicklow. "Spoke to your gardener."

I gave a nod. Not in the way of an answer, more to show I was listening.

"It doesn't really matter if you don't. You see, my colleagues and I have been busy sorting through the pieces of the puzzle, and we had a problem. You see, the pieces don't fit." He patted the pile again. "You won't believe how difficult it can be to build a case against the main suspect when none of the parts fit comfortably. As you know, it's your right to remain silent until your solicitor arrives. But please feel free to interrupt me during this little chat."

I straightened up in my seat.

Heythorp picked up his cup again and took a sip. On setting it down, he said to his colleague, "I don't know about you, Hayden, but it pisses me off when the criminals get all the rights, while the victims' families suffer. A single act of murder destroys so much. It makes me sick."

"Bloody awful I know, Sarge." Wicklow placed his hands on the table and leaned forward. "All those wasted man-hours on circumstantial evidence and for what? So that some jumped up little lawyer can say you're damaged goods. It's not your fault."

I shrugged.

"You mislead us with your so-called missing paintings. Were you hoping we'd see you as a victim?"

I raised an eyebrow.

"Oh yes, they were stolen. Amazingly, without that lead from you, it might've taken us a little longer to make a connection. You see, Ravencroft, your problem made us step back from ours and gave us a different viewpoint." He picked up the envelope Wicklow had brought in, pulled out some photos and fanned them across the table. "That's when we realised what the common link was between everything. Art, as simple as that art."

Heythorp tapped the photographs with his forefinger. Close-ups of nine angels' faces. Each of loving brushstrokes was clearly visible for all to see.

"Before we go any further, I want an answer to something that has bugged me for years. At the time you should've been questioned further. If I had maybe Annie Linton would've been alive today."

"Annie Linton?"

"Please don't pretend you don't know who she was, Ravencroft!"

"Was? Are you saying Annie Linton is dead?"

"You were there when Tamsin Loring crashed her car. After all, a blind spot without witnesses is an ideal place for murder, don't you think?"

"Just now you were talking about art being the link. Now you're linking Mrs Loring and Annie Linton. I don't get the connection. Mrs Loring died because she'd been drinking and misjudged a corner."

"Our duty is to the victims to find out the truth, Ravencroft," Wicklow stated.

"Right, I get that! What's this art link you're talking

about?"

"You went to speak to Mrs Loring about painting a portrait."

"I don't paint portraits." I glanced down at my nine.

Heythorp ignored my comment. "Basil Hallward is an art dealer who introduced you, the artist, to her."

"That's it?" I stretched my leg again. "Not really evidence of a crime."

"Annie hasn't made any contact with her family, just like the rest of the girls, so what other conclusion can we draw?"

I leant forward. "It's guesswork on your behalf then?"

"God willing we'll find a witness when a man commits a crime," Heythorp said. "Let's get back to my question, shall we?"

"So you're putting faith in God to do your job. Why's that? You've no faith of your own ability?"

"In our line of business, Ravencroft, we use whatever is available. You'll be surprised what reveals itself to us these days. Forensic science they call it. Your agent Basil told us about some cushions you lent him. It's surprising the amount of forensic evidence we'll be able to recover from them. So back to my original question about a blind spot without witnesses is an ideal place for murder. We know you were there when Tamsin Loring was killed."

"Your question sounds a little loaded."

He smirked.

"Yes, I was at the golf club, with my agent, on the same day she died. You already have that on record."

"You told us you left before her. Do you mean the building and the car park or just the building?"

"Where are you going with this? I had nothing to do with Mrs Loring's death. I would rather not answer any more of your questions."

"You can wipe that fucking grin off your face, you smug git," Wicklow snapped. "We know for a fact that you're Tommy Blackbird."

I straightened up again. It was going to be a long day.

Once we had the right information everything quickly

dropped into place." Wicklow slid the first photograph forward. "Candela Waterbrook lived in the squat with you."

"With me?"

"Yes, you!" He counted through the photos and selecting my fifth angel. "Also, Jackie Nolan worked in an art supply shop. The shop's ledger recorded anyone collecting an order over a certain amount. Jackie wrote the name Tommy Blackbird against a large order on the day before she went missing. An eyewitness described a man fitting your description hovering in the doorway of a disused shop where Jackie had been waiting for her friend prior to her disappearance."

"And that's your proof?"

Wicklow tapped the photographs. "You gave us all the proof we needed. Only it took Tina Whiteoaks to point it out to us. By the way, she's doing fine. Doctors tell us she is recovering well. One thing in your favour. You had the decency not to rape her."

"No beauty in violence, Heythorp," I said. "Art's about capturing beauty."

"That's all very well, but you made her suffer in other ways." Wicklow slammed his hand down on the photos.

I shrugged.

"She's safe now. Thanks to her colleague. We'll make you pay for what you have done. Tina uncovered your secret. Having the paintings' faces enlarged we saw that Tina's theory checked out. We already have your signed confession, you might say." Heythorp laughed.

"I can see a similarity," Wicklow said, pointing to the jawlines and high cheekbones. "Don't you think so?"

"So what? It proves nothing. I copied them from photos in the newspapers."

"If my memory serves me well, Ravencroft," Wicklow said, flicking through his notebook. "You told us back in 1966, you didn't have time to read the papers, nor did you have a television. So I find it hard to believe your inspiration came from the newspaper."

"Jenny gave me a copy."

"That'll be your agent's secretary, Jenny Flood," Heythorp said, making a note.

"Yes. She always had papers in the office."

"Right, you've admitted to kidnapping Tina, so why not the others?"

"I'm not admitting—" I began to say just as the door burst open and a tall, well-dressed man carrying a briefcase entered.

"Stop right there!" he exclaimed, his face set hard. "You've no right questioning my client without me being present."

"Who might you be?" Heythorp asked, rising from his seat as Wicklow gathered up the documents along with the photographs.

"I'm here on behalf of Mr Ravencroft's father. He has engaged my services for his son. I request that you stop questioning him immediately until I've had a chance to speak with my client."

"His father?" Heythorp and Wicklow said in unison while looking at me.

I shook my head, unable to decide which one of us was more surprised.

Chapter Thirty-Two

1972

Once again I found myself waiting alone. A heated discussion was going on outside the room between Heythorp, Wicklow, and the solicitor. When the door opened again, the last person on earth I was expecting to see walked in.

"We have such little time. I'm sure you have much you want to say to me," he said, with a slight nod of the head.

Finally I get to meet my mother's agent, Chuck Sparks. As I look into his dark stormy-blue eyes it's clear to me why Basil kept us apart. Chuck studied me at great lengths, but I guess I was doing the same. His reddish-brown skin stretched over the same high cheekbones, together with the same long straight nose, almond-shaped eyes, and fullness of lips that I possessed. Mother had undoubtedly betrayed Donald Ravencroft.

"What took you so long to make contact with me, if indeed you are my father?"

"I understand your animosity, James." Chuck spoke in a slow easy tone with a hint of his Native American accent.

"If you're here hoping for forgiveness, I'm sorry but I'm all out."

"No, never. I am sorry I did not make contact with you sooner. If I had, then maybe we both would not have been misled."

"Then why are you here now?"

"Two reasons. Firstly, I owe it to the man you called your father."

I laughed, whether out of shock or surprise, I didn't know.

"Yeah right. What about my mother?"

He lowered his head.

"Oh, you've forgotten about her. She was good enough to fuck, but not to marry."

Chuck's eyes darkened and he let his breath out slowly. "I do not care whatever you may think of me, but do not talk about your mother in those tones. You know nothing of your mother's life before you were born."

I slammed my fist on the table. The sound rattled around the room while some of the foul tea leapt from the cup. It raced across the surface of the table and dripped off the end, to pool on the floor.

"My whole life has been a lie. My mother betrayed my father. Sorry, the man I thought of as my father, and then she killed herself, going to her grave without loving any of us," I said through clenched teeth.

"Your mother was an emotional person. She loved the idea of being in love. Unfortunately she directed her love towards the wrong person. If only she had recognised the love Donald had for her. It's why her paintings had such a powerful message. Jane's creative soul could not recognise the world for what it is, as the rest of us do." He paused, realising what he had said.

He was right. I didn't see the world as others did. "All great art is about death. Mother killed herself because you betrayed her."

"We were never lovers."

"Then how can I possibly be your son?"

Chuck covered his face with his hands and then swept them over his head. "I made a mistake. It should not have happened. Yes, I invited her to London. Yes, I financed the exhibition of her earlier work. I hoped if it were successful, it would be enough to get her to exhibit her latest works. Only Jane misunderstood my intentions, she believed I was creating a means in which we both could deceive our loved ones. Your mother returned to England after suffering a breakdown. She hoped by returning to her homeland she would regain her ability to paint again."

“So she suffered from depression?”

“Yes. But do not blame me for it. You need to understand I made it clear to her, I did not love her in the way she wanted.”

“You were married at that time?”

“Yes, very much so and happily. I have four fine sons. They help run my business. We manage a wide array of different artists including Native Americans. It was while I was managing your mother’s career in America that the misunderstanding came about. Jane misinterpreted my gentle words of encouragement as being a declaration of love. She contacted me not long after she arrived in England to say she was happily married and painting again. I was elated. At last she had what she needed, love and her art.”

“Why didn’t you stay away from her then?”

Chuck looked down at his hands. “If I could turn back time, undo what happened that night, I would.” He inhaled and let it out slowly. “Do not think that I am not aware of the damage caused in a moment of weakness. We allowed the excitement of a successful exhibition mixed with too much drink to destroy everything.”

A noise outside made us both look towards the door. As the voices faded, Chuck continued.

“Donald was a far better man than I was. He told me about you, not for any malicious reason, only because he thought I should know.”

“So he knew I wasn’t his son?”

“Oh yes. Your parents did not have an intimate relationship. I don’t think she was punishing Donald at all. More herself unable to live with what she had done, by betraying him and their marriage vows.”

“You’re right. I came across her journal. After she slept with you she didn’t feel good enough for him.” I was wondering whether he would class me as one of his fine sons. I guessed not, not after what I had done in the name of beauty and art.

“When I bought the gallery, it was a bit of a gamble, but I decided to specialise in individual artists. That’s when I stumbled across Jane Elspeth Maedere's work. Her paintings were so powerful that they spoke to me. I was introduced to her through a mutual friend. I thought she was both beautiful and talented, but also very naïve which made her vulnerable."

"So you took advantage."

"No, I did not. If anything, she took advantage of me."

"But you just said she was vulnerable!"

He hesitated. "You're right. Nothing quite like an old fool, James. I am not here son to destroy the image you have of your mother."

"You are not my father!"

"Please, our time is short. My lawyer will be in soon. They are getting ready to charge you. I will do all I can for you, though I do not see any way of getting you off, only a more lenient sentence maybe."

"I don't need your help."

"That maybe so, but I am not doing this for you. I'm doing this for Jane and Donald. I feel it is the right thing to do."

"You knew my father?"

"In a way yes, I did. He was a compassionate man who truly loved you and Jane. Jane was fond of taunting him, telling him that you were not his."

"It wasn't only my father who suffered her wrath."

Chuck closed his eyes as though he too felt the pain. "I am sorry." His voice no more than a whisper. As his tone deepened, his accent became clearer. "Donald sent word of Jane's death. Did you know that?"

When I didn't react to his statement, he went on. "A few years later he wrote and told me about the onset of his illness. I do not think he expected me to reply." Chuck paused as though contemplating the letter.

I noticed that someone had tried to paint the ceiling tiles and began to wonder what else I had missed. I recalled Donald clearly struggling to breathe as he sat in his chair beside the fire, constantly cold and reading a letter. Had that letter been from this man, my mother's lover, years after her death?

"Donald always wrote to me as though we were old acquaintances, sharing the news of a mutual friend. He kept me up to date on you. I guess he took comfort in knowing you had a relative left in the world after he had gone."

I rested my elbows on the table. The handcuffs rattled as though reminding us of my fate. "Maybe if you had married Jane, she would've been a different person. Maybe if she had fallen in love with Donald, she would've been truly happy, but unable to create her stunning works of art."

"True." Chuck pulled a chemist's photograph envelope from his pocket. "Oh yes. I was given these." He flicked open the envelope, and I recognised the photos as the ones I had given to Wicklow. Chuck fanned them out, each one recording mother's descent into madness.

I looked away, knowing what he was thinking.

"It is a shame that I could not have seen these for myself. Basil Hallward had deceived me. For years, I believed he was paving the way to bring us together. Instead, I found out too late that he was taking your mother's paintings without consent from you. Clever of you to use her code, the one Jane and I had created to stop fake copies of her paintings making their way onto the black market all those years ago. It's ironic that your trap to catch him caused your own downfall."

"So it was you who went to the police then?"

"Yes. In America I reported the theft believing I was helping you."

"What about my *Stone Angels*?"

"Basil has sold all of them, but I have the tenth one. The police gave it to me."

"So he has profited from me in the end."

"For a while, yes. But do not worry, James. I am planning to sue Mr Hallward on the grounds he has ruined my reputation by selling me stolen paintings."

"Thank you. Please keep mother's paintings. I've no use for them where I'm going."

"I will look after everything for you as your father wished me to do."

"Thank you, Chuck. I'm not a son you can be proud of,

am I?"

He shook his head. "You have made quite a name for yourself. I have heard that the other nine paintings have changed hands for large sums already. Going by the many offers I have received for the tenth one, your fame will be far greater than your mother's in more ways than one."

The sound of the door opening made Chuck reach for my hand. "I'm glad for the chance to speak to you. I will see if I can visit you again before I return home."

"I'm sorry Mr Sparks, but your time is up," said the stern-faced solicitor.

David Chamberlain, the solicitor, had finished introducing himself and explained what my charges were, when Heythorp and Wicklow returned, both were clean-shaven and wore freshly pressed suits. Wicklow laid the folder back on the table and opened it. The enlarged photographs of the stone angels' heads lay on the top of the pile.

"Now to get down to business," Heythorp said in a dry tone, "You're under arrest for the kidnap and imprisonment of Tina Whiteoaks. Do you understand?"

I nodded.

"I'm sorry but you need to voice your answer."

"Yes." My mind was still on what Chuck had told me.

"I also need to ask you some questions about the remains of the bodies found at your property today." Wicklow leaned forward.

"Now wait a minute," Chamberlain said. "I haven't briefed my client about this new information."

"Oh, haven't you?" Wicklow said. "That's because we've only just received the information this afternoon."

"Understandably we had to follow up on it before we were in a position to pass it on to you," Heythorp said, his expression darkening. "Our informant led us to the burial site of the other eight missing women. So we're now in a position to charge your client with abduction, imprisonment, and the murder of those eight women. We hope to add Phoebe Browning to the list once we have received further forensic evidence. Also we are able to link some missing chicken wire to the body of Miss Browning and your client."

"There's still the evidence of the photograph showing Mr Hallward speaking to the first victim," David Chamberlain said.

"There's a problem with that as we now have the negatives which that single still came from, and show Mr Hallward wasn't the last person to see Candela alive."

The voices of the two police officers and my solicitor faded as my thoughts returned to my stone angels, captured forever on canvas. No one but me will ever truly appreciate their beauty.

As their painted faces stared back at me from the photographs spread out on the table, I wondered whether they will ever find a home with those who truly loved them for their beauty. Now I understood mother's madness and recognised that art was about monetary gain and not beauty after all.

Printed in Great Britain
by Amazon

62146842R00201